LOCUST
LANE

LOCUST LANE

STEPHEN AMIDON

CELADON
BOOKS

NEW YORK

LOCUST LANE. Copyright © 2022 by Stephen Amidon. All rights reserved. Printed in the United States of America. For information, address Celadon Books, a division of Macmillan Publishers, 120 Broadway, New York, NY 10271.

www.celadonbooks.com

Designed by Michelle McMillian

Library of Congress Cataloging-in-Publication Data

Names: Amidon, Stephen, author.
Title: Locust lane / Stephen Amidon.
Description: First Edition. | New York : Celadon Books, 2023.
Identifiers: LCCN 2022004416 | ISBN 9781250844231 (hardcover) |
    ISBN 9781250844248 (ebook)
Subjects: LCGFT: Novels.
Classification: LCC PS3551.M52 L63 2023 | DDC 813/.54—dc23
LC record available at https://lccn.loc.gov/2022004416

Our books may be purchased in bulk for promotional, educational, or business use. Please contact your local bookseller or the Macmillan Corporate and Premium Sales Department at 1-800-221-7945, extension 5442, or by email at MacmillanSpecialMarkets@macmillan.com.

First Edition: 2023

10 9 8 7 6 5 4 3 2 1

For Clementine

He has seen but half the universe who never
has been shown the House of Pain.
—EMERSON

LOCUST
LANE

Prologue

PATRICK

He hit the dog on Locust. It came out of nowhere, a blur of dark motion. He swerved, but not enough—the bumper's edge caught the animal's hindquarters, sending it spinning back into the night. Its yelp harmonized with the shriek of braking tires. And then he'd stopped in the middle of the road, his heart racing, thinking that maybe going out for a drive wasn't such a good idea after all.

It took him a moment to locate the stricken animal. It had fled back the way it had come, but only made it as far as the nearest lawn, where it was now turning in circles, nipping at its flank, locked in futile pursuit of its pain. It finally lay down and began to lick furiously at the point of impact. The dog was big and black. A Labrador, maybe, or a Labrador and something else. Patrick didn't know dogs.

He checked the nearby houses to see if lights were flaring as homeowners in robes emerged onto front porches. All was quiet. The dashboard clock read 3:11. It was entirely possible the event had gone unnoticed by the residents of Locust Lane. The setbacks here were deep, the windows tightly sealed. Trees shrouded most of the housefronts. Things that happened on the street were a long way off.

The dog continued to nurse its wound, though its movements suggested a recovery was in progress. Patrick told himself to drive on. He wasn't at fault. Dogs weren't allowed to run free in Emerson. Everybody knew that. A six-foot leash was required. There were signs everywhere. And he was not necessarily under the legal limit. The last thing he needed was to wind up walking the sobriety tightrope for some yawning cop. *Go home*, he thought. *Finish the bottle, hit the sack. You know the drill. Dawn will come, followed by another barren day.*

But he couldn't do it. He'd injured a living thing. That made him responsible for it. He had to help. He didn't need another item in the overladen shopping cart of guilt he was pushing around. He'd made a deal with himself not to abandon decency. He could leave behind everything else, but not that.

He pulled the car to the side of the road. The dog remained curled on the grass, although it was fussing with its flank less avidly. Having committed himself to helping, Patrick now understood that he had no idea what to do. Loading a large, frightened, and potentially bloody creature into his M3 and transporting it to an all-night animal hospital was out of the question. And he certainly wasn't dragging it back home. Whatever he was going to do would have to be done right here. The best he could come up with was to see if there was a tag on its collar, a number to call.

He got out of the car. The dog watched him, waiting for the human being to define the situation.

"Good boy," Patrick said, although he had no evidence that the dog was either of these things.

It emitted a brief whine, more of a radar ping than a call for help.

It was taking the measure of this creature who'd brought the pain. Its tail quivered in an unfriendly way. Patrick held out his right hand as a gesture of peace, palm down, fingers dangling, like royalty expecting a kiss. This was more or less the extent of his knowledge of canine communication. He'd never had a dog.

The wounded animal rose shakily, holding its back right paw a few inches off the grass. Standing was a good sign. No spinal damage; presumably no vital organs ruptured. It could limp back home to be cared for by the idiot who let it run free in the middle of the night. Patrick turned back to his car but froze when the dog growled. Low and ominous, like a waste disposal ready for debris. He turned to face it. Previously flat fur on the back of its neck had risen into a staticky bristle. It took a menacing step forward. That injured leg seemed to be getting better by the second.

Okay, Patrick thought. *Time to call it a night*. He showed the dog his hand again, this time offering his flat palm, a cop stopping traffic. There was no need for drama. Whoever's name was on that collar could take it from here. Get themselves a six-foot leash and obey the damned law.

He took a backward step. The dog took a mirroring step forward. Patrick wondered if his hand gestures meant something different to the dog than what he'd intended. He cast a quick glance over his shoulder. He'd left the car door open. That was good. Safety was just five quick strides away. He was pretty sure he could make it there before a three-legged dog.

But then the animal turned its head, its attention drawn to something in a thick copse of trees that separated the residential behemoth directly in front of Patrick from the even larger house next door. Patrick followed its gaze. At first, all he could see was varying degrees of nothingness. The trees were dense, knotted together by a network of vines. But then something defined itself. A man-sized delineation of the darkness. A human being—tall, broad shouldered—watching from a hundred feet away.

What the fuck?

"Is this your dog?" Patrick called out.

There was no response.

"Hello?"

Nothing. This made no sense. Why would the dog's owner be hiding in the trees? The town's leash law penalties weren't *that* harsh. Unless it wasn't the dog's owner. But vagabonds and lurkers weren't exactly common in Emerson. As far as he knew, the town's homeless population consisted of a small, ever-shifting squad of men cooling their heels at the Hilton after getting booted by aggrieved wives. He should know, having been one of them last year.

He looked back at the dog just as it made up its mind about whomever it had seen in the shadows and turned back to Patrick. At which point it made up its mind about him as well, and not in a positive way. Its growl deepened. It took another ominous step forward, the kind of murderous stealth on display in cable shows about the Serengeti. That injured leg appeared to have undergone a full recovery.

Time to go. With haste. Resurrecting a move from his wide receiver days, Patrick emphatically stamped his right foot forward, then pivoted and headed in the opposite direction. All he needed to be home free was five strides, a nifty spin into the car, and a slammed door. And he almost made it. His front foot was already in when there was a sharp explosion of pain on his trailing hamstring. The dog had bitten him. Luckily, its jaws didn't find purchase. Patrick's momentum allowed him to reach the driver's seat and pull the door shut behind him. It didn't latch, however, slamming instead into a cushion of bone and tissue. The dog's head. There was an ear-shattering yelp, followed by a whimpering retreat. Patrick pulled the door all the way closed as the dog limped off toward that dense copse, where a hidden man had just impassively watched it attack another human being.

Patrick gingerly probed the back of his injured thigh. The trousers were torn but there was no evidence of blood. The adrenaline continued to pump, fueling anger now. What the hell had just happened? Why hadn't that asshole intervened? Had he given the dog some sort of secret attack command? Patrick turned on his engine and maneuvered until his high beams illuminated the woods. But there was no one there. Just trees and vines. And of course the darkness, patiently waiting for the end of this frantic little interruption of its dominion.

Back at the town house, Patrick stripped off his torn pants and inspected the wound. The skin hadn't been broken, though he suspected there was a nasty bruise to come. He slathered it with antiseptic cream just to be safe, then applied an ice pack. For the relief of pain, a large tumbler of Suntory and two ibuprofen.

It was now approaching four. He should be in bed. He should have been in bed when the dog was biting him. He should have been in bed when he decided to go for a drive. But a dream had awakened him, driving him clean out of the house. Not a dream, really, but a disembodied voice, clearer and closer than any dream could ever be. *Dad, can you come get me?* It had not been from when Gabi was a girl, sunny and carefree, needing to be picked up from soccer practice or an afternoon at the mall. Nor was it her latter self, pleading and ravaged and shattered, calling from a borrowed burner or reversing the $24.99-a-minute charge from a jailhouse pay phone. No, this call came from the here and now, from the young woman she would have been. Confident and a little impatient. On the cusp of her adult life. Doing her father a favor by allowing him to do this favor for her.

He wasn't in bed when she spoke to him, but rather in his old recliner, the only piece of furniture he'd extracted from his vanished life. It took him a minute to find his bearings. He wore the clothes he'd changed into after work, Dockers and a polo shirt. There was a tumbler filled with whisky-tinted ice melt and a bowl of pistachio shells on the table beside him. The Discovery Channel was broadcasting a muted show about bearded men on a boat, fighting the elements.

Sleep banished, he'd driven. He followed a random course through town. He turned left, he turned right. It didn't matter as long as he kept moving. Adams to Cabot; St. James to Smith, and then on to Rockingham. On Centre through the town's center, where nothing was open but everything was brightly lit. Past the high school, where a lone car sat in the vast lot, sodium light raining down over it like warm drizzle. Past the Mobil Mini Mart, where a Hopperesque figure sat encased in bulletproof glass. And then onto Locust, where the black dog crossed his path.

He should try to get some sleep in the small patch of night remaining, although that wouldn't come unassisted. Not with the pain in his leg, the residual adrenaline still coursing through his veins. And so he topped up on the Japanese wonder drug and contemplated that figure in the woods. The more he thought about it, the more it pissed him off. He couldn't imagine anyone in this town failing to intervene as their pet got hit, attacked a stranger, then was pancaked by a slamming car door. That animal had probably had more spent on its well-being than three-quarters of the world's children. And yet, not a peep from the woods. If the man just happened to be there by coincidence, then *what* was he doing there? It didn't add up.

He contemplated calling the police to report a prowler, a dog on the loose. But he could see how such a call would go. They'd listen patiently, send a patrol car to Locust, find nothing. Besides, Patrick wasn't exactly on the best of terms with the local cops. No, this was over and done with. He decided to allot himself two more drinks. That would do the trick, filling in the three looming hours before he'd have to rise and shine; before the wasteland of the morning would finally creep into view.

Midday Wednesday

DANIELLE

She was on duty when they came through the door. Everybody was—lunch was their heaviest time for traffic. People liked to buy jewelry in the middle of the day. Mostly office workers on their lunch break. Couples, single men—you got a good mix. If you wanted to make sales, you either ate early or you ate late or you didn't eat at all.

But these two weren't customers. She saw that right away. They weren't even a couple, at least not the sort of couple who usually rolled into a jewelry shop. A middle-aged Black woman who looked like a high school principal accompanied by a white knucklehead who could have been the wrestling coach. The woman was a little on the heavy side but carried it well, her clothes spotless, not a hair out of place. The man had a body built of free weights and beer; his hair was shaped by electric razors and gel. No, they were definitely not here to buy an engagement ring. There were credentials dangling from their necks she couldn't read from this distance. Tax people, she guessed. Steve would have seen them on the CCTV in his office. He was probably shredding documents already.

Tomi was closing a deal on what looked a half-carat solitaire, so that left Britt up. The little dummy thought they were customers, so she came at them with that shitshow she called charm. But her smile vanished the moment the woman explained herself. She turned and pointed to Danielle.

Here we go, she thought. Again. Eden had called last night, just after midnight, but Danielle missed it. She'd gone to bed early, turning her ringer off because of a recent spate of Scam Likely calls. So she didn't see that her daughter had called until she woke this morning. She hadn't left a message. Danielle tried to call back but there was no answer. Which meant she'd been unable to forestall whatever nonsense was about to be laid at her feet.

Danielle had no issues with the tax people and her daughter had no money, so maybe they were social services. Although they tended not to come in pairs. The snakes who served summonses and warrants tended to work alone as well. And then she saw the gold shields and that feeling of annoyance shifted to something deeper.

It was the woman who spoke.

"Danielle Perry?"

Her voice was surprisingly kind. In most situations you could say it was soothing. Just not in this one.

"What has she done now?"

"My name is Dorothy Gates. I'm a detective with the state police. This is Detective Procopio from Emerson."

Gates looked around. Another couple had just been buzzed in. The showroom wasn't that big. It was getting crowded.

"Is there somewhere we could talk?"

The fear was starting to come harder. Eden had been in trouble, God only knew, but it had never required two detectives and privacy to explain.

"Ms. Perry?"

There was the storage room, but that was just a walk-in safe with no seating. Which left the manager's office. Steve wouldn't be happy having cops in there.

"I'm not . . ."

And then, on cue, he appeared, Steve Slater himself, with his chest hair and loafers. His eyes were locked on the cops; his frown was so profound it looked like he was in the early stages of a stroke. He said nothing as he approached, as if already following his lawyer's advice.

"These are Detectives Gates and Procopio," Danielle, good at names, explained. "Could we use your office for a minute?"

"My office," he repeated flatly.

Among the many things in Steve Slater's office that he wouldn't want the detectives to see was a gleaming Colt 1911 tucked in a holster he'd affixed to the well of his desk, an instrument of mayhem that may or may not be licensed with the Commonwealth. On the rare occasions he buzzed in suspicious characters, he had a charming habit of stuffing the pistol into the front of his action slacks.

"Yes, I would appreciate that," Gates said.

Which put Slater on the spot. A refusal would get the cops wondering.

"Certainly," he said, sounding like someone had superglued his molars together.

He unlocked the door with the key at the end of his elastic chain and held it open for them.

"Do you know how long this will take?" he asked as they passed by.

Gates turned and smiled sweetly, her face just inches away from his.

"We'll take just as long we need."

If honey were corrosive, that was her voice. The security door shut heavily behind them. There were two chairs facing his desk. Gates, immediately and fully in charge, motioned to one of them.

"Ms. Perry, I'd like you to take a seat."

That's when Danielle knew it was the worst kind of bad. She'd been asked to take a seat once before. Her grandmother after the heart attack.

"I'd prefer to stay standing," she said, as if remaining on her feet could ward off what was coming.

"Please," Gates said, her voice absolute in its kindness.

And so she sat. Gates took the other chair, perching right on its edge, ready to get back to her feet at a moment's notice. Procopio remained standing, his arms crossed in front of his chest. His eyes had not left Danielle since Britt had pointed her out. They betrayed no emotion. It was as if she was a test he was studying for.

"Ms. Perry," Gates said. "There's really no good way to say this. I'm afraid Eden is dead."

Danielle held the woman's eye for a moment, just to be sure, then looked around for something to focus on beside that unbearable sympathy. Her gaze landed on a photo of Slater and his daughters in front of a muscle car. She looked back at the detective.

"I'm so sorry," Gates said.

Danielle wondered why she wasn't crying and carrying on. She knew it was happening somewhere inside her but it hadn't arrived yet.

"What happened?"

"Again, this is hard news, but we believe she was murdered."

"How?"

"It appears she suffered a blow to the head."

"Where was she?"

"At a house in Emerson. Do you know . . ."

"Wait, were Bill and Betsy . . ."

"They were out of town."

"You're sure it's her?"

"Her driver's license was at the scene. We've spoken with the homeowners. Danielle, it's her."

"Was she . . ."

"We're looking at that."

Danielle had run out of questions.

"When did you last speak with your daughter?" Gates asked.

"Last night. Around seven."

"Did she indicate there was anything wrong?" Procopio asked, his voice what she'd expected, practice fields and dive bars and roofing gigs.

"No," Danielle answered. "Where is she now?"

"We're looking after her."

There was a knock on the door. Procopio answered it. His conversation with Slater didn't last long. And then it was just the three of them again. Danielle remembered something.

"She called. I mean, a second time. Last night."

"And when was that?"

"Just after midnight."

"What did she say?"

"I missed it. I was asleep."

"Did she leave a message?"

Danielle shook her head.

"I tried to call back this morning but . . ."

But she was dead.

"So what am I supposed to do now?"

"We're going to need to ask you some questions," Gates said.

"Can it be later? I'm not . . ."

She didn't know what she wasn't.

"It has to be now and let me tell you why. At this point in time we're still trying to piece it all together. And every moment that passes makes that a little harder to do."

"Can we not do it in here, at least?"

"Tell you what. Come down to the station with us. I think that would be best all around."

"Is she there?"

"No, she's being looked after by the Medical Examiner."

"Can we go there first?"

"We can talk about all of that after we get to the station."

In the showroom, whatever everyone was thinking vanished when they saw the look on Danielle's face. Steve said something and then Britt said something but she couldn't process their words.

Eden.

Their car was double-parked just outside the door. There was a Watertown cruiser as well. It took off after a nod from Gates. Danielle sat in the back. It wasn't far to Emerson. Procopio drove. He used his lights and siren a few times to clear people out of the way. They didn't speak, though Gates turned around every minute or so to check on her. Danielle was finding it hard to hold on to her thoughts. It felt like that moment right before you fell asleep, when your mind was pulling you into dreams. Things were still familiar but also completely different from your normal life. You could imagine Eden being just about any old thing. Under arrest. In the ER. In need of rescue from a fender bender or a disastrous one-night stand or angry people who'd been dumb enough to trust her. Laughing her head off over something nobody else even understood. But not dead. She was always alive when you thought about her. More alive than anybody. Fidgeting and talking and asking. Sipping your beer, taking food off your plate. Never quite getting it but plunging ahead anyway, as if the world was a big, rubberized playground where nothing truly bad could ever happen.

"You wouldn't happen to know the password to her phone?"

"1526," Danielle answered immediately.

Gates was surprised.

"It's her birthday plus mine," Danielle explained. "I bought it for her on the condition I knew the password."

Gates sent a text and then the silence resumed. They arrived in

Emerson. Big houses, big cars, quiet streets. As always, Danielle was struck by how *safe* it all looked.

"This must not happen here much," she said. "People getting killed."

"Things happen all over," Gates said, a trace of weary wonder in her voice.

Emerson Police Headquarters looked more like some high-tech firm on Route 128 than a place where the grubby business of law enforcement took place. There was a van parked outside emblazoned with the name of a local news affiliate. A tiny bottle blonde in skyscraper heels spoke into a camera beside it.

"Terrific," Procopio muttered.

They parked in a spot near the back entrance. Inside, there was an open-plan office that was both busy and hushed. People glanced at her as she passed, only to look quickly away. A uniformed man—tall, older, silver-haired—awaited them at the door of a glass-walled conference room. He introduced himself as the chief of police; she couldn't catch his name through the oceanic buzz now filling her ears. When he shook her hand, he covered it like it was a waffle in an iron.

"I am so sorry about your child," he said.

A strange choice of words given the fact her daughter was twenty, but unintentionally accurate. Eden was nothing if not a child. They entered the room. She was once again shown where she needed to sit. Gates and Procopio sat across from her; the chief remained standing. There was a manila envelope on the table. Gates produced a small tape recorder, pressed a button, then placed it on the table between them.

"I'm going to be recording our conversation. There's also a camera."

Danielle nodded. As if she had a say in any of this.

"Okay, what I'm going to do is show you two photographs. We're going to need you to look at them and tell us if they're your daughter. I have to warn you that this is not an easy thing. But it has to be done."

"Yeah, I get it."

"Okay. Here we go."

Gates pulled two big photos from the envelope. She looked at them for a moment, as if having second thoughts, then placed them on the table in front of Danielle. They were close-ups of Eden's face. Her eyes were half-open. The white of the left one was purply red; its lid was swollen like waterlogged bread. You could see the smallest bit of her tongue.

"Her eye."

"That would be from internal bleeding," Gates said.

Danielle touched the edge of one of the photos, adjusting it so it squared up with the other. She nodded. There was silence.

"You're confirming that the person in these photographs is your daughter, Eden Angela Perry?"

"Yes."

There was movement behind her. The chief. He put something on the table next to her. A pen. A very nice pen.

"We're just going to need you to initial the back of each photo."

She did as told. Gates collected the two photos and put them back in the envelope.

"Can I see her?"

"Not quite yet."

"I'm going to need to do that."

"We understand." The detective shifted in her chair. "Now, when you spoke to your daughter last night, what did you talk about?"

"Nothing, really. I was mainly after her to, well you probably know this, she has a court date coming up."

"The shoplifting thing."

"Which is a crock. Anyway, she needed to touch base with the lawyer."

Gates gestured dismissively. Nobody cared about shoplifting now.

"Did she mention if she was seeing anyone last night?"

"No."

"What exactly was she doing at the Bondurants'? On the phone they said something about them being relations."

"Distant cousins. Betsy can tell you the exact number. We were connected through my aunt Nancy. We met at her funeral . . ."

Her voice caught for a second on that word.

"Take your time."

"The Bondurants had taken Eden under their wing. She's . . . a handful. She's not bad. She's just, sometimes she does dumb stuff because the dumb stuff is easy. She trusts people who should have never been trusted. But she wouldn't hurt a fly."

"I'm sure," Gates said.

"She drives you crazy about ten times a day, but she's also kind of an angel. It's hard to explain. You have to know her."

Danielle started to cry. She never cried, but there it was. The tears were like hard little stabs to her eyes. A box of tissues materialized—the chief again. *Okay,* she told herself after twenty or thirty seconds. *That's that. You've cried, and it did all the good it usually does.* She dabbed at her eyes, turning the snowy-white tissue coal black.

"How long had she been there?" Gates asked.

"Almost three months."

"And she seemed happy?"

"She did."

"And what did she do, exactly?"

"Well, Betsy just needed a companion. Somebody to help her get around. I think mostly she was just lonely for her own kids. I guess you know about their eldest."

"Yes. Very sad."

"And the others grown and gone. She just wanted someone to fuss over. I was skeptical at first. Eden isn't exactly a seasoned caregiver. But they really hit it off. Oh, and there was the dog, too. She looked after that. Was it . . . ?"

"The dog's fine. What did you know about Eden's social life?"

"Not a lot. She didn't like to tell me things. We were often at odds on that particular subject."

"Why was that?"

"She'd made some poor choices in the past and so I guess I could be kind of hard on her about the company she kept."

"So no friends that you knew of? I mean out here in Emerson."

"Not that I knew of. Though I'm sure there were, knowing her."

"So she didn't have a job? I mean, outside of the Bondurant house?"

"Beyond walking the dog and keeping Betsy company, no. They paid her. A lot. And gave her a room. It had its own bathroom and a king bed and a big TV. I mean, you saw the place. Maybe that's what it was? A robbery or something?"

"We're certainly looking into every possibility. Back to something you said, about poor choices. Is there anyone from Eden's past who you think might have wanted to harm her in any way? Like an ex-boyfriend?"

"They're pretty much a bunch of losers, but none of them seemed violent."

"Do you have names?"

"There's Matt and Rayshard . . . you know, I'd have to think."

"If you could come up with a list, that would be helpful."

"I can do that."

"Now, did your daughter do drugs?"

"Not to the point of it being a problem. No needles or anything like that."

"And so, this midnight call, you don't know what that was all about?"

"No."

"Was it like her, to call that late?"

"Not recently."

Gates looked at her for a bit.

"So how would you characterize your own relationship with your daughter."

"I'm her mother."

"Could you be a little more specific?"

"I guess you can say that Eden and I were taking a time-out. I mean, saying that, it sounds worse than it was. It was just, you know, after twenty years, I think we decided a break might be in order."

"Oh," Gates said, as if the thought had just occurred to her. "Where were you last night? I know you said you talked to her at seven . . ."

Danielle knew it was only natural that they would suspect her. They didn't know her. She knew how she looked, with the tats and the dyed-black hair. But still.

"I was at home."

"Doing what?" Procopio asked.

"I had dinner and then I watched a movie and then I went to bed."

"What movie was that?"

"It had Julia Roberts in it. She pretends to fall in love with a gay guy to get another guy jealous. I can't remember the name."

"*My Best Friend's Wedding*," Procopio said immediately.

The two women looked at him. Gates turned back to Danielle.

"You didn't go out at all?"

"No."

"Okay. Good to know."

They spoke for a while longer. The chief left them to it. Gates asked her about Eden's ex-boyfriends and her habits and if she said anything more about her weeks in Emerson. They asked about her daughter's moods, which was a bit like asking about the flight plan of a house-fly. Danielle knew she wasn't being much help. They started repeating themselves.

And then the chief reappeared, summoning the detectives for an urgent conversation outside the door. After that, they couldn't get rid of her fast enough.

"Can I see her now?" she asked.

"Tell you what. We'll let you know as soon as possible."

"That will be today, right?"

"They got their own way of doing things over there. But should be."

"Thank you."

"We'll get an officer to take you home now. Is there someone you can be with?"

"I'll be all right."

"Are you sure? There are people we can call."

There was only one person she needed to be with. For a long time, there had only been one.

"I'll be all right," she repeated, even though she suspected she'd be anything but.

CELIA

She'd spent the morning waiting for Alice to answer her text. It was odd. She usually responded right away. But it had been almost three hours. Of course, it was possible that she was still asleep. Alice was not exactly a morning person. It would be a shame if they were unable to meet. They really needed to talk about the kids.

She also had to get out of the house for a while. The builders were making much more of a racket than she'd anticipated. They'd started to destroy the patio just after seven. By doing so, they were violating the Emerson ordinance that prohibited yard work before eight. Not that it mattered. Nobody was going to complain about noise at the Parrish house at any hour. After all, it was Oliver who'd drawn up the rules.

There were four workmen in all. One wielded a jackhammer. Another drove a backhoe. The remaining two watched with analytical expressions, like Olympic judges. Celia was already sitting in her sunny kitchen nook when they arrived, a cup of coffee in front of her. Oliver was away and she found it hard to sleep past dawn when alone. She'd felt a brief shudder when they started cracking the corrupt stone, not unlike the feeling that accompanied the first snip of a major haircut. But then there was no turning back and she could think about the next thing, which this morning happened to be her youngest son. Specifically, his nightlong absence from the house. He'd texted just after midnight. *Staying at Hannah's.* She'd asked if he meant the entire night. He'd responded, eventually, with a simple *yeh*, thereby putting her in a difficult position. She could try to continue the conversation by text, although that would go nowhere. She could call him, but he was with his girlfriend, and that would cause trouble. Provided he even picked up. No, she'd simply have to wait for him to return.

And so she let it be, then woke early the next morning and perched in her favorite place in the house, the kitchen alcove, which afforded her a panoptic view of the house's front, garage, and French doors. When all the boys had still been living at home she'd felt like an air traffic controller, directing landings and takeoffs on multiple runways. With Jack, her youngest, leaving at summer's end, she supposed she'd soon feel more like the lighthouse keeper in some sad movie. She caught herself immediately. Where on earth had *that* dreary thought come from? He was going to Dartmouth, not Afghanistan. She'd still see him plenty, as she did Drew and Scotty. Just not in the daily manner that had her doing things like waiting for him to get home at the crack of dawn.

What exactly she intended to say when he stepped through the door remained an open question. She wasn't ready for this. A sleepover. With a girl. It wasn't expressly forbidden, but only because it had never been discussed. Hannah was Jack's first actual girlfriend, provided you discounted last year's entanglement with Lexi Liriano, which Celia was only too happy to do. She knew they were doing the deed and it didn't bother her. She'd already raised two sons. She was neither a fool nor a prude. She hoped she never got too old or too jaded to forget what it was like, the unrepeatable bliss of those early lovers. Giving every inch of yourself over to someone else. In her case it had been Teddy Vier in the chalet at Killington while their families were off on the slopes. Doing just about every last thing they'd been warned against. Teddy, with his mop of unruly blond hair, his muscular arms encased in sheaths of baby-soft skin.

But they would have never spent a whole night together. Not in high school. It was too much, even for second-semester seniors. There were rules, unwritten but indelible, and everyone needed to follow them, even a family as unconventional as Hannah's. Celia would have to intervene. But she'd need to tread lightly. She didn't want to jeopardize things. There was Jack's temper to consider. And Hannah was proving good for her son. Unexpected, but good. Quiet and sweet. A bit passive, a bit *poetic*, perhaps. Not the prettiest girl in the world, but there was nothing wrong with that. And she certainly adored Jack. Frightening her off would be a mistake.

Truth be told, it wasn't as if he had other choices. He'd never had much luck in the romance department. Drew and Scotty always had some loyal lissome creature who hung on their every utterance, but Jack never could attract much interest from girls. At first, she put it down to his youth. But then he sprouted to over six feet and his voice deepened and he was too old to be seen as being just young. As hard as it was for a mother to admit, he didn't share the undeniable male beauty of his brothers and father. He was not-quite-handsome, which could be as bad as ugly. Eyes too close together, lips a little too thin, lacking his brothers' grace when he moved. And there was something a little too spiky about his personality—that piercing laugh, and the way he resorted to sarcasm when nervous or insecure. She'd hoped that things had changed last year with Lexi. After that ended so disastrously, she was forced to consider the prospect that girls were going to be a long-term issue for her youngest son.

But then Hannah arrived and his girl troubles really did seem to be a thing of the past. She had the patience of a saint, seeing all his good qualities, putting up with the stubbornness and peculiar views and flashes of temper, smoothing out his rough edges with her gentleness and quiet manner. They really were a perfect young couple. It would be a mistake to upset their odd equilibrium. Celia would definitely have to finesse this one as she figured out a way to communicate to Jack that there were boundaries.

Her phone made one of its noises. It was Oliver, calling on Facetime. Which was unusual. She walked into the quieter living room before accepting the call. And there he was, his face too big for the tiny screen.

"Good morning from deepest darkest Connecticut," he said. "What's that unholy racket?"

"The men are here for the patio."

"Oh, that's right. How's it looking?"

"They're still in the destruction phase. How's Stamford?"

He twisted the phone so she could see out his hotel room window. It looked like just about everything else down there.

"You look a little beat."

"We were at it until midnight," he said. "From boardroom to bar."

"How's the deal going?" she asked with trepidation.

Oliver was in the final phases of enabling his clients, a massive German conglomerate, to merge with a Connecticut-based machine-parts manufacturer. It had not been smooth sailing, which meant long hours worked, but also long hours billed. The Faustian bargain of his profession.

"We're getting there. These guys are funny to socialize with. They tell terrible jokes. Everything basically comes down to passing wind and large breasts."

"Hopefully not in the same joke."

He laughed. That was better.

"So when will you be home?" she asked.

"Meetings all morning and then lunch. I'll be there for dinner at the absolute latest."

There was a brief pause. This was the part of the conversation where she should have told him about Jack's absence, but there was no reason to pile anything else on his plate. She'd sort it out with her son first, then present it to her husband as a fait accompli tonight over Manhattans.

"Okay, I better get back to it. I'll let you know when I set out."

"I love you," she said.

"I reciprocate," he answered, their old mantra.

They broke the connection. She stayed where she was, fretting over her husband. He really shouldn't be working so much, especially after that decidedly ambiguous read-out from last year's treadmill test. But old habits die hard. As long as there was a child in the house, he would feel the obligation to provide, no matter how much money they had socked away. Possessed by the need to be everything his own father wasn't. It was simply how he was built.

And then Jack walked through the front door, even though he usually used the garage. His expression was grim, somewhere between troubled and confused. His eyes were on the kitchen as he clung close to the far wall and started tiptoeing upstairs. He was trying to avoid her.

"Hello, sweetheart," she said after he'd taken two steps.

He turned in surprise.

"Oh," he said. "Hey."

"Is everything all right?"

"Tired," he mumbled, avoiding eye contact.

The jackhammer started.

"Come on in here," she said.

After releasing a theatrical sigh, he obeyed. He collapsed on the sofa opposite her.

"Are you sure everything's all right?"

"Why wouldn't it be?" he asked, a sharp edge to his voice that she chose to ignore.

"You look upset."

"Just tired."

"What did you guys do last night?"

"Just hung out."

"At Hannah's?"

"Yeah." He finally made eye contact. "Is that a problem?"

More defiance. She decided not to get into it now. It was useless trying to reason with him when he was like this.

"We can talk about that later. You want breakfast?"

"I'll grab something at school. Can I go now?"

She nodded and he fled upstairs. Celia wasn't thrilled about the attitude, but she told herself he was only tired. After all, he'd just spent the night in bed with a girl for the first time. It would be strange if he didn't look and act like he'd been put through the wringer.

She went back to the kitchen. The workers continued to wreak havoc. It had taken them just over an hour to turn the majestic old patio into six hundred square feet of rubble and churned earth. She surveyed the rest of the yard. The slate pool, the recently painted gazebo, the maze of rose trellises, the tastefully tarnished birdbath. The lawn itself, a tranquil sea of green from which periscope-like sprinklers emerged every evening. A place for games and barbecues and parties. Twenty-five years they'd been here, since just before Drew was born. She wondered what it would be like when it was just the two of them. She'd envisioned them on the new patio on a summer Sunday morning, their bare feet on cool slate, sipping coffee as they passed the sectioned *Times* back and forth. Or entertaining in the evening beneath bug-zapping devices that would spit-roast interloping mosquitoes. *But would it really be like all that? Or would it just be two aging people rattling around a house far too grand for them?*

Once again, she had to catch herself. *Where on earth is all this gloom and doom coming from? They'd be fine. They'd have a blast. A few months in Italy, nights in the city, trips to Broadway or Jackson Hole or wherever they pleased. They'd be fine.*

Jack thundered downstairs and vanished out the front door after a shouted goodbye. So much for that heart-to-heart. And then the jackhammer resumed its bone-rattling chatter. That's when Celia decided to text Alice. They could discuss this sleepover business over lunch. Establish some guidelines; forge a united front. It had been a long time since she'd seen her crazy friend. Too long. She felt guilty about that, even though Alice had been the one making excuses the last few times she tried to get together. This time, however, Celia would insist.

And then there was nothing to do but try to escape the noise and not think about that look on her son's face. Finally, just when it seemed like it was going to be too late, her phone lit up.

"Papillon?" Alice wrote.

"That would be lovely," Celia replied.

ALICE

The Ambien-and-Chablis nightcap had not been a good choice. There was no reason to pretend otherwise. She'd had it sometime around midnight, after hearing Hannah get home. It had bought her four hours of dreamless, deathlike sleep. She checked her phone the moment she woke, although she knew full well that there was no way he was going to message her in the middle of the night. He wasn't even doing it during the day, for God's sake. She kicked free of the twisted covers and went downstairs to irrigate her sandblasted tongue. Light leaked from beneath Geoff's office door. He'd been working later and later, fueled, no doubt, by nootropics he scored from his buddies, the buzz-feeders and focus-pullers that were too new to even have nicknames. His all-nighters had evolved from the exception to the rule. Which was okay by Alice. She was perfectly fine conducting her marriage in shifts. There was light edging through Hannah's bedroom door as well, but she often slept with the lights on, darkness being high on the long list of things she feared.

Alice went to the kitchen and opened the fridge. She pondered another glass of Chablis. It wasn't as if she had anywhere to be in the morning. Or the afternoon, for that matter, now that Michel had dropped off the face of the earth. But that would kill the bottle, and she'd then have to deal with her husband knowing she'd killed the bottle. Geoff could be a real substance snob. Ingest an oblong pill freshly minted in a Malaysian lab and you were a consciousness pioneer, kicking open the doors of perception; drink a couple of shots of stomped grape or fermented potato and you had a problem. She should just get a liter of Stoli and keep it in her underwear drawer, like her mother. It wasn't as if Geoff was going to be getting into her panties anytime soon.

Although maybe it wasn't time for her to turn into her mom quite yet.

She reached for one of the exquisitely packaged bottles on the top shelf. Glacier water. For God's sake. It was like eating a polar bear burger. Ah well. If the world was going to melt, she might as well put it to good use.

"Hey," a voice said behind her.

As she spun in surprise, her hand struck a glass jar in the fridge, propelling it to the floor, where it shattered emphatically, leaving a viscid, bright red substance smeared across the tile. A sharp smell now filled the air. Harissa. Not the thing you wanted to deal with on an iffy stomach.

"What the fuck!" she whisper-shouted.

It was her stepdaughter, as tentative and spectral as ever.

"God, Hannah, you scared the shit out of me."

As she watched the girl's expression collapse, Alice regretted her harsh tone.

"Sorry," Hannah said, miserably.

"Is everything all right?"

"Yes."

And then she started to cry. She collapsed into Alice's body with such force that she almost sent them both tumbling down into glass-studded harissa. The sobs moved through her like a shaken rug.

"Hannah, sweetie, what is it?" Alice asked, truly alarmed now.

"Nothing," she whimpered.

The girl pulled back and swatted at the tears covering her cheeks.

"I'm just being stupid."

"Did you fight with Jack?"

"No."

"Then what is it?"

"I don't know. Just . . . never mind."

"Well, is there anything I can do? I'd offer you some harissa, but . . ."

It was a pretty funny remark, but Hannah wasn't laughing.

"He's here," she whispered, like an actress with a single line in a horror film.

"Who? Jack?"

"He's staying over. Is that okay?"

"Of course it's all right. As long as you don't have sex or anything."

Hannah's eyes widened.

"I'm *joking*," Alice said as she thought: *Stop joking*. "I mean, do you *want* him there?"

"Yes!"

"Then it's fine."

"Do you think Dad will be okay with it?"

"I'll handle your father. But I am a little worried about you being upset. You're sorta supposed to have the opposite reaction to these things."

"I guess I'm just being emotional."

"Emotions are good, right? We like emotions."

Finally, a wan smile. Hannah looked at the floor, illuminated by light from the still-open Sub-Zero, which had started pinging like an elevator locked in endless descent. The harissa glistened thick and red. Shards of glass emerged like broken teeth. It looked like a gangland slaying photo.

"I should clean this up," Hannah said.

"I'll get it. You go back to your boyfriend. And cheer up. These are the good times, kiddo."

Hannah grabbed two bottles of water from the fridge and vanished. Alice was tempted to leave the mess for the morning, but Geoff was given to barefoot nocturnal wanderings, and their relationship had not yet entered the booby-trap phase. It took half a roll of paper towels to clean up. As she worked, she contemplated what she'd just learned. Jack was staying over. This was new. The tears weren't necessarily cause for alarm. Her stepdaughter was prone to weeping, barely able to last through a Sally Struthers commercial without dissolving into a puddle of sentiment. It was probably just an excess of feeling bubbling to the surface.

On the other hand, Alice still wasn't so sure about Jack. Although she'd never seen concrete evidence of bad behavior, there was a faintly sulfuric whiff about him that needed to be watched. Those creepily close-set eyes had a way of cutting into you that didn't feel accidental; his default tone was dismissive sarcasm. He'd recently expressed some strange opinions about what women wanted that Alice hoped he'd be growing out of soon. And there was a lacerating tone to his laughter that gave her pause. Alice had taken her eye off the ball during her recent adventure, but that didn't mean it was no longer something that needed to be watched.

She walked to Geoff's office and paused outside the door. She listened for a moment—he was never happy to be disturbed while working. But he needed to know what was going on under their roof. It was unusually silent inside. She knocked gently. Nothing. She knocked again. More nothing. She opened the door a few inches.

"Geoff?" she whispered into the gap.

There was no response. She poked her head inside. He lay on the sofa against the far wall, dead to the world beneath the Hüsker Dü poster. The slack cadence of his breathing suggested he'd recently visited the deep end of his pharmaceutical pool. Trying to wake him would be futile. She backed out of the room. They'd discuss Hannah in the morning.

Back in bed, glacier water in hand, Alice pondered her own romantic travails. She should go ahead and text Michel, even though she'd resolved not to. It had been three days. Well, four, now that morning approached. She'd written him eight times during that spell, usually in midmorning, the quietest time of his day. Each message had gone unanswered. It was starting to frighten her.

She typed, *hey can't sleep thinking about you*. Not exactly a sonnet, but it got the point across. Her thumb hovered over the arrow. Something was stopping her. She could tell herself it was prudence, but she knew it was really fear; fear that this, too, would go unanswered. And so she erased the feeble girlish words and nestled the phone against her stomach. Just in case. Her eyes came to rest on the canister of Ambien on her nightstand, nestled inconspicuously between the Xanax and Excedrin Plus. *What the hell*, she thought as she reached for it. *That's what it's there for*.

The next thing she knew it was 11:17. Harsh, headachy light poured into the room. Her limbs felt like they'd been filled with cement. Geoff's side of the bed remained unoccupied, extending his three-week absent streak. Her phone had wound up beneath her body, like an egg she was trying to hatch. There was a single message, but it was only from Celia.

"Lunch?"

She was tempted to decline and go back to sleep. Pull the plug on the day. Maybe take a Xanax this time, just to make sure she didn't develop any bad habits. But that was another of her mother's tricks, sleeping the day away. Not-turning-into-Mom might not be the most laudable of goals, but at least it got her out of bed in the morning.

She had the idea while seated on the toilet. It was brilliant. She snatched the phone from the counter.

"Papillon?" she wrote.

"That would be lovely," came the immediate reply.

Which was pure Celia. Anyone else would have sent her back a simple thumbs-up. But Celia was not one for emojis or partial sentences or conflated spelling. If you sent her a text, you got a reply, usually immediate, always grammatically sound and perfectly punctuated. They settled on noon. A bit early, but Alice was suddenly extremely eager for lunch.

It was a smooth move, choosing Papillon. Showing up at Michel's restaurant alone was out of the question. She'd pulled that stunt one time too many. But rolling in with Celia Parrish could not be criticized. It would be frustrating, of course, to inhabit the same space as him without any intimate communication. Especially that space. Their space. And she'd have to be careful around Celia. She still had no idea how she'd react to news that Alice was having an affair. Although Celia clearly took vicarious thrills in Alice's tales of a wild past, this might be a transgression too far.

Most decisively, Michel had made her swear to keep their secret. It was deeply important to him, even though she'd tried to convince him that people wouldn't care as much as he thought. This wasn't the 1600s. And if he was worried about the racial thing—people didn't give a shit. Not these people, with their Ivy League educations and their third-generation Kennedy congressman. Michel might not be a WASP, but he was a French-educated Lebanese Catholic who owned a restaurant you needed to book weeks in advance for a Friday-night table. The only flak he was liable to get from this crowd was for putting an unhealthy amount of butter in his béarnaise.

She needed to get a move on. Her instinct was to throw on a pair of jeans and a sweater. Michel liked it when she dressed young and American. Last week, when they finally got to spend some quality time together, she'd worn a pair of Daisy Dukes and he'd more or less flipped his wig. That had been one for the books. But this was Celia they were talking about. Conversation might be relaxed with her, but not appearances. You brought your A game with Mrs. Parrish. The woman could stroll through a car wash and come out perfect. When they met, Alice's first thought was *God, I hope I look like this in twenty years. Fuckable at fifty.* The porcelain skin that carried a fine network of lines like an artwork that would just keep increasing in value. The extra few pounds that had accumulated in all the right places, distinguishing her from the anorexic voodoo dolls who populated Emerson. Most of all, those sparkling blue eyes, which still made men of all ages sit up and take notice.

Alice chose a simple black skirt and a tan cardigan; a touch of lipstick and blush. She'd do hair and mascara on the drive over. She swung by Geoff's office on the way out—she still needed to alert him to his daughter's middle-of-the-night distress. His door was shut tightly. She heard him clacking away. She really wished he'd bury the hatchet with his boss. Having him around the house 24/7 was getting oppressive. She knocked twice. It took him several annoyed seconds to answer. In his Clam Shack T-shirt and food-stained sweatpants, his too-long hair and unshaven cheeks, he appeared to be exactly what he was: a dweeb desperately trying not to look like a dweeb.

"How's the work going?" she asked.

"No, yeah, it's good. You going out?"

"Ladies who lunch. So Hannah was up in the middle of the night. She seemed pretty upset about something."

"Did she say what?"

"Not sure. You know that Jack stayed over, right?"

"Yeah, I saw him head out around seven."

"And we're okay with that?"

"She's a big girl," he said.

Alice could have debated the point, but she let it go.

"So you got this? You're going to talk to her?"

"It's all good," he said.

Having discharged her stepmotherly duty, Alice headed out into what proved to be a fine spring day. As she rocked over the formidable array of speed bumps that stood between her and the town's center, she allowed herself to get excited by the prospect of seeing Michel. Their last time together had been so perfect. Six blissful hours spent alone in his house last Friday, luxuriating in the knowledge that his son, Christopher, was attending a concert in Boston with Jack and Hannah and then staying at Jack's grandmother's Back Bay mansion. If not for Geoff, she could have spent an entire night with her beloved. Although her husband probably wouldn't have noticed if she rolled in after dawn. These days, he wouldn't notice if her hair was on fire, except to complain about the smell.

It had been the longest period of time they'd spent together. Before that, their encounters had always been brief. Usually in the morning, after the kids were at school and Geoff was at the lab. Or late at night. Sometimes they'd use their homes, although it was impossible to relax at either place. Geoff kept odd hours, even before falling out with his boss. And, because of his son, Michel was weird about using his own place. They'd rented a room at the Hilton once, but that felt as gross as some no-tell motel out on Route 9. Mostly, they'd been confined to his office at the restaurant, with its massive, redolent sofa she liked to imagine he'd brought with him from Beirut, even though he'd only lived there as a boy. *Their divan*, as she came to think of it. Once, after closing, they wound up in the kitchen, where she'd gripped the smooth hot steel bar on the oven door as he had at her.

They'd met at Papillon, during her first visit. She'd gone for lunch with

Celia. Michel had emerged from the kitchen; their eyes had met; he'd come over to say hello. It turned out his son was Hannah's friend Christopher, a slight boy with a shy smile he'd figure out how to use one day.

She'd spent the next hour catching him staring at her through the swinging door. She'd stare back, their eyes launching darts of passion through the food-perfumed void. She'd returned a few days later, alone, and he'd joined her at her table. They talked and then she left her number on a napkin. It was cotton, fine quality, like everything at Papillon. Not the sort of thing you'd normally jot a note on. But he'd handed her a Sharpie and told her to go right ahead. It belonged to him, after all.

He'd texted her that night, inviting her to dinner on Monday, when the restaurant was closed. Her own private meal. The menu was etched eternally on her parietal lobe. Fillet de Cabillaud in a saffron broth, jasmine rice laced with thinly sliced almonds, steamed mangetout that seemed like so many little green dirigibles ready to float away. White wine whose austere label made it clear it was doing her a favor by letting her drink it. They ate and they talked and then he took her back to his office and fucked her brains out. He wasn't particularly gentle. He didn't dilly-dally, didn't ask permission, didn't try to find out what it was she was into. He just let her have it; rough because he was not necessarily in control of himself. Which made her lose control as well. The result of this onslaught was her first non-auto-induced orgasm in a long time. In fact, she had four of them, one after the other. A pileup on a foggy highway with no survivors except the lone woman who staggered from the wreckage, eyes glazed, hair and clothes in disarray.

Driving home that night, all she could think was that she had done this terrible, forbidden thing and there was going to be hell to pay. When she encountered Geoff she expected him to see right through her lies about a girls' night out. But he was too lost in the neural pathways he was fabricating. And so she kept it under wraps. It wasn't easy. It required strategy. She had to create a counter story for everything she did. Another self, a double to provide her with cover. And thus was Good Alice born, a virtuous version of herself who would be out doing Pilates or lunching with a friend while the real her, Bad Alice, was in the arms of an absurdly handsome restaurateur with a French accent and slightly aloof manner. Sometimes she wondered what Good Alice would have made of her bad version had they ever met. Would she be jealous? Loathe her? *Judge* her?

And then came last Friday. He'd finally overcome his reservations about his place, at least for one night. Luxuriating at his sweet little house had changed the way she thought about what they were doing. Before that, she hadn't seen the need to give it a name. It was just another crazy thing that was happening to Alice A. Hill. But that night had made it real. They were a couple. She suddenly saw how this might actually work. No longer having to borrow time or steal moments. No longer having to lie. And so, as they lay entwined, she'd let herself get carried away by the moment.

"Do you ever think about buying the restaurant?" she'd asked. "The building itself, I mean?"

"Only about ten times a day. But property values here . . ."

"I have money."

"What do you mean?" he asked after a surprised silence.

"Geoff and I have a prenup. I get half of everything."

"But you would have to get divorced for that."

She rose herself onto an elbow.

"Yes, Michel. I'd have to get divorced. That's how a prenup works."

"I might not be so popular around here after that," he said.

"Are you serious? Nobody would care. But if that's really an issue for you, then we could move somewhere else."

"Where?"

"Boston. Paris. You name it."

"How much is this prenup?"

"My part's like nine million."

The sum had driven him into a silence she couldn't fathom. She decided to leave it at that. She wondered if it had something to do with him being raised Catholic. And then there was the matter of his dead wife, who'd undergone an apotheosis to saint since succumbing to breast cancer. The Virgin Maryam. There'd been a photo of her in his office that had vanished after their first romp. She was hot as hell, surprise surprise, but there was something in those obsidian eyes that frightened Alice, reminding her of the moralizing zealots in the benighted Pennsyltucky shithole she'd fled as a seventeen-year-old. Forget about that death-do-us-part business, said those eyes. Your narrow ass is mine 'til kingdom come.

In the days that followed, he hadn't answered. There had been no "yes," no "no." Time became a slow, corrosive drip that ate away at her initial elation. She'd pushed too hard, too soon. But every time she'd reached the edge of despair, she'd console herself with a simple thought. He loved her. He understood they were a perfect match. He also loved his restaurant—and hated paying rent. His four-day blackout had to have a perfectly good explanation. A problem at work, an issue with his extended family, spread out as it was over three continents. *Stop worrying*, she told herself. She'd see him; they'd find a few whispered seconds together and he'd touch her and let her know that everything was all right.

Papillon was still mostly empty when she arrived, a few minutes early. Michel would already be in the kitchen, working his wizardry. He'd emerge at some point in his white smock to take a tour of the dining room. It was Sofia, the hostess, a raven-haired, liquid-eyed beauty, who emerged from the kitchen, carrying a stack of menus like a warrior princess's shield. She was some sort of relative of Michel's. She was also on to Alice—there'd been the tiniest trace of a knowing smile the last time she'd come alone. Which had spelled the end of those solo lunches.

"You're our first," she said, a seemingly benign greeting that she managed to infuse with quasi-pornographic insinuation.

Alice felt like giving her waterfall of black hair a quick yank. Instead, she silently followed her to a booth, thinking what she wouldn't give for a caboose like that. She positioned herself so she could keep an eye on the kitchen. It didn't take long until the door swung open and there he was, bent over a tray like a surgeon. She tried to catch his eye but he was totally absorbed in his work. *Look up*, she willed him. *See me. Toss your head slightly toward the office and let's sort this out the good old-fashioned way, with some panting and friction.* But he continued to work, creating delicious things for others to eat.

Water arrived, reminding her that she was actually about to have lunch. Despite all the tension and drama, she was looking forward to seeing Celia, the one and only true friend she'd made since moving to Emerson. They'd bonded immediately at their first meeting. This was early last autumn, not long after Hannah and Jack had started dating. Alice was thrilled for her stepdaughter, who hadn't exactly moonwalked through puberty. To bag a guy from one of the town's dynastic clans was quite a turnaround. She'd started combing her hair instead of using it as a veil; she began wearing clothes that actually fit. The bingeing and purging and cutting appeared to be a thing of the past. She even managed a smile every once in a while.

And then Celia had called, professing a similar delight that the kids were together. She suggested they meet the next day so they could get to know each other. She proposed the Emerson Country Club, a place Alice had passed a thousand times but never entered. It was every bit as neo-puritanical as she'd expected. The dining room was saturated with the impossibility of audible laughter. She briefly suspected Celia's choice of venue was to gain home field advantage for some sort of attack, perhaps her opinion that Hannah was not good enough for her princeling. Well, if the woman wanted a scrap, she'd get one. Hannah might not be a show pony, but she was sweet and constant and had a heart of gold. Jack was lucky to have her.

But she couldn't have been more wrong. The first words out of Celia's mouth expressed the obviously sincere opinion that Hannah was a fine young woman.

"I wish I could take more credit," Alice said. "You know I'm not her actual mother."

"Yes, she told me. Terrible thing for a girl to experience."

"I don't know. Sometimes I wish my mom had abandoned me."

Celia scrutinized her for a moment, and Alice thought she may have blown it before the raspberry iced tea even arrived.

"But then who would we have had to belittle us?" Celia asked with a smile.

And what have we here? Alice thought. After that it turned into a regular lovefest. At one point, Celia asked what it was like to be a stepmother. Alice gave a potted version of her history with Hannah. She was ten when they met; Alice was twenty-six. They hit it off from the first. They shared secrets, they did things together. They talked and often laughed. They shopped, they rated guys, they snuck wine, like a couple of naughty teens. She left out the stuff about Hannah's weeklong speechless sulks and her capacity for self-harm, which shocked even Alice, who'd been around some crazy bitches in her day. Razors, she got. But pliers?

"She sounds like a very lucky kid," Celia said. "It's just so gratifying for Jack to be with a nice girl after . . ."

She caught herself.

"After . . . ?" Alice prompted.

"Oh, he just had an unfortunate experience with a girlfriend last year. Bad breakup."

"I've had my share of those," Alice said.

"Well, I imagine you were never as hurtful as the girl in question."

"That's what you think," Alice said with a jolly little laugh.

But Celia clammed up after that. Alice wanted to press her for more, but it was too early in their relationship. That night, Alice plied Hannah with Pinot Grigio and asked her to spill the beans, which she did only after making Alice swear never to tell a living soul. It turned out there'd been an incident the previous spring between Jack and his erstwhile girlfriend, a senior named Alexa Liriano.

"Lexi? She's a hottie."

"Not that hot," Hannah said.

"No, right," Alice said.

They'd dated for a few weeks and it had ended badly. There'd been a big argument, followed by Lexi accusing Jack of inappropriate conduct.

"Inappropriate as in . . ."

"Nothing happened. Lexi made the whole thing up. She was just butt-hurt because he dumped her. Typical female bullshit."

Typical female bullshit? Alice thought.

"But what did Lexi say happened?" she asked.

"She said he got rough with her. Which if you knew Jack, you'd know was totally ridiculous. His parents only paid because there are people out there who are jealous of the Parrishes."

"Wait, his parents *paid?*" Alice asked as she reached for the corkscrew.

"Yeah. Like, a lot."

It took her several more heavy pours, but she finally got the whole story. Despite Jack strenuously maintaining his innocence, money had indeed secretly changed hands between the Parrishes and the Lirianos. An NDA was signed. And so the accusation never became public, even as gossip. Although Hannah continued to swear that Jack was the victim in all this, Alice kept an eye on him. Because she could kind of see him strongarming some young thing. He had a hint of the bully about him. Those big hands and the harsh laugh that erupted at strange moments. And once or twice he'd hinted at a worldview that sounded a tad Paleolithic when it came to matters romantic.

But he'd always proved a perfect gentleman to her stepdaughter, even though there were times when Alice suspected it was something of an act. And then there was the fact that Hannah's rules as to what constituted abusive behavior might be a bit more elastic than the norm, given her own history of self-harm. But look though she might, there were never any actual grounds for complaint. So Alice kept out of it. No way was she going to jeopardize the girl's happiness on a hunch.

Meanwhile, her friendship with Celia blossomed. They exchanged texts, they shared stuff they found online. The only bump in the road had been the strange dinner party with the husbands. With Oliver, she'd expected some sort of white-shoe Visigoth, but he turned out to be witty, handsome, gracious, and utterly charming, with a voice aged in oak and a face etched in granite. Even his eye-to-temple scar was magnificent—it looked like a dueling wound worn by a dashing archduke. Geoff, clearly cowed by the setting, wound up playing the rebel, provoking the other guests with opinions Alice knew he didn't really hold. But Celia had handled it all with surpassing grace. She was the best. Alice didn't know what she'd do in Emerson without her.

And then, there she was, arriving right on time, looking as poised and perfect as ever.

"Are you all right?" Celia asked after the hug. "You look a little stressed."

"Just the usual stuff at home."

"So Geoff's not being any more responsive?"

"As if."

Celia frowned sympathetically. She knew things weren't great with Geoff. The waiter swooped immediately; they ordered salad specials, as was their habit. And then they caught up. Colleges and summer plans. Celia's renovation of her back patio; Oliver's herculean travails at work, which had just forced her to spend another night alone.

"How long's he gone for?"

"Just until this afternoon," Celia said. "Actually, I'm kind of glad he wasn't there last night."

"Why's that?"

"I'm not sure what he would have made of Jack spending the night with Hannah."

"Oh. Right."

"I mean, are we okay with that?" Celia asked.

"I am, but I get the feeling you might not be."

"It's just, I'm not sure they're ready for this yet."

Normally, Alice would put this down to Celia being a fuddy-duddy, but then she recalled Hannah's stricken expression in the Sub-Zero's spooky light.

"You might have a point. I found Hanns wandering around the kitchen in the middle of night in floods of tears."

"Oh dear. Did she say what it was about?"

"Not really."

"Because something was eating at Jack as well when he stumbled in this morning."

Alice waited, correctly guessing that more was coming.

"It just seems that we shouldn't be sanctioning it," Celia continued. "Obviously they're going to do what they're going to do, but allowing them to spend the night together seems a bit extreme for high schoolers."

Alice could have debated the point, but she understood she might not be in the mainstream on this one. Her first sleepover with a guy had been when she was fifteen. The fact that he was the associate pastor at her father's church complicated matters. As did the fact that he was married.

"I'll have a word with Hannah," she said.

"I'd still like to know what all the drama was."

"I'll ply her full of wine and get the full scoop."

Celia smiled. She thought Alice was kidding.

"So I presume that everything was hunky-dory when they were at your house," Alice said.

Celia looked confused.

"What do you mean?" she asked.

"I mean before they showed up at our place. They were with you, right?"

"No. Jack left right after dinner. He said he was going to your house."

"Are you sure?"

"Yes. In fact, he said it again this morning."

"No, it was definitely after midnight when they wandered in."

They stared at each other for a moment.

"Maybe they were at Christopher's," Alice said.

"Then why wouldn't they say that?"

"Oh well," Alice said. "As long as they were together."

Celia didn't seem particularly mollified by the words.

"It just seems odd they would mislead us."

"Not to me. The only time I told my parents the truth is when I said I hated them."

Alice had intended the remark to lighten the situation. It didn't.

"So you're not bothered by this?" Celia asked.

"Not really."

"Well, I suppose it's different with you."

Alice reared back.

"Different how? Because I'm not her mother?"

"I'm sorry," Celia said. "That came out wrong."

"Because, you know, I'm trying here."

"I know. You're wonderful with her. Strike that remark. It was a stupid thing to say."

Alice let it drop, though it was hard to see how that could have been a slip of the tongue. It was clearly something Celia had been thinking. Their salads arrived. They chatted as they speared lettuce, although things had suddenly turned awkward. Now Alice was wondering what else Celia secretly thought about her. The woman had hidden depths, there was no doubt about that. Alice just wasn't sure she necessarily wanted to navigate them.

And then Michel stepped through the swinging door to survey his kingdom and Alice wasn't thinking about Celia's depths anymore. He saw her but, after a momentary pause, made his way to another table, engaging the people there in that serious-but-friendly manner he had. Making you feel like you were the only diner in the place. Celia kept talking, now about some woman or other who'd done some thing or another. Alice picked distractedly at her vegetation. He stopped at another table and then another. Taking his merry old time. Finally, he arrived.

"So how are the salads?"

"Amazing, as always," Celia said. "You hardly ever see actual fresh beets anymore."

He looked at Alice's plate.

"But you aren't such a big fan."

Really? Alice thought. *Four days I hear nothing from you and now we're talking about root vegetables?*

"Oh, Michel, maybe you can clear something up for us," Celia said. "Were the kids at your house last night?"

His polite smile disappeared.

"They weren't with you?"

Celia shook her head.

"But Christopher said . . ."

Michel stopped himself from finishing the sentence. He seemed genuinely aggrieved by the news. Celia and Alice waited. But he said nothing more. And then the kitchen door opened and his beleaguered assistant was beckoning to him. He disappeared with a polite nod that was calibrated equally between Celia and Alice. They looked at each other in confusion.

"So where on earth were they?" Celia asked.

MICHEL

He did not like abandoning the two women so abruptly. Alice would certainly not be happy about it. Even Celia, always so proper and gracious, had been bewildered by his flight. But he needed to figure out what was happening with his son before he started discussing the situation with others. Better just to leave now and face the music later.

In the kitchen, he was immediately engrossed in work. The day's specials were Salade de Betterave and Sole Véronique, but there were always plenty of à la carte orders. Usually, cooking was enough to drive away bad thoughts. The world would shrink to the size of the next plate. But not today. There was no escaping it: Christopher had lied to him. He'd said he was at Jack's house when he was not at Jack's house. Michel now wondered if this was his only deception. There had been other times recently when he'd been out late, supposedly at the homes of friends. Last Saturday he'd spent the night at Jack's grandmother's house. Had that been a lie as well?

He badly wanted to go straight home; he wanted to wake his son and force him to explain where he'd been, what had caused him to return so late and in such a state. But Wednesday was his busiest lunch, and leaving Jerome and Sofia to handle things courted disaster. So it would have to wait. But the moment he was free, he'd confront the boy. How many times had Michel told him? *I need to know where you are.* That was the first rule. Followed closely by rule number two: he was due home by midnight. Period. No exceptions, unless they'd made other arrangements.

Christopher had finally arrived at four in the morning, just as Michel was contemplating getting in touch with Jack's parents, a prospect he did not relish. He looked tired and upset and unhappily surprised to find his father awake. His shirt's collar was flipped up and he kept his jacket on throughout their conversation. Michel's first reaction was relief, followed closely by confusion. No car had pulled up outside. Did this mean he'd walked the two miles back from Jack's? Why hadn't he called? When this first round of questions was met by silence, Michel—hardly believing the words were coming out of his mouth—asked if he'd been drinking or doing drugs. This was denied with a terse shake of the head. And so it went. Question after question was answered by silence or shrugs or muttered meaningless words. Michel could feel his anger rising. His son had never been like this. There might be occasional tears; every once in a while he might be sullen or talk back. But they always spoke.

"Do you even remember the last few hours of your life?" Michel finally asked. "Are you suffering from amnesia? Do you need to have your brain examined?"

Cruel questions, born of desperation. And futile, as well.

"Christopher—talk to me!"

But he simply sat there, sinking deeper into some inexpressible torment. Michel finally backed off. Confrontation clearly wasn't working. The boy was out on his feet. He needed to sleep. So Michel sent him to his room after ordering him to stay in the house until he got back from Papillon. Michel would call school with an excuse. They'd talk the moment he returned, and silence and shrugs would no longer be acceptable.

It was a girl. It had to be. That would explain why Christopher had become so edgy and secretive of late. Michel had suspected that there was somebody for the past few weeks, even though Christopher said nothing about it. The math just didn't add up. There were Jack and Hannah and Christopher. There needed to be one more. There needed to be a girl.

Time and again, he'd been tempted to challenge his son about his moody distraction. But that was difficult when Michel was hiding something of his own. How could he advise openness when he was secretly sleeping with another man's wife? How could he speak to his son about right and wrong when he himself was sinning? Perhaps Christopher knew. There'd been a chance sighting, an overheard conversation. Although it was more likely that he felt his father's hypocrisy in his bones. All those lessons about right and wrong were lies. You could be secretive and evasive, after all. You could let yourself be ruled by irrationality and lust.

Now, as he labored over blanquette de veau and fattoush and the sole, Michel understood that it all came back to Alice. The matter of Alice. Until that situation was resolved, it would be impossible for him to deal with his son. Or anything else. And that wasn't going to happen by avoiding her. Her unexpected arrival at the restaurant today made that clear. A woman like Alice wouldn't just disappear.

He still couldn't understand how he'd let things go this far. He wasn't looking for a lover. She was there, suddenly, and things began to happen that neither of them could control. For the first time since Maryam's death, emotion ruled him. And it had been good. Better than good. It would be a lie to say otherwise. They laughed together. When was the last time he'd laughed? And the sex, the abandonment. It was sacrilege to say it, but it had never been like this with his wife.

But it couldn't last. It would run its course; the flames would burn out. He knew it and he thought she'd known it as well. But then, four nights ago, she'd made her proposal. Divorce. And not just divorce, but one that would allow him to realize a dream he'd had since he was a young man. But it was wrong, to take another man's wife and money. Wrong to destroy a marriage, even one as unhappy as hers.

He'd said nothing at the time, even though the answer was obviously no. He told himself he wasn't saying it because he didn't want to hurt her. But in truth, he was deeply tempted by the prospect of being with her, fully and without secrets. In his heart, he didn't want to lose her. He didn't want to go back to being the man he was before meeting her, his empty days following each other like ants, dutifully building a colony without knowing why. The loneliness would be even worse this time, with his son starting college. He wasn't sure he could bear it.

But still, it was wrong. Not in the burn-in-hell sense he was taught as a little boy. He'd abandoned all of that after his wife took her last breath. And yet this was still wrong, cheating and sneaking around and now, possibly, taking another man's money. No matter what he and Alice did after they stepped out of the shadows, the original sin, the stain and the stink of it, would still be there for his neighbors and his customers and his son to see and smell.

The rush ended. The restaurant emptied. Alice was long gone; Sofia had left for her break. He checked his phone to see if there were any messages from his son. Nothing. He was still asleep. There was nothing from Alice either, which he supposed was good as well. Amid the usual spam and work matters, he saw a lockdown notification for the high school that had arrived a couple of hours ago, followed by news that it had just been lifted. Michel wouldn't have been particularly concerned even if his son had been there. Americans and their paranoia. If people had been this sensitive when he was a boy in Beirut, he'd have never been allowed out of his house. No one would have. Although maybe that would have been a good thing.

He spent an hour prepping dinner and dealing with deliveries, then headed home. This was not his normal practice—he usually stayed at the restaurant straight through dinner. Working or, recently, seeing her. As he drove across town, a familiar, nagging feeling settled over him. It was something he'd experience from time to time, ever since he moved here almost four years ago. A sense that there was something not quite right about his new hometown. He knew it was irrational. Emerson was a perfect place to live. There was little crime and no litter, and traffic would only snarl briefly when school was letting out. There was money—a lot of it—but you never really saw it, certainly not like you did in the cities. You felt it, like a cooling breeze, a reassuring hand. And besides, Michel had inhabited fine restaurants his whole life. He moved among the rich without friction. The town was white, yes, but not exclusively. There were Blacks and Chinese and Arabs and Latinos. And in the morning they, too, emerged from their million-dollar houses and piled into their Suburbans to take their beloved children to the beautiful shining schools; firing up their German sedans to head off to the hospitals and banks and law firms where they worked.

Moving here was the easiest decision he'd made since Maryam died. When he'd heard that a main street restaurant space was available, he'd called in every favor he possessed to raise the capital. He'd timed the move so Christopher would start high school from the beginning, as a freshman. And after a few terrified weeks the boy had settled in. True, Michel would have preferred another best friend than Jack Parrish, but Christopher was happy enough. And the restaurant succeeded beyond all expectations. After a year, they were booking weekends a month in advance. He was able to cook what he wanted. His mountain of debt slowly began to shrink. He had started thinking that maybe this place could wind up feeling like home.

It didn't take him long to get to Smith, the strange and singular street whose small brick houses had been built by the Italian stone masons who'd settled here to build mansions for the natives. Now, they were seen as starters for young families and odd cases like him. Not that they were cheap. His own modest three bedroom had cost almost eight hundred thousand. The house that backed onto his was worth three times that much. But it was quiet and clean and safe. And no one bothered you here.

Except today. As he drew close to his house he saw two people standing on the front porch. A man and a woman. She was Black; he was white and in the act of swinging the brass knocker. Both turned as Michel pulled into his driveway. Their expressions made clear what he already knew. They weren't selling anything.

He got out of the car and approached them slowly, warily, as if holding out the possibility of retreat.

"Michel Mahoun?" the woman asked when he was in earshot.

"Yes."

He could see now the gold shields dangling from their necks.

"We're with the police," she continued. "We're going to need to speak to your son."

Wednesday Afternoon

CELIA

Celia knew better than to panic. Lockdown could mean anything, and usually that thing was nothing. They'd had one last fall after the school received two hang-up calls in the space of an hour. When Scotty was a senior, they'd locked down after a report of a school shooting in Concord, which was a good twenty miles away. And that had turned out to be a false alarm. It was shelter-in-place you had to worry about. That meant the wolf was no longer at the door. He was inside the house, doing what wolves did.

She saw the alert as she left the restaurant. It was almost an hour old—she never checked her phone while eating, it was rude. She called Oliver before reaching her car. He'd seen it as well and had put in a call to Bart Zorn, the police chief, and a friend. He was checking out of the hotel in Stamford now. He didn't sound worried, but then he never did. Oliver was the sort of man whose heartbeat actually lowered in a crisis. She texted Jack next, instructing him to be careful and let her know what was going on.

She drove by the school, even though parents were advised to stay away. What she saw was reassuring—a single police cruiser parked out front, the officer inside casually staring at his phone. At home, she turned on the espresso contraption, feeling a strong need for another coffee. Her phone rang while the machine was still warming up. It was Milly Williams. Although Celia usually let the inveterate gossip's calls go to voice mail, today she picked up on the first ring.

"There was a murder at the Bondurants'," Milly said breathlessly.

"Say that again."

She did. Celia felt a cold wave of shock pass through her.

"My God. Was it Bill or Betsy?"

"Neither. It was a young woman."

Which meant it couldn't be one of the Bondurant kids. They had three sons. Well, two now.

"Who was she?"

"Nobody knows yet."

"Has somebody been arrested?"

"The police aren't saying anything," Milly said. "Although I do know Bill and Betsy were out of town. What does Oliver say?"

"He's away, too. He'll be home in a bit."

"Well, let me know what he says. Because we're all kinda going crazy here."

"Of course."

Celia hung up, still trying to take on board what she'd just heard. A murder? At the Bondurants'? She really wished her husband were here. True, there were four burly men currently occupying her backyard, armed with sharp tools. They would deter any spree killer stalking the township. But still. She'd feel better when he got home.

A strangulated noise erupted behind her, causing her to jump. But it was only her coffee. Oliver called back as she took her first wincing sip.

"First of all, Bart says there's no need to worry," he said. "The lock-down is just a precaution. Evidently there's been a murder in town."

"I heard it was a young woman."

"That's what I'm hearing as well."

"But who was she?"

"Not a local. That's all he'd say."

"So we shouldn't be worried?"

"The nature of the attack suggests it's an isolated incident."

She texted Jack again after they finished speaking—he still hadn't responded to her first message. Although the sense of emergency had receded, she was still having trouble getting her mind around this. A murder. In Emerson. At the Bondurants'. It was a reminder that, despite the alarm systems and threats of armed response and a police force that was better equipped than some Third World armies, they were vulner-able here, too.

She took her coffee to her sunny alcove, where she checked the news on her computer. No new facts, although on Twitter, speculation was running amok. There were claims that it was a burglary gone wrong. Someone else said the victim was Bill's lover. There was a photo of squad cars and official-looking vans swarming Locust. It was an eerily discor-dant sight, like a school of sharks in the country club pool.

But the kids were safe. That was the main thing. Her thoughts re-turned to the more pressing problem of what she was going to do about her son when they released him from school. She didn't like this part, imposing discipline. She had to be careful not to make too much of it. Celia had raised three teenagers—she knew that lying came with the territory. But in this case, it made no sense, at least none that she could understand. Why would Jack say he was at Hannah's house if he wasn't? He could go where he pleased. He was weeks away from turning eigh-teen, months away from attending college. He had all the freedom a boy could ask for. He'd traveled alone to tennis camp in Florida three years ago; he'd flown unaccompanied to London to visit his uncle last summer. Just a few days ago he'd spent the night in Boston with Hannah and Christopher. And yet he'd still looked her in the eye and lied.

She contemplated calling Oliver to see what he thought, but that risked reopening the old tensions between father and son. Things had been peaceful between them recently—there was no reason to shatter the cease-fire. Oliver had a tendency to overreact where Jack was concerned, turning misdemeanors into federal cases. He'd always been easier on Drew and Scotty. And why not? They idolized him. And they didn't exactly present the same difficulties as their youngest brother. They would never deviate from Oliver's plans for them. What sport to play (lacrosse and baseball), what college to attend (Dartmouth or, if absolutely necessary, Amherst), what career to pursue (law or finance)—they would always heed their father. It amazed her how easily he could command respect without ever being cruel, without even a hint of the brutality her own father, the fearsome John de Vissier, had inflicted on his own offspring.

But it had always been different with Jack. From the time he was little, he'd bucked against paternal authority. And Oliver, in his own calm and reasonable way, would never give an inch. He loved the boy, there was no doubt about that. Perhaps best of all. But he was hard on him. Maybe because, beneath their surface differences, they shared a stubborn streak. Drew and Scotty might be upset at their rare Little League strikeouts, but they were able to shake it off before making it back to the bench. Jack, however, would rage like Lear on his blasted heath over every missed swing.

Although she did not care for the tantrums, Celia sympathized with the boy. As the youngest, he was acutely aware of the examples set by his father and brothers. Not that Drew and Scotty were all that perfect. Not if you knew them as well as she did. Drew's fierce blue eyes always seemed to be judging what was happening around him, and the verdict was usually guilty. His face was settling into a permanent scowl; he'd developed a rasping, solitary cough whose sole purpose was to express impatience. He'd taken to drumming his fingers, sometimes so loudly that it would stop people speaking. As a boy, the power in his broad shoulders and unbreakable wrists had been deployed for athletic triumph. Now, as he abandoned sports, she could see that his strength was transforming into that of a boardroom bully.

Scotty's flaws went in the opposite direction. His once-sharp eyes were now smudged by a vacant satisfaction, his thin lips were always a little slack. He was every bit as strongly built as Drew, but he seemed to be in the process of powering down, as if he'd used his strength to exit the turbulent atmosphere of adolescence and was happy to glide through a frictionless manhood. Never a talker, he was now encased in a silence that she feared signified an expanding void. His friendly smile attracted people to him, yet it was distributed indiscriminately, as if it was more of a buffer against intimacy than an invitation to it.

But most people, including their little brother, only saw a pair of tall, broad-shouldered, strong-jawed young men who succeeded at everything they tried. Jack lacked their ability to hide his flaws. And he was well aware that big things were expected of him. But the world was not exactly proving to be his oyster. Fearing failure or, worse, invisibility, he drew attention to himself by misbehaving. Talking back to teachers. Staying out past curfew. Being a little too rough on the playground. Using his intelligence and sharp tongue as weapons.

Eighth grade had been particularly bad, his rebelliousness now fueled by puberty. His anger focused on the female of the species. There were tense phone calls from concerned mothers. It all reached a nadir when he came perilously close to getting suspended for calling his art teacher a bitch. Celia had to pull out all the stops to keep that from happening. She began to worry that the pressure that had turned her first two sons into diamonds was grinding her youngest into toxic dust.

His freshman year was worse. Scotty was a senior then, the big man on campus, whose triumphs Jack took as a personal affront. And so he acted out. First, he got kicked off the tennis team after throwing a profanity-laced, racket-splintering hissy fit that would have made McEnroe blush. There were more run-ins with faculty; more calls from parents. The most disturbing incident, however, came on the evening Celia stepped into his room to find him seated shirtless at his computer, his back to the door. She'd knocked, unheard—his earbuds played some brutal growling music. On-screen, a horrifying video clip played: a woman kneeled, naked, her breasts pinched painfully together by leather straps. Her gagged mouth and chest were smeared with blood that streamed from her nose. Her frightened eyes, rimmed with mascara or bruises or both, skittishly roamed the hooded, hairy-shouldered men encircling her, all of whom stroked grotesquely swollen members that they pointed at her like muskets.

Celia looked at her son. The muscles on his back rippled as his right arm pistoned. She quickly backed out of the room, the still-warm laundry pressed to her chest. She spoke with Oliver the moment he came home and he had a word with the boy. They were in the study for a long time. When Jack emerged, he looked chastened and wouldn't meet his mother's eye for days.

"It was just natural curiosity," he explained. "Goddamned internet."

Celia said nothing more. But she couldn't help but think about the frenzied way her son's arm moved. And as for being natural, the only other male in her life she could imagine watching such a thing was her father. Which was hardly a source of comfort.

This was not the only time Jack had been summoned to Oliver's study. If the goal of his bad behavior was to get his father's attention, it worked. Whenever he acted out, Oliver would conduct him behind his closed door, where he'd have a quiet word with him. He never raised his voice, he never lost his temper. He certainly never struck him—Oliver abhorred violence. He'd simply explain what was expected of a Parrish. Jack would take his medicine, but it would only be a matter of time before he acted out again. Father and son were locked in some generational male struggle from which she and the rest of the world were excluded.

Finally, after Scotty went off to Hanover, things changed. Jack's temper abated. He began to read voraciously. His grades improved. He grew interested in his classes, psychology in particular. Dinners became disquisitions on Laing and Jung. His expression took on the furtive, self-satisfied cast of someone in the process of figuring things out for himself. He smiled more, but in a knowing, inward manner that left you wondering what exactly he found funny.

By his sixteenth birthday he'd come into his own. The man he was to become was taking shape. A thinker. An intellectual. Strong-minded, decisive, commanding. When people asked what he was planning to study in college, he'd simply answer "the mind." He could be a little too opinionated and argumentative, his views often a tad extreme for Celia's taste. But these were things that would change as he grew older. He'd finally put his difficult boyhood behind him. In the stuff that mattered, he'd become every bit a Parrish.

Her mother called. Katharine had heard about the killing through the grapevine. Not surprisingly, her Dubonnet-fueled views on the matter tended toward the apocalyptic. Celia's mother had spent her whole life waiting for the murderous hordes to descend and always seemed disappointed when they didn't. Now, she was in no doubt that they had struck a blow against all that was pure and good, and that more widespread havoc was coming. Celia was able to escape the call when the landscapers knocked on the sliding glass door to let her know they were finished for the day. They'd flattened the ground; stones would be laid tomorrow. Once they were gone, she watched a blue jay land on the newly exposed dirt, hopping and pecking frantically, unable to believe its good fortune.

Finally, just after three, an alert arrived announcing that the lock-down had ended. She texted Jack and instructed him that she wanted him to come right home so they could discuss last night before Oliver got back. There was no response. She tried him again fifteen minutes later, and then a half hour after that. Still nothing. Four o'clock came and went without Oliver's return. She called him but it went straight to voice mail.

At four-thirty she tried Jack again. Still nothing; nor was there any-thing from Oliver when she called him for the second time. She phoned Alice to see if Jack was there, but she wasn't picking up either. This was getting ridiculous. Meanwhile, the victim was identified—a brightly smiling twenty-year-old Watertown girl named Eden. Such a hopeful name. If Twitter was to be believed, a "person of interest" was now being questioned. At least the women who'd been whipping themselves into hysterics on the Emerson Moms Facebook page were simmering down now that it was clear that no one was marauding through the township's streets, cutting down their young.

Five o'clock passed in silence. Celia was now officially worried. She called Oliver's office, but his assistant was under the impression he was traveling straight back to Emerson. Finally, just when Celia was thinking about contacting the authorities, she heard the garage door rumble. Oliver entered, followed by Jack. Her husband looked grim. His middle finger traced that decades-old scar on his temple, like it always did when he was stressed. Her son was ashen. Neither seemed very eager to meet her eye.

"What is it?" she asked. "Oliver, what's wrong?"

ALICE

She'd lingered at Papillon after Celia left, trying to look plausible as she sipped a refill of coffee she neither wanted nor needed. What the hell was going on? The situation with Michel was getting out of hand. He wouldn't even meet her eye when he came to the table. And the way he simply left her was totally unacceptable. Granted, it had to be alarming for him to learn that his beloved boy had lied to him. But that was no excuse to abandon her, especially since Hannah was involved as well.

She checked her phone for the first time since arriving. Nothing from him, but there was a message announcing that the school had gone into a lockdown. She experienced a short pulse of panic, but it faded quickly. She'd need to hear sirens and the shudder of helicopters to get truly concerned. They had a couple of these things every year and they invariably turned out to be nothing more than soundings of the current depths of communal paranoia.

Still, she should get a move on, just in case Hannah needed to be picked up. The girl was not built to handle emergency alerts. And Michel wasn't coming back out now that things were picking up. As the seconds dragged on, she couldn't escape the feeling that everyone was staring at her, especially the suspicious cousin at the hostess's podium. The table was needed. It was time to go.

She drove by the school after leaving Papillon. As expected, the place looked as placid and protected as ever. She went straight to Geoff's office when she got home. They needed to discuss Hannah's lie. Coupled with her meltdown in the kitchen, it suggested that something serious was going on. Alice could hear raucous music as she approached—his door was open a few inches, which was unusual. Geoff usually kept it tightly shut, whether he was in there or not. His secretiveness about his work had become obsessive. He seemed to be laboring under the delusion that either Alice or Hannah had some deep larcenous interest in neural prostheses, agonist-antagonist muscle pairs, or myoneural interfaces.

She knocked, pushing the door open further, spilling music into the hallway.

And keep your money boys made of silver and gold.

He wasn't inside. She checked down the hall. Light leaked from beneath

the bathroom door. She looked back in the office, a room she hadn't entered in months. There were books and papers; a framed photo of Geoff
poised to skydive; another taken of him at that machine-gun camp in Ar-
kansas. And of course one of him perched atop his beloved Indian Chief
motorcycle. At the center of it all, his desktop computer, with its massive
screen. Indecipherable hieroglyphics covered it, a cave painting from the
future. The human brain, or at least a bite-size chunk of it, mapped and
tagged.

You say your pain is better than any kind of love.

The table around the screen was littered with Post-its, index cards,
scribbled-upon legal pads. There was a laptop as well. It was unprotected;
the music had kept it awake. After a quick look down the hall—he was
still in there—she stepped inside. Another forbidden thing. She had to
lean forward slightly to read what was on the laptop's screen. It was an
email from his boss at Tactilitics.

Geoff—

*So it failed, big deal. Stop sulking. You need to get your butt back in here so
we can get this thing up and running before Bain come a knocking.*

Sid

There was motion at the edge of her vision. Geoff, standing in the
doorway. He looked at her and then he looked at his laptop. There was
no reason to try to explain herself. She'd been busted.

"I didn't know you were home," he said stonily.

"We ate early," she said. "You got the alert from school, right?"

"I talked to Hannah. She says it's all quiet over there."

"Do we know what it is?" Alice asked.

"Sounds like there was a murder in town."

"A murder? Are you serious? Anybody we know?"

He shrugged and stepped into the office. She made way for him as
he put his computer to sleep. The music cut off. He turned and looked

at her. The office suddenly felt as small as an elevator trapped between floors. This was as close as they'd been in a long time.

"Failed?" she asked.

"Sid's being a drama queen."

"Okay. But."

"Alice, it's fine. I got a few bugs to work out. That's all."

"But what's this about Bain?"

A question too far. Geoff did not like to talk about business, especially the venture capital side of it.

"Did you need something?"

"Yeah. I wanted to talk about Hannah."

"Okay," he said, his voice neutral.

"She wasn't where she was supposed to be last night."

"She got home at midnight."

"No, I mean before that."

"Where was she supposed to be?"

"At Jack's. But she wasn't."

"Where was she?"

"I don't know."

"I'm not really getting the significance of all this. They're kids. They run around. She wound up back at the mother ship."

"But she lied about it. As did Jack. And Christopher. Which means they were doing something they don't want the grown-ups to know about."

"How did you find this out?"

"I had lunch with Celia."

Geoff nodded, his face blank. This guy definitely belonged in robotics.

"So what exactly do you want me to do about it?"

"Talk to her. I mean, there's the lie, plus she's so upset when I see her in the mid—"

"Okay, I got it."

Alice, who loved nothing more than to be interrupted by men, held her ground, wondering what would happen if she slapped him in the face.

"Is there something else?"

Oh, fuck it, she thought. *What's the point?*

"No," she said. "There's nothing else."

She was halfway out of the room when he spoke again.

"And for future reference, I'd appreciate it if you didn't come in here and look at my stuff."

She froze. *For future reference?* Was he fucking serious? What was she, the woman from Mighty Maids? She turned to face him.

"Excuse me?"

"It's a simple request."

"I wasn't *looking at your stuff*," she said. "I was coming to tell you that I'm concerned about Hannah."

"What does reading my computer have to do with that?"

"I don't know, Geoff. Maybe I was curious. You have some sort of big beef with your boss that keeps you from going into the lab for two weeks and I see there's a message from him and I'm interested. Maybe I looked at it because we're married and I was wondering how your life's work was going. You know, husband and wife stuff."

He stared stonily at her. *You're wasting your words*, Alice thought.

"Whatever," she said. "Look, I'm sorry I intruded upon the sanctum of sanctums."

Once again, she started to leave.

"Well, just don't do it again."

That's when it truly flipped, the old switch, the one her father had tried to beat out of her, the one that helped drive all those men away. Bad Alice had been conjured from the mists. She spun around this time.

"Are you fucking kidding me right now? This is the first time I've *ever* stepped foot into this, this, grotto!"

Grotto didn't land with the weight she'd intended, but she stood by it.

"I don't know that," he said.

"Well, there are a lot of things you don't know."

His eyes narrowed. *Careful*, she thought. *Cut and run*. But Bad Alice had her by the scruff of the neck. She wasn't going anywhere.

"What is this?" he asked slowly. "I'm just asking one simple thing of you."

"*This* is me. Fed up me."

"Fed up with . . . ?"

"Everything."

"Everything."

"Yes, Geoff. Everything. Every last fucking thing."

"That's a lot."

"It sure is. It's a whole hell of a lot."

For a brief moment, his righteousness wavered. They both knew that she was capable of going a lot farther off the rails than he was.

"I'm going to turn around and walk away from you now," she said. "And I highly recommend you watch me do that in silence."

To her grim satisfaction, he did just that. Her blood still up, she was tempted to hop in the car and drive straight to Michel's house, sort things out with him as well. But that would not be a smart move. So it was back up to her room to stew in her percolating adrenaline. She lay flat on her back and stared at the ceiling. *Take a breath*, she thought. *Get a grip*. She'd just come perilously close to blowing everything up. Arguments and tantrums and threats were not a good strategy for her at this point in her life. If a split with Geoff really was inevitable, then she should take a more measured approach. A preemptive, surgical strike was winnable. A berserk domestic meltdown was much less of a sure thing.

Besides, there was no telling now where she'd wind up if she fled her marriage. Before making any sort of move, she had to deal with the unthinkable—that Michel might be done with her. What a catastrophe that would be. She'd have nothing if he left her. He was her lifeboat, her escape pod. Although maybe she'd been wrong to believe he felt the need for a breakout as strongly as she did. He'd still have things if he ended it with her. A sweet son who idolized him and planned to follow in his footsteps. An amazing restaurant. His looks, which would probably stay with him until he turned seventy. He could find a new lover in ten minutes. But Alice was stuck, especially with Hannah going off to college. Marooned in the burbs. Getting older by the day.

It wasn't supposed to be like this. Marriage, the move to Emerson, settling down—it should have ended her lifelong meandering. It was her father who cut her adrift, with his bottomless silences and his tobacco-stained fingers that folded so neatly into a fist. Grasping, angry, suspicious of the world outside Shithole, Pennsylvania; this angry little man who devoted all his energy to the small chain of hardware stores he owned, joylessly hoarding every last penny he squeezed from his customers. It was as if he'd emerged, fully formed, from the anus of capitalism, to be forever streaked and redolent with its shit. Despite amassing a small, lonely fortune, he rarely spent a penny on Alice. He'd developed dementia in his early sixties and clung on to life long enough to drain the family's savings on the best eldercare available.

Her mother had been no help. She'd discovered vodka just after Alice was born and it remained her bestie until breast cancer got her when her daughter was sixteen. Her father had grudgingly agreed to pay her tuition at a minor outpost of the state university, where she'd partied and fucked and daydreamed her way into academic oblivion. She fled to Hawaii, but returned to the mainland after a guy she'd been deeply involved with for all of three hours drove his Mazda into a banyan tree, ejecting himself into the afterlife and leaving Alice with a broken ankle. She wound up in Los Angeles, though the plaster cast and lack of money made life there impossible. She city-hopped her way back East, stopping in whatever was supposed to be the new hip paradise. Santa Fe. Austin. South Beach. Atlanta. Her stays in each city were measured in months. There was always a guy; in Santa Fe, a guy and his wife—Leander and Jill, about whom the less said the better. It was always the same. A sudden rush of attraction, followed by the slow drip of disillusionment that concluded with a curtain-dropping bust-up that sometimes involved the authorities. And then it was off to the next cool place. Jobs were just for money. Hostessing at a sports bar. Hotel reception. Telesales, for the better part of a Monday. That ill-advised week as a "muse" for a photographer mono-named Roman in Miami. She bypassed New York, suspecting it would eat her alive, and finally landed in Boston. She figured she'd better stop there. She was getting *way* too close to Shithole, Pennsylvania. She was twenty-six but felt much, much older.

It was in Boston that she met the man who changed everything. Geoff Holt had been a guest at a biotech hoedown she'd worked at as a server. To say he stood out in that crowd was an understatement of the first order. He seemed like that rarest of occurrences in her life—a nice guy who wasn't a complete loser. His manners were impeccable; there was a nerd lurking beneath the perfectly stressed leather bomber jacket, but he made that work for him. He asked for her number, she let him have it. His wide-eyed, needy daughter was no trouble whatsoever. He derived a substantial income from the medical robotics company he'd founded with a half dozen other eggheads from MIT, where he'd earned his PhD in neurosomething. He never lost patience with her; he found her insanely sexy. He almost never talked about his ex-wife—in fact, Alice didn't even know her name until two months into their relationship. They had fun. Grown-up fun. Money fun. He took her to see *The Book of Mormon* on Broadway. They drank very expensive champagne on their ten-week an-niversary. He was able to get his hands on amazing drugs, stuff that wasn't even illegal yet. They skied, they Jet Skied. They flew to Italy to get mar-ried at Lake Como, just the two of them and Hannah, who shared Alice's Milanese stylist for her bridesmaid duties. For the first time in her life, Alice was happy in the way that happy people were supposed to be.

And then Geoff cashed out of his company and everything changed. He'd been complaining about his partners since she first met him. They were basically glorified gadget makers. The work was becoming rote. He'd had enough.

His passion returned when he met Siddhartha Chetty, a hot-shit BU professor who specialized in neuromuscular prostheses. Sid had a dream: creating prosthetic limbs that could actually *feel*. It sounded like borderline-creepy sci-fi stuff to Alice, but, as Geoff explained it, the technology wasn't actually that much of a reach from what was currently out there. It was already possible to wire a prosthetic device to the recipient's neural and muscular systems to perform basic manual functions. The next challenge was transmitting feeling back up to the brain. This would be particularly useful for prosthetic fingers, since the sensation of touch was needed for the user to judge how much pressure to apply when typing a sonnet or picking up crystal or playing Bach. Sid's dream was to create a prosthetic hand so finely tuned that it could feel the caress of a loved one's cheek. It all sounded nifty to Alice, especially the part where Geoff stood to make imponderable amounts of money. It got even better when he informed her that he'd extracted just under twenty million dollars from his old firm as his buyout.

Those first days of Tactilitics were heady, even though she started seeing a lot less of her husband. She coped by buying herself a vibrator—speaking of robots and neural pathways—and upping the cable to premium. But the promised breakthrough was proving tougher than anticipated. The body's neural pathways were a lot easier to replicate for motion than feeling. Deadlines were missed. Prototypes failed. The venture capitalists at Bain got antsy. The stress started to take its toll on Geoff. He became snappy and brooding. The romantic gestures dried up. He stopped sharing his hopes and dreams, though he had no problem with unburdening himself of his frustrations. Sex was a distant memory. His quest for artificial feeling had significantly degraded his attention to the real stuff. Alice began to understand why Hannah's mother had hit the bricks without looking back.

She put a brave face on it. She told him it wouldn't be the end of the world if Tactilitics failed. There was still all that cash in the bank. He could write a novel or build craft furniture or snorkel. He could do anything his heart desired. As long as he was nice to her. As long as he loved her. Or even just fucked her every now and then. What she couldn't accept was being ignored; being treated as if her need to achieve even a modicum of intimacy with him was some sort of intrusion on his mad-scientist act. But Geoff wasn't listening. He was a man obsessed. Failure was not an option.

Alice became miserable. In the suburbs. Surrounded by women who divided their time between spin class and school pickup lines. So when the impossibly handsome, well-mannered, French-accented man who owned the only decent restaurant this side of Back Bay offered to cook her dinner, she accepted, sensing that it was her best means of escaping this ice-cold android universe in which she was trapped.

The afternoon dragged on. The lockdown ended. Geoff, still in a huff over her incursion into his lair, finally went into Tactilitics, rumbling away on his motorcycle, shattering the neighborhood's calm with a great eructative parting blast. Hannah sent her a text from school saying she was fine. Celia called, but Alice didn't pick up. She was still a little pissed off at her friend. It had been shitty of her to pull rank with that step-mother remark, especially since she knew how hard Alice tried to look after Hannah. She did, however, listen to the voice mail.

"Just me. Thanks again for lunch, that was nice. I'm sure you've seen they lifted the lockdown. Oh, I was wondering . . . is Jack there? If he is, have him give me a call. I was also wondering if you found out anything more about what the kids were up to last night? I'm still in the dark about that. Any light you could shed . . . okay, bye."

Sorry. No Jack. No light. She started to surf on her phone. On Twitter, she read about the murder. There were photos of the house where it happened. It was on Locust, just a few blocks away. The victim had just been identified. Eden Angela Perry of Watertown. In the photo they'd dug up, she had a sweet face and an antic smile. There was something familiar about the girl she couldn't put her finger on. Who *was* she? It was right on the tip of her tongue. Not school. She went on Facebook and looked at Eden Perry's page. Friends only. She tried Instagram. That was restricted as well. Eden was a careful girl. Just not careful enough.

Through the cracked-open window, she heard the sound of a car stopping out front. Thinking it was Jack and Hannah, she went to the window to check. It was just a neighbor, leaning in to speak with the car's driver. Her obnoxious Boston terrier strained at the leash. Alice watched them chat for a half minute, until the car drove away and dog and woman strode off, disappearing from view a few seconds later.

A sluggish neural pathway in Alice's brain fired. Of course. Now she remembered where she'd seen Eden Angela Perry. She was the redhead with the big black dog. Alice would see her walking by the house regularly, bouncing along without a care in the world, the girl who always seemed to have a smile for everyone.

MICHEL

When he was seven, Michel wandered unexpectedly into the aftermath of an explosion. He was walking from his father's restaurant, the original Papillon, to his uncle's, La Coupole. It was a journey he made often—the two families were completely intertwined; child-minding duties were shared. No one worried too much about his walking the streets of Beirut alone. The Mahouns, after all, considered themselves immune from the horrors so abundant around them. Though Maronite Catholics, they were not political. They had nothing to do with the Phalange, whom his father and uncle privately considered thugs. As for Hezbollah and the Druze and the Syrians and the Palestinians—they all had bigger fish to fry than a couple of urbane Francophile chefs, whose restaurants appeared to exist separately from the rest of the chaotic city.

On this particular day, however, Michel had deviated from the approved route to take the shortcut recently shown him by his older cousin Claude. This took him close to the Green Line that separated the eastern part of the city, where his family lived, from violent and chaotic West Beirut. He'd heard the blast, but it had seemed far away, and some acoustical oddity made it appear to be coming from a different direction. It may have been an errant shell or a prematurely detonated car bomb. It was the eighties, after all. A time of explosions. Israeli F-16s and Syrian artillery. The marine barracks and the U.S. embassy. Fadlallah's shattered headquarters, draped in the MADE IN USA sign. A time of massacres, of roadblocks and retaliation. A time of bad-news phone calls followed by heavy silences. A time of funerals.

Whatever the bomb's origin, it exacted a terrible toll, exploding right next to a café where a group of old men were drinking tea. The scene was one Michel would never forget. The stinging smoke suspended in the air; the small fires; the slowly spinning tire of an upended Citroën. And the silence, so profound it was as if the explosion had sucked the possibility of sound from the air. Ambulances had yet to arrive, there were no police around. Just victims, including a few bodies that looked more like meat his father stored in Papillon's freezer than anything human. Most of the living lay on the ground, their shattered limbs twitching. One man, miraculously, still sat in his chair. His body from the neck down was drenched in blood, but his face remained unblemished, and he still held his unshattered glass between his fingers. What Michel remembered most clearly was his expression. It didn't show pain or sorrow or fear, but rather a sort of bewildered indignation, an anger aimed far beyond cordite and shrapnel. *I don't have anything to do with this*, it said. *This is a big mistake. Please, will someone explain what this madness has to do with me? Will someone take this nonsense away and pour me another glass of tea?*

That was how Michel felt when the police on his porch asked to see his son. Their presence was a mistake. Shocking, certainly. But wrong. It might look bad, it might cause damage and pain, but it was still just a misfire that needed to be remedied before he could return to the normal business of his life.

"What is this about?" he asked from the bottom of the porch steps.

"This is about us needing to speak with him," the woman said, her agreeable voice at odds with her insistent words. "Is he home?"

Michel did not want these people in his house. He did not want them speaking to his son.

"I believe he's at school."

"Actually, he isn't," the woman said.

"I'll need to know what this is about."

"Sir, there's only so long we're going to stand out here having a conversation with you," the man said.

His voice was not like hers. There was a threat in it. Michel knew men like this. Arguing with him would be pointless.

"Let me see if he's inside," he said. "Wait here."

The man started to say something but the woman stopped him.

"We'd appreciate that."

They made way for him. Michel opened the door, his mind scrambling to figure out what he was going to do next. Whom to call, what to say. But the thinking stopped when he saw Christopher standing halfway down the hall, looking small and terrified. He wore sweatpants and a rumpled T-shirt. Last night's torment had increased a thousandfold. He understood that the police were out there and he appeared to know why. Michel wanted to slam the door shut but the woman was already speaking.

"Christopher?" she asked.

Her voice was layered with friendliness and warmth. Michel gestured with his head for Christopher to return to his room, but the boy's eyes were on the detectives. He started to approach slowly, like a sleepwalker.

"So it's probably best if we do this inside," the woman said through the still-open door as Christopher arrived.

Michel hesitated. In America, you didn't have to let the police inside your house without a warrant. He knew this.

"Or we can take him with us," the man said, guessing his thoughts.

Michel led everyone to the living room. He gestured to the two chairs facing the sofa. The detectives didn't move.

"We'd like to speak with him alone," the man said.

This was too much.

"No, I need to be here. He's only seventeen. I have the right."

The detectives exchanged a look. He waited for them to sit before he conducted his son to the sofa.

"I'm going to be recording us," the woman said as she placed a small device on the coffee table between them.

"Christopher, my name is Detective Gates. I'm with the state police. This is my colleague Detective Procopio. He works here in Emerson. Do you know why we're here?"

"No . . ."

Michel looked at his son. He knew. It was in his voice.

"We'd like to ask you if you know a young woman named Eden Perry."

Christopher stared at them in blank terror. He shook his head. It seemed to be more convulsion than denial.

"We have her phone, Christopher," Gates said.

"Lotta texts from you," Procopio added. "Including one from last night saying you were coming over."

"Yes," Christopher said, his voice almost a whisper. "I know her."

"And you saw her last night?"

Christopher hesitated. Michel's heart thudded against his ribs. A terrible knowledge was blooming in his mind. The police being here was no mistake. The shell had landed where intended.

"You need to tell us the truth, Christopher," Gates said. "This is incredibly important. You understand that, right?"

"What is this?" Michel asked. "What are we talking about?"

The woman gave her head a slight silencing shake, though her eyes remained on the boy.

"Yeah," Christopher said, his voice somehow softer. "We hung out."

"Where?"

"The house where she's staying."

"You know what happened to her, don't you?"

Christopher shook his head.

"I think you do."

Gates's voice managed to be both comforting and merciless.

"I just woke up. I saw it like ten minutes ago."

"What is this?" Michel asked. "What's going on?"

Gates finally looked at him.

"Eden Perry was murdered in the early hours of the morning."

The pounding in Michel's chest grew even more powerful. Gates turned back to Christopher.

"You sure there isn't something you want to tell us about that?"

But words were beyond Christopher now. He couldn't even seem to move his head. Gates stood and walked over to him. She put her index finger beneath his chin. It was a gesture so intimate and gentle that Michel did not even think to object. She raised his head until he was looking at her.

"What's this on your neck, Christopher?"

There were four scratch marks, like the vapor trails of fighter jets.

Michel hadn't seen them last night. He remembered his son's flipped collar, his refusal to remove his jacket.

"How did you get these?"

Christopher pulled away from her and covered his neck with his hand.

"I don't know. I must have scratched myself."

Gates nodded, as if this made perfect sense. The man stood.

"You're going to need to come with us," he said.

"You're arresting him?"

"Nobody's under arrest," Gates said. "But your son is a material witness to a murder. We need to formally interview him at the station."

"Do it here."

"Mr. Mahoun, there are procedures we are all going to need to follow from this point forward."

"Then I'm coming with him."

"Christopher? Is that what you want?"

He nodded. Stunned.

"Speak up," Michel said.

"Yes. I want my father there."

"You got your phone on you?" Procopio asked.

"Yes."

"You can bring that along."

They wanted Christopher to ride with them; Michel could follow. He agreed, but only after he extracted a promise that they'd ask his son nothing until Michel was with him again. Gates seemed to be decent but he did not trust the man. There was an anger in him that Michel had seen when he was younger, at roadblocks, in the markets.

The drive over took a very long time. Thinking had become difficult. He could not make things fit together. A girl named Eden. *We have her phone.* His son arriving home, speechless and distressed and late, far too late. Those scratches on his neck, the way he'd hidden them. At the station, he parked in the visitor lot while they drove Christopher to the back of the building. A small group of people had gathered out front. The press. They watched him suspiciously as he approached. One of them raised a camera.

"Sir, who are you?" a woman's voice asked as he passed.

"Nobody," he said without thinking.

The officer behind the glass told Michel to wait. He started to pace, terrified that they'd lied, that they were holding him out here while they tricked his son into saying things. But then the door swung open and Gates was beckoning him with a manila folder. He followed her to a small windowless room with a table. Michel took the place next to his son. Christopher looked completely bewildered now, as he had in the days after Maryam's death. The world had changed and he couldn't understand why.

"Just so you know, we're still recording," Gates said.

The camera was tucked up in a corner of the ceiling, like a sleeping bat.

"So, Christopher, we're going to read you something now that you've probably heard before on TV. But I still want you to pay attention and let us know if you have any questions."

Procopio took a laminated card from the inner pocket of his sport coat and read the familiar words about attorneys and silence. When they were done Christopher numbly said he understood.

"So," Gates continued. "You've asked for your father to be present for the interview but waived your right to an attorney. Is that correct?"

"Yes."

"Maybe he should have a lawyer," Michel said.

"Your call. But if you do get representation, that person will replace you. You can't both be in here."

"No, I want to be here."

"So, just to be clear, no lawyer?"

"For now."

She turned back to the boy.

"Christopher, why don't you tell us about last night. In your own words. Take your time. Don't leave anything out. We'll decide what's important."

"We hung out at the house where she was staying . . ."

"Eden Perry."

"Yeah, Eden."

"We being?"

"There was me and Jack and Hannah."

"Could you provide us with full names?"

"Jack Parrish and Hannah Holt."

"So it was just the four of you."

"Yeah."

"What time did you get there?"

"Like, eight. Some other kids were supposed to come but they didn't show. I got there first and then Jack Parrish and Hannah Holt got there . . ."

"You can just call them Jack and Hannah now," Gates said.

"Okay. And then Jack and Hannah got there and we just, I don't know, hung out. Listened to music and talked."

"Did you drink? Smoke weed? Do any other kind of drug?"

Christopher cut his eyes in the direction of his father.

"Nobody was wasted or anything, if that's what you mean."

"See, I'm not sure if that's a yes or a no."

"No."

"Okay. Go on."

"So we hung out and then Jack and Hannah left."

"What time was this?"

"Around midnight."

"But you stuck around?"

He nodded.

"Why was that?"

"To be with Eden," Christopher said after a moment's hesitation.

"Was there something going on between the two of you? You in a relationship?"

"Not really. Sorta. I don't know."

"You're going to have to explain that, Christopher."

"You just never know with her. What she's thinking about stuff."

"How about you? What did you think about stuff?"

"I liked her."

"Okay, go on," Gates said, after it became clear Christopher wasn't going to say more.

"So we hung for a while. And then I left."

"Did you two make out? Have sex?"

"No."

"What time did you finally leave?"

"I don't know. Late."

"And you went home?"

"Yes. I mean, I may have walked around for a while."

"Why?"

He stared at the table.

"Christopher? Were you upset? Was something wrong?"

"No."

"You sure?"

He nodded. Gates watched him for a moment. If she was frustrated by his evasiveness, she hid it well.

"So I'm a little confused here. How would you characterize your relationship with Eden?"

"I don't know."

"But you were into her," Procopio said.

After a moment, Christopher nodded.

"But she wasn't into you."

"You just gotta know Eden."

"Well, that's not possible now," Gates said, "so we're going to have to rely on you for that."

"She's very . . . unpredictable."

"In what way?"

"Just hard to pin down."

"Not that hard, it seems," Procopio muttered.

"So, Christopher," Gates said. "We gotta talk about these scratches on your neck. How'd you get them?"

"I don't know. I must have just done it to myself."

"So Eden didn't give them to you?"

"No," Christopher said, his tone incredulous, as if it was the craziest thing he'd ever heard.

"You guys have a fight?"

"I said no!" he answered, raising his voice.

"Christopher," Michel said.

Gates looked at him and shook her head.

"How long did you walk around?" Procopio asked.

"I don't know. A while."

"Five minutes? Two hours?"

"He said he didn't know," Michel said.

Procopio looked at him, with his anger. But it was Gates who spoke.

"I think it's best if you don't interrupt, Mr. Mahoun." She turned back to the boy. "Can you tell us what time you got home? Specifically."

He shook his head. Gates turned to Michel once again.

"Can you help us out with that one?"

"I can speak now?" Michel said, instantly regretting the words.

"Yes, please," Gates said, ignoring the sarcasm.

His first impulse was to tell the truth. Just before four a.m. But Christopher knew the time and he wasn't telling them. Michel needed to know why before he said a word.

"No, I'm sorry. It was late."

"I'm curious about one thing, though," Gates said. "You didn't text her after you left."

"What?"

"You texted her a lot. But you didn't after you left."

"I thought she was asleep," Christopher said, feebly.

Gates stared at him without reacting. It suddenly struck Michel that this was a mistake. He shouldn't be letting them question his son without a lawyer.

"Christopher, look at me." His son turned to him. "Do not say another word. Do you understand me? I'm going to find someone to help us and until I do you must remain silent. Tell me you understand me."

Christopher nodded.

"Not a good move, Dad," Procopio said.

"We'd like to go now," Michel said.

Neither detective responded. The door opened and a tall, uniformed man with silver hair entered. He did not look at Michel and his son. He nodded at Gates, then took up a position against the wall, his arms folded. He finally looked at Christopher. His expression was not reassuring.

"Okay," Gates said. "Christopher, I want you to listen to me, because this is important. Is there anything more you want to tell us about what happened between you and Eden last night? Anything at all?"

"No!"

"Did you guys have a fight? Did you shove her? It could have just been one of those things. Something you didn't even mean to do."

"No," he said, his voice plaintive now.

"Enough," Michel said. "My son needs a lawyer."

Everyone watched Christopher. But he was obeying his father now.

"So here's what's going to happen next," Gates said finally. "We're going to put something called a forty-eight-hour hold on you. Which means that you're going to be staying here with us for the time being."

"No! Dad . . ."

"Wait," Michel said.

"The reason we're doing this is we believe you have vital information about what happened to Eden that you aren't sharing with us. We need you here with us until you're ready to do that."

"I don't understand," Michel said. "Is he under arrest?"

"Technically, yes, he's in our custody. But he's not being charged with a crime at this point."

"Then let him come home with me. I'll make sure he doesn't go out."

"Mr. Mahoun, we're going to need you to leave now."

"I want to stay."

"Sir, we're really going to need you to leave."

Procopio said this. Michel felt his anger rise, but he knew that conflict with this man would only hurt Christopher. He looked at his son, who wouldn't meet his eye.

"You'll be home soon."

Christopher nodded, suddenly a million miles away. It was as if he was locked inside his own head even more securely than inside this building.

"Mr. Mahoun?"

There were more people gathered outside now. There were vans with antennae protruding from their roofs. The questions were more aggressive as Michel came through the doors. They understood now that he was involved. He passed them without a word and drove quickly out of the parking lot. It wasn't until he was on Centre that he realized he had no idea where he was going. He pulled to the side of the road, suddenly finding it hard to breathe. The thought of his son locked up was like a hand on his throat. He rolled down the window but that didn't help.

He needed to find a lawyer. He had two of them. The first was for immigration; the second dealt with the restaurant. Neither would do for this. Sofia. She'd had a boyfriend. David. He'd been a prosecutor in

Boston but was in private practice now. Supposedly a big deal. He'd come to Papillon a few times. A little arrogant, but friendly and obviously smart as hell. She would be at the restaurant now, prepping dinner, dealing with the chaos caused by Michel's sudden departure. She'd been texting and calling ever since he left. Her latest message had come just a few minutes ago: *Okay now I'm getting worried. You have no idea,* Michel thought as he put his car in gear and drove to the only place in the world that made sense for him to be now.

PATRICK

The pain in his leg woke him. Otherwise, there was no telling how long he might have slept. Last night, he'd wound up finishing the liter of Suntory he'd been working on for the last couple of days. He'd greeted the dawn with a can of Ruby Grapefruit hard seltzer that had left a metallic aftertaste in his mouth. After that came an oblivion that was blessedly free of voices, dreams, anything at all.

He staggered to his feet and examined his bite wound. The two-inch-long bruise had settled into various shades of yellow and brown. The dog had really done a number on him. He supposed he was lucky it hadn't broken the skin. He recalled boyhood myths about rabies, long needles jammed into your stomach, zombified dads chained to radiators to keep them from harming loved ones.

His phone was dead so he went through to the kitchen to check the microwave clock: 2:43 p.m. Not good. At least there was still plenty of time to make his five o'clock with Ann Nichols. It was the only thing on his calendar for the day. He didn't particularly want to go to the office, but dared not cancel, given his recent track record. Last time he checked, he was looking after eighty million dollars of client wealth, from which he drew a base fee of just under a million. It might be worthwhile to show his face every now and then.

He showered, brushed his teeth to rid himself of the rotted citrus taste, then downed a cup of coffee. For reasons he did not care to examine, he wasn't hungover. Nor was he hungry. Still, he should eat something, since the last time he'd had food—if you discounted last night's fistful of pistachios, whose shells were currently scattered around his recliner—was the breakfast croissant he'd microwaved before work yesterday.

He drove to Whole Foods and parked in a remote corner of the lot, beyond the delivery trucks and dinged employee Hondas. He had to keep his eyes open as he walked to the store. There was often a demolition derby atmosphere out here, destroyer-class Suburbans and Escalades heedlessly backing out of tight spaces and barreling toward the exit like they were fleeing hunter-killer subs. The end might be nigh for him, but not like that.

The store was busy. Nearly everyone was on a phone, which reminded him that he'd left his own charging on his kitchen table. There was no reason to go back for it. There was a landline in his office for no one to call him on. He went straight to the deli section and grabbed a sectioned container. The choices were abundant beneath the scrupulously polished spit shields. Orzo salad and shrimp fried rice and cauliflower cheese. Meat loaf or turkey meat loaf or vegetarian meat loaf. Honey-braised carrots and ratatouille. Pizza. Wraps.

He chose chicken tikka masala with saffron rice, toasted-almond broccoli, and a cube of corn bread. The sugar cookie went into one side pocket of his suit jacket, a plastic knife and fork into the other. He closed the container, then headed toward the front of the store, pausing to pick up a bottle of spring water. He bypassed the registers, exiting instead directly in front of the service desk. The woman working there—her badge read *Soo*—looked up and smiled. Patrick smiled back. Just after he passed, he realized that he'd forgotten napkins. He turned back to Soo.

"How can I help you today?" she asked.

"Do you have any napkins?"

She looked over Patrick's shoulder.

"Daniel, could you go get this gentleman some napkins, please."

She spoke to a slim young man, Central American by the looks of him, who'd just finished filling a bag at the closest register. Off he went.

"How is it out there?" Soo asked.

"Warming up."

"Springs are getting so much shorter."

"Tell me about it. It's April and I'm using my car's AC."

She shook her head in affable commiseration. Shame about the planet dying. The odor from the food he was in the process of stealing filled the air between them. Soo's phone rang. Patrick stepped back a little to give her privacy. Daniel returned. He handed over a one-inch stack of recycled paper and nodded shyly when Patrick thanked him.

"Take care," he mouthed at Soo.

She cupped her phone's speaker.

"You too," she mouthed back, warmly.

He walked out of the store without further ado. Free and clear, once again. In the unlikely event someone had challenged him, he would have simply said he'd paid at the café. Nobody would have doubted it. The thought of him shoplifting was inconceivable. He was a white man with a hundred-dollar haircut and a two-thousand-dollar Italian suit who walked with his chin up and his spine stiffened. People like him didn't shoplift.

There was an unopened fifth of Suntory in the trunk, but he decided to let that continue aging for the time being. After he set himself up in the driver's seat, he put on Mozart's clarinet quintet and spread napkins in a symmetrical grid on his lap. When he opened the container, the BMW's interior immediately filled with the smell of spices from the other side of the world. The chicken was still warm. He took a bite, washing it down with a three-dollar bottle of water.

He sometimes thought what a strange sight he must make, dining contentedly in his car like a first-class passenger jetting above the Atlantic. Although there was little chance of him being seen back here. Occasionally, there might be an employee who'd just clocked out, but they only wanted to get away. Once, a father and daughter had come to practice parallel parking in a sporty little Jetta. Patrick had provided an appreciative audience as he picked over his chicken parm, throwing a big thumbs-up the kid's way when she nailed it on the third try.

Now, sitting alone, eating a meal he didn't really want, his leg still aching, he thought about the voice he'd heard last night. It had been a while since Gabi had spoken to him. A few weeks, anyway. In the days following her death two years ago, he used to hear her all the time, often for several nights in a row. He supposed one day the voice would vanish altogether. He'd need to watch an old video if he wanted to hear it. But that wouldn't be the same. Not the same at all.

For now, however, it was still there. It came as no surprise that she endured in his memory. He'd felt closer to Gabriella than any other person in his life. This wasn't something he chose. It was just how things turned out. She'd been such a sweet, beautiful child. He'd push her down Centre in her stroller and watch the faces of passersby erupt in joy when they encountered her smile. Her first dozen years had been one long sunny day. Everything came easy to her. Friends and school. The violin. Soccer and dance. If there were tantrums or sulks, Patrick couldn't remember them.

The transformation began when she was thirteen. Suddenly, she was prey to ungovernable moods, whiplashing between bouts of weeping and nearly hysterical enthusiasm. She became secretive and paranoid. Her relationship with her mother, Lily, turned downright toxic. If Patrick touched her, she reacted like an oft-whipped dog. Unbelievably, shamefully, he found himself avoiding her company.

At first, they put the change down to the usual tempests of puberty. But it got worse. Her eating became sporadic. Empty wine bottles turned up under her bed. And then there was the burning. She grew obsessed with the false idea that she had split ends and decided to torch them off with a lighter. The sickening smell of roasted hair began to fill the house. They'd be eating dinner or watching television and it would arrive like a ghostly visitation. Confiscating matchbooks and lighters made no difference. They lived in fear that she would light her head on fire or burn down the house. They fought with her, they punished her, foolishly thinking that this was simply bad behavior, that this was all something she could control, when actually it was just the first symptoms of the disease that would kill her.

Therapy began just after her fourteenth birthday. They shuffled through a half dozen well-meaning, ineffectual counselors who rolled out words like *depression* and *compulsion* and *ideation*, but never seemed to get to the heart of the matter. Next came psychiatrists and their magic bullets. Lexapro and Ativan and Klonopin—names that appeared to have been yanked from a fantasy novel. The pills made her sleepy and docile; they dried out her mouth and constipated her and messed with her periods. The only thing they didn't do was make her better.

She was sixteen when she discovered the bittersweet deliverance of opioids. Lily had suffered a bad CrossFit accident around the time that Patrick had undergone dental surgery, leading to a glut of painkillers in the house that neither of them used—Patrick had his booze, Lily her innate toughness. They rid the house of any remaining prescriptions, but by then it was too late. The hook was in. Obtaining pills wasn't hard for her. For months, they had no idea what was happening, blinded by their suddenly serene child. But her receptors got hungrier; the agonists agonized; supply couldn't equal demand. The Scotty Parrish debacle happened and there was no more denying reality. She was drifting farther and farther away. She slept for entire days and then she didn't sleep at all. More, her hungry brain called. More.

Heroin came to the rescue. It turned out it was a lot cheaper and easier to obtain than the pills. Which was news to Patrick, who'd always associated the drug with poverty and the outer reaches of bohemia, when in fact it was dangling from majestic suburban maples and oaks, ripe and ready for the picking. The needles you could get at CVS.

Gabi disappeared, right before their very eyes, to be replaced by a shifty impostor who lied and stole and vanished for days at a time. She limped to the finish line of high school and then enrolled at Barnard, while her parents crossed their fingers and hoped the change of scenery would do the trick. A dean called after less than two months to report her missing. Patrick eventually tracked her down to a B-movie motel on Long Island. She moved back home but was soon wandering the streets, a girl gone wrong looking to get right. God only knew where she wound up staying during that last wretched year and a half, except that she didn't leave the area, remaining close enough to summon Patrick to fetch her and drag her to detox when things got too bad. Then the insurance ran out and they wound up spending close to forty thousand dollars on two useless stretches in rehab. It didn't work. Nothing worked.

It was during this time that he came to understand that he was to blame. This was his legacy to her, more than her looks and smarts, more than her tendency to sunburn or her foot speed. The malignant gene that wound through his genealogy, killing his grandfather at forty-two and afflicting uncles and countless distant relatives and, truth be told, him, had now been passed along to her. By him. There was no other explanation. She'd been deeply loved and diligently instructed; there'd been no trauma or neglect. She'd been an angel. It was a sickness. And he'd given it to her.

He was desperate to do something to stop her slide, but it was too late. The cancer had spread too far. And so, to his eternal shame, he gave in to the urge to let go. Although he'd reacted to her first few disappearances with feverish panic, near the end he began to meet news of her latest vanishing with unspoken relief. There were times when he knew that she was sliding into danger and he didn't raise a finger to stop it; times when he could have tracked her down but did not leave the house. Exhausted and weak and cowardly, he surrendered to the sickness he'd given her.

And then came the final abandonment. Her arrest at Whole Foods had been his last stand. Instead of taking her to the next expensive rehab place, he'd let the state load her into a van and deposit her in one of their grim brick junky warehouses. He told himself that it was tough love, but it was simply bone-weary weakness. The phone rang the next night; the institution's name appeared on the LED screen. He and Lily were both in the kitchen at the time, clearing plates from another silent, stricken dinner. They looked at each other, he shook his head, she nodded. They listened as Gabi left a message, pleading to be picked up. The phone rang again and another message echoed through the kitchen, this one even more hysterical. They fled the house, sheltering at a multiplex in front of an absurd action picture. Sixteen more messages awaited them when they got home. Patrick erased them without listening.

The police arrived four days later. He was passed out on the sofa—he was drinking steadily by this point, starting the long pursuit of his own oblivion. After they gave him the terrible news, he looked down at his feet and saw that he was only wearing one sock. He was clearly over the limit, so the cops gave him a lift. At the hospital, people asked if this was his daughter. He was tempted to say no, not even close.

Over the next few days, as he endured the funeral and everything that went with it, a terrible understanding settled over him. He'd failed her. Pure and simple. This was on him. He was her father and fathers saved their kids. Fathers didn't breathe a secret sigh of relief when their daughters disappeared into the wilderness, taking their agony with them. Fathers answered the phone. And fathers didn't slumber on the sofa while their child was finally silencing her depthless and unfathomable pain as other people's kids sat eating Happy Meals a few feet away. He'd failed her and no one, however well informed or experienced or sagacious, would ever be able to tell him otherwise.

He'd had enough of his stolen food after three mouthfuls. This was how it always went, the initial burst of appetite crushed by his body's inability to handle more than a few morsels. It had been months since he'd finished a meal. He stowed his trash in the nearest bin and drove to the office, chewing three breath mints on the way. The receptionist greeted him with a baffled smile. He didn't know her name—Griff liked to use temps to avoid paying benefits. Kara, the assistant he shared with two other brokers, had long ago migrated to a position near her more productive bosses.

Ann Nichols sat in his office. She acknowledged his entrance with a grim, censorious nod.

"Well, I thought you'd abandoned me," she said, even though he was a few minutes early.

She was his oldest client, both in terms of the calendar and the duration of their relationship. She came by once a month to make sure that her nest egg was safe and warm. Really, she just liked to chat. Her position was only three hundred grand—chump change for Emerson Wealth Management Partners—but she fretted over it like it was the Getty Trust. She came across like a widow, though she occasionally made brief, obscure references to "Otis," and it was only on about her tenth visit that Patrick figured out this was her husband, not her dog. He presumed she knew all about his decline, but she was sticking with him. He hoped it wasn't pity, but ultimately he understood that it didn't much matter.

She was scheduled in for a half hour, as always, even though their actual business usually took somewhere south of ten minutes. It was nothing more than a bells-and-whistles tour of her statement. His presentation was usually followed by a much longer chat about anything from the weather to that time she lunched with Ethel Kennedy, who was not the saint everybody made her out to be.

"I'd never abandon you," Patrick answered, though his attention was focused on the ominous Post-it stuck to his keyboard. It was from Griff, the firm's managing partner. *We need to talk.*

"Did you hear about the murder?" she asked.

"Murder?"

"At the Bondurants'."

The name was vaguely familiar.

"They live here in town," she prompted. "On Locust?"

Locust. The word crashed into his mind like a Panzer division rumbling down a narrow city street.

"Their son got leukemia when he was at Waldo," she prompted. "He's who the fun run's named after. He was on the cross-country team."

The Run for Rick. Of course. He knew this family. EWMP had gone after their portfolio a couple of years ago, but Bondurant wouldn't shift from the rickety old Boston firm his ancestors had probably used since before the Revolutionary War.

"Somebody killed them?"

"Nobody's saying who died."

"Wow. Was it a home invasion?"

She shrugged peevishly, frustrated by her lack of gossip-worthy data. Things were picking up now inside Patrick's skull. The dog's yelp; the figure in the trees. His leg started to throb.

"But have they arrested somebody or . . . ?"

She knew nothing more. Patrick rushed her through the presentation, then invented an excuse to hustle her unhappily out the door. Once alone, he looked up what he could about the murder on his desktop.

There'd been a lockdown ordered for the town's schools, but it had been lifted. They'd released a photo of the victim, a young woman from Watertown, some sort of relation to the Bondurants. *My God*, he thought as he looked at her sweet face. His mouth suddenly felt parched. He badly needed a drink.

He found the Bondurants' address in the company database and Google Earthed it. It was one house down from where he'd been bitten, just beyond that dense thicket. He touched the treetops on the computer screen with his index finger. *There*, he thought. He'd been standing right there.

Somebody needed to be told about this. His instinctive impulse was to call Lily, but his ex-wife was currently in Asheville, chasing happiness and rarely picking up. There was Griff, but a breathless report of what happened while he was wandering the streets at three a.m. might not be a good look for Patrick, especially after that Post-it and the reckoning it promised.

The police. Despite their bad history, it had to be them. They needed to know what he knew. He dialed the nonemergency line and was told to come in immediately. He was tempted to take a detour to the trunk of his car, where that Suntory continued to age. Not a good idea. In fact, he decided to leave the car where it was. He needed to figure out what he was going to say before he arrived. As he strode along Centre, he tried to focus on that figure in the woods. Tall, broad-shouldered. Silent, faceless, but very real. He wished his mind could run it through one of those software programs to sharpen the pixels until a clear image appeared.

There were news trucks outside the station, a scrum of media by the main entrance. They tried to question him but he simply nodded amiably. The officer behind the bulletproof glass invited him to take a seat. The inner door opened after just a couple of minutes. A middle-aged Black woman in a dark blue pants suit emerged.

"Mr. Noone?"

He rose, once again aware of his throbbing leg.

"Detective Gates," she said, offering a hand as he approached. "I understand you have some information for us about last night's incident?"

"I think I may have seen someone on Locust."

She tilted her head. He had her attention.

"When was that?"

"Late. Like three in the morning."

Another correct answer.

"Okay, come with me."

She led him across a bullpen pervaded by a sense of hushed urgency. There was another detective in the conference room. Patrick froze when he saw him. It was the asshole who'd arrested Gabi. He was no longer in uniform, wearing instead a too-tight sport coat and a poorly knotted tie. But he had the same bullying presence, all knuckles and neck and scowl. His eyes flashed recognition as well, though he couldn't quite place Patrick.

"This is Detective Procopio," Gates said.

"We know each other, right?" Procopio said.

"You arrested my daughter."

"That's right," he said, as if they'd once been in the same golf foursome. "How's she doing?"

"She died a couple of weeks after that."

"I'm sorry to hear that," Procopio said after a beat.

Gates's gaze traveled between the two men, trying to determine if there was a problem here.

"Go ahead and take a seat," she said finally. "And just so you know, we record everything in here."

Her voice was gentle and polite. It oozed concern. She might have been one of the procession of counselors he'd sat before during his daughter's descent.

"So why don't you tell me what you saw last night," Gates said.

Patrick spoke the lines he'd rehearsed on the way over. They'd seemed plausible on Centre, but here, with two sets of skeptical eyes fixed on him, they sounded less reliable. A lot less. Gates's expression remained polite, but Procopio's face slowly twisted into disbelief.

"Do you think you could provide a better description of this individual?" Gates asked when he'd finished.

"That's all I have."

"But you're sure there was somebody there," Procopio said, as if he couldn't believe what he was hearing.

"I am."

"And yet you didn't feel the need to call it in?"

It was not an unfair question. Still, something in the man's tone brought it all back. Gabi, gray-skinned and shivering, hunched over in defeat. The cop, refusing to listen to Patrick's entreaties.

Patrick looked at Gates.

"Could he be recused from this?" he asked.

"Recused?" Gates asked in surprise.

"I don't feel comfortable with him here. He treated my daughter unfairly."

"Unfairly," Procopio said.

"Yes," Patrick shot back, holding his gaze.

Gates studied the two men, one and then the other.

"Detective Procopio, I wonder if you could leave us alone," she said.

For a brief moment, anger flashed in Procopio's eyes. But then he flipped his pad closed and walked from the room without another word.

"Thank you," Patrick said.

"Now, let's see," she said, ignoring his gratitude. "You said the dog you struck was a black Lab."

"Lab-like."

"How big would you say it was?"

"You know, medium large. Like this."

He held his flattened hand two feet above the floor.

"And you're sure of the time? Just after three?"

"I remember checking."

"I'm curious—how can you be so sure there was someone there if you didn't actually see them?"

"Yeah, okay. I know it sounds strange."

"Not necessarily. I'm just trying to paint a picture."

"I just knew there was someone there. That's all."

"Would you be willing to accept the possibility that it was all in your imagination?"

Rationally, the answer was yes. Of course it could have been in his imagination. So much was these days.

"No," he said.

She stared at him a moment.

"Had you been drinking at all last evening?"

"Not to excess."

"I'm not sure what that means."

"I was under the limit."

"Do you take drugs, Mr. Noone? Prescription or recreational?"

"No. Well, blood pressure stuff. Diuretics. But nothing that would make me see things."

"Understood. Now, let's go back to what you were doing out and about at such a late hour."

Her tone remained gentle, but there was something new in it. Something sharp and cold.

"What do you mean?"

"It just seems odd, a man like you driving around aimlessly at that time of night."

"It helps me sleep."

"You have trouble sleeping?"

"Sometimes."

"And you don't take anything for that?"

"Not drugs, no. Like I said."

"Do you know Bill and Betsy Bondurant?"

"I think I met Bill once. At the office."

"Have you ever been inside their house?"

"Why would I go inside their house?"

She didn't answer his question. Patrick began to suspect that coming here was a mistake.

"So I need to get back to work . . ."

"Just one more thing. Do you know a young woman named Eden Perry?"

"No."

"She's twenty, kinda pretty, reddish hair. Medium height."

"I know who she is. The girl who got killed. I just read about her online. That's why I'm here."

Gates stared at him, the sweetness and light momentarily drained from her eyes. Her question remained.

"No, I don't know her."

"And you didn't see her last night?"

"No. Just the dog."

"And the man."

"And the man."

"I'm going to give you my number," she said, the charm returning. "If for some reason you think of anything more specific, I'd like you to call me right away."

She handed him a card, then led him to the lobby, where someone else was waiting, a woman with jet-black hair. There were tattoos on her hands and neck, suggesting more beneath her off-the-rack work suit. Bright red lipstick failed to soften her locked-down mouth. The thick mascara on her eyelashes was clumped and runny. There was a beauty there, but she seemed hell-bent on masking it. Her eyes met Patrick's with a laser focus.

"Ms. Perry," Gates said, a bit unhappily.

Patrick kept walking. Perry. This was the mother. He glanced quickly over his shoulder but she was already speaking to the detective, her words urgent and angry. He was tempted to linger to hear what was being said, but he kept on walking, out the door and through the growing congregation of press, whose questions he once again ignored.

He walked back down Centre in a trance. He got in his car and drove. Lefts and rights, speed bumps and stop signs. Going to the police had been idiotic, especially given his history with them. He should have known what would happen. Disbelief, followed by suspicion. He should have used a lawyer. But he *had* seen someone. He'd seen a man. A man who did not want to be seen.

Locust was blocked off by a state police cruiser. He pulled to the side of the road. The Bondurant house was largely hidden by the trees in its front yard, though he could glimpse police vehicles and vans through them. The copse where he'd seen the man stood just beyond the property—he'd been driving in the other direction last night. Now, in the bright April glare, it didn't look like a dark forest. It was just a patch of trees the size of a tennis court. And yet. There had been someone there. Patient, impassive, guilty of something. He was sure of it.

DANIELLE

She went straight to the station when she heard about the arrest. She probably should have called first, but calls could be ignored. And she wasn't exactly feeling like doing things their way. The rage inside her had finally boiled over. They'd promised to notify her if there were developments. Well, arresting the person who'd killed your child certainly qualified as a development. And yet she had to find out about it from a stranger.

She was going to have to keep an eye on these cops. That was obvious. She understood this the moment they'd asked for her whereabouts
last night. Yes, they needed to know for the record, she got that. But that
wasn't how it came across, as some sort of formality. They truly believed
she could have hurt Eden.

It got worse when Procopio called. She was in her house—a nervous
young officer had driven her from the station. But being home was a
mistake. She understood that the moment she walked through the door.
Her body began to shake, like at the onset of a fever. She went to the
kitchen and thought, *What the fuck am I doing in the kitchen?* She went
up to her bedroom and shed her work clothes. Finding something black
to wear wasn't hard. There were plenty of holdovers from her tatted-up
bullshit biker chick days. The clothes still fit, even though the life didn't.

She wound up standing outside Eden's bedroom. There was a clipped
magazine headline taped to the door. *Eden Hazard.* Whatever that
meant. Danielle grasped the knob but immediately let it go. The police had instructed her to leave her daughter's stuff alone—they might
need to look through it. She didn't really want to go inside, anyway.
Instead, she put her forehead against the faded, wrinkled strip of paper
and started to cry for the second time that day, doubling her total for the
last twenty years. A minute passed and then it was out of her system.

She was redoing her mascara when Procopio called. Eden had been
transported. That's how he put it. Transported. Danielle would be able
to see her now.

"I gotta repeat—you don't need to do this."

"Yes I do."

"I'm just saying—it might be easier not to."

"I'm not looking for this to be easier."

"Your call," he said in that know-it-all tone she always loved to hear
from men.

"Can I ask you something?"

He paused long enough to indicate his reluctance.

"Sure."

"How long was she lying there before you guys found her?"

"I can't really discuss that."

"You saw her, though. At the Bondurant place."

"Yeah," he said. "I saw her."

"I mean, was she naked?"

"She was clothed," he said, with great reluctance.

"Did she look, I don't know, peaceful? Did she look like she'd suffered?"

"I can't really . . . maybe the docs can help you with that one."

That was when she decided she was done with Procopio. If the guy couldn't even summon the decency to utter a comforting little lie, then to hell with him. Any further interactions would be with Gates, who at least knew how to pretend she gave a damn.

The address he gave her was in Boston. Another building, another parking lot, more strangers. They were expecting her. A young, bearded doctor and a Hispanic woman, a social worker. *Too late for either of you*, Danielle thought. They walked down a few corridors and stopped outside a door with a red bulb burning above the frame.

"There's some damage, primarily to her eye," the bearded doctor said. "You should prepare yourself."

"How do you do that?" Danielle said.

"Excuse me?"

"Prepare yourself?"

The doc looked at the social worker, who for some reason was nodding, like the question had already been answered. The doctor knocked. A young man in scrubs opened the door. Everybody went inside. She'd expected something like you saw on TV, a basement warehouse with track lights and bodies in big drawers. Faucets and sinks. The whine of a power saw. But it was just a bare room with a gurney in the middle of it. They did do the unveiling thing, pulling back a thin green sheet that covered Eden's body. The movies got that much right. Her eyes were half open; there was some caked blood clumped in her hair above her left ear. If it hadn't been for the eye, its white turned a sickening violet, as if someone had daubed it with paint, she'd have looked like Eden, asleep.

"How'd she die?"

"Cerebral hemorrhage," the doctor said.

"From being hit?"

"Striking her head after being forcefully shoved, it seems."

"And that's why her eye . . ."

"Correct. Yes."

"Was she raped?"

"We haven't really made a final determination on that yet."

"Come on."

"There appears to have been some sexual contact. You'll have to talk to the detectives about the nature of it."

Everybody waited. Danielle had thought she'd find it impossible to leave her daughter once she was with her, but after just a few seconds she couldn't wait to flee. She didn't want to touch her or smell her or whisper private words into her ear. This wasn't Eden. This was just a dead body where her girl used to live. If she wanted to see Eden, she'd have to look elsewhere.

"So what happens now?"

"You'll be needing to arrange a funeral director," the woman said. "We can help you with that."

"But we won't be releasing the body for a few days," the doctor said.

"Why's that?"

"Autopsy."

"Don't I have to agree to that?"

"It's automatic in cases like these."

Cases like these. Danielle turned and left the room. She kept walking until the front doors whooshed open for her. She had an overwhelming desire to do something, but she had no idea what that might be. No way was she going back home. Not yet. And the cops didn't want her hanging around. They'd made that clear enough.

That's when Bill Bondurant called. He sounded a lot older than he had the last time they spoke. It turned out they'd been in Albany visiting friends for a few days. They'd just finished with the police and were now at somebody's house in Emerson.

"I don't know what could have happened," he said.

"Can I come talk to you?"

He gave her the address. And so it was back to Emerson, this time in her own car. As she drove, she thought back to her first visit. It had been like crossing the ocean to an unknown continent. She didn't relish the idea of spending time with country-club types, even if they were cousins three times removed, or third cousins, or whatever they were. To her surprise, she'd found the Bondurants to be genuinely good people. They were older than she remembered from their first meeting at the funeral, just on the edge of being *old*. But there was a strength there. Not just money strength, but a sort of unshakable decency. Betsy so warm and welcoming, speaking to her as if the few drops of blood they shared were a mighty ancestral river. Bill was more reserved, but that was just his way. He was older than his wife by a good ten years. A gentleman, courtly and polite. At one point he said something that explained the whole strange undertaking.

"Betsy always needs someone to be looking after. With the kids long gone, well . . ."

As for Eden herself, she sat contentedly with her big glass of sweetened iced tea, her traveling circus of nervous tics closed down, at least for the time being. And she really hit it off with the dog. Yes, the Bondurants sure loved Eden. But that was just the way she was. People who hardly knew her were drawn to her. It was the ones who were already close to her that she could drive around the bend.

And so she moved out to Emerson. She and Danielle took a time-out, as they called it nowadays. Eden was also, by her own admission, taking a breather from the boys who'd always been such a big part of her life. As the days and weeks passed, it became harder and harder to argue with Betsy's assessment that everything was *just grand*. Danielle only visited a few times, the last being just over a month earlier. And Eden did not come home at all. But that was fine. She needed to start figuring out how to look after herself and this was a good, safe place to start. Everybody was happy with the arrangement. On the drive home from her last visit Danielle had even allowed herself to think she might be able to stop worrying about her daughter.

And now she was dead. Laid out on a gurney, her left eye like a squished raspberry.

Their own house suddenly uninhabitable, the Bondurants were staying with another elderly couple in one just as big as theirs. After profoundly awkward hugs, the three of them gathered in a vast living room. The dog was there. It came toward Danielle to say hello.

"Thor, come here," Betsy said, sensing the other woman's discomfort.

Danielle noticed its limp as it retreated.

"We're just so sorry," Betsy said, for the fifth time in the last two minutes.

"I can't imagine what happened," Bill added.

"So what did the police tell you? They're not telling me anything."

"They weren't very forthcoming with us, either," Bill said. "We do know there was no forced entry. Which means that Eden must have let them in."

"I don't think she would have done that with a stranger."

"No, it's my impression that they're thinking she knew the attacker."

"Had she made any friends here?"

They exchanged a look.

"Well, yes, I believe she had," Betsy said, a little stiffly.

"Did you meet them?"

"She was always pretty guarded about her personal life," Bill said. "Especially after the party fiasco."

"Party?"

"Didn't she tell you about this?"

"No."

He frowned.

"I specifically asked her to."

"Okay, I'm kind of in the woods here."

The Bondurants exchanged another glance.

"We attended a dinner in the city last month," Betsy said. "We stayed overnight and wound up coming home first thing in the morning. It was clear when we arrived that she'd had herself quite the shindig. There'd been drinking and, well, I think they'd been smoking something. Things looked like they might have got out of hand."

"There wasn't any damage but there was certainly a mess," Bill said. "Let's just put it that way."

"So we had a little sit-down the next day. We told her we didn't mind if she had friends over but, you know, we'd rather know about it."

"And underage drinking," Bill added. "People can be pretty touchy about that nowadays."

Goddammit, Eden.

"She promised she'd never do it again," Betsy said, reading Danielle's anger.

"And you don't know who any of these people were?"

"Well, we didn't actually see them, but Eden indicated they were kids from town," Bill said.

"Presumably some of them will be coming forward," Betsy added.

"Do you think something like that happened last night? A party?"

"Well, it's impossible to know without getting into the house," Bill said.

"What do the police say?"

He spread his hands. Something occurred to Danielle.

"Do you have security cameras?"

"No," Bill said, wistfully. "There never seemed to be the need."

They lapsed into a profound silence.

"I'm so sorry," Betsy said. "We should have looked after her better."

"Don't say that. She loved you guys. You were incredibly generous."

Betsy started to cry.

"I'm just thinking about Rick and how that was and I'm just so sorry."

Danielle felt as if she should comfort her but Bill was already on it. He rose creakily and leaned over his wife and gathered her in a loose hug and spoke quietly to her. Danielle watched them, wishing she was far away from here.

"Is there anything you need help with?" Bill asked when his wife had gathered herself. "I mean, in terms of arrangements?"

It took Danielle a moment to understand that he was talking about the funeral. Her immediate instinct was to politely decline, but that would lead to a conversation she didn't have the energy for.

"That's very kind of you."

There were probably a thousand more questions she should ask, but she doubted she'd hear anything that wouldn't frustrate her even further.

"She was an angel," Betsy said suddenly.

There was a vehemence in her voice that caused both Danielle and Bill to rear back in surprise.

"I understand that she had her peculiarities but she was a good soul."

"Bets," her husband said.

"No, it's true. I knew it the moment I met her. For someone to have done this . . . *this*? It's just barbaric."

Her birdlike body was suddenly shaking with rage. The emotion was contagious, at least to Danielle. The anger she'd felt earlier returned. This was wrong. Wrong, wrong, wrong.

"Well," Bill said, daunted by what he now found himself in the middle of.

As if sensing that intervention was necessary, the woman of the house appeared in the doorway, something on her mind that couldn't wait. She gestured for Bill to come have a word. The dog accompanied him to the door, then returned after he was gone. Danielle once again noticed it was favoring a hind leg.

"He's hurt."

"Yes," Betsy said.

"So I guess he was there when it happened."

"Thor was the one who alerted people. The oil man came for a delivery and heard him barking."

"So he was in there with her the whole time."

Betsy nodded woefully—the thought had occurred to her as well. Danielle looked into the animal's murky eyes. *Tell us*, she thought. *Come on. Fess up.* Bill came back into the room, frowning and rubbing his hands on his khakis.

"What?" Danielle asked.

"There's a rumor going around that you should probably know about." He frowned and nodded. "It appears that they've made an arrest."

There were reporters at the station when she returned. She donned her big sunglasses and walked right through them. They sensed who she was but she was inside before they could start braying. The officer on duty told her she'd have to wait. She sat beneath a poster that told you what to do if someone was choking. The door opened after a few minutes. Gates emerged, accompanied by a man. He was very good looking, dressed in an expensive suit, not a strand of his wavy brown hair out of place. Danielle wondered if he might be the mayor or a big lawyer but then she noticed that there was something about him. The way he carried himself, in his eyes. The gut-punched expression of so many men she'd known. She met his gaze as he passed. Wondering who he has, what he had to do with this. What he knew.

"Ms. Perry," Gates said, unable to mask her unhappy surprise. "What can I do for you?"

Evidently they'd be having this conversation in the lobby.

"I heard there's been an arrest?"

"No, we haven't arrested anyone. But we're making progress."

"Well, people out there are saying there's been an arrest."

"Okay, look," Gates said, lowering her voice even though it was just the two of them. "We're talking to a person of interest."

"Was that him?" Danielle asked, pointing over her shoulder.

"No."

"Then who is it?"

"I can't really talk about that."

"You know about the parties, right?"

Gates twisted her head, like she did.

"What do you know about that?"

"Nothing. I just spoke to the Bondurants."

"We're on top of all that. Believe me."

"But you think this person of interest, he's the one?"

"We simply don't know at this point," Gates said. "To be honest, what would be most helpful to me right now is if you were to leave. I know that sounds harsh, but we're going to have a bunch of people coming in here any minute and it makes no sense for you to mix with them. In fact, it might even be harmful."

"I'm not going to cause trouble."

"I know that, Danielle. You're just going to have to trust us on this. We *are* making progress. Let us do our job. This will be difficult for you to understand or accept, but we're looking after Eden now."

Danielle nodded. She'd go. She'd trust the smart woman with the gentle manner and the Glock on her hip. She had no choice. But Gates was wrong about one thing. They weren't the ones looking after Eden. Danielle was. It had always been her, and only her. Just because the silly girl had gone and gotten herself killed didn't change that. Not for one minute.

Wednesday Night

CELIA

From the back of the Mercedes, Oliver and Jack seemed very far away. Even though she could have reached out and touched them, their words sounded as if they came from a distant room. She understood perfectly well that the car was moving swiftly along well-paved streets, but when she closed her eyes, it felt as if they were drifting away on some deep, slow tide.

It reminded her of how she'd felt just after Jack was born, when she'd been gripped by that mystery fever. For three days, she'd run a temperature; at one point it had shot up to 103. A fever of unknown origin, they called it. Part of her understood that she should be worried. She could see the concern on Oliver's face and the grim expressions of the looming doctors.

Her newborn son seemed especially strange and distant. Jack wouldn't stay on her nipple. Nor would he take the bottle. He'd just wail. After a day of this, he began to feel like somebody else's child, and then not a child at all, but some shrieking creature she'd been condemned to carry around for the rest of her life. There was talk of putting him on a feeding tube. A sense of panic began to pervade the birth suite, even as she continued to dwell so serenely in her feverish neverland.

Finally, after three days, the fever broke. She was once again Celia Parrish and Jack was her baby. All the normal things happened. He settled on her breast, he put on weight. He stood and smiled and walked and talked. He became a beautiful boy and a fine and brilliant young man with a wonderful girlfriend. But every once in a while, when she witnessed him react with an anger out of proportion to events or saw his brow crease in frustration, when she caught him watching that horrible film on his computer or saw the look on his face after Lexi Liriano fled their house, she'd think back to that wailing creature she'd held, so oblivious to all the usual solace. And she'd wonder if she really ever knew him at all.

The story he'd told in the kitchen upon arriving home from school with Oliver was deeply alarming, at least at first. They'd been at the Bondurants' last night. They'd been at the house where the murder took place. Jack and Hannah and Christopher and Eden, whom Hannah had met a few months earlier. It was something they did when Bill and Betsy were away. They'd lied about it because the Bondurants didn't want kids partying there. At first, they just hung out. But there had been tension between Christopher and Eden. Evidently Christopher wanted them to be a couple but she had other ideas. It got a little heated, but by the time Jack and Hannah left around midnight, things had calmed down. Or so they thought. And then there was a lockdown the next day and they found out she was dead. Jack called his father, who'd been on his way home from Connecticut.

Oliver took over the story at this point. He'd instructed Jack to stay put at school and talk to no one. When he finally arrived in Emerson that afternoon, he picked him up, along with Hannah. Once he'd determined that the kids had done nothing wrong, he took Hannah home to tell her parents. And now here they were, father and son, ready to speak with the authorities.

"You could have called," Celia said. "I was worried sick."

"I know. That was wrong of me. I wanted to get all the facts before I spoke to you but . . . that was wrong."

"So what happens now? Have you called the police?"

"Actually, they called me a little while ago. I'm going to touch base with Elaine Otto and then we'll give a statement."

Elaine headed his firm's criminal defense division. Celia was tempted to ask if calling her was absolutely necessary, but Oliver wouldn't be doing it if it wasn't necessary.

"They're saying there's a person of interest," she said instead.

"It's Christopher," Jack said. "Gotta be."

"Christopher? They're saying he killed that girl? That's inconceivable."

Jack said nothing, though his expression suggested it wasn't so inconceivable to him. Oliver's phone rang; it was Elaine. He went into his study to take the call.

"How are you holding up?" Celia asked her son.

"Kind of in shock. But okay."

Celia studied him. Something wasn't right. True, his story explained the lie he'd told about his whereabouts. They were partying in a place they shouldn't. What it didn't explain was why he'd been so upset this morning. The timing made no sense, given that he'd just said he only learned about Eden's death this afternoon.

"Jack, what was wrong with you this morning?"

"What do you mean?"

"When you got home. You were upset."

"I was just tired."

"But it seemed . . ."

"Mom, I was just tired, all right?"

Oliver emerged. He was less gloomy than when he'd first arrived home. He was in his element now, solving problems.

"All right," he said decisively. "Let's go."

As they pulled into the police station's parking lot, Celia came crashing back to earth from her little cloud of serenity. It was time to be herself again. The scene outside the building was hectic. There were vans with antennae and logos, bright lights and agitated people. The press was in attendance. Before leaving the car, Oliver announced that only he and Jack would be going into the interview. They needed to keep this simple. Celia didn't like being left out, but she knew better than to argue. Her husband was in charge. For the time being, he was Jack's lawyer as well as his father.

They walked quickly through the crowd, Oliver in the lead, his large body clearing the way, Celia and Jack swept along in his wake. She gripped her son's arm and kept her chin up. Once inside, they were instructed to wait. Oliver paced; Celia sat beside Jack, trying to radiate the reassurance she wished she could feel. Chief Zorn finally appeared, accompanied by a Black woman Celia presumed to be a detective. Oliver went to shake their hands. They spoke somberly for a moment, then Oliver beckoned for his son to join them. Zorn did not meet Celia's eye, even though he'd been to her house on numerous social occasions. The detective did, however, giving her a polite nod. And then they were gone.

Celia sat perfectly still, concentrating on giving nothing away should any of those reporters be watching her through the glass. It was something she'd learned to do when she was a girl. Turning herself into a statue of obedient goodness who wouldn't attract her father's attention. Just don't move, her mother had said, and nothing bad will happen. Yet another lie.

The outside doors whooshed open and there were shouts and then there was Alice, her arm around a terrified Hannah's waist. They were accompanied by a uniformed policeman. There was no sign of Geoff.

The policeman went to talk to the duty officer behind the bulletproof glass; Hannah collapsed into a plastic chair next to a pay phone on the other side of the lobby. Alice spotted Celia and rushed over.

"What the hell is going on?"

"Didn't anybody tell you?" Celia asked.

"As if. The cops just showed up and dragged us down here."

"They were all with that girl last night, the one who was murdered at the Bondurant house. Jack and Hannah and Christopher."

Alice's green eyes lit up with shock.

"Jesus Christ. That's insane. I mean . . . what? How does that even . . ."

"It turns out they'd gather there while Bill and Betsy were away."

"But what happened?"

Celia snuck a look at Hannah. She was pulling her hair in front of her face, creating a curtain through which she watched the two women. Hiding in plain sight.

"It looks like Christopher might have done it," she said in whisper. "Jack says that he and this girl were fighting."

Alice's jaw actually dropped.

"No way."

"I think he's in there right now."

"Christopher? Our Christopher?"

Celia nodded.

"Jack and Hannah weren't, like, there when it happened?"

"No, they'd left beforehand," Celia said. "They only just found out about it this afternoon. None of us knew anything until the police called Oliver."

"Have you seen Michel?" Alice asked. "Have you talked to him?"

"No."

"Do you think he's in there with him now?"

"Alice, honestly, that's all I know."

"I can't even begin to process this."

"Is Geoff coming?"

Alice didn't respond. It was as if she'd suddenly forgotten she was in a conversation.

"Alice?"

"Yeah, no, he's on the way."

"So what do you know about this Eden girl?"

"Celia, I don't know anything about anything."

Geoff arrived. Alice went to meet him. Celia watched them, this miserable couple. Whatever they were saying quickly degenerated into a whispered argument. And then Geoff went to see his daughter, who rose to embrace him. They spoke quietly. Alice, meanwhile, left the building, running the gauntlet of the press like a star arriving late to her premiere.

Jack emerged a few minutes later, followed by his father and the detective. Oliver looked calm. He nodded to Celia and she felt the big fist of tension that had clutched her chest for the past few hours finally relent. The detective gestured for the Holts to enter as Oliver led Jack to Celia. As the two young lovers passed, Jack met Hannah's eye. He gave his head a quick shake. A simple gesture, yet one that seemed so heavily freighted with secret meaning that Celia was certain the detective was going to stop everything and demand an immediate explanation. But she hadn't seen it. Neither had Oliver, or Geoff. Only Celia.

ALICE

Geoff was at work when the cop arrived. Alice was asleep, having polished off the bottle of Chablis after their fight in his office. She no longer worried about his criticism regarding her drinking. She had more important things to think about. She needed to connect with Michel. She desperately wanted to text him and demand an explanation for the cold shoulder back at Papillon, but sensed that would only make matters worse. As much as she hated to admit it, there was nothing she could do but wait.

Before passing out, she'd rummaged around online. They were now saying that a suspect was being held. An Emerson youth. Unnamed, although Alice knew that wouldn't last long. The local gossip machine would be going apeshit on this one. It was creepy that the killing had happened so close by; that the victim had been someone she'd seen at least a dozen times. They were saying she was from out of town, staying with relatives. Alice wondered if she'd been hiding out from a stalker who'd finally tracked her down. She could certainly relate. She'd dealt with her own share of overly attentive suitors, including the charming Nate in Nashville, who'd shown up on her doorstep with a pistol after she'd suggested they might want to start seeing other people. The cops had offered to beat the shit out of him in lieu of formal charges. She'd demurred, though she suspected they did it anyway. What with Nate being Black and Nashville being Nashville.

She put her phone to sleep and finished the bottle. A familiar urge was now dancing around the edges of her consciousness, dormant for the past few years, but clearly still part of her DNA. *Just leave. Fuck it. You tried settling down. You traded freedom for security. You tried being Good Alice and it didn't work out. And so you unleashed Bad Alice. But this isn't the place for her, either. Whichever way you sliced it, Alice shouldn't live here anymore. Just pack your bags and cash out.*

Alone and miserable and more than a little drunk on a Wednesday afternoon, Alice started to wonder if she was destined to fuck up every last thing she undertook. Every relationship, every job, every aspiration. She wondered if Bad Alice would always be lurking in the shadows, waiting to pounce. *Knock it off,* she told herself. *You don't fuck up everything.* This was just her self-pity talking. Things were different now. *You have Hannah. You'd certainly worked miracles with her, given what a basket case she was when you first arrived. And Michel. You're still in love with him.* Capillaries still dilated when she thought about him; her heart went boompity-boom. She'd turned her back on just about everything she could think of during the course of her life, but not on true love. He just needed to talk to her so she could make him understand that the scenario she'd hypothesized the other night was just one of many. Divorce, no divorce; money or no money; bed or sofa or the back seat of a car. For fuck's sake, she would even become a Catholic, whatever that entailed. If he really wanted to be done with her, he'd have to look her in the eye and say as much. But he didn't want that. He was just freaked out by the notion of taking another man's wife—and of finally saying adieu to his own dead one. Once she made everything clear to him, they could be together again.

Having settled on a course of action, she closed her eyes, plummeting into a deep, dreamless sleep that ended with the sound of someone speaking her name. It was Hannah, standing in the doorway. She was terrified, even more so than last night. As Alice struggled to consciousness, she realized that there'd been another sound as well, just before her stepdaughter spoke. A hammer-rap that had echoed through the house's vast empty spaces.

"Okay, I'm awake," she said as she swam to the sitting position. "Wait, is there someone at the door?"

As if in response, there was another thundering knock, followed immediately by the doorbell.

"What is it, Hanns? Who's at the door?"

"The police."

"What do they want?"

But she just stood there, catatonic with fear. Alice leapt to her feet and walked to the alarm pad. It took her a moment to figure out which button to push to make the front porch come up on the screen. The policeman's fish-eye face was young and grave. Her first thought was Geoff. He'd Allmaned himself on 128. She pressed the speaker button.

"Be right there."

The man said something she couldn't make out. But it didn't sound like he was telling her to take her time.

"Hannah, what's going on? Do you know what this is about?"

She shook her head, though the look in her eyes argued that she had a strong suspicion.

"Where's your father?"

"He's not answering."

Alice was tempted to question her further, but there was a cop at the front door who didn't look like he was going to wait much longer before doing something besides wait.

"Stay here," Alice said as she passed her stepdaughter.

The policeman was tall and muscular and dead-eyed. He skipped the pleasantries.

"I need to speak with Hannah Holt."

"Okay, why's that?" Alice answered, her voice sounding like she'd just been awakened from a two-hour wine-fueled midday nap.

"Is she here?"

"Can I ask what this is about?"

"Are you the mother?"

"The stepmother."

"You're going to need to get her for me. Right now."

For an Emerson cop to be speaking to an Emerson homeowner like this was extraordinary, and not in a good way. Everything was happening far too fast.

"I should really speak to her father first."

"Ma'am, she needs to come immediately."

"I mean, are we going to need a lawyer?"

"You can clear all that up at the station. But right now you need to get her."

"I don't suppose saying no is an option."

"It is. But it's not a good one."

It was a nice line. In any other context, she'd have enjoyed it.

"Okay. Wait here."

She started to shut the door but something stopped it. His hand. She looked into his eyes and he looked back at her. She imagined that at some distant time, in some unknown courtroom, a judge would determine that the officer had not been entitled to do this. But for now, he was.

Hannah was on the stairs, just out of view but well within earshot. She looked exactly like she had when Alice had let her watch *The Exorcist* a tad too early in her development.

"You're going to need to talk with this guy."

"You gotta get Dad," she whispered.

"I will. But for now we need to do what he says."

Hannah descended. At the door, she remained standing directly behind Alice, letting her stepmother do the talking. After a short, robust conversation, it was decided that Alice would accompany Hannah to the station. And so off they went, into the unknown. It was Alice's fourth ride in the back of a patrol car. The first had been for possession of a bottle of Oxy with somebody else's name on the label, which she didn't even know was a crime. The second was for simple battery, which apparently was what they called defending yourself against an abusive asshole in Key West. And then there was the DUI—no excuses on that one.

She called Geoff once they were moving. He usually didn't pick up when he was at the lab, wandering those neural highways and byways. To her immense surprise, he answered on the third ring.

"What the fuck, Geoff, we've been trying to call you."

"No, yeah, my phone was off. What's going on?"

"Well, I'm sitting in the back of a police car with your daughter."

"Why are you doing that?"

"Because they urgently want to interview her at the station."

"And you let them put her in a car? Who said you could do that?"

"The guy with the gun."

"You should have waited for me."

"Well, you know what, Geoff? I couldn't."

"What is this about?"

"I have no idea."

"Well, what does Hannah say?"

"Nothing," she said, staring at the back of the cop's thick neck. "What, you want me to put her on the phone, given our current location?"

There was a brief pause as he understood what she was saying.

"I'll be at the station in twenty minutes. Do *not* let them talk to her until I'm there."

She hung up and looked at Hannah, who was whispering something to herself. All Alice could think to say to her was that everything was going to be all right, but that seemed wildly optimistic at this point.

"He's coming," she tried instead.

Celia was in the station's waiting room, which made sense. If Hannah was in trouble, Jack would be as well. She immediately hit Alice with two bombshells. Jack and Hannah and Christopher had been at the house on Locust. And then, before Alice could even register the depth of her shock at the first statement, Celia told her that the police were accusing Christopher of the killing. Alice understood the words when she heard them. They were simple enough. But she couldn't make them real. Sweet, gentle Christopher Mahoun being accused of, well, you'd have to say murder, although putting it like that made it even more incredible.

Geoff arrived. She went to fill him in before he dealt with Hannah.

"They were with the girl who got murdered," she said before he could speak. "Hannah and Jack and Christopher. They were hanging out at her place last night."

The color drained from his face. She'd always thought that was a figure of speech, but there it was, happening right before her eyes.

"What does she say?"

"Nothing. To me, at least."

"Jesus. Okay, I'd better . . ."

"Geoff, wait. They've arrested Christopher."

"No fucking . . . hold on. Do you think they're going to accuse Hannah?"

"I don't think so. Celia says she and Jack left before it happened."

"Okay, I'll handle this," he said as he walked away.

He went to his daughter, who'd been watching them from her chair. She rose and collapsed into his arms. Alice wanted to join them, but Geoff had just made it clear that he was taking it from here. And she had to see Michel. If Christopher really was being blamed for this, then he would be losing his mind. She wondered if he was in there right now with his son; if she should hang around and try to catch him as he left. But that would be insanely risky. Wherever he was, she'd have to meet him somewhere else.

And so she left. Without a word to anyone. She waited until she was free of the reporters before she called. She was sent straight to his voice mail. She left a message, letting him know that she was at the station, that Hannah and Jack were talking to the police, that she needed to know what was happening, that she was here for him, that she loved him.

She summoned an Uber, instructing the driver to meet her in front of Papillon. She half-ran there; it took less than two minutes. As she suspected, it was closed, a hastily scrawled sign taped to the door. There was only darkness inside.

At home, she got her keys and drove straight to Michel's house. She couldn't begin to imagine how alone he must feel now, how trapped and beleaguered. She still couldn't process what was happening. Some girl had been murdered and Jack and Hannah knew enough about it to have the police drag them unceremoniously down to the station. And Christopher was being accused of the crime.

As she sped across town, a thought struck her. Celia had just said that Hannah and Jack only found out about the girl's death this afternoon. They'd left the house on Locust before anything happened. But Hannah knew something was wrong last night, when Alice saw her in the kitchen. Could she have already known that Eden was dead? And if so, why hadn't she said anything to Alice or Geoff or the cops? Jack had known something as well. Celia had said earlier he'd been upset when she saw him in the morning. They knew something, huddled all night in Hannah's room. They knew something that they'd kept secret.

At Michel's house, a few wan lights burned behind drawn curtains. He was in there, alone. She could feel it. There were vehicles parked outside. An Emerson PD patrol car, an SUV with a news station's logo plastered on the door, a dinged-up sedan. A bored-looking man in a leather jacket and an overdressed woman wearing what appeared to be a blond hair-helmet stood beside the cruiser, speaking to the cop seated inside. If the press knew about Christopher, why weren't they reporting it? He was still seventeen. Of course. A minor. Alice, a veteran of calculating age-based legality, knew that anonymity protected minors in the press. Not online, though. There, nothing was protected. The crowd on Smith Street would soon be metastasizing. If she was going to see Michel here, she needed to do it now.

She parked several houses down. His kitchen was at the rear of the house. It had a door. The backyard was small and she remembered a fence. She looked at Google Earth on her phone, summoning a bird's-eye view of this little patch of the planet. It took her a minute to get the lay of the land, to plot her course to him.

She drove around the block, stopping in front of the house she reckoned backed onto his. People were home. Lights flickered. They'd be watching television, staring at phones or computers, desperate to find out more about this thing that had happened so close by; this horror they were soon to discover may have been perpetrated by their neighbor's son. She walked as casually as you could down some stranger's driveway on a weeknight with no plausible explanation for being there. At least she was shrouded by darkness, she thought, a split second before being illuminated by a blinding motion-activated security spotlight. She picked up the pace, sidling through a stand of shrubbery at the bottom of the driveway, then hurrying past a trampoline on the lawn. More lights flared and now she was in a prison-break movie. She reached a wood fence separating this yard from Michel's. It was a few inches taller than she was, made of picketed slats. She looked around. For a brief, insane moment she thought about maybe using the trampoline. Then she spotted a wheelbarrow. She moved quickly, putting herself back in the bright light.

"Hey!"

A man had appeared on the house's elevated deck. *Just keep moving and act casual,* she thought as she grabbed the wheelbarrow's handles.

"Who is that?"

The wheelbarrow banged into the fence, causing the whole thing to wobble unpromisingly. She climbed aboard, achieving less altitude than she'd hoped. Luckily, she'd climbed fences under duress in her life. Between the unexpected wife and freedom stands . . . chain link. She grabbed on to two of the pointed planks and slotted her right foot between two others. She hoisted herself with all her might. She'd hoped to pause gracefully at the summit, but her momentum was greater than she'd anticipated. Suddenly, she was plummeting ass-first into Michel's yard. Her forearm scraped something sharp on the way down, though her contact with the planet was cushioned by damp earth and dead leaf.

Should have just used the fucking trampoline, she thought as she struggled to her feet. Michel's yard was smaller than his neighbor's, as was his house. There were no spotlights here. At the kitchen door, she looked through the window. A light burned above the stove, another down the hall. She knocked, then knocked more loudly. As she did, she noticed that her arm was bleeding pretty badly.

Michel appeared in the hallway. He did not look happy. It wasn't until he'd almost reached the door that he saw it was her. He didn't look much happier. For a moment, it seemed as if he wasn't going to open it. So she held up her arm, showing him her wound.

"Little help here," she said.

MICHEL

He almost didn't answer the back door. Journalists had already come twice to the front. They were polite, he was polite. They wanted a comment. They said it would be anonymous—they didn't name minors. And he almost gave them what they wanted, sat them down and made them understand that this was a terrible mistake. His son would never hurt anyone. But the lawyer had told him to say nothing and so he simply requested that they leave. There had been calls as well, although at least these came on the house phone, which he was able to unplug.

He was tempted to seek sanctuary at the restaurant. But they would only follow him. It might be a while before he went there again. He was starting to understand that closing Papillon was not going to be the temporary matter he'd believed earlier in the day. Watching the police search his house had made it clear how quickly his old life was slipping away. They'd arrived a few minutes after he got back from the station. He'd just finished speaking on the phone with the lawyer, who'd warned him that this was coming. Two uniformed officers and Procopio arrived; they had permission from a judge. Michel watched them from the kitchen chair to which he'd been confined. They looked in every corner and cabinet and closet and cavity. They took Christopher's and Michel's computers; they bagged his son's toothbrush and the sheets from his bed and the clothes scattered around his bedroom floor. Outside, they searched the garbage and recycling cans. The one thing they didn't take was Michel's cell phone. The lawyer had told him to hide it and tell them it was lost—he'd get it stricken from the warrant before they could come back for it. He'd be needing that so they could speak.

His name was David Cantor. He arrived soon after they left. He'd dropped everything and driven straight out from Boston following their initial call. He wanted to touch base with Michel before seeing Christopher at the station. He was a tall man with thick eyebrows and large hands. He looked like a young Elliott Gould. His voice was soft, but it carried authority. Michel liked him immediately.

"So, you're from Lebanon?" he asked after Michel handed him his coffee.

"I was a boy there. But I was educated in Paris and worked there for a time before coming to America."

"Are you a Muslim, Michel?"

"I'm Catholic. I was raised Maronite. Do you know about them?"

"Yes."

Michel was impressed. Most didn't.

"Have you been to Lebanon?"

"No. I got pretty close, though."

"Israel?"

"I lived there for a while before law school. You should know—I served in the IDF for a year."

"Don't be worried. That makes us allies."

"So. No problems?"

"Between our nations or the two of us?"

"Let's try to leave the homelands out of this."

"David, we're both Americans."

Cantor pointed at him with his pen.

"Right answer." He took a legal pad from his bag. "So. In your own words, in your own time."

Michel told him what he knew. Christopher's late arrival home, his stricken silence, his refusal to tell him about being at the Bondurant house. He told him what his son had said during the two interviews, here and at the station. Cantor nodded neutrally throughout the account, although he did appear interested to hear that Jack Parrish had been present at the house.

"Oliver Parrish's son?"

"Yes. You know the father?"

"Like Tokyo knew Godzilla. What's Jack like?"

"He's Christopher's best friend."

Cantor picked up on the disapproving note in his voice.

"And?"

"I don't like him."

"Try to be a little more specific."

"He pushes Christopher around. The way he talks to him, the way he teases him. It's not good."

Cantor wrote something down on his pad.

"Okay, going back to last night. Christopher said he left after Hannah and Jack."

"Right."

"And did he specify what happened during the time he was alone with the victim?"

The victim, Michel thought.

"He said they just spoke."

"About?"

"Christopher liked her. Romantically. She didn't return his affection."

"Okay. Anything else I need to know?"

"There were scratches on his neck."

Cantor pursed his lips and watched him for a moment.

"Scratches?"

Michel formed his hand into a claw and indicated where they had been on his own neck.

"Did he say how he got those?"

"He said he must have given them to himself."

"To himself."

Michel nodded.

"And you knew nothing about his relationship with Eden Perry?"

"I suspected he was interested in a girl, but he was very secretive about it."

"Why do you think that was?"

"He's seventeen?"

"So, Michel, is there anything I'm going to need to know about Christopher, going forward?"

"What do you mean?"

"Arrests. Bad habits. He punched a guy in a bar."

Michel laughed quietly.

"What?" Cantor asked.

"You'll see when you meet him."

"I'll take that as a no."

The first reporter knocked at that point. Cantor nodded with approval after Michel shut the door, telling him he'd handled it just right. Give them nothing, but give it politely. He also explained that he should expect Christopher's name to be on social media soon, if it wasn't already.

"Well, then, people will see how ridiculous this is. Anybody who knows my son will understand this is a huge mistake."

"Michel, let me explain something to you. A white girl just got killed in a three-million-dollar house in a place where there's one murder a decade. Somebody's going to have to be guilty of this, and quickly. The only mysteries these people allow are the ones they control."

"These people?"

"The ones you serve dinner to."

There was silence.

"Okay, I better get over there and talk to your boy."

"What can I do?"

"Sit tight and don't talk to anybody, and that includes friends and relatives. Oh, and a woman named Courtney will be calling about money. We're going to need that wired as soon as possible."

"How much?"

"Ten thousand. Obviously, if they don't charge your son, you'll be getting most of that back."

Michel almost asked him what would happen if they did charge him, but he didn't have the heart for the answer.

"Do you think they might release him tonight?"

"That's what I'm going for, but it's unlikely if they've got him on a forty-eight-hour hold. I'll file a petition with the court first thing in the morning, though judges don't like to overrule cops at this point in a proceeding."

After he left, there was nothing to do but draw the curtains and pace. Reporters kept him busy at the door. The woman phoned and they took care of the money. Sofia called and he told her that he liked David. And then he was alone with this terrible new reality.

His conversation with Cantor got him thinking about his son's friendship with Jack Parrish. Michel had never liked the kid. He didn't appreciate the way he talked down to Christopher, the way he bossed him around. Although his son's English was excellent, he still sometimes made small mistakes—a vowel softened, a verb tense shifted—and Jack would pounce mercilessly, no matter who else was present. When they horsed around, Jack often took it a step too far. There was a bloody nose; there were bruises. All coming with an innocent explanation. Michel knew what was happening. Christopher, the newcomer, was drawn to

Jack's power and status. And Jack enjoyed having this moon circling his bright planet, constant and reflecting and never likely to stray.

Michel never really spoke to his son about it. He'd seen Christopher lonely and didn't want to exile him back into that wasteland. Only once had he felt the need to intervene. This was last summer. Christopher was hanging out with Jack at World Taco; Michel came by to pick him up after his own restaurant's closing. Michel was surprised to find Christopher on the sidewalk, even more surprised to see that he appeared to have been crying.

"What?" Michel asked as the boy dropped into the seat beside him.

"Jack can be a dick sometimes."

"What did he do?"

"He just said something."

"What?"

"Forget it," the boy said, swiping the back of his hand angrily beneath his inflamed nostrils.

"Christopher . . ."

"About Mom, all right! About me talking about her so much."

Michel knew he should let it go. The boys would work it out. If he really felt the need to intervene, he could take it up later with the parents. But Jack had mentioned Maryam. He reached for the door handle.

"No, Dad, wait . . ."

Jack sat in a booth, staring at his phone. Michel stopped at the end of the table. Its surface was littered with cheese-smeared foil, bucket-sized drink cups, crumpled napkins. Jack looked up.

"What did you say to Christopher about his mother?"

"I was just telling him that it wasn't healthy to dwell on her so much," he said reasonably. "It's a morbid ideation."

"What business is that of yours?"

For the briefest of moments, there was a flash of something dark and tribal in the boy's close-set eyes, the fury of a young chieftain challenged.

Michel remembered this from his childhood. A precursor to violence and mayhem. But it passed after just a few seconds.

"Look, I'm really sorry," he said, his tone chastened. "That was stupid. I was trying to help but . . ."

"This is my wife."

"No, you're totally right. Stupid . . . You want me to go apologize to him?"

Kids from other tables were watching now.

"You can do that later."

"I'm really sorry, Mr. Mahoun. I got a big mouth sometimes."

"We'll put it behind us."

And then the boy offered his hand. Michel took it. His grip was gentle, but there was a crushing force behind it. Michel wondered if that was the point of the gesture. As he left the restaurant, he couldn't decide if his son's friend was genuinely contrite or the best liar he'd ever met.

Night wore on, and Michel tried to wrestle his thoughts into some sort of order. It was how his father had taught him to deal with a rush. Look at one problem at a time, the biggest first. Each one you solve makes the next easier. And then the diners are happy and you're drinking a brandy.

So. First things first. Christopher was innocent. There was no sense wasting time trying to figure out if it was true. But what had happened at that house, in the hours he was alone with her? Why had he wandered the streets? She'd spurned him. That had to be it. She'd rejected him and he was humiliated. And so the problem was one of perception. The police had simply jumped to what they thought was a logical conclusion. Once they looked deeper, they'd see it wasn't Christopher. It couldn't be him.

Michel couldn't believe that his son was enduring yet another terrible thing, something unfair and beyond his control. Hadn't Maryam's death been enough? It had split the boy's life in two. Before her illness,

Christopher was happy. He loved to spend time at L'Étoile, where Michel was the head chef and Maryam worked as a maître d', one of the few women who held this job in Paris. He was always underfoot yet never in the way. Michel dreamed of him following in his footsteps, just as he had with his own father. Working side by side. The son learning, equaling, surpassing.

But then Maryam developed a cough that would not go away. There were blood tests and scans and bad news. Nine months later she was dead. Christopher turned eleven during her decline. At first, he wouldn't leave her side. He slept with her, he helped her walk, he constantly embraced her. Near the end, however, as her body deteriorated and her mind slipped, he changed. He wouldn't touch her; he barely spoke to her or even looked at her. He grew quieter and quieter until, on the day of her funeral, he stopped talking altogether. The silence lasted for two months. Nothing Michel did could break it. Teachers, priests, doctors; friends and family—no one could get through to him.

Finally, one morning, Christopher simply walked into the kitchen and asked Michel to make him eggs. Just like that. Michel was so overjoyed that it took him a few hours to understand that his son's voice was different. It wasn't the natural break of puberty—that didn't happen for a few more years. His voice wasn't lower so much as hollow. There was an echo to it, as if he were speaking from deep inside his own body. Like the real Christopher was trapped in there.

He stopped coming to the restaurant. On the few occasions he absolutely had to be there, he'd avoid the kitchen. His fascination with cooking vanished. There were no more tutorials about butter and cream, no more tastings or stirrings. Michel feared that his dream of his son following in his footsteps had died along with his wife.

It was only after they moved to Boston that the true recovery began. Michel's cousin Claude—Sofia's father—needed an executive chef for his Back Bay restaurant, Corniche. Tired of living in a place where every last thing reminded him of his dead wife, Michel had leapt at the opportunity. Christopher took to America the moment he stepped off the plane at Logan. He learned English with startling speed. His voice changed again, this time the natural deepening of puberty. His interest in cooking renewed. He started wearing a Celtics leprechaun cap everywhere. He reinvented himself. Which, after all, was the point of America.

And yet, Michel sometimes saw the pain that had driven him into that two-month silence. He had a particular problem with rejection. Small things—a slight from a friend, an indifferent response from a girl—would drive him into days-long sulks. But mostly, he was the buoyant, happy kid the rest of the world saw. Michel took over the Emerson Grille, using money Claude loaned him for a down payment, and Papillon was reborn. French cuisine with the slightest Lebanese accent, just like his father's restaurant. Christopher began to work there, first as a busboy, then as a waiter, sometimes in the kitchen. Recently, Michel had been teaching him about sauces. The possibility of his working with Michel when he finished college was once again alive.

And now this. Another blow. Another nightmare. One from which it would be difficult to recover, no matter how quickly and thoroughly he was exonerated. He could already see hints of the reemergence of the old, shattered boy in the interview room. He wondered what kind of voice his son was speaking in now; if it was once again hollow and echoey, or if he'd be driven into an abyss so deep that Michel wouldn't hear him at all.

Alice arrived. At first, he was shocked and angry to find her at his back door. But then she showed him her arm, smeared with blood and mud.

"What happened?" he asked as he let her in.

She gestured toward the back of his yard.

"Fence mishap."

Despite everything, he managed an incredulous smile. This woman.

He led her to the sink and turned on the hot water, then handed her a fistful of paper towels. There was a first aid kit in a nearby drawer. Three decades in frantic kitchens had made Michel adept at dressing wounds. He sat her at the kitchen table and set to work. The cut wasn't as bad as it first seemed. He lathered it with antibiotic and then wrapped it in gauze. It felt good to be this close, to be touching her.

They spoke as he worked.

"Tell me that it isn't true that they're actually holding Christopher."

"As a witness, supposedly," he said. "But they think he did this."

"That's insane."

"I tried to tell them."

"I just came from the station. They're talking to Hannah and Jack."

"Then they'll clear it up," Michel said.

"But what's Christopher saying happened?"

"They'd gathered at the house," he said. "It was something they'd do. The girl, Eden, was looking after the place. Jack and Hannah left around midnight and then Christopher left later. Nobody knew anything bad had happened to her until this afternoon."

"I don't think that's true, Michel. I saw Hanns at four in the morning and she was freaked out. I mean, *really* freaked out. And Celia says Jack was acting weird when she saw him first thing this morning."

"It was the same with Christopher. When he got home . . . I've never seen him like that."

They sat through a silence as Michel worked on her wound.

"There were scratches on his neck," he finally said.

"What kind of scratches?"

"Fingernails."

"The cops saw these?"

"They found them. He said he must have done them to himself."

"Do you believe that?"

He finished dressing the wound. He met her gaze. There was no suspicion in her eyes, no doubt. She was simply waiting for his answer.

"There's no possibility that he hurt that girl, Alice. He just . . . wouldn't. You believe that, right?"

"Of course I do."

And it was true. She did. This woman he'd been ready to spurn. She believed it with all her heart.

"Okay," she said. "Let me talk to Hannah. If I get her alone she'll tell me what the fuck's going on."

She put her hand on his forearm.

"Don't worry, Michel. I got this."

And then something gave way in him. The doubts he'd been having since last Friday vanished. Here she was. Another man's but his as well. A sin but also deliverance. Four nights ago it had been strange having her here: alien and wrong. Now, it felt only right. He found himself wishing that time would freeze and they could stay like this forever; that the bad things that happened today would vanish and nothing bad would ever happen again.

His phone rang. It was Cantor.

"So. I just finished with Christopher."

"How is he?"

"He's holding up. Look, I know it's late, but I'm coming over."

"Why, what's happening?"

"Let's put it this way. It looks like it was a much more eventful night at the Bondurants' than initially reported."

PATRICK

They were saying it was an Emerson youth. A seventeen-year-old boy. Because of his age, news organizations weren't releasing his name, but that didn't mean it wouldn't be available soon. If he was a student at

Waldo, it would be whispered throughout town by midnight. The internet would follow, and then he would be the wrong kind of famous.

Patrick had been following the story ever since he got home from his disastrous visit to the police station. Mostly on Twitter, though some of the local Facebook pages were frenzied as well. Early discussion had been tinged with a decidedly hysterical note, but that died down with the news that someone was in custody. Panic turned to gossip. It had become so intense that the cops had been forced to put out a statement on their own Facebook page: "EPD is currently questioning an Emerson youth over the killing of Eden Perry. Details will be released as they become available."

Maybe seeing his photo would shake something loose in Patrick's brain. Not that he relished another go-round at Public Safety Plaza. His visit had been a mistake. He must have seemed like a drunken fool. To date, he'd taken pride in his ability to conduct himself with decorum as he moved about his hometown. Friends and colleagues were concerned, but no one could point to a specific incident that allowed them to say definitively that Patrick Noone had gone off the rails. Rushing over to the cops with an improbable story might possibly be overlooked, but another visit would certainly peg him as delusional.

And then there was Procopio. He'd had enough of that prick for one lifetime. He couldn't believe they'd made that knuckle-dragging brownshirt a detective. Although perhaps it shouldn't have been that surprising. Bullies with badges seemed to be all the rage these days.

The incident with him had been Gabi's first actual arrest. There'd been a few near misses with the authorities before that, the closest being when she was picked up in Framingham in the company of a couple of veteran junkies. One of them had tossed a bindle of heroin on Gabi's lap as they were being pulled over. Luckily, this transaction was viewed by a tall, broad-chested police sergeant named Marquez. He'd met Patrick in the station's lobby an hour later, where Gabi sat shivering on a bench, clutching a small collapsed bottle of supermarket water. He explained that she was not under arrest, although he made it clear that he could have charged her, as he had her two running mates, who had record sheets the length of Russian novels. But he could see that she was a good kid who came from a good family. Truth be told, he was arresting too many people like her these days. She belonged in rehab, not jail. Muttering his strangulated thanks, Patrick had collected his child and carted her off to detox.

Procopio had proved a very different story. By chance, Patrick had been present for the actual arrest. It took place just outside of Whole Foods, which his daughter had just exited with a forty-three-dollar cut of tenderloin in her purse. Evidently her dealer was a steak enthusiast and willing to barter. Patrick was returning—alone, thank God—from a client lunch. He was on foot; it was a beautiful summer day, hot but free of humidity. He saw a lit cruiser first, then a small crowd gathered by the front of the store. He would have kept on walking if he hadn't spotted his old Cornell football jersey, hanging loosely from Gabi's painfully thin shoulders. She stood beside the latest junkie boyfriend, a cadaverous figure who looked like he'd received his neck tattoos in an earthquake. Both wore plastic cuffs. They were faced by a uniformed Procopio and the store manager, a bearded, aproned man who looked more worried about the forty dollars' worth of meat slow-cooking on a nearby bench than the human drama unfolding before him.

Gabi briefly met her father's eye as he arrived. Her pupils were pinpoints, her lids thick. Patrick identified himself. At first, Procopio wouldn't acknowledge him. But Patrick insisted, finally forcing the officer to reveal that she was under arrest for shoplifting.

"Can't we just settle this here?" Patrick asked.

"You'll need to come to the station."

"But I'm standing right here."

Procopio went back to ignoring him. Patrick looked at Gabi. He felt no anger. These days it was only pity and damage control. And a crippling desire to break the voodoo thrall of the poison coursing through her veins; to bundle her into his car and drive her to five years ago. She sensed his gaze and met his eye, as if finally understanding now what was happening.

"Dad," she said.

He nodded. He'd take care of it.

"Come on, this isn't necessary," he said to the cop. "Just write her a summons. I'll make sure she shows. We'll pay whatever needs to be paid."

Procopio didn't answer. Nor did he move to take her away.

"Can I do something about this?" the manager asked.

For a moment, Patrick thought he'd found an ally, but the man was referring to the steak. Procopio nodded. The manager snatched it up and disappeared into the building, trailing an archipelago of pinkish droplets. At this point the tattooed boy chose to make his sole contribution to the proceedings, a contemptuous guffaw that came to an end the moment the cop looked at him.

This was absurd. Passersby were watching. His friends and neighbors. Were they going to stand here all day? They might as well break out the communal stocks. Patrick wondered what would happen if he simply took his daughter gently by the arm and led her away. That plastic band could be easily clipped off at home. But of course that was not possible. The other man had the gun and the badge and the whole massive apparatus of the law behind him. Plus, he was an asshole.

The reason for the delay became clear when a second officer arrived. A woman, a state trooper. Procopio said a few words to her and she took control of the tattooed zombie and led him to her car. Procopio put his hand on Gabi's emaciated triceps and conducted her off toward his vehicle. Patrick continued to appeal as he followed them to his cruiser. As they reached it, he may have veered a little too close to the officer, causing Procopio to turn angrily on him.

"Sir, you need to stand back," he said, loud enough for anyone within a hundred feet to hear.

Patrick held his eye for a moment. He hadn't been addressed in that tone since he wore the jersey currently hanging so loosely from his daughter's shoulders. He'd never really had a problem with cops—why would he?—but at that moment he hated the man standing in front of him more than anyone in his life. Later, his wife would suggest that what he really hated was his own powerlessness. Perhaps. But he also hated this fucking cop.

Patrick took a step back as Procopio placed his daughter in the back of the cruiser; he watched them drive off. At the station, he learned he'd have to wait until five to bail her out, during which time she was locked in a small, windowless cell. It was there, he came to believe, that something finally broke in her, an invisible fracture that slowly deepened as she went from detox to rehab and then right back to the streets; a fracture that would soon leave her dead in the men's room of a McDonald's in some godforsaken precinct of Boston where no one Patrick knew ever went.

He fell asleep in the recliner with his phone on his lap; he woke a few hours later when his next-door neighbor slammed a door. It was just after ten p.m. He checked Twitter. The Emerson youth had been named. Christopher Mahoun. Patrick was suddenly sober and very awake. Michel's son. He'd seen him often, working at his father's restaurant. In fact, he'd refilled Patrick's water and cleared his plates just last month. He was a slight, attractive kid who looked a little like Prince. His permanently averted eyes suggested a shyness completely at odds with his father's dignified gregariousness. Patrick couldn't imagine him being violent.

He got his keys. It was unlikely that he was legally sober, but there was no chance that he'd be pulled. Not today. The cops were otherwise engaged. Nothing impeded his progress onto Locust now. The roadblock and yellow tape were gone. The authorities had their man. Their youth.

He parked just where he had after hitting the dog. His leg throbbed with a memory of pain. He found what he guessed to be the exact spot where he'd stood last night, a few yards onto the lawn. The lighting was different here, but he could see that silhouette in his mind's eye. Just not clearly enough to discern a face. Only to know that the person who'd been watching him wasn't Michel Mahoun's son.

He walked back to the street and headed to the mouth of the Bondurants' driveway, two dozen steps farther along the road. The house was almost entirely hidden behind the stand of trees in its front yard. He wondered if there was anyone home. He doubted it. Why would there be? Just a few hours ago there'd been a dead girl inside.

The scuff of an approaching footstep broke the spell. He turned, expecting to be challenged by a cop or a neighbor. But it was the woman he'd seen at the police station, with her jet-black hair and dark, suspicious eyes. Eden's mother. She stopped a safe distance away.

"I saw you earlier," she said.

"I remember."

"Yeah, so I got a question. Who exactly are you?"

DANIELLE

She had not followed Gates's advice. She did not go home. She did not change into her pajamas and start calling back the people who'd been filling her phone with messages. Her mother and her sister and Steve Slater; her friends and Eden's friends and people she didn't know from Adam. She stayed in Emerson, because going home would be an admission that this was out of her hands, that all she had left to do was remember and suffer.

That time would come. But not yet. There were still things that needed to be taken care of before she started wistfully looking at old photos. Such as making sure they caught the person who did this. How could she trust anyone else to look after Eden? That was on her. She'd known as soon as they'd placed her slimy screeching body on Danielle's too-young chest. She'd worried about dropping her, but after a few seconds she understood that wasn't going to happen. She stuck, like a bur you picked up cutting through a vacant lot. They'd always been attached. It had always been Danielle she'd called when there was trouble. And Danielle had always answered the phone.

Except for last night. Last night she'd failed. She'd missed the call. She'd neglected to move a switch a millimeter to unmute her phone; she'd allowed some towels to fall off the back of a chair to muffle its vibration. She'd done this because, somewhere inside her, she'd believed that the world had become a safe enough place for her to sleep with both eyes shut. Twenty years of vigilance and patience had prepared her for a brief interval of absolute need, and she'd failed. But that didn't mean she could stop. Even if every last person on Earth told her to stand down, she wouldn't do it. Because that would be the end of Eden.

She couldn't imagine a world without her daughter. Even during their time-out, she'd been the most undeniable presence in Danielle's life. Which was funny, because she hadn't even wanted the stupid kid. When the dipstick turned blue, her first thought was to get rid of it. She was only seventeen. And although the father, Mike McMichaels, was good in the sack and a barrel of laughs on a Saturday night, he wasn't exactly dad material. The only regular job he ever held was buying lottery tickets. But after the initial shock had worn off, the thought of a baby took hold. Having something that was hers, just hers. Something that would love her absolutely.

At first, that'd been exactly how it was. Eden had been such a sweet baby. Quiet and soft and warm. All the stuff that people said was going to be hard turned out to be true, and yet it also turned out not to matter. And Mike tried, bless him. He hung around, mostly; he was sober, basically. He got an actual job, roofing. He combed his hair when the occasion required. When she looked back to those first few years, she could honestly say that she was happy.

But then her luck turned, as it had a tendency of doing. Mike got a job offer in Texas and he took it without discussing the matter with Danielle. It seemed he'd had enough fathering. Eden was three when this happened. Not long after, she started to become a handful. It gradually became clear that there was something not quite right about her. It wasn't like she was some dummy. She was perfectly smart. She was just different. She had trouble mastering the whole human-being-on-planet-Earth thing. She'd wander off. She'd get too close to strangers. Yes, it could be cute at first to have a child who insisted on hugging every last person at Price Chopper, but it was also worrying if you were the one in charge of making sure she didn't wind up sold as a child bride in Saudi Arabia. Danielle often thought her daughter saw the world as a sort of psychedelic magical amusement park, full of wonder and adventure and cuddles. If ever a child was born to run with scissors, it was her.

People said she'd outgrow it. They tested her at school but she passed with flying colors. Teachers shook their heads when they talked about her but they were smiling, too. Everybody loved Eden. Why wouldn't they? She was cute as a button and up for anything. It was all well and good when she was a little girl. But Danielle also knew there was a tsunami coming. She felt like one of those people on that beach in Thailand. You could turn and run but that only meant you wouldn't see what was about to hit you.

She was thirteen when the wave finally crashed. Boys entered the equation. They sure liked Eden. And they just kept coming. It was like the Walking Dead. Except they were very much alive and none of them seemed to be walking. Eden wasn't the prettiest girl in town but something about her lit the fuse. Danielle tried to explain about the birds and bees, with special emphasis on the part about getting stung and swelling up. But Eden was focused on a simpler biological truth. If you let boys kiss you, they liked you. Danielle tried to school her in the fine art of making them work a little, but if she was willing to hug any old gross homeless person when she was little, she wasn't going to practice self-restraint when some hot young stud in a Charger and a Gronk jersey rolled up outside. Not that Danielle was one to give relationship advice. She had so much baggage by this point that she felt like she should give anyone bold enough to date her a tip.

But Eden was no slut. Danielle had known nymphos. Hell, there was a period when she was in her early twenties when she probably was one. But that wasn't Eden. There was always only just one boy at a time. Sean or Ryan—there were a lot of Seans and Ryans. Rayshard, with his smile. She'd go crazy after one date and then that was all she could talk about. The boys always seemed stunned by the torrents of affection coming their way. More than one was scared off by it. Most, however, hung around, like a kid who discovered a busted gumball machine.

But then the gumballs ran out. It amazed her how quickly Eden's head could turn. Danielle thought of herself as a hard bitch, but *damn*. The girl lost interest so quickly, so absolutely, that it was like she'd suffered romantic amnesia. It led to some awkward moments, a few of which wound up with Danielle at the front door, armed with whatever weapon she'd been able to grab off the kitchen counter. It wasn't easy, warding off an enraged ex-boyfriend with only a whisk in your hand.

It was all so exhausting. Which was why the move to the Bondurants' had seemed like such a good idea, especially after her daughter swore off boys for the time being. Maybe here, away from all that working-class testosterone, Eden could break the chain of dumb decisions. But clearly Danielle was wrong. As far away as Emerson seemed, it wasn't far enough.

After an hour of aimless driving, she stopped at a diner on Route 9, just beyond the town's northernmost edge. The place reeked of old smoke.

An ancient couple frowned in unison over their his-and-hers Salisbury steaks; a fat weirdo with tinted glasses stared out the window at the late rush-hour traffic, probably imagining sniper scenarios. Two junkies emptied packet after packet of sugar into bottomless coffees.

Danielle ordered a chef's salad, a coffee, and an apple juice. She checked her phone to see if there were any updates from the cops. Nothing. Just more messages from friends and relatives and work. Her mother up in New Hampshire was offering to come down in a tone of voice that made it clear she didn't really want to. Her sister in Florida actually did want to come. Danielle knew she should probably deal with all that. They'd be hurting. They cared. She'd get some food in her and then do her duties. Accept the sympathy she knew wouldn't do her a damned bit of good.

And then she saw it on Twitter. The Emerson youth now had a name. Christopher Mahoun. A senior at the high school. Somebody had posted a photo of him. He was thin, smiling, wide-eyed. He sure didn't look like a killer. In fact, he had such a harmlessly likable face that it took a moment for the hate to come. The initial comments reinforced her confusion. Despite the Middle Eastern name, there didn't seem to be much bigotry. People who knew him were saying he was a good kid. Nobody could believe it.

She looked up his family. If he lived in Emerson, they must have money. His father owned a fancy restaurant in town where they'd cook you a rabbit for a mere thirty-six dollars. There was a photo of him from the local paper—he'd donated food to some charity run. He was very handsome, his smile reserved but genuine. He'd come from Paris, although his roots were back in Lebanon. How did Eden know this kid? Had she been involved with him? He didn't look her type. He seemed too civilized.

Gates would have known about this when they spoke earlier, after she left Bill and Betsy. The kid was probably locked up just a few steps from where they were standing. Why hadn't she told her? Why did Danielle have to hear about this from Twitter? The suspicion she'd been feeling on and off all day returned, stronger than ever. Local kid, local cops. *You need to trust us with this.*

Her phone buzzed. Her mother again. She took the call.

"Oh my God, I was beginning to think they got you, too," she wailed, before dissolving into tears.

It took her a while to get the old bat off the phone. The sniper guy was looking like he was working up the nerve to take a shot at her. She paid her bill and did the rest of her calling from her parked car. She started with her sister down in Bradenton. Danielle told her to stay put until they had a funeral date. Steve Slater told her to take off as much time as she needed, which she figured meant she had until Monday. It seemed inordinately important to him to send flowers. Danielle told him she'd let him know. She called her friend Jackie, who sounded a bit offended when informed her presence was not needed. After that, she decided to put off the rest of the calls. She really didn't need to manage the grief of others.

Still not wanting to go back home, she drove around Emerson. Left turn, right turn. Stop signs and traffic lights. Not looking for a clue, exactly. Just a sense. An inkling. The feeling she'd had when she first brought her daughter out here returned with a vengeance, although this time not in a good way. This was another country. The houses, the yards, the schools. The speed bumps twice as high as where she lived. Most of the houses glowed with inner light; you could see people inside. Tonight, they'd be staring at some screen or another, feeding on her child's death.

She wound up parked across the street from the Bondurants'. The house was protected by its wall of trees. Not a place you'd randomly approach. But also a place where you wouldn't be seen from the street if you did show up at the front door. This would have been how things were when it happened. Quiet, dark, apparently safe. She thought about Christopher Mahoun arriving. Had Eden invited him? Or had he come unannounced and unexpected, someone she knew only in passing, a near stranger who secretly coveted her?

Danielle became aware of another presence. A man had appeared, walking along the side of the road toward the house. He didn't seem to be a cop or a reporter. He wore nice clothes and his hair was cut right. He stopped at the top of the driveway and it was then that she placed him. He was the one she'd seen earlier at the police station.

She got out of the car, shutting the door quietly so as not to scare him off. He turned, unsurprised, as she drew near.

"I saw you earlier," she said.

"I remember."

"Yeah, so I got a question—who exactly are you?"

"Just a curious bystander," he said after a moment.

Her eyes were getting used to the light. He was attractive but, as she'd glimpsed back at the station, soft. Like he'd been basted in a light batter of money. His Beemer, which for some reason he'd parked in front of the house next door, looked like it was worth about two years of her salary. Men like this tended not to be bystanders to anything. If they were present, it was about them.

"But why were you talking to the cops?"

"You're her mother, right?"

"Yeah. I'm her mother."

"I'm really sorry," he said, his voice so gentle she had to lean forward a little to hear it.

"Thank you. But I'm still sort of wondering who you are and why you're here."

"Really, I don't want to intrude."

"You kind of already have, though."

He continued to look toward the house.

"Come on, help me out," she continued. "The cops sure aren't."

"I wouldn't put too much faith in our local police."

She could now detect the slightest slur. Everything was a little too slow. He'd been drinking. It took a minute to see, but it was there.

"Oh yeah?" she asked. "Why's that?"

He shrugged. She decided to try a new approach.

"What's your name?"

"Patrick."

"Danielle."

Shaking hands would have been too weird.

"I mean, look at this from my point of view," she said. "I see you at the station, talking to the detectives. Then I see you here. There's got to be a reason for that. Please."

It wasn't a word that usually came tripping off her tongue. For infrequency, it was right up there with *sorry*. He seemed to sense that.

"I hit a dog."

"Okay."

"Last night, when I was driving by here."

"What, like a big black dog?"

"You know it?"

She pointed toward the house.

"That's theirs. The Bondurants. My daughter was looking after it. Thor. I just saw him a couple of hours ago."

"How's he doing?"

"He'll live."

"He bit me."

"Really? He doesn't seem like a biter."

"I guess he was having a rough night." He winced. "I'm sorry."

She shook off his apology.

"So you hit the dog and . . ."

"It didn't seem too hurt so I just went home. And then when I saw the news, I thought it was something the cops should know."

"And you're here now because, what, you're this big dog lover?"

"There was . . ."

He stopped. The words were there, on his tongue. He was trying to decide if he should say them.

"What? There was . . . what?"

He shook his head.

"I just wish there was something I could have done."

"Yeah, me, too."

He looked at her and she knew her words had come out far more harshly than intended.

"What I mean is, I wish there was something I could have done, too."

"I should go," he said.

Damn it, Danielle, she thought. *This isn't some drywaller you're dealing with. Use some finesse.* He reached into his pocket and took out his wallet. For a moment, she suspected he was going to give her money. But he'd produced a business card.

"If you want to talk."

"We're talking now," she said.

"Things might come up later. They might be clearer."

Now what the hell did *that* mean? He continued to offer the card. She took it. She had to angle it toward the streetlight to read the name.

"No one?"

"It's pronounced 'noon.'" He smiled. "But I answer to both."

Once again, he seemed to regret his joke immediately.

"I'm really, really sorry about your child."

Parting words, though he stood his ground. He met her eye and it occurred to her that this guy, this Patrick Noone, wasn't crazy and he wasn't a creep. No, there was something there that she didn't understand but couldn't turn away from.

"Just because she's dead doesn't mean she's gone," he said, the drink suddenly vanished from his voice.

"Okay," she said after a stunned silence.

"But you'll find it's up to you to keep her alive."

"It was up to me last night."

"No, this is different."

"How?"

"It's hard to explain. But you'll see."

He smiled at her, then turned and walked away. His car sounded like three cars when he turned over the engine. As he drove past he gave her a brief blind wave. She used the card he'd given her to wave back.

Thursday

- - - - - - - - - - - - - - - -

CELIA

J ack was just about to leave for school when the police called. Celia hadn't wanted him to go—the place would be pulsating with gossip and histrionics. The police holding a Waldo student for murder was the biggest thing to happen in this town in living memory. And Jack was right in the middle of it. He needed to be protected until the hysteria died down. But Oliver had overruled her. Their son had done nothing wrong, so there was no reason for him to act like he had.

Despite her concern, Celia had believed that the worst of it was over when she woke this morning. Yes, more testimony would be required. People would talk. But yesterday's sensation of a failed-brakes emergency had passed. Oliver was right. Jack was blameless. He'd been long gone when his friend had taken leave of his senses. Hannah had confirmed the story. Celia still wasn't thrilled about his lying to her about his whereabouts, but Oliver was inclined to let it go as a lesson learned.

And then the police called for the second time. They reached Oliver in his car—he'd headed off to work before dawn but had turned back after they called. When he came through the door unexpectedly, his finger was worrying his scar.

"Detective Gates called. They need to speak to him again."

"About what?"

"That's not clear. But it seemed urgent."

"Did you call Bart?"

"He didn't say much. Except that the district attorney's involved."

"Well, what's your guess?"

"I honestly don't know. As far as I can tell, they're still building a case against Christopher."

Celia would have taken more comfort if her husband's demeanor had matched his words. But he looked even more concerned than he had yesterday. She went to get her son, who was getting ready for school. He answered the moment she knocked. She told him what was happening; he claimed to have no idea what it could be about. And yet he looked every bit as worried as his father.

"Jack, what is this?"

"I'll be down in a minute," he said, gently shutting the door on her.

She wanted to go with them to the station, but Oliver thought it was best that it was just him. He was in full lawyer mode now. Elaine Otto would be meeting him there. Celia grew even more alarmed when she heard this, but Oliver assured her it was just out of an abundance of caution.

"I can't wait to get to the part of this where I don't need to keep being reassured," she said.

She spent the next two hours pacing the house. She checked online. Nobody was talking about new developments, certainly nothing that could damage her boy. All speculation remained about Christopher, mostly from bigots who had no idea what they were talking about. Suddenly everybody was an expert on the Mahouns, who were quickly morphing from sophisticated French Catholics into Arab fanatics stitching together suicide vests in their Smith Street basement.

She'd given the landscapers the day off, although now she wished they were out there making noise. She felt very alone and a little pan- icky. Something wasn't right. The involvement of the head of Oliver's criminal defense department was not a good sign. Celia couldn't stop thinking about Jack's distress yesterday morning, before the girl's body had been discovered. Last night, in her rush to stop thinking the worst, she'd convinced herself it was nothing. Now, however, it was hard not to believe he'd known something had happened long before the police forced open the Bondurants' door.

As if sensing her concern, her older sons called, one after the other. Scotty from Dartmouth and Drew from his office in New York. That made her feel better. She filled them in on the most recent develop- ments, although they already seemed fully briefed. Emerson was a small town with a long reach. People ventured far from here, but they stayed connected. Neither boy was very concerned. Dad was on it. Things tended not to go wrong when he was involved.

There were more calls after that, friends and acquaintances eager for gossip. She tried Alice—they still hadn't connected after she'd fled the police station last night—but she didn't respond. Which wasn't surpris- ing, given the fact that she and Geoff were dealing with the same thing as the Parrishes. She'd swing by later. It would be good to speak with her. Her voice had a way of soothing Celia.

They got back just before noon. Jack, looking upset, walked past with- out making eye contact and disappeared to his room. Oliver's expression was even more somber than it had been this morning. The tastefully weathered skin and strong bone structure seemed to have undergone a temporary collapse, revealing the aging man beneath.

"So, Christopher has been making some pretty serious allegations," he said once Jack was out of earshot. "He has a lawyer. A good one."

"And?"

"He's saying that Jack assaulted the girl."

"What? He's saying *Jack* did this?"

"Not the murder. Not specifically. He says that Jack assaulted her and then he and Hannah left. Christopher stayed behind to comfort her. Evidently the girl was very upset. But she was alive when he left her in the early hours."

"What exactly does he mean by assault?"

"The allegations are sexual in nature."

"But that's insane. Hannah was there."

"Exactly."

"Well, what does Jack say?"

"Obviously that Christopher's lying. There *had* been some tension between Christopher and her earlier in the evening, but our son's behavior was aboveboard from start to finish." He smiled ruefully. "Jack has a theory about it, of course. He says Christopher is projecting."

"What do the police think?"

"They're skeptical of Christopher, to say the least. Changing his story once he got representation—it's a real red flag. And we got the distinct feeling that there's forensic stuff they aren't talking about yet."

"And Elaine?"

"As far as she can see, there's little risk that Jack faces any sort of legal jeopardy," he said gloomily.

"Then why don't you seem happier?"

"Because if this allegation gets any traction, it can do all sorts of damage. Especially if last year's nonsense gets out as well."

"What can we do?"

"Nip it in the bud."

With that, he went to his study to make some calls. Celia collapsed into her chair in the alcove. She wanted to share Oliver's certainty that Christopher was the only one lying, but she couldn't help but think about that bound woman on her son's computer screen; about the look on his face right after Lexi fled the house last year, how similar it had been to the one he'd had when he arrived home yesterday morning.

Whatever had happened, Oliver was right about one thing. An accusation of sexual assault was very bad news, no matter how nebulous. Proof wasn't necessary. There wouldn't have to be a trial. All it would take was a critical mass of radioactive whispers to drag their son—and the whole Parrish family—into a never-ending nightmare.

Oliver was particularly sensitive to this. He'd already lived through one devastating family scandal. Celia heard the story soon after she started dating him. He was in law school; she was at Wellesley. He wanted to make sure she knew about it before things went any further between them. Celia listened quietly and then told him it didn't make the slightest bit of difference. She could already see the type of man he was. Besides, she was the last person to judge someone for their father's behavior after what her own had done to her in his Back Bay study.

Frederick Parrish was a successful attorney, specializing in criminal law. Mostly white-collar offenses. It was all so low-key and genteel that it was often difficult to remember that many of them were criminals. With their wireless spectacles and pillowy jowls, they looked like the sort of men you'd find in a business lounge at a regional airport, waiting to connect back to their suburban homes.

His last-ever client, Matilda Czerny, was one of the few women he defended. In her late thirties, she'd been senior assistant to the CFO of a big farm insurance company. It was a position she'd used, according to prosecutors, to siphon just over two million dollars from the firm to a location currently unknown.

It was a complicated case. Two things happened during the long meetings between lawyer and client. First, it became clear to Frederick that Matilda Czerny was guilty as charged. The second was that he fell in love with her. Mixed together, these two factors proved combustible, causing the well-respected lawyer to vanish with his client on the eve of the trial. Frederick was detained in Mexico City five days later after being discovered unconscious in a hotel elevator. He had no money or ID, and one of his shoes was missing. Matilda was never heard from again.

It made no sense. With her broad hips and small, squinting eyes, Matilda wasn't exactly a femme fatale. But something that had been building up in Frederick for years suddenly percolated over as he passed those quiet hours with her in his plush Loop office. Boredom, fear of aging, proximity to all that easy money. Whatever it had been, it sent him south of more than one border.

He pleaded guilty and was sentenced to five years in a minimum-security prison in Missouri. Oliver, seventeen at the time, had driven to visit him only once. He was surprised to find his father largely unchanged. They spoke about Oliver mostly, particularly his enrollment at Dartmouth in the fall. Understanding that he wasn't going to get an unsolicited explanation, Oliver had flat-out asked him why he'd done it. Frederick had removed his glasses and cleaned them with the tail of his coarse denim shirt.

"Life is messy," he said eventually, and then he said nothing more.

Instead of heading straight home, Oliver had gone on a three-day drunken road trip that ended with him being pulled from a hump of crumpled, smoking steel by volunteer firemen using the Jaws of Life. The deep gash on his head had left him with a permanent scar. Four months later he enrolled at Dartmouth; four years after that he was at Harvard Law. But in many ways he was still driving that Gran Torino as fast as he could, putting as much distance as possible between himself and his father's humiliation. Trying to atone for the corruption. Trying to become the man his father had only pretended to be.

Celia mounted the steps quietly. Jack's door was shut. He hadn't made a peep since returning from the station. She knocked once, then knocked more loudly. There was no response. She hadn't walked in on him since that horrible incident when he was a freshman, but circumstances now seemed to warrant it. She twisted the knob and pushed the door open. He was sitting up in bed, his thumbs working his phone at a mile a minute, his head vised in noise-canceling headphones. She pointed to her ears and he removed the buds. The music that leaked from them sounded as if an enraged next-door neighbor was shouting at his children.

"We need to talk."

"That's all I've been doing recently."

"Jack, that poor girl's dead. You will speak as much as deemed necessary. And turn that dreadful music off."

Shocked by his mother's angry tone, he did as commanded.

"What was wrong with you yesterday morning? Why were you so upset when you came home from Hannah's?"

"I wasn't upset."

"Jack, I swear, if you lie to me, I'm going to get your father up here."

He closed his eyes and sighed and shook his head.

"I was tired. I'd been up all night taking care of Hanns."

"Was she sick?"

"She'd taken something."

"What?"

"It was supposed to be Molly. But I don't think it was. It was really strong. She and Eden and Christopher took it."

"Why would they do that?"

"To experience feelings of euphoria."

"But you didn't take any?"

"Of course not. I don't need stuff like that."

"Where did they get it? Was it Eden's?"

"Yes," he said after a moment's hesitation.

Suddenly that sweet-faced girl didn't seem so sweet.

"Did you tell the police this?"

He nodded.

"So your father knows?"

"I made him promise not to tell you."

"Why not?"

"Because I didn't want to have this conversation! Look, I shouldn't have lied about it. Or where we were. It was just easier not to explain."

"But how do you think that girl wound up dead?"

"Honestly? I think after we left Christopher made a move on her and she turned him down. He lost his shit and killed her."

"But *Christopher*?"

"He was crazy when it came to her."

"And now he's blaming you."

"It's just all so messed up," he said, on the point of tears now.

She hugged him, suddenly overwhelmed by guilt. Of course he hadn't done anything. She couldn't believe she'd entertained even a moment's doubt. Jack's lie was wrong but understandable. He didn't want to get his girlfriend in trouble. For now, all that mattered was that her son was safe.

"Get some rest," she said. "And turn the music down. You're going to ruin your ears."

Oliver was still on his conference call. At some point they'd need to discuss his not telling her about the drugs. She was getting tired of being cut out of things. The person she *did* need to talk to immediately was Alice. She must be going crazy with worry. She should know that what had been bothering Hannah in the middle of the night wasn't as bad as it might now seem. She started to compose a text, but then saw the others she'd sent in the past twenty-four hours, all of them unanswered. Better just to drive over. They could have that coffee they'd put off yesterday.

ALICE

It had been an endless night, an agonizing mixture of good and bad. She was back with Michel, but only because his life had fallen apart. He wanted to be with her, but he was trapped in his house. Hannah wasn't in any real trouble, but Christopher, the son of the man Alice loved, was being accused of murder. It was as if she were teetering between a life she'd always wanted and one she'd always feared.

She'd expected an inquisition when she returned from Michel's, but Geoff was too preoccupied by what was happening to his daughter to notice anything amiss. In fact, he was being sweet. For him. He popped her a beer and split the roast turkey sandwich he'd just fixed himself. His normally impassive face was creased by worry. A surge of pity rose in her, dragging with it feelings of guilt.

"So," he explained, "they were hanging out at the house this Eden girl was looking after. You remember her? She was the one who used to walk by here with the dog."

"Yeah, I remember. Red hair, full of beans."

"That's how Hannah knew her. They just started talking one day out front. Evidently this was a regular thing, hanging out at the Bondurants'. Kids knew about it. But last night it was just the four of them. Turns out Christopher had a thing for Eden but she wasn't interested. Anyway, Hannah and Jack left around midnight. Christopher stayed behind, presumably to press his case. The next morning she turns up dead and Christopher is behind bars."

"But come on. Christopher?"

"Stranger things," he said before taking a sip.

"Is this why Hannah was so freaked out in the middle of the night?"

"No, she didn't know until this afternoon. Everything was hunky-dory when she left."

"Are you sure? She seemed pretty upset."

"Come on, Alice. This is Hannah we're talking about. It was late. Maybe she wasn't acting as weird as you thought she was." He nodded to her bandage. "So what happened to you?"

"Scraped it getting out of the Uber."

"Looks serious."

"No, yeah, it's not as bad as it looks."

He met her eye. It looked like he was deciding whether or not to say something.

"I'm sorry to bail on you like that," she said, mostly to break the weird silence. "But it didn't seem like my presence was required."

"Yeah, I'm the one who's sorry. But this is all a shock."

A normal couple would have hugged at this point. Instead, Geoff took another bite of his sandwich and Alice went to check on her step-daughter. She was sitting up in bed when Alice eased open the door. She quickly placed her phone facedown on the covers. She wasn't crying, exactly, but the runways were definitely open for the next arrival of tears.

"So how was it?"

"Scary."

"Your father told me what's going on."

"I just feel so bad for Christopher."

Alice crossed the room and sat on the edge of the bed.

"So you really think he did this?"

"Looks like."

"But does that even make any sense?" Alice asked. "I mean, had you seen any sign of this? Because I've been around some pretty violent men in my life. And Christopher Mahoun isn't one of them. Not by a long shot."

"He was pretty crazy when it came to Eden."

"How crazy?"

"I think she was the first girl he ever loved. And she could be pretty unpredictable. He was a lot younger than her. Eden had been through some stuff and he's, you know, like Bambi."

"Bambi went through some stuff."

"Oh yeah. Well, you know what I mean."

"Hannah, I have to ask you something. Last night, when I saw you in the kitchen, you were really freaked out. But you didn't know about Eden yet. I mean, nobody did, right?"

"I wasn't freaked out."

"You kinda were, though."

Hannah stared at the bedspread.

"You can talk to me, Hanns. You know that, right?"

"You can't tell Dad."

"Cross my heart."

"I was just really strung out. I'd taken something and it really messed me up."

"Okay."

"It's why I was up all night."

"Do the police know this?"

She shook her head.

"We didn't want to get in trouble."

"So everybody took it?"

"Not Jack. But the rest of us, yeah."

"So that was it? The only thing that was bothering you last night?"

She nodded, though she wouldn't meet Alice's gaze.

"You know if there was something else, you could tell me."

"I know," Hannah said. "But there wasn't."

"Well, come here."

They hugged.

"What did you take, anyway?"

"It was supposed to be Molly but it musta been a bad batch because it really wiped us out for a couple of hours."

"I know this is going to sound weird coming from me, but be careful around that stuff," Alice said.

"No, yeah, lesson learned."

She left her alone after that, although she couldn't help but feel that there was something more going on here. Yes, what Hannah was saying certainly made sense as far as her kitchen outburst was concerned. The girl didn't exactly have a robust constitution. Two glasses of wine and she crumbled into a disorganized mass of giggles and blubbering. And Alice had seen enough people bent sideways in her life to know that all bets were off when chemicals were introduced. But still. It didn't feel right.

Michel needed to know about this. She went up to her room and texted him, but the message went unread. She knew that he was considering turning off his cell if his number fell into the hands of the rabble. Simply communicating, much less being together, was going to get even more difficult. She considered emailing him but then remembered that the cops had taken his computer. She climbed into bed, exhausted by the last few hours but also knowing that sleep was unlikely without pharmacological assistance. But she needed to stay sharp. Her arm began to throb beneath the dressing. God only knew what kind of evil shit was lurking below.

Undrugged, the night fragmented into short intervals of shallow slumber interrupted by bursts of panic and dread. Michel didn't write. Nor was there any real news online. There was, however, plenty of gossip. After an initial wave of shocked disbelief, public opinion was solidifying against Christopher. The racists and trolls arrived, lending their measured insights. Osama became the go-to insult; Obama wasn't far behind. The comments subdivided into three main schools of thought. First, there were those concerned with policy: *so I guess were just going to keep letting these fuckers in until they dehead us all.* There were also those whose interest was more in the mechanics of due process: *Kill him. No trial. Rope + tree. Summary execution.* And finally, a more nuanced element, focused on the romantic and erotic side of the emerging story: *Their own women are pigs so they go crazy when they see a white girl I bet he fucked her with his little brown dick after she was dead.*

More damningly, local kids were coming forward to say Christopher had been acting weird of late. It was emerging that Eden was known around Waldo. Evidently she'd let the Bondurant place become something of a party house. Hannah's classmate Jessie Beverly, a certifiable imbecile, wrote, *I don't know why ppl are't talking about the parties this girl through there not surprised something happened.* To which Sergei Letved, the state champ pole vaulter, replied, *Mahoun was crazy to try to get with her lol outta yer league bro.* And some young sophisticate who went by the name Biggusdikkus16 suggested that *anybody who'd let Jack Parrish bitch them out like Mahoun did is too big a pussy to kill anybody.*

That last comment got Alice thinking about Christopher and Jack. Although she'd never seen Jack treat Hannah badly, she couldn't say the same for the way he acted toward his best friend. There was an undertone of nastiness there. It rarely manifested itself in straight-up bullying, but you could always feel it. With Christopher, as with Hannah, he'd found himself a captive audience for his often-bizarre insights into the workings of the human psyche. Jack saw himself as top dog, a status he reinforced with commands and insults wrapped in a thin layer of jokiness.

The worst episode came last September. Fortunately, Alice had been there for it, or it could have been a real disaster. Hannah had just started dating Jack. There was a small Saturday gathering of kids enjoying a spell of early autumn heat at the Holts' backyard pool. Alice had just emerged from the kitchen to see if they needed anything before she headed off to Trader Joe's. Kids lounged about, languorous, dappled with water and sun. The smell of marijuana was in the air; there were half-heartedly hidden beers. Music played. One boy stood in the shallow end, his phone aloft, ready to film the object of everyone's attention— Christopher, perched on the diving board, preparing to perform a dive. Uncharacteristically, he was basking in the attention. What he didn't see was Jack, sneaking up behind him. The kids saw it, though. Jack stepped gingerly onto the board and tiptoed toward Christopher, whose concentration on his upcoming feat made him oblivious to the other boy's approach. Alice thought Jack was simply going to push him in, but then he slowed, hands lowering, fingers pincering, preparing to grab the bottoms of Christopher's trunks.

"Jack!"

Her voice echoed through the backyard like a lost spelunker's cry for help. Jack pulled back his hands; Christopher turned and understood what was going on. The boys faced off for a moment, watched by the others, whose smiles had vanished. Jack was so much taller than Christopher, so much stronger. There was a defiant smirk plastered on his face as Christopher's expression ran through a rapid sequence of shock, anger, and confusion.

And then Jack pushed him in the pool. Everyone laughed. Just a couple of best buds horsing around. But Alice didn't laugh. She was aghast. Maybe it was the angle she had; maybe it was the fact she'd seen a lot more evil male shit than any of these kids had, or ever would. But Jack really had been about to pull down Christopher's trunks, exposing him to his peers, one of whom was set to capture it on film. An act of unfathomable cruelty, especially for a boy as shy as Christopher. Later that evening, when she mentioned it to Hannah, she insisted that he'd just been messing around. No way would he actually *pants* Christopher. Alice had let it go. Maybe Hannah was right. But now, she couldn't help but wonder if maybe she'd been wrong.

Time passed. The clock ticked. Michel didn't write. And then, just before dawn, as she hovered between sleep and wakefulness, she heard a car pull up. She went to the window, wondering if the media's traveling circus was now pitching tent here. A large Mercedes blocked the end of the driveway. The passenger door opened. Geoff emerged; the dome-lit man behind the wheel was briefly visible. It was Oliver Parrish.

Alice quickly stepped back from the window. What the hell had she just seen? These two weren't exactly close. Geoff couldn't come up with enough bad things to say about Oliver after that ill-fated dinner party, even though the other man had been the personification of charm. And yet here they were, driving around together in the middle of the night, locked in secret confabulation hours after their kids had become involved in the local crime of the century.

Her husband quietly entered the house and went straight to his office. She gave him a minute to settle, then crept downstairs. His door was off the latch. She gently pushed it open. He didn't notice her. He wore headphones; he was completely engrossed in his screen. Instead of the usual neuroglyphics, there was an image of the front porch of a house. This house. It was dark and empty. The image danced a little, as if it was scrolling rapidly, forward or backward.

She closed the door and retreated to her room. *What in the literal fuck?* she thought. First a clandestine meeting with Oliver, and now this. Why was Geoff surveying home security footage? This wasn't right. This wasn't even in the same area code as right. Something seriously hinky was going on here.

Fully awake now, she decided to check her wound. She removed the dressing in the shower, half-expecting to find writhing maggots feasting on gangrenous flesh. But it was fine. It was just a scratch with attitude. By the time she emerged from the bathroom, dawn had finally shown its stupid face. Downstairs, she made herself a coffee and once again waded into the social media swamp to see if there were any new developments. But there was nothing. Last night's narrative was holding. Things were definitely not looking promising for Christopher. The hive mind had decided on his guilt.

The house phone rang. She scooped it up immediately—Hannah was still asleep. She'd be going to school late today.

"Ms. Holt?"

"Yes," she said, letting the mistake stand.

"This is Detective Gates. Is your husband available?"

"Not just now," Alice said, even though he was currently sitting about fifty feet away. "Can I help you?"

"Could you have him call me as soon as possible?"

"Sure. Can I tell him what this is about?"

There was a pause.

"Thing is, he might not be available for a bit."

"In that case, you're going to have to help us out," Gates said. "We need to speak with Hannah again. As soon as possible."

"Shall I have her call or . . ."

"We'd like you to bring her in. Immediately."

They'd found out about the drugs. That had to be it. In Alice's youth, the presence of drugs at a gathering like last night's was a given. But the good folk of Emerson took a darker view of controlled substances. Here, getting caught with them had dire consequences for that holiest of grails— *the future*.

She headed down the hall, passing Geoff's quiet office. She thought about him in Oliver's car and that flickering security footage. There was no need to tell him about this just yet. She pushed Hannah's door open. She lay sprawled at an acute angle on her bed, looking for all the world like she'd just plummeted to her death from a great height. Her face was buried in the pillow, hidden by a plume of hair. Her sheet was half-wrapped around her, exposing a lightly freckled thigh.

Alice crossed the room. Hannah's phone was charging on the bedside table. Without really deciding to do it, Alice reached out and touched the ID button. The phone lit up. There were four banners on the locked screen, each a message from Jack. They'd arrived within the last minute. The first read *Hannah don't freak out*. The next said *Just stick to the story*. And then *You tell them what E was saying I'm fucked*. Finally, *ERASE*

THESE. Alice, her heart pounding, desperate to read more, swiped the third message. She understood her mistake the moment she was faced with the invitation to enter her pass code.

Goddammit. Hannah stirred. Alice put her hand on her shoulder.

"Hannah?" She gently rubbed her shoulder. "Hanns? Sweetie?"

The girl's eyes slowly opened.

"Time to get up. The police want to talk to you again."

"Did they say why?" she said, fully awake now.

"No, but I presume they know about the drugs."

"Shit."

"Don't worry about it. There's nothing they can do at this point. Unless you still have some of them?"

"No."

"But you're going to have to tell your father about it."

"He'll be pissed."

"You want me to deal with him?"

"No. Shit. I'll do it."

Hannah's gaze migrated to the phone, as if she sensed there were messages behind its now-dark screen.

"I better get dressed," she said.

You tell them what E was saying I'm fucked. The words played through Alice's mind as she went to Geoff's office. She didn't bother knocking. His screen was now covered with its usual luminous bioscribbles. He pulled off the headphones and turned to her. His bloodshot eyes shimmied; his parched lips were coated with a fine milky film.

"The cops just called," Alice said. "They want to talk to Hannah again."

He didn't seem surprised by the news. Unhappy, but not surprised.

"It sounded urgent," she added.

"Okay, I got it," he said, his words urging her out the door.

She was tempted to hit him with the things she'd witnessed, his meeting with Oliver and the security camera footage and Jack's texts.

But she once again chose silence. She went to the kitchen, where she paced, trying unsuccessfully to fit the pieces together. It was all coming at her too fast. But one thing was clear. This wasn't about drugs. Not only. This was suburban DEFCON 4. Or 1. Whichever was the worst, this was it.

Geoff soon arrived with Hannah, whose eyes flexed with worry. She would have just read Jack's messages. Read them and then erased them. As instructed.

"So what's going on?" Alice asked.

"They just want to clear up a few details."

"Geoff . . ."

"Everything's fine." He immediately understood how harsh his words must have sounded. "Sorry. We gotta go. We'll talk when I get back."

She texted Michel the moment they were gone. *MICHEL IT'S ME. I need to see you asap. Something weird's going on.* Like last night's message, it was delivered but remained unread. And so she was once again cast into the no-man's-land of waiting for him to contact her. There was nothing to do but pace the house. Time passed. Minutes, and then it was an hour. She was upstairs when there was a knock on the door. Tentative, friendly, unlike yesterday's doom-laden cop-rap. Celia was all smiles and sweet light when Alice greeted her.

"I thought you'd disappeared into thin air!"

"It's been a madhouse here," Alice said.

"Tell me about it. But I bring a little sanity."

"In that case, come on in. Coffee?"

"I'd love one."

They went to the kitchen. Celia looked around as Alice started to work the big Italian caffeine machine.

"Are Geoff and Hannah here?"

"They just got summoned back to the station."

"Yes, Oliver and Jack were there as well."

Was there something not quite right about Celia's voice? It seemed a little too shallow and breathy.

"Do you know why? Nobody tells me anything."

"This is obviously just between us, but it turns out Christopher's now telling some cockamamie tale about Jack assaulting this Eden girl."

"Really?" Alice asked after a brief pause, during which she jettisoned her temptation to tell Celia about seeing their husbands together earlier.

"It's desperation speaking. I mean, he says nothing at first and then his father hires a hotshot attorney and suddenly this story miraculously materializes out of thin air."

Alice handed Celia a steaming cup and started to make her own.

"Did you talk to Jack about it?"

"He says it's nonsense, of course." She tried to take a sip but it was too hot. "What does Hannah say?"

"They left at midnight; everything was copacetic. That's it."

"So, Alice. There's something else. I'm only saying this because I love Hannah. But it appears she was doing some pretty heavy drugs."

Celia might love Hannah, but that wasn't why she was here. There was definitely something not right going on.

"Really?" Alice asked, playing along.

"Something called Molly? You've heard of it?"

If by heard of it you mean did I do it more or less daily in the summer of 2013, Alice thought, *then the answer would be yes.*

"Yeah," she said. "It's like speed, only not so . . . speedy."

"It turns out this Eden girl had some."

This Eden girl. She kept calling her that.

"Okay. Not good."

"According to Jack, it really threw all of them for a loop."

"Did he take it, too?"

"No, but that doesn't excuse his behavior. Anyway, I imagine that's why Hannah was acting so strange when you saw her. And I guess it also explains why Christopher . . . did what he did."

Alice's phone vibrated on the table. It was a call from an unknown number. She ignored it.

"Wow," she said, still trying to figure out what was happening.

"I thought you should know." She sighed. "I just wish Oliver had been home. Jack would've never pulled a stunt like this unless his father was away."

"Well, thank you for telling me," Alice said.

Celia must have caught something in her tone, because she tilted her head slightly, her pretty eyes crinkling in concern.

"Is everything all right?"

And then it hit her. The vague suspicion turned into an absolute certainty. Celia was lying. Geoff was lying. Even Hannah—she was lying as well. They all were. Oliver's predawn presence and Jack's texts and the security footage and now Celia turning up to assure her that everything was hunky-dory. This wasn't about recreational drugs. Her son had done something horrible to Eden, just like he had to Lexi Liriano. *You tell them what E was saying I'm fucked.* He'd done something and now they were covering it up, just like they had before.

"Just tired," she said with a tired little smile.

"I'll leave you be. I just thought you should know."

"I appreciate it, Celia. I really do."

"This will all be over soon and we can have a proper lunch. Only not at Papillon."

You cunt, Alice thought as they hugged. *You complete, total, and absolute cunt.*

"That'd be good."

"And you let me know if you find something out," Celia said.

As if, Alice thought. The moment she was alone, she checked her phone. That unknown caller had left a voice mail. It was probably spam. She played it, anyway. She'd be checking everything from here on out.

It wasn't spam. It was Michel.

"This is me now . . ."

MICHEL

He almost didn't see her message. He'd come upon it just before he finally switched off his cell phone for good. Someone had posted his number online last night, setting off the avalanche of hate. Hundreds of strangers telling him, some calmly and grammatically, others in enraged gibberish, that they wished pain and death upon him and his son. He had to dig through this sewage to find the messages from people he knew. Sofia had texted twice and left a voice message—she needed to know what to do about the restaurant, but mostly she was sick with worry over Christopher. Friends back in Paris, who were only now getting the news. And, finally, Alice. *Something weird's going on.*

That much I know, he thought. The story Christopher told Cantor last night was very different from the one he'd given in front of Michel. The lawyer arrived at the house just after Alice left. She went out the back door once again, although this time Michel opened the vine-encrusted gate in the fence for her. He watched her sprint across his neighbor's backyard, keeping one step ahead of security lights. It was a beautiful sight. For a moment, he could forget everything. *This woman*, he thought.

And then Cantor arrived and he was brought crashing back to reality. Apparently, the interview with his son hadn't started well. It took Christopher a while to understand that Cantor was an ally. He was also worried about getting his friends in trouble. But after Cantor painted him a graphic picture of what his life would look like if he was found responsible for Eden's death, the story came tumbling out.

"Turns out the gatherings at the Bondurants' were a regular thing,"

Cantor explained. "It started as an open house, but the owners got suspicious, so by Tuesday night it was basically just the four of them."

He took a slow, dramatic breath and explained that Eden had accused Jack of sexually assaulting her.

"What does that mean? Assault?"

"Rape."

The two men were momentarily silenced by the enormity of the word.

"And Christopher let this happen?"

"He and Hannah were apparently in no fit state to intervene."

"Christopher said there was marijuana."

"I think it was a lot more than pot. Anyway, Eden becomes hysterical and attacks Jack. This rouses Christopher and he gets involved— this is where he sustains his neck wounds. Jack flees the house, Hannah goes with him. Christopher stays behind to deal with Eden. He settles her down, although she's making it clear she intends to make Jack pay for what he did. Your son eventually leaves and the next thing anybody knows she's dead."

"So what does Christopher think happened?"

"Jack came back to the house to shut her up."

"But how exactly did she die?"

"She hit her head falling. Cerebral hemorrhage."

"So it could it have been an accident."

"No. She was propelled backward. With force. There were marks on her upper chest consistent with a hard shove. She was definitely killed."

"But why didn't Christopher say any of this during the first interview?"

"I'm not sure. Maybe because you were there and he didn't want you to know about the drugs. Maybe because he's scared of Jack."

"So what happens now?"

"Christopher and I talked to the cops."

"Did they believe him?"

"Impossible to know. They're going to reinterview Jack and Hannah first thing in the morning. That goes right, we wind up in a better place."

"So what do I do?"

"Stay put. I'll let you know the second there's any news. We'll know where we are soon. Oh, they got your cell number, don't they? I've been hearing it buzz. Either that or your takeout's doing big business."

"Yes. They have it."

"Okay. Turn it off."

"But how will we talk?"

He reached into his satchel and took out a flip phone, the sort Michel hadn't used in years.

"Is that necessary?"

"If you've been doxxed, then we have no idea who's listening to your old phone. The cops, the press, some asshole in Latvia. Have you looked at Twitter? People are invested in this."

"Okay. Thank you."

"Don't thank me too much. It'll be on your bill."

The relief Michel felt at Cantor's news soon gave way to anger at his son. Why had it taken Christopher so long to reveal the truth? Why hadn't he told him? Shame about the drugs didn't explain it. No, he'd been protecting Jack. Because he was afraid of him. He knew the right thing to do, and yet he was too weak to do it. For almost twenty-four hours, he'd kept quiet. What would have happened if the police hadn't come for him? Would he still be protecting his friend? Stupid boy. Stupid, stupid boy.

Michel didn't sleep all night. He turned off his old phone, unable to bear the hate being directed at his son. He was tempted to call Alice on the new one, to ask her to return to him, but that would be insanely reckless. By dawn, he'd entered a sort of limbo. Time no longer existed. He no longer existed. It was just Christopher, behind a locked door.

Strange to think that there was a time when he would have prayed for help. He'd had faith before Maryam's death. Absolute and unshakable, or so he thought. It had been born during his boyhood in Beirut, where he attended Saint Georges several times a week. Some of his first memories were from that massive cathedral. The stern saints on the wall; the smell of incense and the echoed voices from the choral platforms. God was always there, a deep and lulling hum, a constant gentle breeze.

But then Maryam fell ill, and when he asked for mercy God showed his true face. Just after she died, he'd walked out of Salpêtrière, down to the Jardin des Plantes, and then to the river. A ragged man, a drug addict, had tried to sell him stolen flowers. Michel reached for his wallet, then remembered she was dead. Thinking he'd been mocked, the man cursed him, his face transforming into something terrible. Bloodshot eyes and sharp, yellowy teeth; thick lips and a flat nose. His gray beard chaotic; his rough skin leathered and filthy. And Michel suddenly knew that this was the true face of God. One that cursed you and brought only death. He made you believe in mercy and hope and then he left your wife screaming in delirium and pain, unable to see anything but the greasy walls of the abyss she was sinking into; her skin turned to brittle parchment, imprinted with the calligraphy of her bones. From that moment on, there was no consoling presence in Michel's life, no gentle breeze. It was just him and his son, whom God wouldn't protect any more than he did Maryam. That was on Michel.

Cantor finally called late morning, sounding gloomy and overwhelmed.

"What's going on?" Michel asked. "I've been waiting."

"Yeah, well, dragging in Oliver Parrish's son in the middle of the night was not an option." He took a breath. "So we didn't get the result we were after. Hannah and Jack both denied everything. The assault, the accusation, the fight between Eden and Jack."

"But we knew they would do that."

"Yes, but not so well. They were definitely reading from the same textbook."

"So the police believed them."

"That's certainly my impression."

"Where does this leave us?"

"Not in a great place. Right now it's a he said, he said sort of deal with one he having a much louder say than the other. And a witness to back him up. Well, two. Hannah's father also gave a statement, and he's swearing Jack didn't leave the house from midnight 'til morning."

Hannah's father. The husband of his lover.

"Christopher didn't do this," Michel said.

"Well, that's certainly our position. I'm on my way to file a motion now to get your son released. But I wouldn't hold your breath."

"Please. I haven't breathed in two days."

There was an ominous pause.

"They're still doing forensic tests but initial reports aren't promising. They're being very meticulous. Those scratches on Christopher's neck aren't a good look for us. Michel, I think you're gonna need to prepare yourself for the possibility that your son is going to be charged with homicide."

Michel sat perfectly still on the sofa after they hung up. It was as if the air itself had become heavy, miles and miles of it crushing down on him. Finally, he got up and walked to the window, peering through the sheer curtains. The reporters were still out there. He wondered how it would go if he simply walked out the front door and told them what Christopher was saying about Jack Parrish. But of course he wouldn't. He'd do as told. At least until it was time to do something else.

And then, when he finally summoned the nerve to check his old phone, there was Alice, telling him she'd found something. He called and left a message and then he was waiting again.

"How's Christopher?" she asked when she called him back.

"They're still holding him."

"I'm so sorry, Michel."

"Jack raped her. He attacked her and he made them keep quiet about it. And then he went back later and . . ."

"I knew it."

"You did?"

"I saw Hannah's phone this morning. Jack's pressuring her to lie. God knows what bullshit he's told her. And I saw Oliver and Geoff together before dawn, having a big heavy conversation. After which Geoff starts messing around with our security camera. And then Celia just happens to drop by a few minutes ago. Talking shit about Christopher, making sure I toed the party line. Jack did this, Michel. And his parents are protecting him. They've got everybody involved. Hannah and Geoff and the cops and their friends. This happened before, you know."

"What do you mean?"

"Lexi Liriano. You remember her, right?"

"She was one of the kids from Boston."

"She accused Jack of the same shit last year. She was going to expose him to the world. But then Oliver pays a visit to Lexi's mom and suddenly the whole thing goes away."

"So what should we do?"

"Call your lawyer. Tell him."

"He'll want to know where I heard it."

"Look, if you have to tell him about us, go ahead." She paused. "But maybe you shouldn't say anything for now. Maybe it's better if they think I'm one of them. That way I can figure out what's happening."

"All right. You're right."

"We're not going to let them do this, Michel. I promise you."

They were silent for a few seconds, joined together by a cheap phone.

"I need to see you," she said.

"Not yet. But soon. I promise."

He called Cantor immediately. The connection was poor; there were voices in the background.

"I'm filing the motion right now," the lawyer said, a little impatiently.

"We need to talk. There's something new."

"I'll call when I'm done."

"Come by."

He arrived an hour later, smelling of coffee.

"Christopher is telling the truth," Michel said the moment he closed the door on the braying voices from the street. "I'm sure of it."

The lawyer studied him for a moment.

"Is there something you have to tell me, Michel?"

He wanted to tell him about the meeting between the fathers, the erased security footage. But this would make it clear Alice was the source and he wasn't sure how much he could trust this man yet. There was one thing, however, that he could say.

"Jack did this before. Last year. It was a girl named Lexi Liriano. Oliver paid to keep her quiet."

"And you know this, how?"

"I just do."

"Michel, I'm your son's lawyer. Everything you say to me is confidential."

"You just have to trust me."

Cantor didn't look happy, but he also understood it was as much as he was going to get.

"Okay, I'll look into it."

"Will you tell the police?"

"Michel, I guarantee you the cops will not be interested in this unless I can give them something more concrete. Right now it's just hearsay."

"Can't we just go to the press with it?"

"Sorry, I don't play those games."

"We could look at Jack's phone. Maybe there's something on there."

The lawyer winced.

"What?" Michel asked. "Is that not possible?"

"Technically, yeah, we could request the cops get a court order. But I don't see them asking a judge to do that right now."

"Why not?"

"First of all, they like your son for this. Plus, they've already dragged Oliver Parrish's kid down to the station twice. I think they've probably exhausted their goodwill in that department."

"Does that matter?"

"He's managing partner in one of the city's biggest law firms. He's the town attorney, or at least his firm is. He golfs with the chief of police."

"Then what do we do?"

"Like I said, I'll look into this Liriano thing. Could it be the basis of a defense down the road? Yeah, if we can get some confirmation. But I have to tell you, I really don't want to get to the point where this is all we got."

"But it's true."

"I hate to say this, but as of right now, the truth ain't what it used to be."

PATRICK

He was awakened by a call from his ex-wife. The sound of his buzzing phone sent adrenaline coursing through his sluggish bloodstream. He didn't like getting phone calls. The news was never good. It hadn't been since the disease took hold of his child.

"Were you asleep?" Lily asked.

It was 11:13 in the morning.

"No."

"Are you at work?"

"Yes."

There was a brief, censorious pause. It had been a while since he'd lied to his ex-wife. He must be getting rusty.

"So I was reading about this murder," she said, cutting to the chase, as was her habit these days.

"Yeah, crazy."

"What are you hearing?"

Patrick hesitated. For the first time in quite a while, he actually had something consequential to say to Lily. But she would not respond kindly to reports of middle-of-the-night roaming and ghostly visions. She'd done her time.

"Only that they're questioning Michel Mahoun's son."

"Yes, I saw that. So you don't know who the other kids in the house were."

This was not a question, but a statement that indicated she did know. It didn't surprise him that she was ahead of him. He hadn't checked the news in twelve hours. He'd started drinking seriously the moment he left Danielle Perry outside the Bondurants'. The last thing he remembered was watching a documentary about Stalingrad. And then a Russian winter had descended inside his head.

"Sounds like you do."

"Jack Parrish, for one," she said.

"No shit. Is he, I mean, involved?"

"Only as a witness, it seems."

"Wait, he was there when it happened?"

"That's not clear."

"Man, his parents must be thrilled."

"So how are you doing, Patrick?" she asked after a pause.

Talk of murder and mayhem was over. It was time to move on to the real horror show. Him.

"No, I'm good."

"Are you seeing someone?"

For a brief moment, he thought she meant dating. Which, weirdly, caused an image of Danielle Perry to flash in his mind. Had people seen them outside the Bondurants'? But that was not what she meant at all.

"Oh, now and then. Meetings mostly. Got my chair-folding technique down cold."

"That's good," she said. "Are they helping?"

Patrick didn't necessarily want to get into specifics about something that wasn't happening.

"Definitely. So how are you, Lily? How's Sam?"

She was only too happy to change the topic to their remaining child.

"He's fine. We're starting to think about colleges."

They talked about that for a while, SAT tutors and campus visits. He offered to split the latter duty with her and she said that she would have to get back to him, which was code for the fact that there wasn't a chance in hell that she was going to allow her fifteen-year-old son to occupy a motor vehicle operated by his father. With that, the conversation ended.

He closed his eyes after hanging up and experienced a particularly intense desire for a drink. Conversation with his ex-wife had lost none of its sting. Sometimes, he preferred their turbulently doomed last days, as the artillery fire of his misery and misdeeds drew closer and closer to their suburban bunker. But that sort of drama wouldn't be forthcoming, ever again. After finally bringing down the curtain on the calamity that was their post-Gabi marriage, Lily had become coolly solicitous and mostly indifferent. He wasn't her problem anymore.

The Parrishes. He wished he was sorrier to hear they were being dragged into this mess. Unlike most of the town's residents, Patrick was not a member of their fan club. His animus stemmed from an encounter with them six years earlier, when Gabi had dated Scotty. They were both juniors at Waldo. This was before heroin made its appearance, although Patrick was later to learn that Gabi was already downing painkillers regularly. Even so, nobody was surprised she'd caught the eye of one of the legendary Parrish lads. Gabi was always popular with the boys. She was funny and as sweet as could be most of the time. And smart—she collected As easily. She was also extraordinarily beautiful. This wasn't just Patrick talking; everybody said so. Take away the drugs, and she was pretty close to being the perfect girl.

Problem was, try as you might, you couldn't take the drugs away. Her romance with Scotty had ended when she suffered a panic attack at the Parrish house. Lily was tending her sick mother in Providence at the time, leaving Patrick to deal with things on his own. He'd had a few beers when the call came in but was perfectly capable of operating a motor vehicle to Emerson Heights. After all, it wasn't as if there was an actual summit to achieve—the neighborhood stood just a couple dozen feet above the rest of the town. The name didn't describe geography. It conferred status.

Celia answered the door; Gabi stood behind her, looking like she'd just wandered out of a Japanese horror movie. Hair curtained her face; her chin was pinned to her clavicle. Scotty hovered at the hall's midpoint like a free safety who hadn't decided whether to play the run or the pass. Oliver, whom Patrick would only ever meet on the phone, was nowhere in sight.

Before anyone could speak, Gabi hurried out the door, making a beeline for the car, her feet never seeming to hit the ground.

"I'm sorry about this," Patrick said.

"Don't be ridiculous," Celia answered, the personification of charm and grace. "I just hope she feels better."

As he dealt with his daughter that night and the following morning, he didn't give much thought to the Parrishes, except perhaps to feel grateful for how nice Celia had been. The problem came later that day. He was at work when his assistant told him that Oliver was on the line.

"How's Gabriella?" he asked.

"A little shaky, but better."

"I'm glad to hear that."

"Thank you. I appreciate your calling."

They'd reached what should have been the natural end of a polite conversation. Oliver Parrish was a busy man. He'd discharged his duties as a host. And yet he stayed on the line.

"So, this isn't pleasant, but I wanted to alert you to the fact that some medications are missing from the house."

"Okay," Patrick said, seeing immediately where this was going and wishing somehow it wouldn't.

"The only explanation we can come up with is that Gabi took them."

"I see. Well, I guess I can ask her about it."

"Look, Patrick, I may be overstepping here, but there seems to be a lot of this going around these days. I see it with clients and colleagues. And from what I can tell early intervention appears to be the best strategy."

Patrick said nothing, his nerves quivering with shame.

"If you want, I can connect you with some people who can help. They have a place out near Stockbridge that is really doing some cutting-edge stuff."

Patrick knew that a hundred people could listen in on this call and ninety-nine of them would only hear a well-intentioned, powerful man offering assistance to a neighbor in need. One father to another. But Patrick was the hundredth person. He didn't feel gratitude or reassurance. He felt humiliation. It was as if his own pathetic attempts at fathering were being corrected by the master, with his perfect wife and his castle on the hill and his Ivy League boys. He muttered feeble thanks and hung up.

Gabi was in her room when he got home. The panic was gone, but in its wake she'd withdrawn even further into herself. She sat up in bed, legs folded, computer balanced on her lap. She avoided eye contact as he explained what Oliver had reported. Silence descended once he'd finished.

"Well?" he asked after it had gone on long enough.

"Scotty just dumped me."

"He did?"

"He said his parents thought it was for the best."

She'd never looked so helpless. Not as a child, not as a baby.

"What is *wrong* with me?" she asked.

The pain he felt at this moment had been unbearable. He muttered some fatuously conciliatory words and backed out of the room. He went downstairs to fix himself a drink and get even more pissed off at the Parrishes. Even at the time, he knew his anger wasn't justified. Oliver and Celia were just doing what any parent would have done—protect their kid. But that didn't lessen the sting. His daughter, his family, were being dismissed. Sent down from the heights they'd foolishly tried to ascend.

Of course, the Parrishes were by no means the worst. But they had been the first to treat Gabi like she was a suburban succubus out to corrupt their young. People just couldn't accept that his daughter was sick. They believed she had a deficient character. She lacked willpower or moral fiber. It was inconceivable to them that what afflicted her was a case of synaptic haywiring over which she had no control. To them, she was selfish and wicked. Poor Rick Bondurant had a 5K named for him; the only race Gabi inspired was for the door. Although Patrick had eventually grown numb to this attitude, he'd never forget the Parrishes' underlying message: *Your child is less than my child. She's bad. Keep her away from him.*

After hanging up with Lily, he checked the latest news. Word on the virtual street not only put Jack Parrish at the Bondurant house on Tuesday night, but also another girl. Evidently they were long gone before the actual crime took place. In fact, they currently appeared to be in the process of providing evidence against Christopher, which earned them a certain amount of online grief from peers.

Patrick dragged himself from bed. There was still the day—well, half of it—to organize. There were a couple of clients coming in, calls to make, markets to fathom. He knew he should just quit. His heart had left the job months, maybe even years ago. And his mind was now in the process of following. But it would be better to let Griff fire him. That would ensure he got severance, COBRA, the whole nine yards. Even though they were drifting farther and farther away from him, he still had Lily and Sam to think about.

Before going to the office, he'd need to manage the colony of cockroaches writhing beneath his skin. His usual morning drink was vodka and water, topped off by a sachet of effervescent vitamin C powder. But all he currently possessed was water. So whisky it was.

This needed to be done right. He poured himself a quarter tumbler of Suntory and positioned himself at the sink. After taking a deep breath, he tossed down the entire drink. A fire broke out immediately in his throat and spread quickly to his stomach. In response, his body's sprinkler system dampened every inch of his skin with sweat. He hunched forward, gripping the sink's stainless-steel edge with all his might, like a prisoner being rectally searched. He stood his ground. He hung in there. The first thirty seconds were crucial. If he didn't puke by then, all was well.

He didn't puke.

After another shot, he got the coffee going, then ran the electric razor over his face and climbed into the shower. The hot water and the booze brought on a spell of vertiginous clarity, the sort he imagined someone falling down a well must feel. For the second time that morning, thoughts of Danielle entered his empty mind. When she emerged from the shadows last night, he suspected she was going to accuse him of being a voyeur, a creep, perhaps even a suspect. But she simply wanted his help. He'd been tempted to tell her what he saw in the trees. Problem was, he still didn't understand what he'd seen. And she was obviously still too raw to be handling that kind of unexploded bombshell. The woman had a hard road ahead. On top of everything else, they were now raking her over the coals online. She didn't exactly fit the mold of grieving mother. She looked *hard*. Lashes thickly covered in mascara, like they'd just been rescued from an oil spill. Tattoos spilling out from her clothes onto her hands and her neck. People around here would take one look at her and think, *Yes, all right, I get it*. She was exactly the sort of person whose daughter got killed.

And then it hit him. He wasn't sure where it came from but boy did it come hard. He turned off the shower and wrapped himself loosely in a couple of towels. Still dripping, he googled *Jack Parrish Emerson* on his phone. There were plenty of pictures of the boy. Facebook, Instagram; at school and parties and the beach.

It was him. It had been Jack Parrish he'd seen in the tangle of trees.

He should go to the police. The problem was, he didn't want to go to the police. The nice detective had given him her card but she'd also made it plain as day that she didn't want to see him ever again. No, he wouldn't be returning to Public Safety Plaza. Not yet, at least.

He dried and dressed and drove to work, at a loss what else to do. His route took him by Papillon, whose front door was now covered with an impromptu sign. God, this had to be rough for Michel. Patrick knew the feeling. Your kid's name out there, a talking point for the world. The mix of private helplessness and public shame. He was a good guy, Michel. Friendly, without overdoing it. He remembered names; he'd pull up a chair. He was always giving you tastes of things, unsolicited desserts and appetizers that never turned up on your bill. And there was never even the slightest glimmer of judgment in his eye when Patrick ventured a little too deeply into the drinks side of the menu.

He slipped into his office without incident, just in time for his meeting with Benny Karim, an anesthesiologist who'd expressed concerns about his portfolio. It was one of those meetings that reminded Patrick that most of his clients knew his business as well as he did. It was right there online. To get access to the real druidic mysteries of the markets, you needed billions and billions. Patrick was just a caretaker. Pruning and seeding and, mostly, fertilizing with feel-good bullshit. The real growth happened in the jungle, where he'd long ago proven himself too timid to dwell.

As they spoke, Patrick began to suspect that the good doctor was not here to talk about investment strategies so much as to give his adviser a diagnostic eyeball. Word was getting out. The exam's results must have been bad, because Karim was frowning noticeably by meeting's end. Patrick presumed he'd be calling Griff the moment he'd cleared the building.

His phone rang seconds after the client was gone. *That was quick*, Patrick thought.

"It's a Danielle," his assistant announced. "She says you know her?"

"I do," Patrick said, realizing he'd been expecting this call all day. "Put her through."

DANIELLE

She called him after the funeral guy left. She'd wanted to get that over with as quickly as possible, but the guy wouldn't take the hint. It wasn't as if she was being difficult. Small ceremony, no church, cremation. And no frills—she doubted that a Book of Remembrance would be something she'd treasure in coming years. She'd planned on using the same firm she'd used for her grandmother, but they'd gone out of business. Which was strange, when you thought about it. A funeral director going under. You'd have thought there'd always be another body. This outfit was called Dermot Costello and Son. Dermot had been the one to knock on the door. He had the most profound bags under his eyes she'd ever seen—they made his face look like a used candle. There was no sign of the son, who she'd have bet good money was also named Dermot. For the down payment, she gave him Betsy's cell number. The woman had called twice about paying. She wouldn't take no for an answer, so Danielle stopped saying no. The only thing Dermot couldn't do was schedule a day. That would need to wait until Eden's body was released.

Once alone, Danielle checked the news. They continued to hold Christopher Mahoun, but only as a witness. She considered calling Gates to see what the delay was, but they'd already spoken briefly when Danielle checked in this morning, and the detective still wouldn't even confirm that it was Mahoun. Just that they were holding an unnamed youth as a material witness while they were conducting further investigations.

There was, however, one major new development online. Two additional names had appeared. Jack Parrish and Hannah Holt. Both, like Mahoun, seniors at Emerson High. Danielle checked them out. The boy looked like somebody the heroine of an eighties movie would date until she figured out the nerdy star was really the one for her. He had a snide, superior smile and a lean, muscular body. In one photo he posed by a late-model GTI; in another he was whacking a tennis ball like he was trying to teach it a lesson. Hannah Holt had suspicious eyes and a hesitant smile. Danielle dragged their photos onto her desktop, as well as the one of Mahoun making the rounds. She arrayed them side by side and stared at them for a long time, trying to figure out what the hell Eden had been doing with this crew.

She thought about Patrick Noone, wondering how he fit into it all. Lost on the streets of his own town at three in the morning. Drunk, probably; maybe even crazy in a way Danielle didn't yet understand. His story about the dog would have been difficult to believe if she herself hadn't seen the thing limping. She should be taking everything this man told her with a boulder-sized grain of salt, but for some reason she trusted him. And yet there was something he still couldn't bring himself to say. For the thousandth time since their improbable late-night meeting outside the Bondurants', she could hear that unfinished sentence. *There was . . .*

The card he'd handed her was in her purse. It was black and white, yet somehow radiant. The letters were raised a little—it made her want to run her thumb over them, like she was blind. It suggested the world she'd never inhabited—the place where things were easy. To her surprise, she was put right through. To her even greater surprise, he agreed to meet her. But it was no surprise at all that he suggested a bar out on Route 9.

The Royal Lounge looked like it had been in business continuously since they invented liquor. She arrived first. Finding a booth wasn't a challenge. The REO Speedwagon song playing softly over the cheap speakers sounded like someone was vacuuming the back room. A fat drinker at the bar turned laboriously to check her out. She narrowed her eyes and he kept turning laboriously until he was facing the bar again, a surprisingly graceful pirouette of rejection.

Patrick Noone arrived, wearing an expensive suit and sunglasses that the boys she'd grown up with would have risked prison time to steal. Whatever else he might have been, the man certainly was attractive. He had the good grace not to smile at her as he slid into the booth. When he took off his glasses the whites of his eyes were as clear as his business card and he didn't smell of alcohol, at least not more than the booth's ruptured Naugahyde seats.

"How are you holding up?" he asked.

"I don't know. Functioning."

"Functioning is good. Better than the opposite, anyway."

"Is it?" she asked.

He asked her what she wanted to drink. She said Chardonnay because she wanted a drink but didn't want that much of a drink. He went to get their refreshments. The bartender, a short woman in her sixties who looked like she'd rather be working just about anywhere else on God's green earth than the Royal Lounge, greeted Patrick Noone familiarly. He stared at the bar as he waited for the drinks. Danielle took the opportunity to study him. To say he didn't belong in this place was an understatement. He looked like he belonged in one of those downtown clubs whose heavy doors were guarded by men dressed like they were protecting the queen of England.

"This could be colder," he said apologetically as he placed the glass in front of her.

She shrugged. She hadn't come for the Chardonnay. He was drinking something clear with a slice of lime. There was an interval of silence that would have normally been filled with small talk. He seemed comfortable inhabiting it with her.

"So I'm wondering why they haven't arrested this Mahoun kid," she said finally.

"What have the police told you about that?"

"Nothing. What do you know about him?"

"I know his father. He has a restaurant in town." He paused. "People are surprised."

"Are you?" she asked.

"I'm not really surprised by much these days. But yeah. I am. It just doesn't fit. I'm sorry if that's uncomfortable for you to hear, but there it is."

He took a drink like he needed it. Not gulping it down, exactly. But savoring it.

"You said something last night," she said. "Well, you started to say something."

He watched her. Not unfriendly. Just guarded.

"You said *there was*. But then you stopped yourself."

"Did I?"

"Yes, you did. Like you saw something other than the dog when you stopped your car."

He looked into his glass as he swirled the ice and lime. This man had something to say to her and she had no idea how to get him to say it except give him time.

"I lost a daughter," he said. "Two years ago."

"Oh no. I'm sorry to hear that."

"She'd been struggling with drug addiction."

"Well, damn."

"The situations aren't really equivalent, I guess."

"Dead is dead. That seems pretty equivalent to me. How old was she?"

"Twenty. Same as Eden."

He met her eye. This lost man.

"What was her name?"

"Gabriella. Gabi."

"That's nice."

"As is Eden. How did you come up with that?"

"I thought, you know, innocence. I was young. I didn't take into consideration the whole apple and snake deal."

He took a sip. She looked at her wine. It brought to mind a urine sample. She left it where it was.

"So that's why you gave me your card?"

He finished his drink.

"You want another?"

"I probably should go ahead and take my first sip of this one."

He headed off for his refill. Once again, she watched him at the bar. If this were a date, he'd have been the best-looking man she'd ever been out with. Also the wealthiest. And the nicest. She thought about that, a date with Patrick Noone. He'd spend two hundred dollars on dinner and be a gentleman when he said good night and then she'd have rushed home so she could tell Eden all about it. But this wasn't a date and she wasn't going to be rushing home to talk to her daughter ever again.

When he returned she resisted the urge to fill up the silence. The man had his own rhythms that she knew better than to disturb. They half-listened to that song about Sister Christian as it gargled inside the nearest speaker.

"You'll hear her voice."

She had to run what he'd just said through her mind a few times to make sure she'd heard it right.

"Okay," she said.

"Has that happened yet?"

Danielle knew that if she said anything at that moment, she might lose control. So she simply shook her head.

"You will. She won't say anything important. I mean, she won't tell you who killed her. No lottery numbers. It'll just be normal stuff."

"I could probably live with that."

"That's why I was out there that night, driving around. I was asleep and then I heard Gabi ask me to come pick her up. I mean, obviously I knew it wasn't real. But it . . . unsettled me."

"So it was a dream."

"Not really. Her voice didn't come from inside the sleep, if that makes sense. It came from somewhere else. And no, I don't believe in ghosts."

Danielle was wishing this didn't all seem so goddamned plausible.

"The funny thing was, her voice wasn't like it had been when she was alive. At least not those bad last years. But she wasn't a kid, either. It was like what it would have been now."

He was still staring at his empty glass. Finally, he looked up at her.

"So. After I hit the dog. I saw someone."

Suddenly, everything in the bar became a lot clearer and a lot quieter.

"What do you mean, you saw someone?"

"When I got out of the car to check on the dog. There was a person there. In the trees at the edge of the property. I tried to speak with him but he didn't answer. He just stood there. Like he was trying to be invisible. And then the dog attacked and . . . when I checked again he was gone."

"Was it Christopher Mahoun?"

"Well, see, that's the thing. It wasn't."

"Do you know who it was?"

"I'm pretty sure it was a kid named Jack Parrish."

Friday

She called the Twitter account Emerson Depths. For her icon, she used a photo she'd found of the quaint wooden sign outside the Emerson Heights T stop. She was careful to cover her tracks while setting it up. She used a dummy email for verification; she turned off location services. Geoff had set up a VPN for her after they got married, so she didn't have to worry about anybody tracking her IP address. It would take a boatload of court orders to discover this was her. If it got to that point, she'd have already accomplished her goal.

The thread consisted of seven tweets. She labored long and hard over the first one to make it just right.

"Anybody who thinks Jack Parrish was an innocent bystander on the night Eden Perry was killed should know that he privately admitted to sexual misconduct with a female Waldo student last year."

After that, the story wrote itself. She simply stuck to the facts, with a few embellishments here and there. It was an impressive bill of particulars. An incident in a boy's bedroom. A terrified girl a long way from home. An enraged mother. Ethnicity and class. Thousands in hush money. An NDA, signed and sealed. And now, it was happening again.

Although she wrote the thread late Thursday night, she waited to post it until just before seven Friday morning, when her target audience would be starting the day. She tagged four gossip super-spreaders. Milly Williams, Cassandra Nilsen-Shapiro, Jean Feddes, and the Emerson High Drama Club. Alice wanted to make sure she covered all her bases. This thing needed to get out there fast. A half hour later, the thread had been viewed over five hundred times. There were likes and retweets. Progress would soon be exponential. It was unstoppable.

Clicking the blue oval made her feel like one of those hot Maoist chicks from the seventies, plunging a detonator and sending some capitalist pig's limo into orbit. And yet, despite the thrill, posting the thread was a big gamble. Whatever her precautions, it could still blow up in her face in ways she didn't anticipate. It was also a pretty shitty thing to do. But she had to do something, especially after her blunder yesterday morning in Hannah's room, when she'd failed to preserve Jack's incriminating texts. It had been a golden opportunity to help Michel bring his son home. But she'd fucked up, leaving Christopher behind bars and her lover in hell.

Last night, her other prize bit of information—the Lexi cover-up—had also looked like it was going to prove useless. Michel had called just before ten to report that Cantor had been unable to confirm that the Parrishes had paid off the Lirianos. There was nothing in the public record, naturally enough, and the lawyer's call to Gloria Liriano, the mother, had elicited only a terse denial. As for Lexi, she was currently a freshman at Bucknell, and Gloria would appreciate it if Cantor left her in peace. He'd called her anyway. She hadn't picked up. If there was an NDA, it was a good one.

After hearing this, Alice got pissed off. The thought of Christopher sitting in a jail cell was horribly wrong. Her rage deepened as she pictured

Oliver driving around in his Merc like it was a chariot of the gods, paying people off, intimidating them. Oliver, whom she'd always thought a beacon of integrity. God only knew what he'd discussed with Geoff at five in the morning. She pictured Jack bullying her stepdaughter while Eden Perry lay dead in the Bondurant house. She couldn't believe they were doing this and nobody was stopping them.

She should have seen this coming. If nothing else, the confrontation she had with Jack in December should have alerted her. It was during their Christmas break; she'd come home from the gym to find Hannah and Jack prowling the kitchen.

"Come on," she said, in Cool Mom mode. "Let me buy you lunch."

She took them to a Greek place. Jack did all the talking, describing his AP Psych project, an admittedly clever variant of the Stanford Prison Experiment set in Home Ec. Evidently, amid the failed soufflés, the worst aspects of human nature were confirmed. When the server arrived, he ordered for both of them. Spanakopita for Hannah, a gyro for himself.

"Since when do you eat feta?" Alice asked. "Or spinach?"

Hannah shot her a panicky look and gave her head the slightest of shakes. When lunch arrived, she put a forkful in her mouth and attempted, without much success, to chew it. *What the hell*, Alice thought.

"Why did you order her that?" she asked Jack. "I don't get it."

"She can never make up her mind," Jack said.

Alice was flabbergasted. If a man had ever ordered unwanted food for her, she'd have made him eat it. Off the floor.

"Women are a lot less decisive than men," Jack continued, authoritatively. "They need us to make decisions. It's an established fact."

Alice knew she should let it go. There was no reason to fight with her daughter's boyfriend. Except for the fact that he was being an asshole.

"Meanwhile, Hannah's lunch gets tossed. Not exactly a win for the male of the species."

"I'm just saying there are proven differences between the sexes."

"I agree. And men have no clue what they are."

"So men never make decisions for you?"

"Only when I tell them what they are."

"Not even Mr. Holt?"

The question was delivered with a knowing smirk. Alice was tempted to impale him with one of the little plastic spears holding his gyro together. Meanwhile, Hannah was making barely audible sounds of alarm beneath the congealing food still resident in her mouth.

"Meaning what?" Alice asked.

"No, it's just, he works like twenty hours a day and makes all this money and is totally stressed, and here you are at lunch after the gym, so it's not like it's this big equal partnership."

It was such an astonishingly shitty thing to say that Alice found herself waiting for him to announce he was just kidding. But he didn't. Because he wasn't.

"Relationships are negotiations, Jack. Don't judge them unless you're at the table when the deal is done."

If he caught the reference to his own entanglement with Lexi, he wasn't letting on. Instead, he took a big, shrugging chomp of his meat-stuffed sandwich. It occurred to Alice this could go one of two ways. She could either wipe the sticky floor with him, or she could let it go.

"Here, have some of my salad," she said to Hannah, choosing the latter course. "The portions here are too big anyway."

And why had she let it go? Because she knew the damage a knock-down brawl would inflict on Hannah. Because she'd believed an entitled cocksure pseudo-intellectual preppy boy was better than no boy at all. But she'd been wrong. The anger, the will to control—it was right there, as plain as the pustule of sauce perched indifferently on the corner of his lip. The kid was bad news. Bad news, and she'd let it go.

So it was on her. She needed to help Christopher before he was beyond help. She had to put the focus where it truly belonged. On Jack. If the Parrishes were going to throw Christopher under the bus, then she'd run an Amtrak over them.

Although her anger had initially been spread evenly over the entire family, she was particularly furious with Celia. Coming here all smiles when she knew the sordid truth. Alice had never been anything more than a diversion for her; the wacky friend whose stories and boho attitude provided a quick jolt, like a midday espresso or a second cocktail. That dismissive remark about Alice not being a real mother should have been sufficient warning. In Celia's eyes, Alice wasn't a real anything. But she was going to be something real now. As real as real could be.

The beauty of the thread was that Celia would never know it was her. She had no idea that Alice knew the whole story about what really happened between Jack and Lexi. As far as she knew, Alice was still a member of Team Parrish. And Alice had every intention of making sure Celia kept thinking that, right up until the moment it was her son being held by the cops.

She finished around two in the morning and it was all she could do not to post it then. But that would risk having it swallowed by the night. Better to wait until the bright morning light could shine on it; when those caffeinated, surfing suburban eyes would be open wide and Celia's reign as queen of this rotten little town would finally end.

Forty minutes after posting the thread, she walked downstairs. It was, despite everything, time to get Hannah up for school. She paused outside her stepdaughter's door to make sure her phone was ready to take a photo immediately. The Parrishes would have seen the thread by now. Jack would probably be issuing more directives. She eased open the door. Hannah slept soundly; her phone was in its usual spot. Alice crept forward and touched the home button. The locked screen flared. There was nothing.

"Hey," Hannah said, a split second after Alice had pulled her hand away from the phone.

Her eyes were still liquid and unfocused from sleep. Alice sat quickly on the edge of the bed, blocking the girl's view of the still-lit phone.

"How you doing?" she asked.

"No, yeah, okay, I guess."

Alice reached down to move a strand of hair from Hannah's face.

"I hate that you're having to go through all this, Hanns."

"It'll be all right."

"I still can't get my mind around it. Christopher. Did you ever see any sign of it? He always seemed so gentle to me."

Hannah rolled onto her back, her eyes now focused on the ceiling.

"I dunno."

"But can you really see him doing it?"

"Not really. But I guess he did. I mean, we left him there and she wound up dead."

For a moment, it looked like she was about to say more. But then she caught herself. *Stick to the story.*

"Hannah, if there's anything you want to talk about, I'm here. You know that, don't you?"

Hannah continued to stare at the ceiling.

"I know how close you and your father are, and of course you love Jack, but maybe I can be a little more objective than them."

"It's not what people think."

Alice felt her heart start to churn.

"No?"

"I mean, Eden wasn't . . . everybody's making out that she was this innocent person but she wasn't."

"How so?"

"She made a lot of stuff up. These weird fantasies. You could tell half the stuff she said wasn't true. You know how girls like her can be."

"Yeah, well, I know how men can be, too."

"And she had this crazy temper. You hardly ever saw it, but when you did, it was . . . outta control."

"So she lost her temper the other night?"

Hannah nodded. *Come on*, Alice thought. *Spill.*

"So something *did* happen before you left."

Hannah nodded, almost imperceptibly.

"Between Jack and Eden?" Alice asked.

Another nod, this one even fainter than the last.

"Hey," a voice, Geoff's, said from the doorway.

Alice closed her eyes for a moment, then turned. He'd clearly just woken as well. Neither father nor daughter had seen the thread yet.

"What's going on?" he asked.

"Just talking," Alice said.

"Are you going to school today?"

"Yeah, I guess," Hannah answered.

"I'll run you over."

Alice gave her stepdaughter's shin a loving tap and tried to make eye contact to let her know the conversation would be continued. But Hannah had turtled back into her shell. And so Alice left the room, meeting Geoff's inquiring gaze with a benign little smile as she passed him.

She waited until they'd left to call Michel. She needed to see him. Immediately. She needed to explain the Twitter thread, to let him know that Hannah had come *this close* to opening up to her. Something had definitely happened between Eden and Jack. One more session alone with the girl—she'd bring booze this time—would surely do the trick. Mostly, she just wanted to see him. To hear his voice and be held by him.

He agreed, although not at his house. She suggested somewhere out on Route 9, but he didn't want to leave town, since word on his son's fate could come down at any moment. She suggested United Unitarian, where she'd attended that waste-of-time poetry class. In a blatant example of sectarian overreach, the back parking lot was big enough to service a Texas megachurch. It was hidden from the street by the big stone building. Nobody ever went back there, probably not even on Sundays.

He was already there when she arrived. She joined him in his car. His eyes were bloodshot with exhaustion. She wanted to embrace him but something about his body language made it clear that they'd need to speak first. She asked if he'd seen the Twitter thread about Jack this morning.

"Cantor told me about it," he said.

"That was me," she said.

"Okay," he said, not particularly surprised.

"Are you mad?"

"No. I'm just wondering what good it will do. The police have made up their minds."

She didn't like the defeated tone in his voice. She could handle scared and frustrated and sad. She could definitely get behind pissed off. But she didn't know what to do with defeat.

"I talked to Hannah this morning," she pressed on. "She's definitely hiding something."

"But what?"

"Geoff interrupted us before I could get her to say. But something definitely happened between Jack and Eden."

Suddenly, his eyes filled with tears. It was a sight so unexpected that for a few seconds she was unable to respond. But then she leaned over and embraced him.

"Oh baby."

"I just feel so powerless."

"Michel, listen to me. I'm going to get Hannah to tell me what she knows. She's going to tell me the truth and then we're going to get Christopher free and clear and put that fucking rapist in a cage."

They kissed. Softly, not for long. There was no sex in it. After a few seconds she wrapped her arms around his shoulders and put her head against his chest. She could hear his heart beating against his ribs, slow and sad. She wished they could stay here forever, invisible to the world.

"I got you," she said.

His phone rang loudly enough to cause her to bang her elbow against the steering wheel as she recoiled.

"Cantor," he said after reading the flip phone's crummy little screen.

She retreated to her side of the car. She could tell by the tone of the lawyer's voice that it was bad news. Michel hung up without responding and stared out the window for the longest five seconds of Alice's life.

"If you're going to talk to Hannah, you should do it soon." He looked at her. "They've just arrested Christopher."

Hannah was in her room when Alice arrived back home. Geoff was at the lab. Seeing her chance, she knocked and entered. Hannah immediately placed her phone facedown on the bed.

"I thought you were at school," Alice said as she sat next to her.

"I had to get out of there. This thing on Twitter."

"Yeah, I saw that."

"Jack says Lexi must have posted it."

"Makes sense," Alice said, bookmarking the self-loathing for later.

"I mean, the only reason Jack's parents gave the stupid girl money was to stop her from lying. And now she's doing it anyway! It's so unfair. He didn't *do* anything. And all this other stuff. That thing at the mall was a prank! It's such crap."

"I know, I know." Alice let a few seconds pass. "Hannah, earlier, you said something about Eden having a temper. What was that all about?"

Hannah stared at her capsized phone. Alice touched her forearm.

"Hey, come on, Hanns. It's me."

"Can I ask you something?" she asked.

"Of course," Alice said.

"If something happened that didn't really matter and I didn't tell the cops, that's okay, right?"

"Well, that sorta depends."

"I mean, if there's something that might make us look bad but telling people won't change anything about Christopher, it's okay not to tell them, right?"

"Hannah, why don't you just tell me what happened at the Bondurant house. Let's start there."

"Okay, but you can't tell anybody I told you this."

"You can trust me. You know that."

Hannah took a deep, memory-fueling breath.

"After we took the pills, I mean, they hit *really* hard. I got totally zoned and wound up in an upstairs bedroom. Their son's. The one who died? They have all these photos of him. I got kind of lost in them and then I lay down on his bed and wondered if this was where he'd died and started thinking about what it must be like to be dead. I mean, like, what if there are new colors you've never seen before? And then I passed out for a while, until I heard somebody screaming. For a second I thought it was the dead boy but then I figured out it was Eden. So I ran downstairs. She was standing in the middle of the room, totally hysterical. She'd wrapped herself in a comforter, like it was a cape or something. I mean all of a sudden she's this fierce goddess. Jack and Christopher were just standing there like they didn't know what to do."

She shook her head in appalled wonder.

"You should have seen her face. She was crazy. She kept on saying, *You're going to pay for this*. Over and over."

"Who was going to pay?"

"Jack. Which made no sense. She was saying he'd attacked her. We tried to reason with her but she was crazy. Finally he was like fuck this, I'm out, this chick has lost it. He tells Christopher he needs to fix this and then we go."

"Christopher stayed?"

"Yeah. What you gotta understand about Christopher, he was *totally* in love with Eden. It was painful to watch, because she basically saw him as this little kid. She'd make out with him sometimes if she was drunk or stoned enough. But no way was she going to fuck him. Christopher just wouldn't take the hint, though. He's not exactly experienced with girls. Anyway, by the time we got home, forget about sleeping. You saw me. That's why I was so upset, this craziness Eden was saying. I was just so worried what would happen to Jack if that got out. And then the next afternoon we heard, you know, that she'd died. We had no idea what was going on. It was surreal."

"What set her off, do you think?"

"The drugs. Jack said she was passed out when suddenly she went all psycho. He thinks maybe it was a flashback to being attacked by one of her mom's boyfriends. Anyway, after we found out she was dead, Jack didn't want me to tell anybody about her freaking out. And I definitely didn't want to talk about the drugs because . . ."

"Because why?"

"You can't tell anybody."

"I won't," Alice said, wishing the silly girl would stop making her lie.

"They were Dad's."

"Wait, Geoff gave you drugs?"

"No. I stole them."

"Hannah . . ."

"I thought it was the Molly he uses! He would've never given it to me so I just helped myself. But I guess I took the wrong ones because these were like the anti-Molly. They really knocked us out for a couple of hours."

"Does he know you did this?"

"Oh yeah. He was royally pissed. Especially after he found out Jack told his father."

"Wait, Oliver knew that you guys were using Geoff's drugs?"

"Yeah."

So there it was. The reason Geoff was helping cover this up. Why he was lying about being awake, why he was messing around with the house's security footage. Because if he didn't, Oliver would let it be known that it was his dope that set off Tuesday night's events. "Local Man Provided Drugs to Eden Killer" wasn't exactly the press you wanted in the run-up to the launch of your new company.

"It doesn't even matter now because the cops know we were using. Christopher told them and I guess they did tests on Eden."

"But they don't know they were your father's pills?"

"That's what I mean! Telling them wouldn't change anything. Except messing Dad up."

"Where did you tell the cops you got them?"

"From Eden."

"But didn't Christopher know?"

"Not that I got them from Dad."

"Hannah . . ."

"Jack didn't *do* anything! If we tell the cops she was talking that shit then . . . I mean, you see what's going on this morning. People have it in for him. They're just so jealous."

"But why would Eden say it, then? Those are some serious charges. You think she'd really lie like that?"

"Girls lie." Hannah shook her head. "It's my fault, too."

"How's it *your* fault?"

"I put the idea in her head. I told her the Parrishes paid off Lexi. We were pretty stoned, I guess, and she was telling me about all the weird shit that'd happened to her with guys. And so I told her about Lexi and Jack. She was amazed by how much money it was."

"But Hannah, really? Doesn't it make more sense that something actually happened? I'm not saying Jack attacked her but sometimes people get their signals crossed."

Hannah looked at Alice, her eyes narrowing.

"What, like he was trying to cheat on me with Eden while I was in the other room?"

"No, no, I don't mean . . ."

Alice stopped talking. That was more or less exactly what she meant.

"Jack didn't do anything to Eden, Alice. He didn't touch her at the house and he didn't go back there after we left and kill her like Christopher and this fucking bullshit on Twitter is saying."

"Okay. I'm sorry. Of course."

"So it's okay that I didn't tell the cops about any of that stuff, right?"

"Yes," Alice said, since today seemed to be the day for lies.

Appeased, Hannah lay back on the bed and stared at the ceiling.

"I just love him so much."

Alice resisted the temptation to whack her stepdaughter on the head with the nearest blunt instrument. Even though it seemed you could get away with that in this town.

"I know you do, sweetie," she said instead.

"I mean, I'd do anything for him."

Evidently, Alice thought. And then Hannah's phone buzzed. She looked at the screen and immediately answered.

"Hey," she said as she sat up.

It was Jack. Sitting up had caused the sleeve of Hannah's baggy T-shirt to ride up a couple of inches, revealing a thin crescent of bruise on her biceps. It appeared to be just the edge of a much bigger one, angry and new. Alice was tempted to pull up the sleeve, to demand to know what the hell she was looking at. But she knew what she was looking at, and sensed that revealing herself now would be a mistake.

Hannah, who hadn't noticed what Alice had seen, was giving her a look that indicated she'd prefer to be alone. Alice lingered outside the door, trying to listen, but—surprise, surprise—Jack was doing all the talking. And so upstairs she went.

Jack was guilty. He'd raped Eden while his girlfriend dreamed of new colors and then, facing ruin, he'd gone back and killed her. And now he was bullying poor lost weak Hannah into defending him. That bruise was fresh; there were undoubtedly more, inside and out. And, for reasons Alice now understood, Geoff was helping the kid as well. The fix was in.

She started to pace the room. She had to convince Hannah to tell the police about Eden's accusations. Christopher had undoubtedly told them, but they'd thought he was lying to save his ass. If Hannah told them, they'd have to start looking at Jack for this. Once they did that, anything could happen. But getting her to tell the truth wouldn't be easy. The girl had it bad. She was a true believer.

Alice had no idea how many times she'd traversed her room before the Indian Chief's motor rattled the windows. She went to the top of the steps. Geoff was downstairs, speaking to Hannah in urgent tones. Alice walked down to them, feeling, for only the millionth time, like an interloper in her own house. By the time she reached the kitchen Hannah had retreated to her room. Geoff stood by the refrigerator, guzzling an energy drink.

"So Hannah's spending the weekend at Jack's grandmother's," he said after unplugging the bottle from his mouth.

"Really? Why?"

"You saw this Twitter thing, right?"

"I know. Crazy."

"Yeah, well, we thought it was best that they lie low for a while."

"Who's we?"

She saw something pulse through his eyes.

"What?"

"No, you said we, I was just wondering . . ."

"We," he said, as if speaking to a child. "Me and Hannah."

"Oh, okay. Sorry. Yeah, of course."

But he hadn't meant him and Hannah. He meant him and Oliver

Parrish. His new best buddy. His lord and master. After Geoff disappeared into his office, she hung around the kitchen, hoping to connect with Hannah before she left. But the girl wouldn't even make eye contact when she came out of her room. Instead, she made a beeline for the front door. As it opened, Alice could see Jack's GTI idling at the curb. And behind the wheel sat the kid who had killed Eden Perry and believed he could get away with it. *As if,* Alice thought. *As fucking if.*

CELIA

Celia hadn't seen the thread until an hour after it appeared. She'd decided to take the day off social media. She'd had her fill of news flashes and insinuations. But then Milly Williams called, a little too eager to be sharing the news that Jack was being slandered. And so she was once again lowered into the cesspit, forced to read about her son attacking a girl and the ensuing cover-up.

She dreaded telling Oliver. This was precisely what he'd been so worried about when they did the deal last year. The stink of insinuation. But it was better that he hear about this from her than from a colleague or client. He was at the office; he'd left before dawn to deal with the increasingly disgruntled Germans. His assistant said he was on a conference call but promised he'd get back to her the moment he was free.

As she paced the kitchen, Celia inevitably found herself thinking about Lexi Liriano. She was a bright Dominican girl from Dorchester who'd come to the school as part of the METCO program, which brought a dozen disadvantaged students from the city to Waldo every year. They were highly motivated and impeccably behaved, but they also kept to themselves. You almost never saw them at social functions or hanging out on Centre. It was a long ride back to where they lived.

So for Jack Parrish to go out with a METCO girl was surprising, to say the least. Celia never did know what to make of Lexi. She was certainly beautiful, with big brown eyes, lovely skin the color of Earl Grey tea, and waves of thick black hair. She was obviously intelligent. She wanted to become a lawyer, much to the delight of Oliver, who was completely enamored of the girl. After their first conversation, he more or less offered her a job upon graduation from Harvard Law, where he would put in a good word for her.

And yet it was impossible for her to relax around the Parrishes. Celia understood how overwhelming her household could be. She'd done everything in her power to set the girl's mind at ease. But Lexi remained guarded and suspicious, treating questions like traps, biopsying compliments for mockery. She was like a lookout perched in a crow's nest, scouring the horizon for bigotry. Once or twice Celia had seen indignation flash in her eyes when they spoke but could not for the life of her figure out why. And then there was the time Celia overheard Lexi speaking hushed Spanish with the Guatemalan housekeeper, Estrella. When she entered the kitchen both fell silent and avoided eye contact. Another brick in the wall between Celia and her son's first girlfriend.

The incident in question happened about a month into their relationship. Jack and Lexi were in his room after school. Celia was in the kitchen, trying to sort out dinner. Oliver would be working late in the city, so it would just be the three of them. She was halfway through an inventory of the fridge's contents when she heard footsteps coming quickly downstairs. The front door opened and closed. Which meant they must be getting something on Centre before Celia took Lexi home—Jack, who'd just got his license, could drive around town, but not into Boston.

Celia's mother called twenty minutes later. She'd *badly* twisted her ankle and needed Celia to come help her *immediately*. Normally, she'd have begged off—the woman was a handful even without injury. But since she was taking Lexi into the city anyway, she decided to give the hobbled old warhorse a hand. She was just texting Jack to tell him to get back home when she heard someone coming down the steps. She froze in confusion. There wasn't supposed to be anyone up there. Jack entered the kitchen with a puzzled smile on his face.

"I thought you'd gone out," Celia said.

He shook his head. For some reason he wasn't meeting her eye.

"But where's Lexi?"

"She went home."

"How? I thought I was giving her a ride."

"Her mom picked her up."

Celia waited, expecting more.

"Is everything all right?" she asked when there wasn't.

"Yeah, 'course. What's for dinner?"

"Whatever you can make for yourself," she said, annoyed now.

She went to her car—Katharine would be waiting—but was stopped in her tracks by a totally unexpected sight revealed by the garage door's opening. Lexi stood at the end of the driveway, statue-still, her back to the house. It was a position she appeared to have held for the last half hour. She didn't turn, even though she'd have heard the door's seismic rumble. Celia was about to go see what on earth was happening, when a car pulled up. Lexi got in without looking back. The car stayed where it was for a few seconds, and then a woman rose from the driver's side. She was tall, dressed in scrubs, with a long, severe face. Lexi's mother. It had to be. Her eyes flashed with anger when they met Celia's. It looked like she was contemplating storming up the driveway. But then Lexi got out of the car as well. After a brief, sharp exchange, her mother got back in, but not before leveling one last furious look at Celia.

Once they were gone, she went back into the house to ask her son what on earth was going on. Their conversation was conducted over the smoking carcass of a just-microwaved Hot Pocket. But Jack would only say that it was no big deal. They'd had an argument, that was all. And then Katharine was calling.

"I am literally in *agony* here . . ."

Celia had no choice but to leave it at that. Forty minutes later she was dealing with her mother, whose injury, not surprisingly, turned out to be less than critical. Celia didn't get home until after nine. Oliver, looking grim, confronted her as she walked in the door.

"What happened between Jack and Lexi this afternoon?"

"They had some sort of fight."

"Her mother called just after I got home," he said. "She accused Jack of behaving inappropriately."

"Inappropriately?"

"She accused Jack of physically mistreating her daughter."

Celia remembered that bewildered smile.

"Well, what did he say?" she asked.

"He said he grabbed her arm, but only to calm her down after she slapped him. Which he thinks was a lot more serious than anything he did."

"Well, isn't it?"

"Come on, Cee. You know it isn't."

She knew. Nobody would think the slender Latina girl from Dorchester, with her straight As and choral group solos, posed any sort of threat to the tall, well-built white boy. Celia understood the damage this sort of accusation could do. It was Jack's word against Lexi's. That was not a fight she wanted to wage in the court of public opinion.

"So what do we do?" she asked.

"We can have Jack apologize. Formally."

"Do you think that would pacify the mother?"

"Frankly? No. The woman was very . . . adamant."

"Okay, then what else?" Celia asked.

"We can deny everything. Paint Lexi to be the instigator."

"Do you think that would work?"

"It depends on what you mean by work. Would it keep Jack out of legal jeopardy? Yes. But as for everything else . . ."

Everything else, Celia thought. She could see it now. The looks, the insinuations, the conversations that ended abruptly upon her arrival.

"Can we compensate her?"

"Compensate?"

"Yes, Oliver. Pay her off. Slip her hush money."

He stared evenly at her. She would have sworn that he'd never so much as entertained the idea.

"Look, if we start flinging accusations back and forth, everybody loses," she said. "Yes, Jack's damaged, but what do they get out of that? But if we give them something, let's say for her education, then everybody comes out a winner."

Oliver frowned, his finger tracing his scar.

"We could try that."

And so that was what they did. He met Gloria the next day at a coffee shop near the dental practice where she worked as a hygienist. It was decided that fifty thousand dollars would be paid into Lexi's 529 after both mother and daughter signed NDAs promising never to discuss the matter again.

Celia resolved to forget it, to put it all behind them. And mostly she did. But there was one thing she couldn't forget. The baffled look on Jack's face as he came down the steps. As if he'd just witnessed something he couldn't understand.

Oliver called back. She read him the Twitter thread.

"Did anyone else know about the payment?" was his first question.

"Just me and Jack. How about on your end?"

"I wrote the NDA myself."

"So you think the Lirianos posted this?"

"It has to be. Lexi, I imagine. She wasn't thrilled by the arrangement."

"So what do we do?" she asked.

There was someone at his firm who dealt with social media issues—maybe they could get the thread blocked or deleted. He'd also try to find definitive proof of its authorship. Once they had that, Oliver could use the NDA to compel the Lirianos to tell everyone it wasn't true.

Not that it would matter. The damage had already been done. After getting off the phone with Oliver, Celia checked—the thread now had sixty-two likes and eight retweets. Nobody had commented yet, but that was sure to come. Several hundred views might be nothing in the general scheme of things, but they comprised a multitude in Emerson, population twenty-four thousand. The toothpaste was out of the tube and there was no putting it back, however savvy Oliver's social media expert might be. There was a lot of goodwill for the Parrishes in town, but there were also people who would take pleasure in seeing them covered with slime. It was inevitable. You rose to a certain point in your life and people suddenly felt the need to tear you down, as if your fall would elevate them.

It was maddening and depressing. She'd awakened with the belief that the nightmare was over. Not *over*-over. There would still be court dates and a susurrus of gossip. But her son would be all right in the end. He'd finish out his senior year. They'd summer on the Cape and he'd start at Dartmouth. They'd move on.

And now this. Before hanging up, Oliver had reassured her that at least the authorities wouldn't give the Twitter comments much credence. They had their prime suspect and it wasn't Jack. Christopher had motive and opportunity; there was compelling physical evidence implicating him, with more that they had yet to make public. His arrest was a foregone conclusion. Everything else was just static.

She wished she could take more comfort in his words. But she couldn't dismiss the notion that there might actually be some horrible, hidden truth here. She thought about Lexi standing at the end of the driveway; she thought about the look on Jack's face when he came through the door Wednesday morning, while the girl's undiscovered corpse was cooling in the Bondurants' rec room. She thought about the smeared and pleading eyes of the woman on the computer screen.

She needed to speak to Alice. She could offer reassurance and perspective. Celia texted her. Her message went unread, so she decided just to pop by, as she had yesterday. Driving across town felt strange now that this vile slander was out there. Suddenly, she took no comfort from all those familiar houses and shops and schools. She pictured the people inside them reading that thread, thinking what it wanted them to think.

As she turned onto Crescent, Alice's sporty little Land Rover sped by in the opposite direction. Celia checked her rearview mirror as it rolled through a stop sign and took a right toward the town center. Wherever she was going, she was in a hurry.

The police station. Something was happening. Celia executed her first three-point turn since her driver's test and headed after her, racing over the speed bumps, eager to intercept Alice before she got to the building. Oliver was undoubtedly already en route, having once again decided to keep whatever was happening secret from his wife. It would be useful to know, for the first time, what was happening before it'd already happened.

She caught up with her a few blocks from Centre, just as she made an unexpected left. She wasn't going toward the station after all, but instead driving toward Emerson Heights. Maybe she'd seen the thread and was on her way to see Celia. But then she pulled into the Unitarian church. Celia slowed in confusion. Why on earth would Alice be going to church on a Friday morning? Some sort of meeting? But she'd know if her friend was in recovery. She'd certainly been forthcoming enough about everything else in her life.

Celia turned into the church's driveway, then stopped in front of the building. Alice was nowhere in sight. She must have pulled around back. Celia got out of the car and considered her next step. She was tempted to look inside. But she didn't want to have to explain herself to somebody wearing sensible shoes. Instead, she went around the far side of the church, following a narrow strip of lawn bordered on one side by maples and the other by stained glass. The play of light and shadow back here was so beautiful it felt otherworldly, as if she were entering heaven. Wouldn't that be funny, if the Unitarians had it right all along.

She paused at the back of the building, then poked her head around the corner. Alice's Rover and a dark Lexus were parked in the capacious lot. Two people sat in the latter vehicle. One was Alice, the other Michel. They began to kiss. Celia stood perfectly still, witnessing their embrace. Alice's wild auburn hair, her soft hands all over him. They separated abruptly; Michel started to speak on the phone. Alice watched him, her hand running through her hair. Even at this distance, there was no mistaking the look of love.

Celia had seen enough. Her hands actually shook as she drove away from the church, still trying to comprehend what she'd just witnessed. It didn't take long for her to get home. Five minutes, during which her brain did not generate a single coherent thought. It was only when she pulled into the driveway that it came to her. She opened Twitter on her phone and started to read. She found what she was looking for in the fourth tweet.

"As if a girl like Lexi would just walk away from this sort of disrespect. As if her mother would let this go without somebody making it worth her while."

As if. Alice said it all the time. She'd written the Twitter thread, not the Lirianos. Celia could hear her voice in it now. Not just that single telltale phrase, but every word. She'd slandered Jack for the whole world to see. And now here she was, celebrating with her lover, the father of a killer. Pawing each other like rutting animals.

She called Oliver. Her husband was in a meeting; she ordered his assistant to pull him out of it, the first time she'd ever done this. He listened in silence and then said he was coming right home. In the meantime, Celia was to get Jack out of school immediately and ship him off to Boston. When she said that it might be difficult to pry him away from Hannah, he told her to send her along with him.

She called Katharine to set things up. Although Celia had hoped that the old woman's aversion to social media had kept her from seeing the thread, a friend had been only too happy to read it to her over the phone. After an insinuating pause that suggested this was probably all Celia's fault, she readily agreed to harbor Jack and his "little friend" while Oliver straightened this mess out. She'd make sure her grandson stayed out of sight. And God help the reporter who came knocking on her door.

Oliver arrived home soon after Jack went to get Hannah. He looked more determined than angry. She told him about what she'd seen, sparing no detail as she narrated the full magnitude of Alice's betrayal.

"So what are we going to do?" she asked when she finished.

"What are we going to do?" he said, grim and incredulous. "We're going to expose the woman for what she is."

MICHEL

Michel called Cantor back as soon as Alice left the parking lot. Christopher would be appearing in court at two that afternoon. Before that, the police would hold a press conference to announce his arrest. Michel, numb and confused, asked if he should be there, but Cantor said that wouldn't be a good idea. It was best if he continued to remain out of sight.

So, more invisibility. Trapped in his house, phone turned off, restaurant shuttered. Venturing out only to lurk in the shadows with the one person he should not be seeing. His world shrinking with each passing hour. He was beginning to suspect that he would soon reach a point where he no longer existed at all.

As he sat alone in his car, still feeling her and smelling her, a terrible suspicion began to echo in his mind. The affair was the cause. It was the root of it all. Just look at the facts. Christopher began secretly visiting the Bondurant house around the time he met Alice. The killing had happened days after she proposed destroying her marriage. And just now, news of his son's arrest had come while he was literally in her embrace. The affair was the cause. Which meant he had to stop seeing her. Until he did, the punishment would continue.

But that would deprive him of his best ally. In the last two days, Alice had become what she'd wanted to be all along, what he'd resisted. His partner. She believed absolutely. She was their salvation. What she'd posted this morning on Twitter—that was just the beginning. She was his spy, smart and cunning, moving freely behind enemy lines. She lied and cheated, because she needed to do those things to get to the truth. Their love had always been based on deception. It was time to use the lies to survive.

The court was in a town west of Emerson, where the houses were smaller and the cars showed their miles. He met Cantor in a nearby coffee shop.

"How is Christopher?" he asked as he sat across from him.

"He's a tough kid."

"Is he?" Michel asked, his voice laced with doubt.

"Right," Cantor said, moving on. "So, today they formally charge him. We plead not guilty, the judge then decides about bail."

"I can get my hands on a hundred thousand cash."

"Well, let's start there."

"You think they'll want more?"

"Possible. Or the judge might not grant it at all."

"Can he do that?"

"He can do whatever he wants. I gotta tell you, I wish your son wasn't a French citizen."

"I'm starting to wish we'd never come to America."

"That's a sentiment you might want to keep to yourself."

"Can I see him before it starts?"

"I'm afraid not. This is a big case, Michel. Everybody's playing it by the book." Cantor watched him for a moment. "So this thing on Twitter—what do you know about that?"

"Just what I read." Michel shrugged. "Maybe Lexi and her mother wrote it."

"I spoke to the mother. That woman ain't posting anything." Cantor stared at him more closely. "Be careful, Michel. Stuff like this can blow up in your face."

It was time to go. They walked through the parking lot to a door at the back of the courthouse. A guard let them in and passed them through a metal detector. The light was too bright in the hallway. There was a dreamlike hum—Michel didn't know if it was in the building or in his ears. Cantor paused to speak with another lawyer and Michel could barely understand a word they were saying, even though he could hear them plain as day. They wound up in a courtroom that could have been a lecture hall at the colleges he'd visited with Christopher. Cantor directed him to the front bench, on the left side. The wood was hard, like a pew.

Cantor went to see Christopher, who was being held in a room nearby. Michel became aware of the people in the court. The benches behind him were already full. At first he thought they'd come to see his son, but most of them had problems of their own. Directly in front of him, on the other side of the rail, lawyers and clerks milled about. Michel wished Alice was here, and then almost laughed out loud at the absurdity of the thought.

There was movement to his right. Two lawyers, a man and a woman, were stepping into the enclosure. Both carried heavily laden shoulder bags that they placed on the table opposite Cantor's. They were trailed by a black-haired woman who took a seat directly across the aisle from Michel. Eden's mother. He recognized her from the news. There was a ferocity about her that reminded him of women he'd seen in Beirut. Widows. Fighters. Believers. A few days ago their two children were, what? Lovers? Friends? The female lawyer spoke to her over the fence; Eden's mother nodded grimly as she took in her surroundings. Michel felt her gaze moving inexorably toward him. He knew he should look away. But that would be like admitting his son's guilt. And then she was staring at him with her black eyes. Michel expected rage and hate, but instead there was a deep curiosity. As if she was asking him a question. Without thinking, he gave his head a single shake. She held his gaze a moment longer, her expression unreadable, before she looked away.

Cantor returned.

"We're up first," he said. "Michel, it's important you don't do or say anything in front of the judge."

Michel nodded. Cantor took a seat at the table in front of Michel and began to pull folders from his briefcase. Christopher entered from a side door, accompanied by two guards. He wore an orange jumpsuit. His hands were shackled in front of him. He looked very small. His eyes were downcast. Making himself invisible, like he would do when his mother was ill. Michel was tempted to speak his name but remembered his instructions. The guards directed Christopher to the chair next to Cantor. He did not sit, however. Instead, he turned to face his father. Michel stood and opened his arms and his son fell into them. He smelled of bitter soap. His body quivered slightly, like an idling machine. The guards spoke to them; Michel felt a hand on his arm.

"I'm going to get you out of this," he said.

He released his son and sat down. There were tears on his face and he wiped furiously at them. Eden's mother was looking at them, her dark eyes still unreadable.

The judge entered, a tall man with wispy gray hair. He spoke to a clerk whose desk was directly below his bench. When they finished, the clerk stood and said that Christopher Paul Mahoun was charged with murdering Eden Angela Perry. Christopher stood and, his voice almost inaudible, claimed he was not guilty. A long discussion broke out over bail. Cantor talked about Michel's place in the community, Christopher's grades, his acceptance at BC. The female prosecutor talked about his relatives in Paris and Beirut, his French passport. Finally, the judge said there would be no bail, although he made it clear that they would be revisiting his decision soon. And then it was over. The judge left; the guards led Christopher out a side door. He didn't turn around.

Cantor tried to be encouraging. He said it was unusual for the judge to offer another bail hearing so quickly. There was still a chance Christopher could be out soon. Michel nodded, though he wasn't really listening. He just wanted to get away so he could call Alice and they could set about the business of liberating his son.

DANIELLE

When she finally saw him, she didn't feel the things she'd expected. She'd arrived at the courthouse believing that confronting Christopher Mahoun would give her certainty. Part of her knew she should be feeling it already. The facts certainly suggested as much. He'd been alone with Eden in the house, the last person to see her alive. He had some sort of fixation on her. The police were now saying that the chunks of flesh beneath her daughter's nails definitely came from his neck. It was him.

But when she saw the boy's father, the doubts Patrick had instilled last night returned. He wasn't what she'd expected. At all. With that name, she'd thought he'd be like one of the wholesalers who dealt with Slater. Coarse, heavy-browed men with pitchy voices and suspicious eyes. But the elder Mahoun was more like a European, with his dark suit and fine features. Of course, that didn't mean anything. Rich European types did evil things all the time. Just look at history. And yet when he shook his head at her, it was hard not to feel that they were both trapped in the same hell.

Her doubts deepened when Christopher appeared, shackled and terrified. She'd seen photos of him but they hadn't prepared her for this. He was just a baby. Danielle had been around violence her whole life and there was none of that to him. She just couldn't see it. Eden could handle herself. She'd seen off much more formidable boys than this. There had to be something Danielle was missing.

She was tempted to express her doubts to the detectives and the DA, but she knew that her words would fall on deaf ears. They'd been so certain at the press conference. What an ordeal that had been. Danielle hadn't wanted to attend. Being paraded in front of all those cameras, having her image broadcast even more widely than it'd been already—the thought terrified her. But Gates, as usual, was very persuasive. They needed her there, standing up for her fallen child. And so it was back to Emerson. Danielle wore the big sunglasses Eden had given her for her birthday. A crowd had gathered outside the police building. It was a real production. Microphones, cops and suits, the press, a small group of citizens who had nowhere better to be. Gates greeted her warmly. She was introduced to the DA handling the case, a large woman named Penny. She looked like someone who lived with a cat and a mother and a lifetime of slights she took out on the shitheels she put away.

"So we're going to make the announcement and then take some questions," Gates explained.

"You don't want me to say anything, right?"

"Oh no," Penny said, a little too quickly, as if Danielle had just volunteered to pole dance. "You're fine as is."

They started on time. The chief spoke first. As Danielle had suspected when she first met him, he was a pompous windbag who seemed more worried about the damage this *horrible tragedy* had inflicted on the community than the fact that her daughter was currently stiffening at the morgue. He was followed by Gates, who was even better in front of the cameras than in person. She opened up by offering her condolences to Danielle. There were a few sympathetic looks from members of the public; the glares from the press felt more predatory. She wanted to flee at that point, but they were right. This was where she needed to be.

And yet, for all the carny atmosphere, the event eased her doubts. It was a show, but a professional one; well funded and well oiled, staged for her child. Standing there, in this forecourt or plaza or whatever you wanted to call it, with its fountain and its fenced-in saplings and its bronze statue of a cop helping a little boy, Danielle couldn't help but feel convinced. How could all of this be wrong? Christopher Mahoun had killed Eden.

But then, in court, she saw the Mahouns and the doubts returned, even stronger now. The show had been just that. A show. Maybe Patrick was right. This shackled hundred-forty-pound weakling was just a whipping boy. The easy option. If they were accusing some rotten-toothed smirking Southie with a Celtic cross tattooed to his neck, she'd at least be able to take whatever comfort you could from knowing that the case truly was closed. But this kid? With his father? In her forty years Danielle had come to know that the only thing she could rely on was the bad feeling she sometimes got in her chest. And that feeling was coming on like a heart attack. This was wrong.

After they denied bail, the lawyers and guards orchestrated her departure so she didn't come in contact with Mahoun senior, even though she badly wanted to ask him what he knew. But her purpose had been served. It was time for her to go home and climb the walls until they needed her again. Suddenly, after being treated like a movie star all day, she found herself alone. She wondered if this was what a trial would be like, this dizzying cycle of exposure and loneliness.

She thought about Patrick on the drive home. The man with the doubts. He was like no one she'd ever met. Gentle and kind and intelligent and intoxicated, wearing his damage like a tailored suit, certain he knew things no one else did. She'd thought she was done with him when they'd said good night in the parking lot of that wretched bar, but now, suddenly, she felt like that was just a beginning. So, instead of going home, she pulled off Route 9 near Emerson and called the cell number he'd given her last night.

"You saw they arrested him," she said when he answered.

"It's all over the news."

"I just got out of court."

"So what do you think?"

"Something doesn't feel right." She watched traffic pass. "You know, there's a version of this where you're a crazy person taking advantage of a grieving mother."

"Well, I make no claims about my sanity. But I guarantee you I'm not taking advantage of you. If you really think that, hang up. I won't bother you again."

"Are you drunk right now?"

"No."

"Can we meet?"

"Yes, of course."

"But not at that bar. Can I come to your office?"

"That might not be the best idea."

"Your home. My home. Fenway. I don't give a shit. We just need to talk."

"Come to my house. But you'll have to forgive the mess."

If messes bothered me, she thought, *I wouldn't be talking to you.*

PATRICK

The reckoning at work had finally arrived. Griff had texted him late last night. A simple message, but all the more ominous for being so. *Let's meet tomorrow at ten. Important. Be there.* He'd texted back a simple thumbs-up, which was as much communication as he felt safe doing in his condition. He'd started drinking seriously when he got back from the Royal, transitioning from Tanqueray to Suntory. The result was the same as ever. Intervals of oblivion interrupted by flashes of shattering nightmare. His nights were becoming predictably similar. That was the one thing about booze. You always knew how you were going to feel after enough of it. His days would soon be like this as well. One of Gabi's counselors had remarked that no matter what an addict's origin story, they all ended up the same person. An arm in search of a needle; a parched mouth in need of a bottle. Patrick sometimes wondered how long it would take him to sandblast away all the particulars of his personality, to become the thing-in-itself. Pure, noxious need. Perhaps not as long as he thought.

He had no idea when he passed out, though he knew exactly when he woke: 4:13 a.m. Moments after Gabi had made another appearance. Her voice, anyway. It was even briefer than on the night of Eden's murder. A single word this time, a question. *Dad?* Uttered as a prompt. She still needed to be picked up.

At least this time he had the sense not to leave the house. That would be pressing his luck. Irrevocably awake, he'd resisted the temptation to continue drinking. He needed to be sober for this meeting. He doubted he'd be fired. Griff was a good guy. But Patrick's behavior was clearly unsustainable. Some sort of ultimatum was coming and he wanted to take his medicine with a clear head.

He got to the office before seven and set to work with the avidity of a twentysomething trainee making his bones on Wall Street. He unleashed an avalanche of memos to colleagues and clients, copying Griff on all of them. He ignored what was happening in the Eden case, knowing that it was a rabbit hole that would swallow his efforts to play the good employee.

But he couldn't stop himself from thinking about Danielle. He was starting to worry that he'd pushed things too far with her. When he told her that he'd seen Jack Parrish standing in the woods, he'd half-expected her to drench him with that septic Chardonnay. To his surprise, she seemed willing to listen as he told her about Oliver and Celia and his own daughter's brief, unhappy involvement with the Parrishes. Danielle Perry, he was beginning to understand, was not the woman he'd expected. She was tough, yes, but beneath the warrior's armor there was a vulnerability and intelligence that suggested her life might have gone another way had her luck been different. She'd spoken about Eden with the sort of hard-eyed frankness so rare in Emerson, where people tended to discuss their kids with the breathless enthusiasm usually encountered in the first round of the NFL draft. She obviously was crazy about the girl, but in a blunt, exacting manner that made it clear she saw Eden as a person and not an adornment.

They were well into their second hour—Patrick had finished his third gin, she was still contemplating the Chardonnay like it was part of an initiation rite—when she announced they should probably go. He agreed, reluctantly. Despite the whirling horror surrounding them, it was easy talking to her. The way she held his eye as he spoke; her refusal to be scared off by his obvious addiction. Their lost daughters provided a bond that was unbearable and unbreakable and more intimate than anything he'd felt in a long, long time. And there was a beauty to her. Hard and indifferent, but also undeniable. He stopped this particular runaway train of thought when he found himself wondering what it would be like to kiss her. Instead, he'd given her his cell phone number and walked her to her car. They'd parted uncertainly, Patrick to go home to drink himself into oblivion, she to travel into a more absolute sort of darkness. He wondered if they would ever speak again. The thought of that not happening added another small boulder to the sled of sadness he was tugging through the frozen tundra of his life.

At exactly ten—this was not the sort of meeting for which you were either early or late—Patrick walked the twenty strides from his office to his managing partner's. Griff was not alone. Also present were the firm's lawyer, Lance Avagyan, and a pleasant-looking woman with an imitation leather folder on her lap. Griff introduced her as Wendy Umans. She was a stranger, but Lance he knew well. He'd been with the firm from the first. He was a snide, thoroughly decent guy who usually comported himself like a frat house prankster. Today, however, he was subdued, so much so that he wouldn't meet Patrick's eye when they shook hands.

"So," Griff said. "My preference is to skip all the stuff where we talk about your performance of late. Can we just agree it's been subpar?"

"Stipulated," Patrick said.

Lance smiled, though he still wasn't making eye contact. The word was a private joke among the three of them, used to agree to another round of martinis or acknowledge the hotness of a nearby woman.

"Patrick, you know me," Griff continued. "You know this guy here. We like it when people are happy."

"And they aren't," Patrick said, his statement somewhere between question and concession.

"*You* aren't. Right? That's kind of why we're here. Your mind clearly hasn't been in the game since Gabi. Which is understandable. I mean, damn. But still. We got some serious assets under management and a client base that is pretty tuned in. The drinking . . ."

"Look, can we just cut to the chase?"

The words came out many times harsher than Patrick intended. Griff stared evenly at him. Waiting to see which way this was going to go.

"Sorry," Patrick said. "I don't mean to be a jerk."

"You're not being a jerk. You're in trouble. And we want to help."

He turned to Wendy. Patrick did as well. Lance continued to look at the carpet with great interest.

"First of all, Patrick, I want to say how sorry I am for your loss," Wendy said.

Patrick nodded his thanks as she opened the folder on her lap and removed a glossy brochure from one of its pockets.

"I'm a counselor at a facility called Brook Farm. We're in Vermont. Near Brattleboro?" She handed him the brochure. "We offer a comprehensive course in recovery services."

Her eyes urged him to look at the brochure. He complied. He vaguely knew the name. It was one of the few places he hadn't dragged his child to. It looked awesome. First rate. Five stars. Log cabins, volleyball, people engaged in meaningful discourse along wooded paths. Beards and smiles and flannel. Hands resting on shoulders. Vermont. Fucking Vermont.

"What we had in mind for you is a thirty-day immersive course of treatment. It would begin with a carefully monitored detox after which you would move into one our programs. It's fully state-of-the art and welcoming. We really do get results. I think you'll like it there."

Like was probably a stretch. Patrick looked at Wendy. It would be so easy to hate her, with her midlength hair and the cloth bracelet undoubtedly woven by a special patient. It really would. He'd despised so many of the professionals who thought they could help his daughter. But that was wrong then, as it would be now. They were good people, especially when compared to the legions of flaming assholes afoot in the land. But they were doomed. They were lightly armed soldiers sent out to battle a hundred-foot-high, laser-shooting lizard. They had no chance.

"So I go here or . . ."

"Patrick, come on," Griff said. "Forget about *or*. You go there. You beat this thing. You come back. Hilarity ensues, wealth is accumulated."

Patrick looked back at the brochure, imagining himself there. Suffering the heebie-jeebies in a sylvan grove. His daughter's voice calling from the pines.

"When?"

"Well, we were thinking, like, now."

"I can drive you up there," Wendy added.

Patrick looked at Griff.

"I know you don't want to talk about this, but just so we know the parameters—what if I don't go?"

"Come on, Patrick. That's not where we're at."

"Then what's he doing here?" Patrick said, tilting his head in Lance's direction.

Once again, he wished he could take back his words the moment they left his mouth. That *he* was just plain nasty.

Lance finally met his eye.

"I'm here because you're my brother and I love you," he said quietly.

"I'm sorry," Patrick said, the small reserve of defiance he'd managed to carry into the office fully evaporated. "I just can't imagine not drinking. Pathetic as that sounds."

Wendy had the good grace not to say anything supportive. A long silence ensued. It was his move. They were right. Obviously. Inarguably. He needed to get his ass to Vermont ASAP. But the thought of getting into Wendy's Subaru didn't feel like the first step to recovery. It felt like the end of something. Himself. It felt like death.

"Monday morning," he said.

Unhappy glances were exchanged.

"Please. Give me that much."

"I can't really do Monday," Wendy said. "In terms of driving."

"For God's sake, I can drive myself to Vermont," Patrick said. "Granted, Maine would be a reach."

There were tight smiles.

"Look," Patrick said. "Just let me have this weekend. There's something I need to sort out."

"Okay," Griff said. "But I'll drive you. And we need to go early. I got shit to do."

"I can be ready any time after 4:13."

He took the rest of the day off. It wasn't a choice, insofar as the second act of the meeting, conducted after Wendy's departure, consisted of him signing a document Lance had prepared stating that he was suspended with full compensation and benefits effective immediately, lasting until such time as his partners determined he was fit to manage client money. Should it be decided that he was not coming back, they would enter good faith negotiations about what to do with Patrick's ownership stake. No one was out to hose him. He knew that. They wanted what was best.

There'd been hugs and brave faces and a little gallows humor at the end of the meeting. Everyone was acting like this was nothing more than a thirty-day hiatus. Patrick played along. And then he got his phone and laptop from his office and left without saying goodbye to anyone else.

Outside, the sky was a cleansing blue, though Patrick took little comfort in the splendor. It felt as harsh and revealing as a doctor's light on a pried-open eye. He drove straight home, where he finally allowed himself to look at the news. They'd charged Christopher Mahoun with murder. There was a lot of satisfied chatter among his friends and neighbors. The prevailing opinion seemed to be that justice was being served.

And then he saw the Twitter thread. He almost missed it in the avalanche of posts about the arrest. It appeared in Emerson Depths, a new account that had been purpose-built for telling this story. Jack Parrish, it seemed, had been a naughty boy with a young METCO student last year. And his parents had gone to considerable lengths to keep it quiet. The implication was clear. He'd been the one to kill Eden Perry.

Patrick looked once again at photos of Jack. He could see it now, as clear as the daylight he'd just fled. The shoulders, the jaw, the hair. It was him. The thread cemented it for Patrick. This was who he'd seen lurking outside the house in the middle of the night.

He watched the news conference, which the Boston stations carried live on their noon reports. The state police detective, Gates, was running the show, surrounded by a bunch of somber-looking public servants. Procopio was there, flexing and scowling. Danielle stood at the end of the line, shrouded in big sunglasses. She looked like an avenging angel. He wondered what she was really thinking; if she was buying this.

He should call the cops. They needed to be told they were making a mistake. Although he could predict how that would go, him showing up, voicing dissent on their big win, just hours after he'd been suspended from his job for drinking. Gates had talked about decisive forensic evidence during the press conference. The chief had mentioned community healing. They had their boy. If Patrick tried to hit them with a counter-narrative they'd probably put him in a much less congenial place than Brook Farm.

Besides, he had his own reckoning to deal with. He'd bought himself three days. The sane thing to do was to use the time to get his shit together. Call Lily. Speak to his son for the first time in weeks. Touch base with his few remaining long-term clients to make sure they didn't freak out when he went missing. Pack. Shave. Floss. Be human.

But he'd meant what he said back at the office—he doubted he could handle sobriety. He'd managed ten days last October and it had scared the shit out of him. Withdrawal had been no joke, although by the third day the hand tremors had abated and the colony of cooties squirming under his skin had retreated. He'd even started to feel some physical benefits. Not puking his guts out every morning was a welcome change, as was having bowel movements that weren't like the first explosive discharge of a clogged garden hose. In spirit and mind, however, he'd wound up feeling much, much worse. What was objectively a stunning New England autumn suddenly seemed coated with a sticky membrane of meaninglessness. His moods fluctuated between rage and despair. And then there were the dreams. Car crashes, dropped babies, futile punches, chronic pantlessness. He'd wake every two hours feeling like he was lying in a just-drained bathtub. The worst was a recurring dream in which he'd down shot after shot of whisky, rendering himself so drunk that he woke up with a drubbing hangover, even though he was perfectly sober. The ache was never-ending, interrupted only by explosions of terror and dread. Sobriety *hurt*. They didn't mention that in the pamphlets. This would be what he was letting himself in for. And not just for ten days. But for thirty. Theoretically, forever. That was their plan. A forced march into a place where sweet relief was no longer at hand.

But here's what all the Wendys didn't understand. It was too late. Maybe last year, he'd still had a chance. Certainly ten years ago, before everything had turned to shit. He'd always intended to quit. Ever since college, he'd sensed that his relationship to booze was a little too cozy. But he'd also believed he could handle it. He had a system. Nothing during the day, unless it was a wedding and Lily had the keys. Sober days, dry months. And it worked. He'd never been breathalyzed. He'd never got into a fistfight; he'd never been drunk at work. Nobody ever suggested he ease off a bit. What he couldn't see, however, was that he was laying a foundation. Or rather, eroding one, with drop after drop of ethyl alcohol. He was a cocky fighter shrugging off jab after jab, unaware that his opponent was simply measuring him up for the thundering left hook that would knock him permanently on his ass.

That blow, of course, had been his daughter's reckoning in the McDonald's stall, which he always pictured to be squalid, shit-streaked, and graffiti-scarred, though it could just as easily have been spotlessly clean. In the aftermath of her death, Patrick took a solemn pledge never to drink again. A return to his old ways was unthinkable. Which turned out to be true, although not how he intended. Three days after that terrible visitation, he took a long swallow from a bottle of Grey Goose that he didn't stop hitting until he'd fallen into what nobody could quite bring themselves to call a coma. The floodgates had opened. The elaborate system of checks and balances finally gave way. Grim milestones were passed. His first had been getting drunk on a workday—at Papillon, of all places, Michel Mahoun himself pouring him the last of a bottle of outstanding burgundy.

"Some days you drink wine," the man said with Levantine conviviality.

First fender bender. First bottle stowed away in his office. First blackout. First ultimatum from his wife. First divorce from same. First bedwetting. First bedshitting. First time he'd heard Gabi's voice. And now, first time he'd been suspended from the only job he knew how to do.

You'd have thought he'd get the message by now. But that was the thing that people didn't understand. The booze worked. *That* was the message. People told you not to drink because drinking wouldn't make you feel better. That was false. Drinking absolutely made you feel better. And if you drank enough, it made you feel nothing, which was the finest feeling of all. If the best thing the world had to offer you was to sit in a comfortable recliner sipping the peatiest single malt available, Pollini's recording of the Chopin études filling the air, then for God's sake, get to it, man. You might be leaping to your doom, but it would be from a great altitude; the wind sweet on your face, the view still pretty good from up here.

But now the ground was coming into view. Three days until impact.

One thing was clear. Whatever he decided to do when Griff rapped on the door Monday morning, there was no way he was going to commence his sobriety before then. He removed the Grey Goose from the freezer. He poured himself a large tumbler and was appreciating the play of late afternoon sun through the viscosity when his phone rang. It was Danielle, fresh out of court. She accepted his invitation to come over without hesitation. He put the tumbler in the freezer without taking a sip. He straightened up as best he could, the house and himself. She arrived after fifteen minutes.

"I expected someplace bigger," she said as he directed her to the rented sofa.

"We sold bigger after the divorce."

"Was it like the Bondurants'?"

"More or less."

"Boy, you guys must have really wanted not to be married."

"That would have been my wife."

"The booze?"

"And the daughter."

"Go ahead and drink if you want," she said. "You look like you need it. I don't give a shit."

"Not alone. You'll have to join me."

"You don't drink alone?" she asked dubiously.

"Not if there are other people around."

He showed her the frosted bottle. She shrugged. He poured her a glass and retrieved his own from the freezer. She did a double take at the latter maneuver but said nothing.

"I don't want to be one of those demanding guests, but can I at least have a slice of lime?"

He found a lime that looked like something being sent to the lab for a biopsy. He pulled a knife from the block and steadied himself over the chopping board to wait for the blade to stop vibrating like a struck tuning fork. And then she was standing beside him, her hand on his.

"I got this," she said.

"So you were at court," he said when they were seated.

She took a sip and then stared into the glass.

"They sat me across from his father. I tried to give him the evil eye but it just didn't feel right. Any of it. The press conference, the court-room. And the kid. He's just a baby."

"Still. People can surprise you."

"I think you might be right, Patrick. Christopher Mahoun didn't do this."

"Okay."

"I just don't see it. But everybody's so sure. Except you."

"Have you looked online today?"

"No, I'm all set with online. If I want to be called a heartless bitch, I can just phone one of my exes."

"It turns out Jack got in trouble with a girl last year."

"Really? What kind of trouble?"

"He was overly aggressive. And it looks like the Parrishes paid the girl and her mother a small fortune to make it go away."

"So have you spoken to the cops about him being the one you saw?"

"There's a problem between the cops and me. I have a history with one of the detectives. Procopio."

"Yeah, he's a piece of work."

"He was the one who busted Gabi right before she died. He was a real hard-ass about it."

"Ah, okay. Shit."

"I don't think I'm seen as the most reliable source over there."

"Still."

"You're right. I'll call them. Just let me collect my wits."

"I really want the person who did this to pay. I think that might make it just a little bit bearable."

"You want justice. You want to move on."

"I want justice, sure. But I don't want to move on."

"You don't?"

"You haven't."

"I'm not necessarily the best role model."

"Well, for now, you're all I've got." She looked into her glass as she gently swirled the thick liquid. "What you said about hearing her voice."

She took her first sip of the drink. And then the glass was empty.

"Hearing my daughter is an auditory hallucination, Danielle," he said. "It's not uncommon in people with my condition."

"But which condition is that? The booze or the dead kid? Because I got one of those."

He opened his hands. He had no idea.

"What if when Gabi spoke to you on Monday, she was actually telling you to go to the Bondurants' and hit that dog and get out of your car and see who did it?"

"You can't . . ."

"No, hold on, I've thought about this. It makes sense, right?"

"What do you want from me, Danielle?"

She handed her glass to him.

"First, I'd like another drink. Hold the lime. And then I'd like you to help me figure out who killed my child."

Monday

- - - - - - - - - - - - - - -

CELIA

She could have read the article online. They posted things at the same time that they released the print edition. But she wanted to read a hard copy, to hold it in her hands. The last few days had convinced her that what she'd always suspected was true—the internet was a festering wound that oozed hatred and lies. The less time spent there, the better. So, as her husband slept, she drove to the Mobil Mini Mart. She didn't read the article until she was back home, in her alcove, coffee steaming beside the paper. Although there wasn't a single unexpected word, it was still shocking. And then there was the cover photograph, a grainy nighttime image of a couple embracing inside in a sedan marooned in an empty parking lot. By the time she finished reading, she felt like she needed a sedative. And a bath.

The article was Oliver's idea. He'd handled everything. From the moment she told him what she'd seen at United Unitarian, he knew what to do. The photographs, the research, the interviews. He took no joy in it. He was like some bow-tied Hercules, cleaning the suburban stables.

But that didn't stop him. This was necessary to ensure the family's safety and the community's well-being. Enough was enough. This had to end.

On Friday, once the kids were safely stowed in Back Bay, the Parrish house was transformed into a command center. Although Celia had been married to Oliver for twenty-six years, she was still surprised by the efficiency of his actions and the swiftness of the results. He really did plan to destroy Alice. A few times, she was tempted to ask him if he really wanted to go after her this hard. But then she remembered that this woman, this supposed friend, had set out to harm her child, and nothing her husband did could be too severe.

First, he made a phone call from behind the closed door of his study, followed by a Friday night visit from two men in a white van. Oliver conducted his business with them in private. By Sunday, they'd prepared a dossier on Alice Ann Hill. It was quite a document. First and foremost was a series of photographs of Michel and her locked in loving embrace, taken on Saturday night. Once again, their assignation took place in his car, this time in an empty parking lot on Route 9. The images left no doubt that they were lovers. In fact, the one of her straddling him on the passenger seat was not fit for a newspaper. But it could, if necessary, be used online. Celia could not believe she'd ever called this woman a friend.

The dossier also contained an extensive ledger of Alice's past transgressions. These suddenly felt a lot less charmingly mischievous than the stories she told over lunch at Papillon. Those vaguely described scrapes with the law turned out to be an arrest for drug possession that resulted in a year's probation, an assault complaint that was dismissed only when the victim had dropped the charges, and a DUI that landed Alice in jail for a few nights. Most damningly, there were Leander and Jill Quade in Santa Fe. They had quite a story to tell about a viperous young woman who'd slithered into their marriage to cause near-terminal havoc. Their entanglement with Alice began with a meeting at Jill's gallery, then moved to the pool house where Alice took up residence. She became the lover of wife, then husband, then both together. The whole thing ended in tears. Money went missing; locks were changed; marriage counseling was required.

"She's not who you think she is," Leander stated.

"She's a master manipulator," Jill added.

On Sunday morning, she had a phone conversation with the two reporters from the *Herald* who'd been the recipients of the information assembled by the white van men. (Oliver explained that the *Globe* would have carried more editorial weight, but he feared that they might not use the more evocative photos.) For the most part, they simply wanted Celia to confirm the facts about her friendship with Alice and express her belief that she was the author of the anonymous Twitter comments about her son. Only at the end did they ask her to comment on her personal feelings.

"She's very good at acting the friend, but I now see she always had her own agenda. She's a very unhappy and disturbed person who has no place in a community like this."

Whatever doubts Celia initially had about the article, by Sunday evening she couldn't wait for it to come out. It hadn't been a good weekend for the Parrishes. Since the Twitter thread posted, there'd been a tectonic shift in public attitudes about the case. If Christopher initially fit the dark preconceptions of a certain segment of the population, then Jack struck a chord with those harboring a more progressive paranoia. Suddenly, people on Twitter and Facebook were casting him as a poster boy for heedless privilege. Someone actually had the nerve to use the term *affluenza*. Other incidents from Jack's past were dredged up, presumably by classmates and so-called friends, all writing anonymously. *Everybody knows* became a refrain. The Lexi incident continued to be blown way out of proportion. And then there were the photos, perfectly normal teenage stuff that now had a sinister aspect. The time had passed for indulging the secret doubts Celia had harbored about her son when this whole thing started. They were after Jack now. There was only one thing to do: protect him.

Most distressing of all was the incident on Saturday night, when somebody came to the house. Celia had been on her way upstairs to go to bed when she happened to glance out the dining room window. A sleek dark sedan was parked out front. A man stood ominously still by the driver's door. At first she thought he was associated with Oliver's investigation, but something about him didn't feel right. The way he just stood there. And there appeared to be someone in his car. A woman. Celia went to tell Oliver in his study. His face immediately stiffened in alarm. He wasn't expecting anyone. He went to the dining room to look.

"Call the police," he said.

"What's happening?"

"Just call."

As she dialed 911, there was movement out at the car. The man had started to walk toward the house. Oliver stepped into the hall and turned on the front lights. This froze the stranger in his tracks, just beyond the realm of light. There was something vaguely familiar about him, though she couldn't place it. After what seemed like an endless interval, he turned and got back in his car.

"Oliver, what is this?" Celia asked.

"The price of notoriety."

A squad car arrived quickly, though the intruder was long gone. The police took a report and promised to keep an eye out. After that, Celia's anger toward Alice deepened, as did her own sense of guilt. She'd put the family at risk by letting this woman get so close. She'd been duped, no matter how pure her intentions. Because Alice was an impostor. She was evil. She didn't belong here. She had to go.

. . .

After reading the *Herald* article, Celia texted Jack and told him to return from his grandmother's immediately. Oliver was still at home—he wanted to speak to his son before he left for the office. Jack arrived back just after nine. His eyes flickered toward the newspaper spread on the table as he sat across from her.

"You've read this, I presume," Celia asked.

"Yeah. Grandma had like ten copies delivered once she heard."

Oliver emerged from his study.

"Did you know about this?" he asked his son, nodding to the front-page photo.

"No. I mean, I knew she's a flake, but I had no idea that she was banging Christopher's dad."

"Did you ever talk to her about Lexi?"

"No! God, I'm not stupid."

"But you talked to Hannah about it?"

Jack's expression answered the question.

"That was a mistake, Jack."

"I know. Stupid girl."

"So she had no idea that this affair was going on, either?"

"God, no. She's more freaked than anybody."

"I presume she's not going to be telling her stepmother anything else."

"Don't worry about it," he said with an ominous chuckle. "She couldn't if she wanted, anyway. Hannah's dad gave her the boot."

"Well, good riddance," Celia said. "So what happens now?"

"What happens now is that people will read this and come to their senses," Oliver said. "They'll understand that all this nonsense that's been written about us is just a load of crap and they'll turn their attention back to the real guilty party here. This is confidential but—talks have opened with Christopher's attorney about a confession."

"Thank God," Celia said.

"It could all be wrapped up by the end of the week."

It was decided that Jack would take the day off from school. But this would be his last absence. Tomorrow, he'd be back in the saddle. Normality would return. The time for hiding would be over.

Oliver left for the office. Celia got ready for her monthly meeting of the steering committee for the library's renovation. She'd been tempted to cancel, but when Jack announced that he was going back to bed, she decided to attend after all. It would be a bad look not to go.

She spent the better part of an hour dealing with fallout from the article's revelations. First, her mother. Katharine didn't hold back. Celia must have been out of her mind to get so close to such a malevolent character. She endured five minutes of abuse before pretending that there was someone at the door. She moved on to her friends. These exchanges, thank God, took the form of texts. Nobody had ever really liked Alice. In fact, several people gently criticized Celia for her friendship with her. She took her medicine. The criticism would fade. This would be over soon.

She checked in on Jack before heading out. He was fast asleep. She left him a note in the kitchen, telling him she'd be back for lunch. They could send out. Chinese, Mexican, whatever he wanted.

As she drove into town, Celia tried to focus on the meeting ahead. Truth be told, the town's massive Margaret Fuller Memorial Library didn't need renovation. It was a little outdated in its architecture—it had been built in 1979—but the building itself was perfectly sound. Someone had commissioned a study, however, that claimed the institution was "too book-oriented." The proposed facility looked like the sort of interactive museum where she used to take the boys. It was approved by the selectmen with the proviso that half of the forty-one-million-dollar budget be privately raised. Celia was asked to cochair the committee. She was always being asked to cochair things. She'd joke that was what they'd write on her gravestone. Mother, wife, cochair.

She stopped at the restrooms on the way in. Not the ladies'—she didn't want to risk a sink-side conversation. Instead, she went into the handicapped one. She was sitting on the railed toilet when her phone buzzed. It was Alice. She was tempted to swipe it away, but that would be unwise. Alice might be wounded, but she remained a danger to the family.

"So you hate me now. I get it. But I couldn't just sit by and watch Christopher be destroyed. Your son did this, Celia. He raped Eden Perry and then he killed her. And he's forcing Hannah to help him hide it. I've seen texts he sends her and she basically told me as much on Friday before you guys shanghaied her to Boston. You don't believe me. Fine, I get it. You don't owe me shit. But do yourself a favor. Ask Jack what really happened. Just do that. Ask why Eden said she was going to make him pay. Look him in the eye and see if you believe him. Because I'm going to keep talking about this until they fill my mouth with dirt."

Celia closed her phone. My God, the woman really didn't know when to quit. She flushed the toilet and washed her hands. She glanced at herself in the mirror and that's when it returned, the feeling she'd had in those feverish days after Jack's birth. The sense that the world was drifting away from her; that things close enough to touch were suddenly far beyond her reach. She remembered Jack's face when he came home on Wednesday morning, before anyone knew there was a dead girl on Locust; the same baffled expression he'd had just after Lexi left the house. As if he'd just seen something terrifying, something he couldn't understand.

She opened the door to a shriveled man in a wheelchair, looking murderously at her.

"Oh, I'm sorry," she said.

"I presume you can read," he answered.

"Of course I can read," she said. "Why else would I be in a library?"

At home, she went straight up to Jack's room. He was still asleep.

"Jack, wake up."

It took him a moment to understand where he was.

"What did you do to Eden?" she asked as he sat up.

"What? Nothing."

"You did something to that girl, didn't you?"

"Jesus, Mom. You sound like one of those people online."

"No, Jack, I sound like your mother."

Her voice was sharp, as sharp as it had ever been. She wasn't going to be tolerating his temper and swagger. Not today.

"Hannah thinks you did something to Eden."

"Who told you that?" he asked.

"Alice."

"And you believed her?"

"Jack, you need to tell me the truth. Right now."

He was awake now. He understood how serious she was being. The anger and the defiant sarcasm were gone. His voice took on a pleading, almost pathetic quality.

"Mom. Listen to me. Christopher's lying. Hannah's crazy-ass mom is lying. I didn't do anything to Eden."

"Do you swear?"

"I'll swear on anything you got."

She held out her hand.

"Swear on me."

His face screwed up at the oddity of her request. Or perhaps at something else, something more worrying—the magnitude of the lie he was about to tell. But then he reached out and grasped her hand, holding it delicately from beneath, like it was a wounded bird.

"Mom, I'm telling you the truth."

She believed him. She had to. He was her son. She'd given birth to him in a fever that almost killed her. She'd raised him. He was her son and you didn't get to judge your children. You didn't owe the world justice where they were concerned. You just believed them. You protected them. No matter what. Whatever he was—that was her job.

"You believe me, right?" he asked.

"Of course I do," Celia said.

ALICE

She texted Celia while waiting for her room. Check-in usually wasn't until four, but it turned out that she was a preferred customer. Something to do with the credit card. They promised to have a junior suite for her in an hour, tops. She waited in the lobby. Her sudden notoriety had closed off most of her usual venues for killing time. Going to spin or Starbucks might be amusing on some perverse borderline-sociopathic level, but she really didn't need to be drenched in chai latte or have a kettlebell dropped on her foot. And Michel's house was totally out of the question. She couldn't even begin to imagine his fury and shame when he saw the article. He must now see her as some sort of succubus, invoked to deprive him of everything.

She established herself next to a potted tree and wrote to her former best friend, even though Celia would probably delete her text unread. She'd know that it was Alice behind Emerson Depths; that her dear friend was in fact her nemesis. But Alice still had to try to get through to her. Otherwise Christopher was going to wind up locked in a cage for a long, long time.

Until the reporter's call the previous night, she'd truly believed they were turning this around. It had been a good weekend. The thread had worked better than she'd hoped. The comments proved that she'd tapped into a deep well of antipathy toward Jack. People genuinely didn't like the kid. He'd humiliated some minimum wagers at the mall. He'd been a dick to multiple classmates. Worst of all, it seemed, he'd cheated at tennis.

It was the Lexi incident that struck the deepest chords. A number of anonymous Waldo girls now claimed they'd steered clear of Jack after detecting hints of his dark side. One wrote that *the only reason Lexi dated him was b/c she was Metco and nobody told her.* To which another unnamed poster added *and the only reason Hannah Holt is with him is because she's a total wimp.*

Not just a wimp, Alice thought. It went deeper than that. Alice got it now. Hannah didn't just tolerate Jack's sadism. It was what drew her to him. And him to her. *That* was their bond, cruelty and pain. Hannah took what he wanted to give. Not just took. Needed.

Alice had thought the self-flagellation was behind them. The cuts and unexplained bruises. The uprooted hair on her sheets. The inexplicable falls, including a tumble down the basement steps that broke her wrist. And most of all, worst of all, that terrible moment when Alice walked into her stepdaughter's room to find her using a pair of needle-nose pliers to unspool a hangnail. Blood streamed down the back of her hand. She'd made it to the first knuckle by the time Alice intervened. By no means squeamish, she'd swayed to the edge of consciousness while holding the girl's hand under cold water in the bathroom. Hannah was unbothered by the blood; her only concern was that Alice not tell her father. And she hadn't. Because she thought she could handle it. Fool that she was.

Alice remembered the bruise she'd seen on Friday and wondered how many more there were, how many more there had been. It was plain as day now. Jack hurt Hannah. And she took it because she thought that was the price of his love. Jack hurt Hannah and Alice should have known but she was too busy chasing her own thrills to notice. Most people worried what kind of secret pleasures their children were pursuing behind closed doors, when all the while Alice should have been wondering about the secret pain.

It wasn't too late to stop it. Of course, that meant betraying Hannah. But she had no choice. The alternative was unthinkable: Christopher imprisoned, Michel ruined, Hannah condemned to a life of cruelty. Alice had never liked the term *tough love*, having experienced all the toughness she needed in the name of love. But suddenly she understood that was exactly what was needed.

And it seemed to be working. Jack was being exposed as the sadist he was. Not only that, but Alice had been able to see Michel again on Saturday night in a Route 9 parking lot. At first, he was gloomy. Christopher had been in bad shape when he saw him earlier in the day. He was having trouble understanding what Michel said to him. It was almost as if he were drugged. All he could say was that he didn't kill Eden.

Alice tried to rally Michel by explaining that she was close to getting Hannah to tell the truth. All she needed was one more conversation.

"But how do we get her to go to the police?" he asked after she told him what the girl had said.

"I'm working on it."

Michel finally allowed her to comfort him. She stroked his hair and they kissed and then desire took over. She conducted him to the passenger seat and then they were in a hidden place, shrouded by their love and desire.

Sunday felt endless. She expected Hannah to come back from Boston in the afternoon, but Geoff informed her she'd be away until the following morning. And then her phone rang. It was a Boston number. Presuming it was a telemarketer, Alice didn't pick up. She was surprised to see that they left a message that lasted for over thirty seconds. She listened, and her world fell apart. It was a reporter from some tabloid. Substantial allegations had been made against Alice that needed to be addressed. She needed to call back right away—they'd be running something tomorrow. She took a deep breath and hit redial.

"What is this?"

"Would you care to characterize the nature of your relationship with Michel Mahoun?"

The woman knew everything. Michel, the Twitter thread. They had photographs of them together on Saturday night. They also had a record of Alice's past. Chapter and verse. Somebody had done a lot more than a Google search. Would she care to comment?

"It's not true."

"Which part?"

"None of it."

"But your legal troubles are public rec . . ."

Alice hung up. An objective observer might have told her that was a mistake, but there didn't happen to be any of those around. *Just us chickens*, she thought. This made her laugh for a moment.

"Just us chickens," she said out loud.

She started to cry. Softly, but with conviction. The house phone rang. It was the reporter again, calling for Geoff. Alice listened as the woman's voice echoed through the vast kitchen. She wasn't worried; Geoff had gone to the lab. After the beep, Alice erased the message. They wouldn't have his cell phone. Nobody did. Geoff and his secrets.

How? was all she could think. Somebody must have been tapping Michel's phone. Something had come up on the computer they'd seized from him. They'd followed him last night. Or her. She thought they'd been so careful, but clearly she was wrong.

She picked up a marble pestle from the counter and threw it as hard as she could across the kitchen. It sailed right through the door into the den, where it harmlessly struck the back of the sectional. She looked around the kitchen. Her eyes came to rest on the Wüsthof carving knives and she contemplated opening a seam in herself from navel to sternum. Probably better to warn Michel about the article. But she couldn't imagine their conversation. *Sorry, hon, I seem to have ruined any chance your son might have of escaping life in the big house. Wanna meet later? Your parking lot or mine?* In the end, she sent him nothing. He might as well have one more night of hope. She also considered calling Hannah, but she would already know all about this. Any chance of her opening up to Alice had evaporated.

Instead, she got the vodka from the freezer and went up to her room. She took a long sip. Hello darkness, my new friend. She should just vanish. The prenup was pretty elastic as far as adultery was concerned. Geoff would fight her, but she'd still wind up with a couple mil. Maybe she'd finally give New York a try, now that she'd added the two missing ingredients needed to make it there—material security and moral bankruptcy.

But she wasn't going anywhere. The idea of abandoning Michel was just too painful to contemplate. Night staggered along. She got through about a third of the bottle as she sat in front of the newspaper's website, clicking refresh every few seconds. Typical, she thought. Two hundred years since her neighbor Hawthorne died and she still managed to get a scarlet letter pinned on her cardigan. The vodka didn't put her to sleep; it only transported her to a much more problematic kind of wakefulness. It was two a.m. and then three a.m. She nodded off at one point but that cast her into a sixty-second free fall that ended with her splattering on the asphalt of a parking lot. So much for sleep.

They posted the article at five. "An Untimely Affair: Secret Dalliance Rocks Eden Murder Case." The photo told the whole story. Michel and Alice up in a tree, k-i-s-s-i-n-g. The article started out plainly factual. The suspect's father was spotted in an intimate situation at a remote location with the stepmother of one of the prosecution's chief witnesses. The writers then shifted gears to innuendo, suggesting "it remained to be seen" if Alice had been the author of the Twitter thread that had "shaken" the community on Friday. And then there was her past, capped off by Leander and Jill back in the Land of Enchantment. Sounding like victims, as if they hadn't had the time of their lives out in the pool house, sharing her like a big bag of movie theater popcorn. Celia had her say, sounding mournful and betrayed. Michel couldn't be reached; his lawyer had no comment. The only small consolation Alice could take was that they hadn't unearthed Roman, the erotic photographer in South Beach. Yet.

Geoff woke just after six. She heard him in the bathroom and then she heard him in his office. A minute passed and then she heard him leave his office. And then he was standing in the doorway. She rarely saw Geoff angry. It wasn't a pretty sight. His face would get so pinched that it looked like he'd entered a denser gravitational field.

"You hurt my daughter."

"It had to be done."

"It had to be done? Are you for real? You publicly accused her of lying to help Jack."

"Jack raped Eden Perry and then he went back later and killed her to shut her up."

"You're wrong. He was here all night."

"You couldn't possibly know that! You were dead to the world. I could have lit your sweatpants on fire and you wouldn't have known until your legs were extra crispy. You're lying, Geoff. To me and to the cops. Because Oliver Parrish told you to."

"Why would I lie for him?"

"Because he knows it was your brain candy the kids took. He knows that if he told the world, you'd be fucked out of a shitload of money."

"Who told you they were my drugs?"

"Hannah."

This stopped him in his tracks.

"And you fucked around with the security footage, too. Don't deny it, Geoff. I saw you doing it. You know I did. I even saw the two of you in his car in the middle of the night."

He stared at her and she thought she had him. She really did. But then he smiled bitterly and shook his head.

"God. You and your imagination. You got it so wrong."

"Do I? How so?"

"Yeah, Oliver came to see me early Thursday. And yes, he wanted me to tell the cops that Jack had been here all night. He was worried they wouldn't believe just Hannah, but if I said Jack was here, too, he'd be in the clear. It was really important to him that Jack didn't become a suspect, even though he was innocent. Just the suspicion could damage him. But I guess you know all about that, don't you?"

She said nothing. Her sense of triumph was evaporating rapidly.

"But I couldn't just say that he was here because, you're right, I did pass out for a while. So he asked me if we had a security camera and I said yes and he asked me to check it. He *asked me to check it*, Alice. Think about that. He knew his son was innocent. There were no threats. The drugs didn't even come up. He was just a concerned dad. So I looked. And you know what? Jack *was* here all night. He arrived with Hannah at 11:57 and didn't leave until 6:58. Nobody in or out in between. Front, back, garage. So yeah, I did the guy a solid. But I was always telling the truth."

"So Hannah telling you wasn't enough?"

"Was it enough for you?"

Touché, Alice thought.

"Did you show the tape to the cops?"

"Sure, I sent them a copy. Jack's not a suspect, Alice. They have their guy. All you did with that thread was cause an innocent family grief." He gestured toward his office. "I could show it to you if you want."

"But the drugs," she said, hearing how feeble her voice sounded.

"They're hypnotics that don't have FDA approval yet. Sid gave them to me. They're kind of like Halcion, only a lot more targeted. They have a real short half-life, like an hour. I took one myself on the night in question." Geoff was resurrecting his rage. "Nobody's blackmailing anybody. Your boyfriend's son killed Eden. The police know it and now he's going to be put in a cage."

She continued to say nothing.

"The chef," he said. "Unbelievable. With his smock. You're done. I want you to leave. Now. Pack a bag and get out. Go stay with your cook. Live under a bridge. Whatever. But you come near Hannah again and I'll slit your fucking throat."

A theatrical threat, but there were those Wüsthofs to consider. Seeing that he'd made his point, he turned and started to walk from the room.

"Geoff, hold on."

He turned, his face cold and resolute, ready to deny any clemency she might request.

"I'm just curious. While all this was going on, did it ever occur to you to talk to *me* about it?"

"Yeah. Wednesday night. When we got back from the station. I wanted to talk to you then. But you weren't here. Because you were with him, right?"

She didn't answer.

"I guess I'd been suspecting something for a while now," he continued. "I mean, I'm not an idiot. But it wasn't until I saw that bandage on your arm that I knew for sure."

"The bandage?"

"No way could you have wrapped that yourself. And I doubted the Uber driver did it. I was going to call you out on it but with everything that was going on . . . I just never thought it would have been him." His voice had taken on a mournful quality she'd never heard before. "You're just so fucked up, Alice. You see yourself as being this wild child but in the end you're just a bad, selfish person."

"But isn't that why you married me? For the wildness? Did you think you could defang me?"

He didn't have an answer for that one. Once he was gone, she did as instructed. She packed a few things and crept to the nearest acceptable hotel. It wasn't until she was checked in that the fear and humiliation really hit her. This was it. She'd lost everything. Michel and her house and Hannah. She'd finally gone too far and now she was going to pay for it.

The room phone rang. She snatched up the receiver.

"What?"

It was a recorded voice, asking her if she would like to take a brief survey on her experience at the hotel.

"I only just got here!" she shouted, slamming the phone down so hard that it was a wonder it didn't break.

MICHEL

He wasn't surprised when Cantor told him about the article. He'd sensed some fresh catastrophe bearing down on him all weekend. Yes, there was a brief period of hope after Alice tweeted her accusations. It seemed as if Jack Parrish really might be brought to justice. But the police had gone ahead and arrested Christopher anyway, and the descent had resumed. People chattered away online all weekend about Jack and his family but his son remained caged. This morning's *Herald* article was just another downward jolt of the elevator to hell he was riding.

After Friday's hearing, Michel had spent the rest of the day trying to figure out how he was going to get his hands on a quarter million dollars. That was the amount Cantor guessed they'd need if the judge were to grant bail. He'd have to take out an equity credit line on the house, max out existing credit cards, and sign up for others. Liquidate the college fund, borrow more from family and friends. With all that, he could just about manage. It would leave him buried in debt. He'd probably have to take a job at the Cheesecake Factory. But he couldn't think about that now. He just needed to get Christopher home.

It wasn't until Saturday that they finally let him speak to him. Since Christopher was being charged as an adult, they were holding him at the county jail. It just so happened that Saturdays were visiting days for inmates whose last name began with M through Z. As Michel left the house, he noticed that the reporters had disappeared. Christopher had been arrested. The waiting game was over. The drama would now be at the courthouse.

The jail was old: bricks, barbed wire, Gothic windows paned with iron bars. The room where they met was oppressive and dank, the only remotely human touch a small area in the corner filled with used toys. Christopher shuffled in with the other inmates. He looked even worse than he had in court. Although contact was not allowed, Michel briefly touched his son's cheek. It was as if he'd been hiking in winter woods.

"Are you cold?"

"I don't know what I am."

They sat across from each other on hard plastic chairs. People had tried to scratch things into the table between them, but they'd been defeated by its impenetrable surface.

"We're going to get you bail."

"Guys here say you never get bail for killing a white girl."

"You didn't kill her."

"I don't think that's the point, Dad."

"Cantor's talking to the prosecutors. You need to keep faith."

"In what?"

Michel had no idea.

"Are they treating you badly?" he asked.

"Mostly we just watch TV."

"Have you seen what they're saying about Jack?"

"There wasn't anything on the news."

"They're saying he molested another girl last year and his family was forced to give her money."

"Lexi, right?"

"Yes."

"I wondered about that."

"Really? Do you know anything that would be useful to us?"

"He never talked about it."

Michel leaned forward a little and lowered his voice.

"Christopher, what happened at that house?"

"You won't like it."

"I know about the drugs. That doesn't matter now."

"No, I guess it doesn't."

Christopher looked at the scratches on the table. As if he was on the brink of figuring out what they were trying to say.

"We were just hanging out. As usual. The girls had these pills they wanted us to take; they said they were amazing. Jack wouldn't, he never did drugs. I didn't want to but Eden would've laughed at me if I didn't so I palmed it and chucked it out in the bathroom later. The girls got totally wasted. It was not good. They got really sleepy but they were both fighting it and that made them into total zombies. Hannah went off somewhere to lie down and Eden passed out eventually on the sofa. I guess at some point I said something to Jack about how I really wished I knew how to be with her. I mean, I loved her, Dad. She was just . . ."

He lapsed into silence.

"Christopher."

He snapped out of it.

"And then Jack said you should just go for it, man. And I'm like, what are you even talking about? She's totally passed out by this point. He started in with all his Jack shit, about how you can't let them call the shots, how they don't know they want it until you give it to them."

"And you listened to this?"

"No! But then he was like, I'll show you. He walked over to her and I thought he was just messing around. But then he puts his hand between her legs. I mean, she was wearing pajama bottoms, they had little kitten faces on them, and he just puts his hand under them. I tell him to stop and then I grab him and suddenly she's awake and screaming bloody murder. And then she attacks Jack, I mean, like, tries to physically kill him. He's holding her off by her wrists and I try to get them apart and so she grabs me by the throat. Her nails are like totally digging into me. Hannah's there by now, she gets involved. I finally break free and now Eden's threatening Jack, telling him he's going to pay. Hanns is totally flipping out and so Jack decides to get the hell out of there. He looks at me and says you better fucking sort this out. And then they leave."

"What happened then?"

"I wanted to talk to her but she just closed down. She called her mom but she didn't pick up and that sort of took it out of her. She slept for a while and I just sat there. She finally woke up and looked at me and just said *Get out*. Real cold, you know? So I left. I walked around a while and then I came home."

"Christopher. Look at me."

He did.

"Are you sure you didn't do anything to that girl?"

He hesitated. It was for just a second. Less than a second. A fraction. But it was there, the slightest catch in the flow of time.

"I swear to God, Dad. You believe me, right?"

"Of course I do," Michel answered.

They made him leave after that. As he drove home, he thought about his son alone in that big house with a girl he loved but couldn't have. He remembered the way he'd acted when he arrived home at four in the morning; the look on the detective's face when she saw the scratches on his neck. That fraction of a second just now, before he swore he'd done nothing wrong. He thought about these things but he could not think beyond them. His mind would not go to the place these thoughts wanted him to go. Because Christopher could not have done this. It was impossible.

He called Alice; they met in the darkness. It was so good, losing himself in her body. The way she moved almost weightlessly over him, the heat of her exposed skin. After she came and he came, they continued to embrace for a long time. He wanted to stay here forever, in this dark empty lot surrounded by shadows and trees. This place that was no place at all.

Then he was alone again. Sunday was endless, waiting for her to call with the news that she'd convinced Hannah to tell the truth. The cheap cell phone finally rang in the late afternoon, but it was Cantor. He was on his way to the house. Michel could hear bad news in his voice. His mind went through a terrible litany of possibilities in the twenty minutes it took for the lawyer to arrive. Christopher had been hurt in jail. Even more damning evidence had emerged.

"Did you talk to them?" Cantor asked as he stepped through the door.

"Who?"

"The paper, Michel. The *Herald*."

"Why would I speak with them?"

"Tell me about Alice Hill."

"What do they know?" Michel asked eventually.

"Everything. There's a photo of the two of you locked in a steamy embrace."

"I don't know what to say."

"Well, how about telling me how long you've been together?"

"Three months."

"And she was behind that Twitter thread?"

"Yes."

"What else has she been doing?"

"Trying to get Hannah to confess."

"Confess what?"

"That she's lying about Jack being in her room all night."

"Yeah, well, something's telling me that's no longer in the cards." The lawyer sighed. "Listen, Michel, first of all, I'm not opposed to any of this. In theory. If we could get concrete evidence that Hannah and Jack are lying to the police, that's a money shot for us. But we have to be

smart. If you're going to make a run at Oliver Parrish's boy, you gotta do it right. And sleeping with Hannah's mom ain't right."

"That thought has occurred to me."

"So, what, this is an irresistible compulsion?"

"I love her."

"Same difference."

"So what happens now?"

"You need to stop seeing Alice Hill. If she attempts to contact you with any other information pertaining to your son's case, have her call me. No exceptions."

"I understand."

"I should fire you," Cantor said.

"Can you do that?"

"This is America. Anybody can get fired."

"I'd rather you didn't."

Cantor nodded, though the friendliness was gone now and Michel doubted it would be coming back.

"I'll tell you one thing. We can forget about bail."

"But it's me who did wrong, not him."

"Yes, Michel. It *is* you. And you're the responsible adult into whose care we are asking the court to place an accused killer. You're supposed to be the man who won't do something rash like spirit your son out of the country. It's going to be hard to convince the judge that's you."

Michel buried his head in his hands.

"So what happens now?"

"I'm going to have some conversations with people in the morning and then we'll see where we are."

"What can I do?"

"Nothing. You think you can manage that?"

The reporters returned in the middle of the night. They knew the

article was coming. By morning the street was clogged. It was worse than before. The old rules no longer applied. They came right up to the house; they shouted his name.

"Come on, Michel. Talk to us. We need a comment. Michel . . ."

A police cruiser was parked outside but the officer made no effort to intervene. Just after dawn, somebody pushed a copy of the *Herald* through the letterbox. Michel looked at the front-page photo and then he read the article. The arrests, the couple in New Mexico, Celia's pained words. He didn't know this woman at all. Her body, yes. But nothing more.

Cantor arrived later Monday morning, accompanied by shouts from the reporters in the street. He looked even more grim than he had last night. He started talking before Michel was able to offer him coffee.

"The judge had postponed the bail hearing, as expected. Which is probably a good thing. You do not want to step into that courtroom anytime soon. He just tore me a new asshole and evidently he's *really* pissed at you."

"And?"

"I think it's time we start to talk about a plea."

"What? No."

"It would be remiss of me not to at least explore this with you."

Michel nodded glumly.

"Okay, here's how it would work. Anybody with half a brain can see that they've overcharged your son. Proving Christopher intended to kill Eden Perry is a very long shot. My feeling is we can probably get manslaughter. That means five, six years if he behaves himself."

"Is there no other way?"

"Sure. We go to trial. But I think we can assume that neither Jack nor Hannah is going to be changing their story. And we also now know that Hannah's father is saying the kid never left the house and that he can back it up with security footage. The forensics are solid and they're against us and evidently there's more coming. I'm not sure yet how your entangle-

ment with Alice Hill plays into this, but I doubt it will be in our favor. I'm a pretty good lawyer, Michel, but I don't see what my play is here."

"Can I ask you a question?"

Cantor nodded unhappily. He knew what was coming.

"Do you think my son is guilty?"

"I really don't think it's helpful to speculate about that."

"Please. Off the record."

Cantor stared at him evenly. There was something on his mind he couldn't bring himself to say. Michel recalled Christopher's hesitation when he asked him at the jail if he'd done anything wrong, that fraction of a second that seemed to stretch for an eternity.

"My job is to provide the best possible defense for your son given the totality of the evidence."

"So you won't answer my question."

"I think I just did, Michel. You just didn't hear it."

Sofia arrived an hour after Cantor left. He almost didn't answer the bell, but then he saw the unmistakable cloud of black hair floating in the front door's small windows. Her embrace was perfunctory. She wore her fierce face. She'd seen the article.

"Are we alone?" she asked as she looked around suspiciously.

"Don't worry. She's gone."

"We need to talk."

"Did David send you?"

"He told me you were a mess, so I came."

He looked at her and she said yes, she and David were seeing each other again.

"Is that a problem?" she asked.

"No. It'd be good if somebody found some happiness in all of this. So—does he think Christopher's guilty?"

"He'd never say that," she said. "But he has his doubts. Big doubts. He says there's something tearing Christopher up inside."

"The girl he loves just got killed and he's been falsely accused of it."

"It's more than that, Michel."

"Cantor said that?"

"Not in as many words."

"Don't tell me *you* think Christopher did this," Michel said.

"Do I think my little cousin deliberately set out to hurt someone? To kill a girl? Of course not. That's crazy talk. But he was in love and people in love lose their minds sometimes. Believe me. I don't carry pepper spray for the strangers."

"I cannot tell my son to plead guilty."

"So you have no doubts? You don't think it's possible that for a moment he flipped out?"

"I don't know," Michel said eventually.

"I knew about her," she said. "What was happening between you."

"You did?"

"Michel. My love. She was out for you from the first."

"It wasn't like that."

"Please. I saw. The way she watched you? Eating lunch on her own? What woman eats out alone? You stay home, you have yogurt, you weep."

"So I was a fool."

"Because you were lonely. After Maryam, you cut yourself off. You became vulnerable. You were a sitting duck for a woman like that. Always with the hair."

"You've got her wrong."

"Who do I have wrong? The part where she betrayed her husband? Where she called her stepdaughter an accomplice to murder? Am I wrong about the criminal in the newspaper article? Was that fake news?" She took a calming breath. "You lost sight of things, Michel. Especially your son. You were so busy with your little dolly that you let Christopher run wild. Maybe he knew—you think about that?"

He closed his eyes and leaned his head on the back of the sofa.

"I sinned. I know that."

"*Sinned?* Please. Don't be so self-important. This is America. There's no sin here. You fucked up." She took a breath, the first, it seemed, since she started speaking. "Listen to me. Your son's in jail. You have a big decision to make. Stop thinking about what you've done and start thinking about what you're going to do."

Her phone buzzed. She angrily checked it.

"Okay. I have to be at work. I'm subbing at Antonelli's this week." She met his surprised expression with a bitter laugh. "What? It's not like *you're* going to look after me."

She left without another word, without a hug or a kiss, taking her pity, leaving her rage behind.

DANIELLE

It was as if the hot water would never run out. At her own house, you had five minutes until it became a drenching slush puddle. Patrick's shower, however, appeared to have an infinite supply. The man seemed to have an infinite supply of lots of things. Money. Patience. Words. Sadness. His capacity for alcohol seemed bottomless as well. His time, however, was definitely finite. No way could he keep on like this much longer.

She'd spent the weekend with him. Well, most of it. But now it was Monday morning and it was time to leave the neverland they'd been inhabiting. On Friday, she'd permitted herself to get drunk. It wasn't something she normally did. She'd been around too much boozed-up shit in her life. But suddenly it felt right. Maybe it was a mistake, but she could make mistakes now. So she sat back on his deep couch and listened as he filled the air with words. He talked about his hometown. The Parrish family and Mahoun's restaurant. His daughter. Why they called the high school Waldo. As she listened to him she kept thinking, *This man was given all the good luck in the world and then he got hit with the worst shit possible.* He'd never seen it coming. His guard was down. He was soft when he needed to be hard and it gutted him. He told her that he was supposed to go to rehab on Monday but she doubted he would. And even if they lassoed him into that, he wouldn't last a week. Where he was going wasn't Vermont and it wasn't good. She had to make sure to remember that in case he asked her along for the ride.

For now, however, this was where she had to be. He knew things she needed to know, such as how the police and courts worked out here. Every second she spent in Emerson convinced her more deeply that she was being handled. That delicate boy hadn't done this. It was Jack Parrish, with his GTI and his smirk. But they were hiding that fact, because of corruption or indifference or just a simple desire to wrap things up.

There was something else, as well. Something more elusive but also maybe even more important. Patrick knew about the pain. Not loss, but this agonizing, tantalizing *presence*. His daughter wasn't dead to him. Somehow, he'd kept her alive. She still spoke to him. Maybe it was tearing him up but it was also keeping him on his feet. Danielle knew that if she thought about it too much or talked to someone with an ounce of sense, she'd see the madness in it. The man was a raging alcoholic who might as well have a LOST SOUL label sewn to the inside of his expensive suits. But as long as she stayed with him, just him, then the terrible reality of her daughter's death could be replaced with the possibility that she didn't have to vanish so completely. And so she stayed with him.

After he finished telling her about Emerson, he told her other things. He explained how money worked, which, surprise surprise, was not at all how Steve Slater believed. He told her about a TV program he'd just watched about the siege of Stalingrad; he explained why Brahms was actually better than Beethoven. But it wasn't all about his universe. He asked about her life and listened, really listened, when she told him about the men and the jobs and the childhood where cruelty was just how people expressed themselves. He asked about the tattoos and she told him how she'd never felt in control of her body when she was a girl. People were always touching her and looking at her in ways that made her feel like property. And sometimes there was other stuff she'd rather not discuss. But with the tats she was in charge. This wasn't the skin she'd been given but the skin she'd taken. She was writing herself. If you touched her, you were touching the flesh she created.

"Show me," he said.

Normally, a slappable request, but from him it felt natural. And so she took off her blouse and she showed him. She knew she didn't look so hot unclothed these days, certainly nothing like she had when she was Eden's age. But she also sensed he didn't care about that. He genuinely wanted to read what she had written.

"What's this?" he asked, grazing her left shoulder with his fingertips.

"It's called an Ouroboros."

"This heart is amazing," he said, almost touching her naked chest above her bra.

"Hurt like hell, though."

He ran his fingertips along her right triceps.

"And these Roman numerals . . ."

"Eden's birthday."

She supposed she could slip off her skirt and tights and show him what was down there, the half-moons and vines and skulls and ankle roses. But he got the point.

"Okay, and now the masterpiece."

She reached behind and undid her strap, then quickly crossed her arms in front of her chest to keep the bra from falling. She turned her back to him. She pictured what he was seeing. The still-vibrant colors and the upturned beak. The spread of the wings and the flames.

"Whoa."

"I had to go to New York for this one. The guy who did it was a real artist-to-the-stars type. It's on his website. My claim to fame."

He was touching it with both hands, like a blind person.

"Do me up," she said, before this became something else.

She turned after he had.

"Anyway," she said. "That's me. Illustrated version."

They slept together but they didn't fuck. It wasn't something they decided. It was just how it played out. He stripped down to his boxers, she finally took off her skirt and tights. But neither of them went farther. He ran his hands over her body, so lightly that there were moments when she could barely feel his fingertips. His body was like everything about him. Slender, beautiful, soft. They kissed but it wasn't the sort of kissing that led anywhere except to sleep. He paced during the night; she drowsily told him to come back to bed. On Saturday morning, she went home to change and decide if she wanted to do whatever they were doing. Animals had got at the casserole dishes neighbors left on the front porch. There were messages on the machine she didn't play. The kitchen sink had developed a drip. The house was starting to settle into a terrible emptiness. She could feel her daughter drifting out, like smoke through an open window.

She slept until the afternoon and when she woke she wanted to see him. He came to get her in the evening. He'd already been drinking but he drove just fine. He took her to an expensive restaurant in Brookline. They ordered a hundred dollars' worth of sushi and barely touched it. Instead, they drank sake, hot and smooth. He was in some sort of state now, talking and talking, weaving webs with his words, entangling himself in his own thoughts. Something was both rattling and exciting him. It felt dangerous in a way she couldn't define.

Her head was spinning by the time they were back in the car. They returned to Emerson, to a part of the town where she hadn't been yet. The houses were even bigger than the Bondurants' here. He pulled onto a street called Fox Chase Lane and parked in front of a particularly grand one. She knew who lived here before he even said a word.

"Have you ever been inside?" she asked.

"A few years ago. There was a party. It's what you'd expect."

"We'll never touch this kid, will we?"

"Let's go talk to them. Tell them what we know."

"Somehow I don't think that would go down very well."

She spoke with a rueful laugh, but she could see that he was serious.

"This isn't the way to do it, Patrick."

"I think maybe it is."

"Please. Let's leave."

For a moment she thought she'd convinced him. And then he was out of the car. He watched the house. He'd seen something. She tracked his gaze. A woman's silhouette filled a window. She and Patrick stared at each other, like two cats before trouble started. And then the woman vanished. Danielle leaned across the seat and rapped on the window with a ring but Patrick ignored her. She looked back at the house; there were two figures in the window now. Patrick started to walk up the lawn but froze when a light came on. Danielle reached for the door handle, ready to end this, but just then Patrick turned and walked back to the car. There was a dead little smile on his face she wasn't thrilled about.

"We go," she said when he got back inside. "Now."

She didn't speak until they were several blocks away.

"You do anything like that again and we're done with whatever it is we're doing."

"I'm sorry," he said.

He offered to take her home but she couldn't abandon him now. So she spent another night at his place, a very different night. The stunt at the Parrish house had driven him into a bad place. He poured himself a whisky the moment they stepped through the door and bolted it and then he poured himself another. She drank nothing. She tried to get him to talk but he was beyond speech. He finally passed out in a recliner chair. She covered him with an afghan and went to bed.

On Sunday morning, she woke to the sound of him vomiting. She nursed him for a while and then decided she didn't want to nurse him. So she went out to get some food. He told her to take some of the cash that he'd cunningly hidden in an envelope lying on the counter with his bank's name on it. She counted it. There was just over two thousand dollars inside. At Whole Foods, she bought groceries that were so expensive she almost broke into laughter at the register. He was asleep when she got back to his condo, so she got an Uber home. She needed her own car. Whatever happened next, she didn't want Patrick Noone behind the wheel.

At home she checked online to see what was happening. The prevailing opinion seemed to be that Jack Parrish was a very bad egg. Reading this, her attitude toward Patrick softened. Maybe he wasn't such a crazy man after all. She remembered how she'd felt when she saw Christopher Mahoun and his father in court. She remembered her daughter's purple eyeball as she lay on the stainless steel table. Just because Patrick was losing control didn't mean he wasn't the one who knew the truth.

He called in the afternoon.

"Did you just leave or are you gone?"

"I need you to stop drinking long enough for us to deal with this situation in a way that doesn't end with us in handcuffs."

"I think I can manage that."

She drove over at dinnertime. He cooked for her from the food she'd bought. She'd never known a man who could cook. He made chicken and rice with a lemon sauce. As he worked, he drank from a wineglass filled with clear liquid. She took a sip without asking. It was water.

They ate. It was delicious. This man.

"So where did you learn to cook?"

"My ex-wife and I took a course in Italy."

"Yeah, I was thinking about doing that."

"Really?" he asked.

She shot him a look and he smiled sheepishly. His neck actually reddened and she thought she could fall for this guy, if only every last thing was different.

"You and I really are from different planets," she said.

"And yet here we are, at the same table."

"So what's the plan, Patrick?"

"What do you want the plan to be?"

"I think you should talk to the police. Positively identify the Parrish kid as the one you saw. Put it on record."

"I'm not sure how much water that will carry."

"All right. Then we go to Mahoun's lawyer. He'll listen to you."

"I'll go to the cops. If you come with me."

She wanted him to call the police right away but he wasn't yet ready for that. They agreed to do it first thing in the morning.

"This needs some wine," he said, referring to dinner.

"As long as we don't graduate to the harder stuff."

"Well, wine can be the harder stuff. But point taken."

The three glasses he drank seemed to be just enough to keep him from crawling out of his skin. She cut herself off at one. They went to bed at some point and finally made love. It was awkward at first. But he was gentle and patient and persistent and after a while she began to lose herself and then they were off to the races. A lot of things were released in both of them. At one point they were basically grappling. She bit him on the shoulder and tasted the sweat. He didn't complain. He held his own. When it was over she cried for the third time in a week and he held on to her until she was quiet. And then there was sleep and there were no dreams and that was the first good thing that had happened to her since the two cops walked into Slater's shop.

She woke up first. He slept peacefully. She could see her teeth prints on his shoulder. Simple indentations, like something you'd leave in an apple you'd changed your mind about eating.

"I've left my mark on you," she whispered.

He didn't hear her.

To her mild surprise, the shower eventually did run out of hot water. He was awake when she emerged from the bathroom, wrapped in a thick white robe he'd been gifted on some holiday or another. The kitchen smelled of coffee. He was smiling ruefully at his computer.

"Any news?" she asked, since it was Monday, a day for new things.

"Well, I've been fired."

"Seriously?"

"I was supposed to check myself into rehab this morning, remember? My partner actually came by to give me a lift to the facility."

She remembered now, someone knocking on the door before dawn. She'd let it go, sensing there was nothing good on the other side.

"Maybe you can do that when we're done."

"Maybe," he said as he shut the computer's lid. "We're meeting with the detectives in a half hour."

Which left her just enough time to get dressed and make herself presentable. She checked her phone—there was a text from Steve Slater, asking how she was doing, which she translated as *When the hell are you coming back?*

"I'll call later," she wrote, even though she had no idea when later would be.

At the station, Procopio was unhappily surprised to see her. He led them to an interview room and asked them to wait. He returned with Gates, who was also surprised to see Danielle, though she did a better job hiding it.

"What's going on?" she asked once everyone was seated.

"It was Jack Parrish I saw outside the Bondurant house," Patrick said.

There was a long silence that Procopio broke.

"And this just dawned on you?"

"I saw his name and then I saw his picture and it jogged my memory."

There was a knock on the door. It was the woman from the district attorney's office. Penny.

"Could you please repeat that for my colleague?" Gates asked.

As Patrick spoke, Danielle could see that they didn't believe him.

"Okay," Penny said. "So this memory came back to you when you saw the photos of Jack on Twitter."

"Well, yes," Patrick said after a moment.

"You see the problem here, right?"

"Not really."

"I'm looking at this from the point of view of you as a witness," the prosecutor said. "You can't identify whom you allegedly saw and then you see a photo of someone who people are speculating is guilty and suddenly you remember it's him. That's a tough sell."

"Isn't that how a lineup works?"

"We call them arrays now," Procopio said. "And that's pretty much the exact opposite of how they work."

"I saw what I saw."

The prosecutor nodded, though not in agreement.

"Have you ever seen Jack Parrish before?" Gates asked.

"When he was younger."

"In what circumstance?"

"There was a party at his parents' house."

"A party? So you're friends with the family?"

"I wouldn't say friends. His older brother briefly dated my daughter."

"The one who died?" Gates asked.

"There's only one daughter," Patrick said with a defiance that felt hollow.

"You didn't happen to visit the Parrish residence on Saturday night?" Procopio asked.

"No. What? No."

"You sure about that?" Procopio asked.

"Of course I'm sure."

The detective cast him a disbelieving stare, then turned to Danielle.

"How about you?"

"No," she said. "I didn't."

"Okay," Gates said, tapping the table once. "Thank you both for coming in. We'll take all of this under advisement."

"What does that mean?" Patrick asked.

"Just what I said," she answered, as pleasant as she could be.

Procopio opened the door. Patrick looked frustrated, but there was nothing more he could do. The conversation was over. He stood. Danielle stood as well.

"Ms. Perry, could I have a quick word with you?" Gates asked.

She sat back down. Patrick looked at her, not wanting to leave her alone here.

"Come on, Patrick," Procopio said, as he might to a child or somebody he'd just busted.

Patrick had no choice but to follow him. The prosecutor stayed behind.

"How you holding up, Danielle?" Gates asked.

"Still standing."

"So what's going on?" she asked, referring to the man who just left.

"Yeah, I know how it looks. But I think he's right."

Gates considered this for a moment.

"All right, I'll cut to the chase here. This is turning into sort of a crazy case but it doesn't need to be. You read the news this morning?"

"No. I mean, what news?"

"It looks like Christopher's father and Hannah Holt's stepmother are romantically involved. They've been stirring things up."

"Seriously?"

"Yes, seriously. We're pretty sure that Twitter thread about Jack Parrish that you've undoubtedly read was cooked up by them in order to deflect blame from Michel's son."

"She'd do that to her own daughter? Call her a liar?"

"Stepdaughter. And the answer to your question is yes."

Patrick had known about this. He'd read it when she was in the endless shower. But he didn't tell her, even though she'd specifically asked him if there was any news. Gates looked at Penny and raised her eyebrows.

"Okay," the prosecutor said. "I'd like you to keep this to yourself, but you deserve to know. We've opened discussions with Christopher's attorney about him pleading guilty."

"You have?" Danielle asked, her voice as small as she'd ever heard it.

"Yes," Gates replied. "He killed your child, Danielle. Not Jack Parrish or Jack the Ripper or any other Jack. Sure, we looked at him at first, of course we did, but not anymore. The evidence against Mahoun is overwhelming. But even without that . . . I've been doing this a long time. Guilty people, you can just tell. There's something about them. And with Christopher—I know. He's guilty of something and I can't think of what else it might be. It's eating at him and pretty soon he's going to confess and then all this craziness will be over."

Danielle suddenly felt very alone.

"I know it seems unlikely, when you look at him. But he did it. Sweet kids do bad things. He did it and everything else is just chatter."

"But what happened?"

"I'm still limited in what I can say until the negotiations are over, but it appears that Christopher was angry with Eden after she told him she wasn't interested in having a sexual relationship with him. An argument broke out. He attacked her, she fell, and . . ."

"So she wasn't raped?"

"We don't have the evidence to charge him with that."

A strange way to say no, but Danielle knew the woman well enough by now to understand that she would say nothing more.

"As for Patrick Noone, he has issues. His own daughter and the drinking. You see that. You're a smart woman."

"But . . ."

It occurred to Danielle that she had nothing more to say.

"People talk about closure but they don't really want it," Gates said. "Most of them, anyway. When my dad died it took my mom a year to record over his voice on the answering machine. Drove my brothers and me crazy but that was just how she kept hold of him."

"What made her erase it, in the end?"

"The tape broke." Gates cast off the memory. "I think you're trying to deal with the fact that once we lock Mahoun away, then Eden's gone. As long as there's something else to be done, you can put that day off."

"He says he still hears his daughter's voice."

"I imagine that man hears a lot of things," Gates said sadly.

Danielle nodded. Gates was right, of course.

"Go home and get some sleep. And then you should get ready to bury your child because pretty soon we're going to be sending her home to you."

PATRICK

They said nothing until they'd reached the lobby.

"You're making a mistake," Patrick said, breaking the silence.

"So I'd like you to do two things for me," Procopio said, making a show out of being reasonable. "First, I'd like you stay away from Danielle Perry. The woman is torn up by this and you're not helping."

Patrick started to answer him but the detective raised a hand.

"Number two is not optional. You need to stay the hell away from the

Parrish house. You go back there and we're all gonna be in a new place. Are you hearing me?"

Patrick didn't respond. Procopio held his eye. Despite the suit and the promotion, he was still the same thug he'd been with Gabi.

"We're going to stand here until you tell me you're hearing me."

"I hear you."

Procopio screwed up his face, no longer bothering to hide his contempt.

"I mean, isn't there somewhere you need to *be*?"

He turned and walked through the door without waiting for an answer. Patrick stood still until he became aware of the duty officer watching him. It would be better to wait for Danielle outside.

It was a glorious spring day. Birds, sun, a slight breeze. He tried to remember what it had been like to take pleasure in this. He pictured himself walking along a shaded path in Vermont, putting the pain behind him. There were just so many impossibilities now. The things he couldn't do were pushing him toward what remained.

Danielle emerged from the building. Although he knew what they'd been telling her, he wasn't ready for her grim expression.

"What is it?"

But she walked silently past him and got into the passenger seat.

"Christopher Mahoun is going to plead guilty," she said once he was beside her.

"That just means they got to him."

"Or it means that he killed my daughter."

"Danielle . . ."

"They think you're a crazy drunk, Patrick."

"Yeah, I sort of got that."

"How wasted were you that night? Was it as bad as Saturday?"

"I know what I saw."

"Why didn't you tell me about Christopher's father and Hannah's mom? You saw that this morning, didn't you?"

"Because it doesn't matter."

She nodded toward the building.

"It does to them."

"I know what I saw."

"Like you know what you hear?"

It was a cruel remark that landed heavily. For an instant it looked like she regretted it, but then her expression grew even harder. They drove in silence back to his condo.

"I'm going to go home now," she said after he'd pulled into his numbered parking place. "Please don't call me."

"You don't have to do this."

"Yes, I do. We both do."

She got out and walked to her car. She didn't look at him as she drove past. It was just after ten in the morning. In two hours it'd be noon and then, after that, the rest of his life. He went inside and woke his computer. Griff's email was still on the screen.

Patrick—

I know you were there when I came by this morning. Whether you heard me or not is irrelevant. Obviously we're going to have to cut you all the way loose. Everybody's gone the extra mile but we simply can't have you associated with the fund anymore. Lance will be in touch about compensation. It'll be fair. I wish you luck. I really do.

G

Cut loose. He checked the news but there was nothing about an impending guilty plea. Not that there would be. Things would be happening behind the scenes from here on out. He read some of the reaction to the news about the affair between Michel Mahoun and Alice Hill.

Public opinion had whiplashed. Jack Parrish was innocent now. He'd been a scapegoat, a straw man. Christopher Mahoun was the guilty one.

He had a drink. The alcohol hit him hard, like it sometimes did. He'd reached the point where he couldn't be sure how that was going to go. He poured himself another and settled into the recliner. He thought about how Danielle's body had felt last night, smaller than he'd imagined, more fragile. He remembered what the detective said. *You're not helping her.* He drained the second glass and poured himself a third.

And then it was afternoon. He drove to Whole Foods. A car honked at him at an intersection but he didn't know if it was for something he'd done or something he hadn't done. As he parked there was a deep scraping sound. The curb.

In the store, he bumped into a sloped tray of limes. A few fell. He watched them spread out across the polished floor and then he kept on walking. *Clean up on aisle P*, he thought, or maybe said. He didn't bother with the bins of redolent food. He just plucked a random sandwich from the refrigerator unit. The cellophane felt like the skin of something dead. He'd almost made it to the door when he heard the voice behind him.

"Excuse me?"

It was a woman, timid but insistent. He kept walking.

"Sir?"

She was next to him now. There was no avoiding her. He turned. She was young. The name tag on her smock read *Rae*. She had a round face; her hair was dyed crayon green and shaved around her left ear. There were tattoos on her bare arms, geometric shapes, sporadically placed, like the doodlings of an early astronomer who was still trying to figure out how it all fit together up there.

"I already paid for it," Patrick said.

"What? No, I just . . . are you okay?"

Patrick struggled for words. It wasn't an easy question.

"You're Gabi's dad, right?"

"Did you know her?"

"We were in the same year. It's just so . . ."

"Yes," he said. "It is."

"Anyway, you looked like you could use some help."

Others were watching him now, employees and customers. A face he recognized, a woman, a mother or client or neighbor. Everyone had the same expression. He looked like he could use some help.

"No, it's just . . . bad day."

Rae released a pent-up breath, as if he'd just explained everything. He offered her the sandwich. After a confused moment, she took it. It was Cranberry Tuna, something he'd never eat.

At home he drank. Time boomeranged. Hours passed and then it was only a few minutes later. He remembered the way Danielle had looked at him as she emerged from the station; he remembered the limes rolling on the polished floor, little green moons escaping gravity's pull. He remembered the two silhouettes staring at him as he stood in front of the Parrish house. Oliver and Celia. Or maybe it had been Celia and Jack. Afraid, perhaps, but also knowing they were safe inside.

He must have slept, because suddenly it was dark. Things had changed again. A process of separation within him that had begun when his daughter died was now complete. The last time he'd felt this way was when he'd been concussed running a crossing pattern back in college. A linebacker lowered his head; helmet struck helmet. He knew he'd just been hurt, maybe badly, but there was a sort of elation in it, a freedom. This time, it felt permanent. He was no longer of his life. The parts of his body that spoke and felt and moved were beyond his control. He was just a passenger. All he could do was watch and wait to see what was going to happen.

He found his phone and summoned Danielle's number and typed.

I'm taking care of this now.

He pressed send and got his keys. His car made an ominous sound when it started. He must have hit that curb pretty hard. His body drove carefully. It didn't take long to get to Fox Chase Lane. He parked down the road this time. He passed three houses walking back to the Parrishes', all of them massive and still. He didn't hesitate as he crossed the weedless lawn. He walked around the side of the house, where he passed a lit window. Through it, he could see a large, book-lined office, a sanctuary of burgundy and chestnut brown. Oliver sat at the massive desk, speaking on the phone, his back to the window, his voice muffled by the thick glass.

At the back of the house there was a patio guarded by a low cordon of ribbon. Furniture had been piled on the lawn beside it. He stepped over the flimsy barrier and walked across freshly laid stone to the French doors. They were open a few inches, but the screen was locked. He used his keys to cut a wound in the mesh, then reached inside and opened it.

The kitchen was empty. A dishwasher churned; Oliver's voice droned down the hall. Patrick waited to see what his body would do next. And then someone was thundering down the steps. He walked deeper into the kitchen. He passed the sink, where a slight vegetable odor emerged from the drain. He kept moving until he was in a recessed alcove that overlooked the lawn.

Jack walked into the kitchen. He wore a pair of sweatpants and a Van Halen T-shirt. His hair was mussed, as if he'd just been sleeping. He pulled the refrigerator door open and started rummaging inside. Patrick's hand took his phone from his jacket pocket. His fingers worked over it and then there was a photo of Eden, the one everyone had seen, with her red hair and her smile. Patrick stepped out of the alcove and walked quietly around the far side of the island, so that he was blocking Jack's path to both the hallway and the back door. The boy saw him just after he shut the refrigerator. He held a cheese stick.

"What the fuck?"

"You have to tell people." Patrick held up the phone so the boy could see her face. "You have to tell them the truth about what you did to her."

The boy understood he was trapped. Even if he went around the far side of the island Patrick needed only shuffle a few steps to block him. And then Jack's eyes widened and he shook his head. Patrick turned. Celia had walked into the room. He hadn't heard her coming. Her body seized up and she took a step back.

"Patrick? Why are you here?"

"Your son needs to tell the truth."

There was a sound somewhere in the house, a doorbell ringing, followed by urgent knocking.

"You should leave."

"Not until he tells the truth."

She turned her head back toward the hallway but kept watching him.

"Oliver!"

"No . . ."

"Oliver!"

He contemplated fleeing out the back door but Jack had to tell the truth. He went toward the boy. Jack started to back away but Patrick was moving quickly now, as swiftly as he had when he was young. He grabbed Jack's arm. He held the phone in front of the boy's face, so he had no choice but to see.

"Look at her."

There was more noise and movement behind him. He turned, lowering the phone as he did, though he did not let go of the boy's arm. Oliver was in the room now. He looked at Patrick's eyes and Patrick looked at his eyes.

"Wait . . ." Patrick said.

There was another man. Procopio. He took his pistol from his hip and pointed it at Patrick and started shouting. Patrick raised the phone to show them Eden. Before he could speak again, before he could explain, Oliver shouted, a single word, and then there was a sound that covered all the voices and Patrick once again didn't see the hit coming. And then he was lying on floor, knowing he'd been hurt, but feeling elation and the possibility of freedom. *So this is it*, he thought. And then the pain came, carrying its own end inside it.

Tuesday

MICHEL

Cantor called just after midnight. He had to repeat the story before Michel, still reeling from that morning's *Herald* article, understood what he was being told.

"But why?"

"He was on a mission. He claimed to have seen Jack on the night of the killing."

It was impossible to imagine. A home invasion, bullets, blood. Patrick Noone. All he could see was a well-mannered, impeccably dressed man seated alone in a corner booth, closing his eyes at the first sip of the bottle of grand cru he would proceed to quietly finish.

"So where does this leave us?"

"It makes it seem like only crazy people think Jack Parrish is guilty. Look, Michel, everything's in flux right now. To say the least. I need to have some conversations, take stock. I'll come by tomorrow and we'll see where we stand."

That night became an endless succession of hours and minutes and seconds. Unbidden images flashed through his mind every time he neared sleep. Those broken toys in the prison's visiting room. The newspaper photo of him and Alice. Patrick Noone, smiling at Sofia as she refilled his wineglass. He dreaded morning's clarity, the pale light and passing cars.

Cantor arrived just before noon. He didn't look happy.

"So?" Michel asked.

"It's like I thought. People see this as exonerating Jack." He shook his head in frustration. "And there's something else. I've finally learned what sort of forensics they have beyond the scratches. It's not good for us."

"Okay."

"They found traces of Christopher's DNA in the victim's vagina."

"That's impossible."

"I'm running out of options here, Michel. At the end of the day the prosecution is going to show the jury pictures of a dead girl who looks like God invented the sun to shine on her. They're going to want to blame somebody for that and I'm afraid when the bottle stops spinning it's pointing at your boy."

He paused. Choosing his words now.

"And there's something else, and I say this with all due respect. Your son isn't necessarily white. Some people are going to look at him and they're going to think the marathon. They're going to think the towers."

"We're Catholic. He's French."

"Yeah, well, this is Massachusetts. There are Catholics and then there are Catholics. As for being French, let's just leave that one alone for the time being. Michel, take a look around. We're not exactly living through the Age of Enlightenment. There are a lot of crazies out there who aren't big believers in reasonable doubt. Or reasonable anything. And they *love* to sit on juries."

"What happens if we lose at trial?"

"Worst case? Life. Best case fifteen."

"So what do we do?"

"Conventional wisdom says the DNA and yesterday's events would harden their position. But this is Emerson and it's turning into a shit-show and I guarantee you the people who run this place, one of whom happens to be named Parrish, do not want shitshows. Staying out of the limelight has served them very well for the last few hundred years. They'll be willing to travel pretty far to keep it that way."

"What does that mean? Specifically?"

"Your son pleads guilty to voluntary manslaughter. We explain the DNA by saying they were fooling around. Seems like they'd accept that. It's not semen, which helps us a lot. They were close, that's known. People had seen them kissing before. But on this night they start to engage in foreplay and then she tells him she isn't into it. They argue, things get heated. He's young and unschooled in the ways of the heart and he loses it for a few seconds. He didn't intend to kill her. There was no blunt instrument, no clenched fist. It was just a shove. Most of what happened to Eden was an accident."

"And if they accept?"

"Fifteen years up front. That's mandatory. But that would get lowered to five once the circus moves on. Christopher gets out, he's in his midtwenties."

Michel couldn't imagine it. And yet he knew he had to.

"Talk to your son, Michel. He needs to understand the stakes."

"How long do we have to decide?"

"The door's open 'til the end of the week."

"I'll talk to him," Michel said. "But I'm not happy about this."

"Yeah, well, happiness is a bit of a reach for us all at this point."

Cantor called the district attorney before leaving the house, arranging for Michel to see his son that afternoon. It was outside normal hours, but they were willing to make an exception. Michel was no longer a combative parent. He was now a potential ally.

At the jail, they gave them a room reserved for lawyers. There was no guard, no time limit. The only decor was a poster listing all the things they couldn't do. Christopher was unshackled when they led him in. They embraced, violating rule number one. His body felt limp, without substance.

"So somebody got shot at Jack's place?" he asked before Michel could speak.

"His name was Patrick Noone. He was a customer. You'd remember him. He said he saw Jack outside the house around the time Eden died."

"Damn. But that's good for us, right?"

"People are saying he was crazy."

"Right. Of course." He met his father's eye for the first time. "So. You and Hannah's mom."

"I'm so sorry."

"She's married, Dad. What do you think Mom would say?"

"She wouldn't like it. At all."

His son stared at him, making another readjustment to his universe.

"So why are they letting you see me today? It's not our time."

"I'm going to tell you something, but before I do, I want you to . . ."

"Cantor thinks I should plead guilty."

Michel reared back in surprise. Who was this knowing, world-weary young man currently sitting in front of him?

"They found DNA in her. Yours."

"Yeah, okay."

"It's just hard for him to understand how to defend you."

Christopher stared at the table, his eyes losing their focus.

"It's bad in here," he said. "I wish I could tell you it wasn't. It's boring most of the time and then it's really scary. And the next place is supposed to be a million times worse."

The next place.

"Are they hurting you?"

"Not yet."

Michel wanted to ask him what he meant, but he wasn't sure he could bear the answer. Christopher met his eye.

"So how long is he saying?"

"Five years."

Christopher thought about this, then let out a dead laugh.

"Like college. If I took a gap year."

His son looked back at the table.

"Okay. I accept."

"Christopher, wait . . ."

"Please, let's just get this over with." He gave his head a bitter shake. "I deserve it anyway."

"What do you mean?"

"I lied to you on Saturday," Christopher said. "About what happened."

He opened his hands on the table and stared into them, as if reading from an invisible book.

"You just don't know how Jack is. Yeah, he can be your best friend most of the time. He gives you stuff and tells you you're his bro. But then he turns on you. He makes you feel like shit. Like you're nothing." He put on a voice, harsh and hateful. "'You're a pussy. You're never going to get with her. If you can't fuck this trashy slut, you're never going to get laid.'"

"Why were you even friends with this monster?"

He looked up.

"Because I was nobody without him."

"That's not true."

"Yes, it is. I was invisible at that school. You don't know what it's like because you're this hot shit chef everybody loves. But I'm just some short brown kid. Yeah, everybody's polite. Nobody's calling you names. But that's only because nobody's calling you anything. And then Jack starts hanging with me. I know he mostly just wants somebody to boss around, but whatever. It was like an initiation. That's how I looked at it, anyway."

"Initiation? Christopher, he *bullied* you."

"It was worth it." He smiled bitterly. "So I thought."

He looked back at that unseeable book in his hands.

"So, she's lying there passed out and he says, 'You're going about it all wrong, Mahoun. Chicks like this, you gotta take it to them. If you respect them they just think you're a faggot. You gotta get her going, get her over the hump. She'll love it.' That's when he pulls down her pajamas and grabs me by the back of the neck. You don't know how strong his grip is. Like fucking iron. He says, 'If you don't fuck this bitch right now, I'm going to tell everybody what a pussy you are.' He puts his mouth right against my ear and he's like, 'Just touch her, man. Just see how good that shit feels.'"

His eyes were tearing up.

"I was, I don't know. Scared mostly. But also like, maybe this really was the way. Nothing else works. And I wanted her so bad. I loved her so much. So I just did it. I put my fingers inside her. One and then two. I'm trying to be gentle because I don't want to hurt her. She started to move and I told myself she was liking it."

"Christopher . . ."

He shook his head. He was going to say this.

"Jack's still got me by the neck, I can hear him breathing right behind me, and then he's like, 'Okay, man, she's ready. Go for it. Fuck her. Do it.' He's pushing me forward, pressing against me, and I feel, I can feel he has a hard-on. That's when I knew how wrong this was. I stop touching her and Jack is swearing at me now, saying, 'If you aren't going to do this, I am.' He tosses me aside and he pulls . . . he pulls it out. I can't move. That's when she wakes up. She sees Jack there with his dick out and me watching and she sees her pants pulled down. You should have seen her eyes, Dad. She was so scared. He comes at her and she starts to kick and twist away. That's when I grab him and pull him back. She starts to attack him and I'm just trying to stop everything and that's when she scratches me. Finally, I get them apart. Somehow they covered themselves up before Hannah comes down. We try to settle Eden down but it's no good. She's screaming about making people pay, calling her mom. She thought he'd raped her already, I think. So we just leave. But when we get outside Jack tells me I have to go back inside and shut her up."

His eyes were full of tears now.

"And then what? Christopher—what happened after that?"

"I went back inside."

"And?"

He angrily wiped away the tears.

"Isn't what I just told you enough? How guilty do you want me to be, Dad? Just tell Cantor I'll confess."

He stood up and walked to the door and knocked. It opened almost immediately. The guard took him away. He didn't look back.

Thursday

- - - - - - - - - - - - - -

ALICE

She had no idea if Hannah would show. The text Alice had sent her had been marked READ, but she hadn't responded. With Hannah, that could mean anything. For instance, it could have meant, "Okay, yes, I'll meet you outside the frozen yogurt place at three this afternoon and we'll work things out and go back to being best friends." Or she could be saying, "You must be joking, you backstabbing bitch." Most likely, it simply meant that she had no idea what she was going to do. Which was, after all, Hannah's default mode.

The meeting point she'd chosen was a small, trellised grove in the shopping plaza on Centre. It served both the fro-yo shop and the build-a-salad place. Its dozen hexagonal metal tables, half-hidden by ivy, were usually unpopulated this time of year, although today they were packed with gibbering kids just liberated from school. Alice decided to stay in her car until Hannah showed. If she showed.

Should that not happen, so be it. It wouldn't be the end of the world. That already seemed to have happened. The last three days had been a hellish wasteland. Already gutted by Geoff's revelation about the security footage exonerating Jack, she could only watch helplessly as the bad news piled up. Monday brought an avalanche of internet abuse. *Slut* seemed to be the term of choice, though there were plenty of others. Geoff sent an email detailing all the ways in which she was banished from his life. There was also a text from Hannah: *How could you do this?* The only person who didn't get in touch was the one she wanted to hear from.

And then word came that a man had been killed at the Parrish house. At first, she was certain it was Michel. He was dead and it was her fault. She collapsed on the bed the moment she heard the news and didn't move for an hour. When she finally did stir, she learned it was some crazed local guy. Her pain and panic receded, but her guilt remained intact. Her thread had lit the fuse, and now some poor soul had been cut down.

After that, she was basically trapped in Room 217, hoping Michel would contact her. Roman from South Beach finally released his nude photos of her, which at least were solo, despite his pleas to join the frame. She read about Patrick Noone. He had a face that had probably never been punched or spat upon or ignored. It was impossible to think about a cop shooting him. Reports had him locked in a downward spiral following the overdose death of his daughter, a recent Waldo graduate. There were two photos of her making the rounds. One pictured a real stunner with a sly, million-dollar smile. The other was a mug shot: emaciated, blemished, dead-eyed, her hair an unwashed medusan tangle. Before and after. Way, way after.

Alice also tracked the resurrection of Jack Parrish. The tide of blame that had flooded over him all weekend had receded. He was now cast as a victim: an innocent boy who'd almost been led to the slaughter by online calumny. This sea change was even reflected in the mainstream press, where commentators were starting to see his treatment as a teachable moment, most notably in a *Globe* think piece portraying his case as an object lesson in the perils of social media.

And then, to cap it all off, rumors began to circulate that Christopher Mahoun was preparing to plead guilty. Evidently they were lowering the charges to manslaughter. A hearing was set for Friday. People were confident that the whole grisly matter would be wrapped up by the weekend.

That's when Alice decided to leave town. As sumptuous as the Hilton's breakfast buffet was proving to be, it was time to go. She'd leave and never look back. She didn't have the stomach for this suburban sanctuary. You just had to sacrifice too much. Trimming away the rough edges seemed like a smart play until you were as smooth and boring and dead as a beach pebble and you understood that the edges were why you got out of bed in the morning.

So, it was on to New York. She'd be arriving late to the party, but she still had her looks, mostly. And now she'd have money. Not the full fifty percent, but Geoff would fork over enough for the foreseeable future, if only to keep her out of his hair. And she'd finally be unburdened of her romantic misconceptions. The search for the perfect man would be over, because she'd already found him, and look where that got her.

Then she'd received Michel's text. It came as she was packing. *We need to talk.* She told him she was still in town and he said he was on the way over. For a brief moment, she allowed herself to believe that he wanted a reconciliation. Love had conquered all. The thought didn't last long. She'd ruined the man's life. There would be no kissing, no making up.

There was a muted knock on the door, and there he was. He looked terrible. Red-eyed and pale. His normally perfect hair chaotic; his normally pristine shirt wrinkled and coffee-stained. He didn't meet her eye as he entered. She wanted to embrace him but she knew that was impossible. He sat on the end of the California king. She perched beside him. Two players on a team getting slaughtered.

"You heard he's pleading guilty."

"Yes."

She waited for him to speak. He was staring at their convoluted re-flections in the television screen.

"Is he?" she finally asked. "Guilty?"

"I honestly do not know."

"What do you want me to do, Michel?"

"Talk to Hannah. You said she was going to tell the truth if you spoke with her one more time."

"Unfortunately, I don't think she's my biggest fan right now."

"But she was," he said. "Maybe you can still get the story out of her."

"I'll try. Of course I'll try."

They sat in silence, still staring at their warped reflections. She put a hand on his knee. They were touching, and yet it was nothing. It amazed her, how quickly it had become impossible. How quickly it had gone away.

"I'm sorry. I knew that what we were doing was wrong but I thought if we loved each other, really loved each other, then that would make everything else all right."

"It looks like we made the same mistake, then."

She pulled her hand away, allowing him to go. He stood and gave her a helpless smile and then he walked out of the room.

Hannah appeared, right on time. She looked around the tables, then peeked inside the frozen yogurt place. Alice got out of the car; Hannah spotted her through the trellis. She tried to look scornful but couldn't pull it off. Alice beckoned her. After a theatrical pause, Hannah approached.

"Let's talk in my car."

She agreed. She didn't want to be seen with Alice.

"I can't believe you cheated on Dad," she said the moment they were sealed inside the Rover.

The words were clearly rehearsed, but there was still real bitterness and pain there.

"I love Michel," Alice answered. "I don't love your father."

"But you lied to him."

"I guess that's the catch-22 of this stuff. You have to start the affair before you know it's real. You can't exactly go up to your spouse and say, 'Honey, I'm thinking about getting involved with another guy, but it might not work out, so just hang tight and I'll get back to you.'"

"It went on for like months."

"I know. And that was shitty. You probably won't believe this, but Michel and I were getting ready to make it official before all this happened."

"Yeah, right."

But Hannah's heart was no longer in it. She'd seen how things had been between the two adults in the house.

"So are you guys getting together now?"

"No. Michel is going back to the Virgin Maryam."

"Who?"

"Never mind. No, we are *not* getting together."

"And that Twitter thread. That was just a terrible thing to do to Jack and me."

"I know. I guess I saw it as some kind of tough love to shake you out of this huge mistake you were making."

"Jack didn't do it. He was with me all night."

They sat in silence, watching the happy kids gossip and flirt.

"But are you really and truly sure about that, Hannah? He and his parents haven't worked something out to hide the truth? You can tell me. I'm done. Nobody in this town will ever listen to me again."

"If I thought that Jack had killed Eden, don't you think I'd tell people?" Her voice was plaintive now. "I know you think I'm a doormat, but there's no way I'd do that. But Jack did *not* do it. She was alive when we left her. He was with me when she was killed."

"Maybe he didn't even intend to hurt her. Maybe he just wanted to talk to her and things got . . ."

"But there was no reason for him to go back. His dad was going to sort everything out."

"What do you mean?" Alice asked after a few seconds.

"His father said he'd deal with it when he got back. He wanted us to stay away from her."

"Wait, when was this?"

"When Jack called him."

"I know, but *when*?"

"Right after we left Eden's house. Jack called and told him everything. Mr. Parrish told us to get back to our house and stay there. He said he'd sort it all out once he was home. Until then we couldn't talk to anybody. And then when he came by school after lockdown he told us what Christopher had done. Jack never even got to talk to her."

"And you left the Bondurant house, what, before midnight?"

"Yeah."

"And Jack called him right away?"

"We were still in the car coming home," Hannah said.

"But Mr. Parrish didn't come back to Emerson until the next afternoon, right?"

"Yeah, he was out of town. We didn't see him until just after the lockdown."

"Did you tell the police this? I mean, about Jack calling him?"

She shook her head.

"Why not?"

"Because he told us not to."

"Did he explain why?"

"I don't think so. What difference does it make?"

Alice could see it now. It was so obvious. One moment she didn't understand anything and the next it was perfectly clear. Hannah wasn't lying. Of course she wasn't lying. Jack was innocent. Of the killing, at least. Geoff had the proof; he'd given it to the cops. But Christopher hadn't done it, either. He couldn't have. He simply didn't have it in him. Neither of them was lying. They were both telling the truth. They were all telling the truth. Hannah and Jack and Christopher and Geoff. They were all telling the truth. The little they knew of it.

Hannah's expression had shifted as well. It looked as if she was thinking the same thing as Alice. The girl was spacey but she wasn't stupid. The doubt only lasted for a few seconds, however. Her eyes soon hardened. She was once again living in the Parrishes' world.

"Let it go, Alice. It's over."

"No, you're right."

Hannah's eyes filled with tears. Alice spread her arms and she folded into them, like she had a thousand times before. Alice was tempted to lock the door and drive off, taking the poor kid as far away from this evil place as she could, shutting her away until she could make her understand.

"When are you leaving?" Hannah asked as she disengaged herself.

"Later today. There's something I need to wrap up before I go."

CELIA

The doorbell rang just after Jack left for counseling. Celia had been driving him for the past few days, but this afternoon he insisted on going alone. He already thought it was a big waste of time. Being escorted by his mother made it downright humiliating.

"Come right home," she said, worried that he might be planning to slip back to Emerson to see Hannah.

To her surprise, he hugged her.

"You got to stop worrying about me."

"Fat chance of that."

Once he was gone, Celia restlessly paced the big house. She didn't like staying here. The place wasn't exactly teeming with fond memories.

Having nothing to do didn't make it easier. For now, Oliver was taking care of everything, dealing with the police and the press and Rapid Response Cleaners. She was supposed to be resting. The plan was for her to return to action when they got home on Sunday. If six days seemed too soon to anyone, that only proved they'd never shared a house with Katharine de Vissier. Granted, her mother had been profoundly sympathetic when they first arrived the morning after. About the attack, of course, but also the vicious slander her beloved grandson had endured running up to it. Celia's mother did not use social media—she didn't even own a computer, and on the rare occasions she operated the iPhone Celia bought her, she touched the screen like someone picking swallowed diamonds from stool. She did, however, listen to the gossip of friends, and they were kind enough to provide her with chapter and verse descriptions about the terrible things being said about Jack.

Her compassion, however, had soon devolved into something less supportive. Katharine, who'd been charmed by Christopher on the night he'd stayed over, started speaking of him as if he was a beturbaned, bazooka-wielding member of the Islamic State, even though she knew that he was a baptized Catholic with an early acceptance at BC and a handshake offer to attend Le Cordon Bleu. None of this mattered to Katharine. His arrest had reinforced a long-held opinion she'd somehow never managed to express. For Celia to let Jack become entangled with this ticking time bomb of murder and mayhem was parental malpractice of the first order.

"It's just odd nobody saw this coming," Katharine said, her tongue loosened by her third Dubonnet. "I'm glad I lock my bedroom door."

"For heaven's sake . . ."

"And I cannot for the life of me understand why you'd confide in that woman." Evidently they'd moved on from Mohamed Atta to Hester Prynne. "Didn't you have any idea that she was a con artist?"

"I knew she had an eventful past. But no, I didn't think she was a con woman. Nobody could have."

Katharine leveled a dark maternal glare at her.

"Don't go too easy on yourself, sweetheart."

"Not a concern, Mother."

They settled into a difficult silence, neither really wanting to enter into a full-on argument with Jack within earshot and Oliver due home.

"Well, just be glad the police arrived before that lunatic did something."

She shuddered, then retreated to her room to start her evening round of cocktail calls. Celia wouldn't go so far as to say she was glad that Detective Procopio had arrived when he did. Not when she remembered the look on Patrick Noone's face. At least her mind had blocked the shooting itself, as well as the moments leading up to it. She'd have thought it would have been the immediate aftermath that was scrubbed. But that was all starkly present. The ringing in her ears and the smell of a thousand struck matches. Jack sitting with his back against a cabinet door, eyes shut, his fists balled, like a newborn. The squawk of a radio. And Patrick lying on his back, his eyes fixed on a point a million miles above the ceiling, his expression one she could only call wonder.

But of the moments before that, nothing. The last thing she remembered was hearing voices in the kitchen. And then she was looking after her son. Her initial temptation had been to take him to her mother's immediately, but he was needed to make a statement to the police. Drew and Scotty arrived just before dawn. Both were ashen. Nobody could understand it. Michel Mahoun would have made a certain kind of grisly sense. But Gabi's father? He'd always seemed so gentle. Even when his poor daughter had been in such dire trouble at the house, he'd handled it calmly and with grace.

Their business at the scene concluded, they went to her mother's. Together for the first time since Christmas, the Parrishes sat in Katharine's drawing room as Oliver explained what he'd learned. Patrick's behavior leading up to his attack on Jack had been bizarre. Clearly, it had been him at the house on Saturday night. He'd gone to the police yesterday morning, spewing conspiracy theories. This came just an hour after he'd been fired from his job for drinking. There had also been some sort of confused shoplifting incident at Whole Foods.

"But I still don't get why he came for Jack," Drew said.

"He'd been claiming he saw him outside the Bondurant house on the night Eden was murdered," Oliver said.

"What was he doing on Locust at that time of night?" Celia asked.

"Wandering around aimlessly. If he was even there."

"And he seriously thought he saw Jack?" Scotty asked.

"Only after he read everything being posted online," Oliver said. "Supposedly that jogged his memory. Hence the visit to the police."

"Jesus, couldn't he just drag him online like any other red-blooded American?" Drew asked, his scowl deepening.

"It gets stranger," Oliver said. "He seems to have convinced the girl's mother that there was something to all of this."

"That horrible witch woman?" Katharine asked, helpfully.

"She actually accompanied him to the station yesterday. Thank God they were able to set her straight. Seems she was the one who called the police to warn them Noone was on his way to our place."

Oliver and Celia huddled in private after that. Plans needed to be made. They decided Jack would speak with a counselor daily; he'd only return to school when he got the green light. Oliver suggested Celia see someone as well. She told her husband not to be silly. His own psychological well-being was not discussed. Drew and Scotty would spend Tuesday night at Katharine's, then return to their respective lives.

Celia kept a close eye on Jack for the next couple of days. He seemed perfectly fine, though the counselor warned of lurking trauma that could take weeks or months to emerge. Tuesday passed slowly; Wednesday was glacial. The police put out a statement saying Jack was not now, nor had he ever been, a suspect. Everyone was waiting for Christopher to plead guilty. Relations with Katharine continued to deteriorate, leading Celia to decide to return home by Sunday. Oliver had wanted to give it two weeks but she put her foot down. She didn't want to wind up like the Bondurants, exiled from her own house.

When the doorbell rang, her temptation was not to answer. It was probably just the press. But it rang a second time, and she didn't want her mother to deal with them. She crept down the hall and looked through the peephole. *You've got to be kidding me*, she thought. Although every molecule of common sense she possessed told her not to open the door, she understood that this woman would need to be dealt with.

Alice's face was haggard and pale, tinged with sleeplessness.

"How did you know we were here?"

"Educated guess. Look, I know you hate me. But can we just talk for five minutes? I'm leaving for good and there's something I wanted to say to you before I do."

Celia shook her head in disgust and prepared to close the door.

"Jack didn't do it," Alice said.

Celia stopped herself.

"I know that now. I was wrong."

"I wish you'd understood that before you caused so much grief."

"Can I come in?"

Celia briefly contemplated a meeting between her mother and Alice.

"I don't think so."

"Just a few minutes and then you're free of me forever."

"There's a Starbucks around the corner. Wait for me there."

She waited for a decent interval before leaving the house and almost turned back once she was halfway there. But she pressed on, like she always did. Alice had found a table far from anyone else, an untouched black coffee in front of her.

"I've been thinking about what you did," Celia said after she sat down. "It wasn't pure malice. I know that. You were operating under some misplaced loyalty to Michel. And Hannah, even. But what I can't forgive was that you were willing to hurt Jack."

"I don't expect forgiveness," Alice said, the contrite tone dropped from her voice. "And my loyalty wasn't misplaced."

"What are you talking about?"

"Christopher didn't kill Eden."

"Oh for heaven's . . ."

"Your husband did."

"You really are crazy. Why was I the only one not to see it?"

"Jack called Oliver right after he left the Bondurant house and Oliver drove straight home. He went to see Eden to shut her up. Which he did."

"That's preposterous."

"Since then he's been orchestrating everything."

"Enough."

"At first I thought he was doing it all to hide the fact that Jack snuck out of our house. But I was wrong. Jack was with us all night."

"But that proves that Christopher is guilty!"

"No. It only proves that Jack isn't. Oliver wasn't protecting your son. He was protecting himself. He knew the minute the cops stopped thinking this was Christopher, once they started looking seriously at Jack, they were going to eventually figure out it was him."

"Oliver never left the hotel. This is where you're wrong. He called me first thing. And he spent the morning with German businessmen. Unless you think they're in on this conspiracy."

"He still could have done it."

"This is preposterous."

"And then there's Patrick Noone. The one person who saw him there winds up getting killed."

"Patrick Noone claimed to have seen Jack, not Oliver!"

"Think about that."

"I'm leaving now," Celia said as she stood. "I strongly suggest you don't breathe a single word of this nonsense to anyone else. If you do, you'll be dealing with Oliver, not me."

"What's he going to do? Bash my head in? Have the cops shoot me?"

"No, Alice. But he will destroy you."

"I'm already destroyed."

"Well, act like it."

Her anger was so intense that she almost walked right past the house. She couldn't believe this woman. She was relentlessly perverse. She'd taken the simplest of things, a parent protecting a child, and twisted it into a sick conspiracy. Because she couldn't understand. Having no children of her own, she couldn't begin to fathom why parents did what they did.

When she got home, she poured herself a brandy and took it to her father's study, now a dark, moldy repository of mismatched furniture, fading photographs, and odd wall hangings, most notably a framed map of the Galápagos Islands. And of course the closet. Katharine's boudoir was directly above; Celia heard her on the phone, berating some poor soul. She collapsed into the ancient leather club chair and took a sip of the brandy, then closed her eyes until her mind was free of Alice's twisted fantasies. After a while Jack returned from his session and went straight upstairs.

She usually avoided this room. This was where John de Vissier administered his corrections. There were good old-fashioned beatings for her brother, John Jr., currently living in exile in Kingston-upon-Thames. His implement of choice had been the belt from his old navy salute uniform. But Katharine had forbidden him from striking her daughters—she didn't want scars on that snowy skin. And so he had to get more creative with Celia and Emily, who was currently raising alpacas in Simi Valley. Hence the airless closet where forgotten things were kept.

She'd only looked in it once since those days, soon after her father died. Its contents remained mostly untouched. The naval dress uniform that would turn into a radiant white ghost as her eyes adjusted to the darkness. The putrid leather shoes that would gather around her like patient rats, waiting for her to nod off. The collapsing cardboard box of damp and swollen books. A tightly tied plastic trash bag whose contents she never did determine.

But the bucket was gone. So at least there was that.

There was no lock on the door, so he'd angle a straight-backed chair beneath the knob. Not that she ever tried to escape. Because he was right there. Sitting in his leather chair, reading about admirals and explorers, battles and mutinies. Sometimes, although not often, he would be at his desk, working on his magnum opus, the infamous nautical novel that disappeared with his death. If it ever existed. Whatever he was doing, he was not to be disturbed. Making a fuss would only mean an extension of her sentence. And so she learned to stay perfectly still. Waiting for the bad time to end. Waiting for the light to return. Waiting to escape to Farmington, to Wellesley. To Oliver, whom she never told about any of this. In fact, the only person she ever spoke to about it outside the family was Alice, after she'd described the beatings her own father administered.

"Do you think it messed with your head?" she asked.

"Well, I suppose I avoid spending any more time inside closets than absolutely necessary. But otherwise, not particularly."

Alice had smiled but said nothing. Celia had only complained to her mother once, after a particularly long internment.

"Well, that's just how our world works, my dear," Katharine said. "If it's not to your liking, go live in the other one. See how much you like *that.*"

The exhaustion and the brandy finally got to Celia. Her mind loosened, like a massaged muscle. Before long it was if she was sitting alone in a dark theater, watching a random replay of the last ten days. The stunning red of the beets in the salad Michel had made. The churned earth of the patio. Oliver's digitized face as he spoke to her from Connecticut.

And then it was there, as well. The lost memory, arriving fully formed. Patrick and Jack stood beside the kitchen island. Her son terrified; Patrick gripping his arm. There was something tentative, almost embarrassed, about the intruder's posture. His words were an incomprehensible jumble about darkness and trees and Eden. And then Jack's eyes widened and Celia sensed the familiar, solid presence behind her, the mass she'd anchored herself to since she was little more than a girl, desperate to flee her father's merciless world. Patrick's eyes were focused on Oliver. The confusion was gone, replaced by something else. Not fear or alarm, but recognition.

"Wait . . ." Patrick said.

He raised his arm, there was something in his hand.

"Gun!" Oliver shouted behind her, before Patrick could say what he now knew.

And then the world exploded and Patrick's eyes were emptying and Jack was fetal on the floor, a phone with the dead girl's face on its cracked screen next to him. Celia went to her son and got him on his feet and led him to the front lawn, where they waited as every siren in town descended.

Wait. Of course. It was so obvious now that she'd remembered. They were spitting images. Dead ringers, provided you didn't look too closely. Everyone always said it. Son and father. Father and son.

Celia stood and walked to the kitchen. Her computer slept on the table. She opened her email and typed the letters e and z into the search box. A long list of identical subject headings appeared. DoNotReply@ezdrivema .com. Monthly Account Statement. She got right on—the password was stored. There was a charge for last Wednesday, from the turnpike: 1:41 a.m. Oliver's Mercedes, heading east. Charlton to Framingham. Coming home. She stared at the page for a very long time. There were no charges going back. But he had gone back. She'd seen him there, spoken to him. He must have taken surface roads. Because something had happened, something he hadn't planned. Something he needed to hide, even though it was too late.

She closed the computer. It was quiet upstairs. Jack would be talking to Hannah, Katharine slumbering. She briefly wondered what it would feel like to inhabit a different life, where she could gently shake her mother awake and tell her about this terrible thing she'd just discovered, and then listen as the steely matriarch provided her with sage advice that would lead them all to a happy resolution. It certainly would be a far cry from where she was now. That was something her father used to say: *A far cry. I sure am a far cry from that life*, Celia thought.

Oliver arrived home. She was still in front of her computer. He came straight to the kitchen.

"Where is everybody?"

"A far cry from here."

He tensed, aware that something was wrong.

"EZ Pass."

He stared at her and then he understood.

"You're checking up on me?"

She didn't answer. His finger began to trace the scar. He wouldn't meet her eye now.

"Celia, she was dead when I got there."

"And so you just left her and drove back to Connecticut without telling anyone? Don't lie to me, Oliver. Please. Give me that."

He pulled out a chair and sat heavily in it. They waited through a silence that stretched the length of their marriage. Their lives.

"She wouldn't listen. That's what you have to understand. She *would not listen*. She was so angry. She'd taken leave of her . . . she used the word *rape*, Celia. Rape. Think about what that would have done to us if it got out. She kept on saying she was going to make us pay. Us. This family. I told her that was why I'd come. To pay. But she wouldn't listen."

"Maybe she didn't mean money."

"People always mean money. Whether they know it or not." He shook his head. "She was pointing at me, spitting out foul language. It was really getting out of hand. The dog's locked outside in the hallway, making a racket, scratching at the door. And then she hauls off and hits me. A real punch, right in the chest. Here, look."

He loosened his tie and yanked it from his collar, then unbuttoned his shirt to expose his right breast. The bruise was the size and shape of the sand dollars she used to collect as a girl.

"She's still coming at me, trying to grab my throat, scratch my face. And so I . . . lost control. For a split second. It was just a shove. I just wanted to get her off me."

"Oliver . . ."

"She hit the coffee table. Just right. Or wrong. I mean, what are the odds? My instinct was to help, every bone in my body. But then there would have been no turning back. So I waited until she'd . . . settled."

He closed his eyes. Worrying the scar again.

"Opening the door was a tricky moment, I thought the dog would attack me. But he went straight to her. He must not have liked what he saw, because by the time I left the house he was bolting past me. And then that drunken fool hit him and instead of just driving on he has to get out . . ."

"And sees you."

"And sees me. After he left I put it inside before it caused more of a commotion. Plus . . ."

"What?"

"I didn't really want her to be alone."

His voice caught. There was an interval of silence and then he cleared his throat, cleared his mind of the weakness that had given him pause.

"And once they blamed Christopher, you never thought to stop it?"

"Why would I do that?" he asked, genuinely confused by the question. "That was the point of the exercise. But I've been pressuring people to go lightly on him. Very lightly."

He met her eye.

"I had to carry my father's shame my whole life, Celia. I couldn't do that to you. Any of you. If it had just been me . . ."

"And Patrick?"

"The man entered our house," he said matter-of-factly.

"But why did Jack even call you? Nobody would have believed her."

"Because he always calls me."

Always, Celia thought. *Of course. It wouldn't have only been once. Or twice.*

"So what happens now?" she asked.

"Nothing happens now, Celia. We go on."

There were footsteps. Jack, coming downstairs. Oliver buttoned up his shirt. By the time their son reached the kitchen, Oliver and Celia had both put on the faces they'd always worn. Jack hardly glanced at them.

"Hey," he said as he tore open the refrigerator. "What's for dinner?"

"Nothing," Celia said.

He looked at her. Oliver was watching her as well.

"We're going out."

Oliver chose a steakhouse where he knew the owner. They got a corner table, so no one would recognize them. But no one did. Eden and Christopher were the faces of this now. Victim and killer. Innocence and guilt. Good and evil. The world had divided along the usual lines and the Parrishes were about to have their dinner.

Oliver and Jack ordered steaks, Celia a salad. As she waited for their meals to arrive, Celia watched her husband. She thought about the self-discipline it would have taken him to get through Tuesday and the days beyond that. Figuring out how he could control this. Anticipating problems, tying up loose ends. Doing it for the family.

The food was served and the Parrish men dug in. Their strong jaws moving, sinew and tissue; their eyes unfocused, their breathing a little heavy. If not for the eyes and the lips, they really did look alike.

He glanced at her.

"Is something wrong with your salad?"

He would have sent it back. Got her another one, or anything else her heart desired. Anything to make her happy. To make sure they were all happy.

"Oh no," she said. "It looks lovely."

He was waiting for her. And so she picked up her fork and dug in.

Epilogue

DANIELLE

They finally gave her back her daughter. Once the judge accepted the confession, they no longer needed Eden. Her body held no more mysteries. As far as the Commonwealth was concerned, her story had been told.

Dermot Costello took it from there, assisted by his son. As Danielle had guessed, he was also named Dermot. He was a carbon copy of his father, cautious and melancholy, with the same barely detectable tic that made him seem like he was always about to wink at you. Despite their comical appearance, the Costellos were competent and caring. There was a sort of grace to their movements and their hushed voices. It made it all a little less unbearable.

More people came to the funeral than she'd expected. There were the usual suspects: her mother and sister, Steve and his daughters. But there were more of Eden's friends than she'd counted on, more friends of her own, more neighbors and acquaintances. And then there were the strangers. A couple dozen of them, even though she hadn't made any kind of announcement. Mostly young women, although there were a few slim boys with long forelocks and tight black jeans. Kids who'd allowed their fantasies to become entangled with Eden's reality. They steered clear of Danielle, sensing that she wouldn't be sympathetic to their dark dreams.

The Bondurants were there, and not only because they were paying the bills. They truly had grown to love Eden. Betsy was especially afflicted. She'd already gone through this once with her Rick. Danielle wondered if she'd risk it again; draw someone else into her life, a new person to worry about. She doubted it.

Gates was there, as well. Danielle was surprised by that—she thought they'd already said their goodbyes after Christopher Mahoun's guilty plea. What a grim affair that had been. The boy as frail as a twig; the father not looking any better. Someone had asked if she thought the sentence was too light. She'd merely shaken her head. She'd taken no joy in seeing him sent away. It was too easy, too fast, too absolute. That bad feeling she'd had in her guts from the first was still there, and she was beginning to doubt it would ever go away.

And then there was the mystery woman. She'd come alone. Medium height, auburn hair, dressed beautifully in black. Green eyes that were revealed only after she removed her big sunglasses. She was Danielle's age, more or less. Well, less. Danielle didn't recognize her, and yet she didn't seem to be a total stranger, either. She'd seen her somewhere, if only in passing. She arrived late and sat at the back of the chapel and was the first to approach Danielle after the ceremony, an envelope in her hand.

"I'm sorry to intrude," she said. "I just wanted to tell you how terribly sorry I am about your daughter."

"You knew her?"

"She used to walk her dog by my house. She always had the most beautiful smile."

"That she did."

The woman handed her the envelope. It felt like there was more than just a card inside.

"There's something in there you're going to want to read."

"Okay."

"My number's there, too, if you want to talk. Which you will, I think."

She held Danielle's eye for a moment, then turned and hurried to a sporty Rover. Danielle looked at the envelope. "For Eden's Mother." She put it in the pocket of her jacket and turned to deal with the other mourners.

She'd gone back to work the day after the hearing. Everybody made a big deal about it but then they registered her attitude toward being fussed over and got back to the business of selling diamond chips to young people rolling the dice on the future. It was good to be working. It kept her from thinking too much about Patrick, at least during the day. Night was another matter. There was no stopping the thoughts at night.

It had been dark when his message arrived. *I'm taking care of this now.* She hesitated before calling the police. She'd already betrayed him once that morning, by leaving. But her resolve to stay out of this lasted only a few minutes. Gates wasn't available, so she wound up being put through to Procopio. He hadn't said much of anything, although there was an urgency to his silence that frightened her.

Suspecting she'd made a mistake, she drove to Emerson. Her fears were confirmed when she pulled onto Fox Chase Lane. There were three police vehicles parked out front, two cruisers and a sedan. There were people on the lawn, Jack Parrish and a blond woman she presumed to be his mother. She kept driving and parked behind Patrick's car. She looked at the scene in her rearview mirror, not knowing what to do next. But then more lights appeared, a fire truck and a state police cruiser and an ambulance.

She got out of the car and headed toward the Parrish property, where she followed a fence to the backyard. Out back, she walked across tightly cut grass until she was just beyond a roped-off patio. From here, she could see inside the kitchen, crowded with police and EMTs; Procopio and a man she immediately knew to be Jack Parrish's father. Someone lay on the floor, almost entirely hidden by the kitchen island. The only thing she could see clearly was his loafers, and that was all she needed to see. She stood in the darkness for a while and then left without alerting anyone to her presence.

Over the next few days, she knew she should feel grief and guilt, but what she mostly felt was nothing at all. The part of her that housed those feelings was already full. Instead, she remembered their weekend together. Not the drunkenness or the fevered speculation or the sex. But the moments of tenderness as they lay quietly in his big bed, drowsy but still a million miles from sleep. At some point he said that it had been almost two years since anyone had touched him. He just seemed so grateful to have her hand on his chest, her warm breath against his cheek. She remembered his voice. She wished they'd had more time together, that he could have met Eden. She imagined him listening patiently to her, trying to understand what was going on inside her head. Who knows, maybe he could have figured her out.

She went alone to the crematorium. They put the body into the oven. There was a whoosh and that was that. The end of Eden.

There was a reception afterward at her house. The Slaters ran the show. They really outdid themselves with the food. And Steve had pried open his wallet to buy too much booze. Gates didn't come; the Bondurants left after less than a half hour. Four of the weird girls from the graveyard showed up. They lurked in the corner, nibbling defiantly on raw vegetables, resisting all efforts to be drawn into conversation.

It broke up after less than two hours. The Slater twins offered to clean up, but she told them to go—they had their hands full with Steve, who'd been leaning pretty heavily on Mr. Jack Daniels. Her sister and mother offered to stay the night, but Danielle didn't want that. If she was going to be on her own, she might as well get started now.

And then there were just cold cuts and an ocean of liquor and the crushing emptiness she'd been dodging for the last couple of weeks. The Bondurants had brought the rest of Eden's stuff, quietly leaving it in a corner of the living room. Danielle had picked up most of her clothes earlier in the week, but there were still shoes and a few cosmetics scattered throughout the house. Her hairbrush was there as well, full of her hair. Danielle lugged it all up to her room. She'd either unpack it later or never. It didn't make the slightest bit of difference where Eden's old Chucks lived now.

At the bedroom door, she thought about what Gates had said about the message on her mother's answering machine, and she wondered how long she'd leave that Eden Hazard sign up there. She'd intended to dump the bags just inside but something drew her into the room. She looked around at the posters, as random as her daughter's mind. *Reservoir Dogs*, Van Gogh's sunflowers, some skinny tattooed nitwit with his shirt unbuttoned. Makeup was scattered on her dresser, surrounding a foul ball she'd got at Fenway.

Danielle lay down on the stripped bed. As she did, something fell out of her side pocket. It was the envelope the green-eyed woman had given her at the funeral home. "For Eden's Mother." She tore it open. The card was a nice one. No corny writing, just a black-and-white photo of an orchid. She opened it to see who this person was. Several pages of notepaper fell out, each of them covered, front and back, with small, neat handwriting. She looked at the last page. It was signed Alice Hill. Of course. Hannah's mother. *There's something in there you're going to want to read.*

She dropped the pages on the bedspread. Reading was beyond her just now. She'd do it later. Even though she hadn't had a drop to drink, she was suddenly overwhelmed by exhaustion. The house's emptiness was like sleeping gas leaking invisibly into the room. She didn't necessarily want to lie here and think about her dead child, but she was too weak to resist the memory when it came. Eden was young, three or four. They'd gone to the mall, just the two of them. Danielle needed a new dress—her friend Maude was marrying the wrong guy, yet again. She'd taken Eden into the changing room, where she'd amused herself by looking at her reflections in the opposing mirrors. An infinity of Edens. And then, at just the moment Danielle's head was hooded by the dress she was trying to squirm into, Eden bolted, moving as fast as an unleashed spaniel. Danielle called out as she frantically finished dressing, first to her daughter, and then to any adult within earshot. By the time she staggered through the curtains, the girl was gone. Nobody had seen anything. Panic ensued. Sales people, security guards, concerned citizens. Their own little Amber Alert right there in Filene's.

It was Danielle who found her. Probably just sheer dumb luck, though maybe it was something more, a homing instinct that took her inside one of the squared counters in the cosmetics section, where her daughter was happily applying lipstick in front of a mirrored pillar. Streaks of it on her lips and cheeks and forehead and neck. She smiled when she looked up at her mother, proud to show off what she'd done. Danielle wanted to yell at her but what was the point? The stupid girl never even knew she was lost.

Danielle fell asleep, a sudden plummet into a dreamless darkness that welcomed her like a warm bath. She had no idea how long she was out. It could have been only a few seconds. It could have been an hour. All she was certain of was the manner of her waking. A voice had spoken to her, not of this world, but too clear and too real to be a dream. Gently urging her to do something.

"Mom?"

Acknowledgments

I'd like to thank my friend and agent Henry Dunow, who has been providing wise counsel and finding homes for my books for more than two decades. I'd also like to thank Deb Futter and Randi Kramer at Celadon—their astute editing proved invaluable to the completion of this novel.

And I'd like to thank my family: Caryl, Clementine, Alexander, Aurora, and Celeste. They are my constant inspirations and best readers. They make it all possible.

CELADON
BOOKS

Founded in 2017, Celadon Books, a division of
Macmillan Publishers, publishes a highly curated list
of twenty to twenty-five new titles a year. The list of
both fiction and nonfiction is eclectic and focuses
on publishing commercial and literary books and
discovering and nurturing talent.